New Beginnings on a Mountain

Love is a Cabin Series
Book 4

Jacque Jacobs

Drawings by
Ken Czarnomski

Cover Photo by
Bill Johnston

An imprint
Drellag Press, LLC

Other Works of Fiction by
JACQUE JACOBS

Love is a Cabin Series

High on a Mountain – Book 1

Life on a Mountain – Book 2

Settled on a Mountain – Book 3

The Community Unites on a Mountain – Book 5 (Early Fall 2022)

Holidays on a Mountain – Book 6 (Late Fall 2022)

Drawings by
Ken Czarnomski

Cover Photos
Bill Johnston

An Imprint of
Drellag Press, LLC
Vero Beach FL

Acknowledgements

Sincere thanks to the great folks at Hagood Mill in Pickens, S.C. for allowing me to use the photograph of a cabin from their historic site on the cover of this book. Bill Johnston, long-time friend and award-winning photographer, visited the mill and captured this cabin which provides a perfect representation of what I imagine Bella's new cabin to be. I hope you will visit Hagood Mill in person, or at least check out their website at *www.visithagoodmill.com* I believe it is important for each of us to support the historic places in our country for future generations.

Thanks to family and friends who have cheered me on and supported my work in big ways and small. For your continued reading and feedback, thanks to Dondra Maney, Ph.D. Peggy Jones, Ed.D., and Paula VanHooser. I offer a sincere apology to Susan Lovelace for omitting her in my acknowledgements in *Settled on a Mountain.* Susan read with a critical eye and continues to encourage me and teach me. Thank you.

Writing is a solitary process, but publishing a book takes a team.

With thanks to my very talented friends for their contributions:

Ken Czarnomski for your drawings

Bill Johnston for your photograph on the cover

Thanks to the team who put it all together for the continued interest and support of my readers:

Elaine Massung, editor extraordinaire at *https://academic-smartcuts.com*

Arkonna, format professional at *http://fiverr.com*

Pixelstudio, book cover designer professional at *http://fiverr.com*

Note: See Author's Note at the end of this book for a list of the acronyms used in this story.

Dedication

This book is a work of fiction that includes stories of the tragedies of young lives lost and others lost in crime. As many of us truly struggle with the loss of the lives of children and teachers in yet another school in the U.S.A, I dedicate this book to the victims at Robb Elementary School in Uvalde, Texas, who lost their lives senselessly, and to the memories of one too many lives lost to gun violence at the schools in our nation. As a former elementary principal, I know the weight of responsibility to protect the lives of the children we serve. May we have the will as a people to right this wrong.

Keep close to Nature's heart... and break clear away, once in a while,
and climb a mountain or spend a week in the woods.
Wash your spirit clean...

John Muir, 1838 – 1914

Drawing by Ken Czarnomski

CHAPTER 1

The Nature of Friendship

THE BARREN BRANCHES OF DECIDUOUS TREES and the dark silhouettes of the tall, evergreen conifers appeared to dance across the ridgeline of the Smoky Mountains. Bella Anderson soaked up the splendor of her surroundings as she ate lunch on her porch. She reached down and rubbed Wizard, her sheprador pup, behind the ears. "We're so fortunate to have this idyllic spot, boy. Even the cold weather seems to enhance the blue of the sky. Of course, I bet you don't feel the temperature at all under that fur coat of yours. Think we should stay here for the winter?"

The pup looked up at her. "Guess you're not going to give me any advice, eh?" She chuckled and wrote a note on the small tablet of paper she now kept on the table by her favorite porch chair: "barren branches," "dark silhouettes," and "stay in the mountains?" *I've been here since early September, and I can finally play with words again.*

The bowl of vegetable soup finished; Bella stood to take her tray to the kitchen. She paused for a moment to take one more look over the ridgeline, her heart leaping as a bird zipped through her line of sight and disappeared into the undergrowth. She missed hearing the eastern towhee's call of "drink-your-tea," but she was pleased with the overshadowing manmade sounds, which had their own musical undertones. The cacophonous hammering of the repairs to her shed, accompanied by the whirring sound of the concrete trucks pouring the footings for her guest cabin, were welcome music to her ears.

Arthur Gillett had explained that the cabin footings would be shallow, but he would anchor them to the bedrock below. Bella was confident he knew what he was doing, and she was fascinated with his explanation of how they "pinned" the rebar into the bedrock to ensure the stability of the cabin. At the same time, new hinges were being installed on the large double doors of her old shed to replace the ones someone had tampered with. Criminal trespass was a new vulnerability in her quiet community tucked in the mountains, and she wanted to be sure there was no easy access. *Drellag Caban, we are repairing the wounds to our land and creating opportunities for new memories.*

The wall phone in her kitchen began to ring as she walked through the living room. She dropped the tray on the dining table and grabbed the handset before her answering machine could switch on.

"Drellag Caban, may I help you?"

"Good afternoon, lovely lady." The kind voice was familiar to her.

"Good afternoon to you too. How are you this fine day?"

The smile in Joshua's voice was evident. "I'm doing better than I might have expected, thanks, but... well, do you have a minute?"

"I always have time for my big brother. What's up?"

"First, let me say I like being referred to as your big brother. I should have asked you to be my sister years ago." Joshua Johnson laughed. "Second, I'm calling to see if you're coming down the mountain for groceries anytime soon?"

"No plans at the moment, but I could. What do you need?" Bella knew Joshua had to struggle with running the Valley Store by himself since his father was killed.

"Need? Nothing, really. Just like to talk with you in person about..." He hesitated, the catch in his voice sending its own message. The recent death of his dad, Joe, was surely the reason for the call. Joshua had never called and asked her for anything before.

"Joshua, listen, I can head down now. It'll give me a break from all the hammering."

"You sure?"

"Absolutely. I'll see you in less than an hour."

"Thanks, Bella. Maybe you could stay for supper?"

"We can talk about it. See you soon."

"Thanks again, Bella. Drive safely."

Problems to Solve

"Come in." Chad Oliver, the sheriff, shook hands with his lead detective, Billy Williams, as he walked into Chad's office.

"Thanks, boss. You sure you have a minute?"

Chad was accustomed to Billy showing up at his door unannounced. Most of the time it was fine, but this was not one of those times.

"A minute." Chad's voice was more terse than he intended. He took a breath and started again. "Sorry, Billy, have a seat. Lots on my mind today. It's already noon, and I haven't managed to reach Quinn yet."

Billy knew he was referring to Agent Quinn Isaacs of Immigration Enforcement. Billy would like to be in touch with her, too. He was surprised how much he had enjoyed her company as he escorted her around the last jamboree, and he was hoping to ask her out to dinner soon.

Chad wanted to find out what was going on about them meeting with the FBI and any further developments on the illegal activities a certain local county commissioner had gotten involved in. *Or orchestrated. I wouldn't put it past Zimmerman to be 'el jefe' himself.*

"I'll be quick." Billy's banter—often playful and usually bordering on inappropriate— was missing.

Chad sat down at the round table in his office and looked at Billy, a glance that said, "Go on."

Billy plunged in without any further preamble; he knew Chad didn't waste time on a lot of chatter. "I heard from Peggy O'Haire, and she asked if I thought one more run at Bobby Kirk would get a straight-up confession on killing Joe, or at least get him to admit his actions made it happen. Although she'd prefer to negotiate a plea deal with him, she can convene the grand jury on Tuesday next week. Her two plea options are reckless homicide, which you know means two to twelve years plus a ten-thousand-dollar fine, or criminally negligent homicide, which is the most she thinks she can get. That sentence is one to six. Thomas and I can push him, but..." Billy paused, out of breath like he had just run a marathon.

"Billy, breathe. Please." Chad knew Billy had been running on all cylinders for weeks, and he had expected Billy to submit a form for leave this morning. Chad's voice was firm but kind. "Listen, I'll take care of this with the DA, no problem. I assume you have that leave form ready for me. I want you out of here no later than three."

"Boss, that's not why I came to talk to you—" Billy stopped. He knew it *was* why he came: he needed Chad to tell him he *had* to take the leave. He sighed. "Yeah, I guess it is. The leave form is on my desk. I just feel guilty not finishing up this case. Joe meant the world to all of us."

"Look, Billy, we're all a bit off-kilter with Joe's death. For you ... for us..." he swept his arms open in a gesture that indicated the whole of the valley community. "It came on the back of more crime than we've seen in these parts in a month of Sundays. Now, tell me you'll do something good for yourself with your time off."

"Think I'll take a ride over to Nashville and take in some good music. Might be just what I need to put some pep back in my step."

"Good idea. Might I suggest you head out tomorrow after a good night's sleep." Chad studied Billy's eyes. "Whatever you decide, be safe."

"Okay, if you're sure I'm not shirking my duties."

Chad stood. Billy knew it meant the discussion was finished.

"Get out of here, Detective. Travel safely and get some rest."

"Yes, sir. See you the end of the week, boss."

Chad returned to his desk. He picked up the phone and asked dispatch to see if District Attorney O'Haire was available. He then had to decide how he was going to handle the interrogation of Bobby Kirk. It had been a long time since he'd been in that role. He decided it would be good for him to get back into the swing of the routine work he expected of others. He sent a text to Deputy Susan Thomas to see him when she had time.

While waiting for a reply, he took out his personal mobile phone and dialed Bella Anderson's number at her cabin. It rang until it went to her answering machine. He debated about leaving a message but decided he'd try later. He didn't try her mobile number as he knew she had no signal on top of the mountain. As he put his phone back in his pocket, there was a knock on his door. Deputy Susan Thomas entered as he opened it.

"Have a seat. Thanks for your quick response. How are you today?"

"Fine, Sheriff. And you?"

"Likewise, thanks. Need your perspective and thoughts on an interrogation."

Susan raised her left eyebrow in a questioning look. She knew to give the sheriff time; he would say what he had to say when he was ready.

"Billy is on leave until the end of the week. I need to talk to the DA first, but I think we'll need to see if we can get Bobby Kirk to own up to his part in Joe's death. What are your thoughts on making that happen?"

She sat quietly for a few moments. "Sheriff, I think Bobby responds to the good-cop-bad-cop routine. Who do you have in mind to go in with me?"

"Me."

She couldn't keep the look of surprise from her face. "Seriously?"

As soon as she said it, she wanted to swallow the word. "Sorry, sir. Not that I don't think you're capable, it just took me totally by surprise. My mind was running through a list of possible deputies." She stopped talking.

Chad had his "gray-eye stare," which is what his deputies called it when they couldn't read any expression on his face.

"Do you think if *you* were surprised, it might be equally surprising for young Mr. Kirk to have the sheriff appear?"

"Good point! I like the idea. I suspect his positive response to me playing good cop will be heightened with the big guy showing up." She paused for a few seconds. "I like it a lot."

"I think we have a pretty good idea he's seen his mother abused and has been abused himself. As much as I hate that for him, he might think twice about stretching the truth with me there."

Susan nodded her head. "No doubt he'll have an image of his pappy being the one in front of him."

"Okay, let's wait until I hear from Peggy, then we'll try to get this done today. I'd like for Joshua to be able to start to heal from all this."

"For sure, Sheriff. Call when you're ready." She stood and walked out, thrilled she was going to work with the sheriff on an interrogation.

Chad leaned back in his chair, locked his fingers together, and put the back of his hands against forehead, hoping for one minute of quiet. He managed to count to twenty-six before his desk phone rang. He sat up and stretched as he reached to answer it.

"Oliver here."

Supporting a Friend

Bella took Wizard out for a walk. When they returned, she made sure there was water and food in his dishes. She checked the latch on the screen and decided to leave him on the porch while she was gone since she didn't plan to be down the mountain too late. "Be a good boy and protect our home. I'll be back soon." Wizard wagged his tail.

Drellag Caban closed up, she grabbed her mobile phone and wallet, slipped on her Merrell mules, her navy blue down jacket, and headed out the kitchen door. She looked to see if Arthur was at the shed but saw him walking down the hill to the location for her new guest cabin. Her Jeep started right up. *I must remember to ask Joshua or Chad where to get it serviced. Hopefully I won't have to go to Round City. It's almost November! Winter is coming.*

Arthur had told her he hoped to get the new garage built before the first big winter storm, but she told him to prioritize the shed and the new cabin. The concrete truck was pulling down the hill, so the whirring sound was finished and Arthur must have heard her start the engine because he turned around and waved. She reached him as he arrived at the new cabin site; she rolled down the window as he walked to the car.

"Afternoon, Bella. Are we driving you out of house and home?"

"Quite the opposite. The sounds mean progress is being made, and I'm just so grateful that you were able to get started so quickly. How are you this afternoon? Anything you weren't expecting with the shed?"

"No. Not a thing. We've pulled the rotted boards along the bottom and done some grading of the ground. You won't have standing water anymore. Your dad did a good job building that shed, so I'm not surprised it didn't settle too much. Gotta figure, just like people, everything settles, and seventy years is a long time. It'll be right as rain when we finish. Have you decided what you're going to have painted on the side of it?"

"I'm finalizing my ideas for that wall, but I also need to find someone who can paint it. Any problem anchoring the foundation of the new cabin to the bedrock?"

"Smooth as butter. The noise was a bit much for you I suspect, but it's finished now, and the footings are poured. This one will be up high enough that you shouldn't have any problems with it settling or having to deal with rot. The log package will be here in a few days. So, it's all moving right along. Can I help you with anything?"

"Thanks for the update. As a matter of fact, there is something you might be able to tell me. I need to get my Wrangler serviced. Know anyone in these parts who can save me going to Round City?"

Arthur pulled a card out of his pocket and wrote a name and number on the back. "This is a boy who went to high school with my oldest, so you know he's been around a while. Has a shop he runs beside his house, but he's a good mechanic and runs a legitimate business—pays taxes just like you and me. You could give him a call. He's not too far from the library."

"Thanks, Arthur. I've been meaning to get this done and just haven't gotten around to it."

"No wonder with all that's happened in the last couple of months. Hope things are settling down for you."

"They are, for sure. Having this work done and the new cabin built makes them seem like distant memories. Thanks for your concern. Well, I'm headed down to the Valley Store. I don't know if I'll be back before you leave, so I'll wish you a nice evening."

"Same to you, Bella. Give my regards to Joshua and Carla."

"Will do, Arthur."

Isn't that interesting? Arthur included Carla in the greeting as easily as if she had been helping Joshua out for years. Does that mean folks are seeing her as part of the Valley Store? Bella slowed as she approached the beginning of the switchbacks. It was important to drive slowly to avoid going over the side of the mountain with the sharpness of some of the curves, but she had also started making it her business to look for unusual patterns of activity in the area. It was deer hunting season now, so tracks from all-terrain vehicles were more evident, but after a trespassing ATV slammed into the side of her shed last month, she wanted to be aware of any tracks that were not on the usual hunting trails. So far, she had not seen anything of concern.

Suddenly, a flash of white caused her to step on the brakes. Straight ahead, right on the edge of the road, someone had dumped a refrigerator; they didn't even bother to send it down the hill as most folks did in their attempt to avoid recycling fees. *At least it will be easier to remove. I'll call the county offices and let them know. I need to talk to Harold soon about how we can facilitate recycling these appliances.*

She eased over as she reached the narrow pullout just before the last run down the mountain. She didn't want to forget to call about the refrigerator, and this pullout was where she began to have a mobile signal.

"County offices, this is Abigail how may I help you?"

"Hey, Abigail, this is Bella Anderson."

"Hey! How are you?"

"Fine, thanks. I'm on the way down my road and there's a refrigerator about half a mile from the final pullout."

"Thanks. Our guys spend a lot of time trying to track down items since most folks don't have a precise location. Sure wish we could get folks to take them to Round City."

"Thanks, Abigail. They won't be able to miss this one as it's an accident waiting to happen. I'll talk to you soon, and tell your guys I appreciate it. You have a good afternoon."

Since she had stopped to make the call, Bella decided to text Chad that she was headed to the Valley Store: "JJ called. Headed to VS to c him. B." Just as she put her phone in the dash holder, it rang. She didn't want to finish driving down the mountain talking on the phone, so she decided to sit and enjoy the view through the trees down to the village.

"Hello, lovely lady."

"My, my! A woman could get a swelled head with two men calling her in the same day, using the same greeting."

"Has that four-year-old grandson of mine figured out how to call you?" The chuckle in Chad's voice caused her to smile. She wanted to find a quick retort but couldn't.

"Not yet. Joshua called..."

"Did I ever tell you I have a green-eyed monster who can rear his ugly head when Joshua Johnson shows an interest in you?"

Bella laughed. "Shame on you, Chad Oliver. I am headed to see my friend... No, my big brother, and he can tell me I'm lovely anytime he wants."

"Fair enough. Fair enough. Wasn't very nice of me, was it?"

"You're forgiven—*this* time."

"Can you stay down for supper?"

"For fear the green-eyed monster might resurface, I should just go home." She paused to see if he would say anything. "However, if you're willing to share dinner with Joshua and Carla, I'll stay down. He asked first."

"Works for me. Hate to run, but duty is calling. Let me know when you have a plan with my nemesis."

"Good vocabulary will get you brownie points. Talk to you soon. Go protect the planet, or at least our little corner of it." She smiled as she hung up. The banter with Chad was easy, and it was something she had missed the past five years since Matt died. *Staying up here for the winter is looking more and more appealing. Of course, I'll need to go to North Carolina and get some real winter clothes and make arrangements for things there.* Her thoughts drifted to what she would need to do to stay in the mountains longer than she had originally anticipated, but her eyes were solidly on the road.

Decisions are Part of the Job

Chad hung up his mobile phone. Since he had not answered his desk phone, the dispatcher had sent a message to his computer that she had the district attorney on the line. He took the call.

"DA O'Haire, how are you this fine afternoon?"

"Just fine, Sheriff Oliver. Are we standing on formalities today, Chad?"

"No, Peggy, just thought I should show respect for the woman we've managed to keep pretty busy these last two months; I wish it weren't so."

"It has felt a bit like full-time work over there. Up until now, if it hadn't been for Round City crime, I might have been out of a job. You've certainly had more than usual. But I'm quite sure my long-term employment is not why you called. What's up?"

"The good Detective Williams is headed out on much-needed leave, so I want to make sure I know what you need from us to wrap up the Kirk boys. Billy said you were looking for a straight up confession from Bobby Kirk. That about right?"

"Honestly, Chad, I have enough to put him away, but I hate wasting taxpayers time and money to convene the grand jury and go to trial if we can get him to recognize his role in the death of Joe Johnson. It's more likely he'll negotiate with me if he accepts his responsibility. He has no priors, so I think the best I'll get is criminally negligent homicide, and probably not even the maximum of six years."

"You sure about that? He was responsible for the death of the oldest native-born European descendant in these hills. I think a judge and a jury might have some pretty strong feelings about that." Chad actually wanted the plea agreement so that Joshua could start to put his dad's death behind him. He knew the judge's docket likely meant it would be months or even a year before the trial. At the same time, he owed it to Joe and Joshua to push for the most serious punishment they could make happen.

Peggy interrupted his train of thought. "You already know there are lots of factors in every case and every sentencing, whether a jury or a bench trial. Since this young man is refusing to have counsel, I think we can wrap it up. It would just be cleaner if you can get a more definitive statement of culpability out of him."

"Thanks, Peggy. Just wanted to know what you needed. Hope to have it back in your court, so to speak, this afternoon."

"Okay," Peggy dragged out the word. "I thought you said Billy was on leave. I assume you'll send in Deputy Thomas, but who's going to be her foil?"

Chad waited a beat before he spoke. "Thought I might see how rusty my skills are."

Peggy paused even longer than he had. "Well, well, you just never know what a day's gonna bring. The finest detective ever in East Tennessee is going back in an interrogation room? I can hardly wait to see the video. See if you can up your technology over there so I can livestream it next time!"

"We're not far off, Madam District Attorney. The fine Sergeant Sylvia Whitehorse has all kinds of new gizmos and gadgets on order. She's even promised that we can increase the bandwidth and throughput." He hoped to high heaven Peggy did not ask him what that meant.

Peggy pulled out her best southern drawl. "Mercy! I am downright faint from the modernity sweeping through the valley. I may need some smelling salts."

Chad laughed uproariously. "Get on with you. I'll be back in touch soon."

CHAPTER 2

People are Interesting

BELLA'S LONG DARK BROWN HAIR kept blowing in her face as she drove with her window down. She parked at the Valley Store and looked in the mirror. There were too many tangles to run her fingers through her hair, so she pulled out the hairbrush and hair clip she kept in the glove box. Her hair brushed and clipped back from her lightly freckled face, she took one more glance in the mirror before heading into the store. *It'll have to do.*

Carla came from behind the cash register to hug Bella when she walked in the door. Bella gave a slight wave to Joshua, who was talking to a customer.

"Yessir, it's about an hour and a half to Gatlinburg."

"Yeah, uh, what'd you say your name was?"

"Joshua, sir. Joshua Johnson. This is my store. Now, like I was telling y'all..." Bella could hear the deliberate drop into his deep mountain voice.

"Yeah, I get it, but I want to know how many miles it is."

"Thirty-four, give or take, but doesn't matter. It's still an hour an' a half."

The man walked out shaking his head.

"Flatlander!" Joshua, Carla, and Bella said in unison as each stifled a laugh.

Joshua walked over, leaned down from his six-foot-four frame and kissed Bella on the cheek. "Welcome. Nice to see you."

"Nice to be seen. How many times a day do you get asked that question? I know I heard. . ." Bella trailed off. She was about to recall a time she heard Joe telling someone the same thing.

"It's okay, Bella. I know my dad loved dragging out that little scenario. In leaf season and summer, we get asked about once a day. Enough of that, though, how are things up on the mountain?"

"Yes," Carla echoed. "How's the construction?"

"Moving right along. You will no longer be able to tell an ATV trespassed on my land and ended up in the side of my shed." Her voice became more animated. "My new cabin is going to be perfect. The logs should arrive by the end of the week, and it will be going up soon."

"Let us know when, we'd love to come see it," Carla said.

"Come any time. My pup is doing great, too. I can't wait for you to meet him."

"We're looking forward to meeting Wizard and learning how you decided on his name. I couldn't believe it when you told me!" Joshua waved his hand like he was casting a spell with a wand.

The silver bell above the door jingled, and three people walked in the store. Joshua turned to Carla. "You okay up here by yourself?"

"Sure."

"Come on back, Bella. Let's chat. Can I grab you a bottle of tea from the cooler?"

"I can get it." Bella turned to Carla. "Put the tea on my tab, I'll be getting a few other things while I'm here." She knew she needed dog food, dog treats, and a few canned goods she had forgotten during her last shopping trip.

Joshua was looking out the back window of the storeroom when she walked through the swinging double doors. She looked around the space.

"Joshua, what's different? Oh, I see. You've moved your table and chairs. I like it in front of the window. It looks like your pallets are stacked differently too. Work better for you?"

"That's one of the things I wanted to talk to you about. Yeah, it works much better. Far more efficient to organize the products by frequency of access. Don't know why I never thought of it."

"Does it matter why you just thought of it? You have now."

He pointed to a chair for Bella and sat down after she did. "That's the point. I didn't think of it. Carla did."

Bella couldn't decide if he was pleased about that or not. She kept quiet. After all, there was a reason he wanted to talk to her.

"I've spent years doing things the way my dad always did. It worked for the most part, but it also meant I did double work. Why could Carla see that in just a week?"

"Does it bother you that Carla is the one who saw it?"

"I don't think so. What bothers me is why I didn't see it."

Bella smiled. She reached across the table to squeeze Joshua's hand then let go. "Joshua, what does our expression, 'can't see the forest for the trees?' mean to you?"

Joshua sat, contemplative as he often was, and looked out the window. "Good point. I was in the middle of it, so I couldn't see it. I know it's a good thing that Carla saw it, just like putting the table in front of the window. Why didn't we? Granted, we mostly see propane tanks against the side of the mountain, but at least we get some sun and look at something other than a cinder block wall." He seemed to wind down like a top skittering across the floor.

"Doesn't matter that you didn't see it. Try to think of it as a fresh start, like cleaning out a closet."

Joshua started to laugh. "Bella, I have never cleaned out a closet. Jan used to say it was worse when I got through than when I started." He stopped.

Bella knew it was saying Jan's name that caught up with him. She waited.

"Here's why I really needed to talk to you. My head is so messed up. First, Jan dies in September, then my dad gets killed in October, I have this business to run... No, I have two businesses to run, and with the propane work I'm having to leave Carla alone in the store a right good bit these days."

"Sounds like a lot to handle. Maybe you want to talk to Pastor Fisk."

He interrupted her. "I've spoken with him and appreciate the spiritual counsel in dealing with losing the two most important people in my life ..." He took a breath and looked at Bella. "I needed a friend to talk to about Carla."

I hope I can help with whatever he needs to share. Bella sat silently.

Things to Do

Chad was mulling over the two messages he had received while talking to the district attorney. The first one was from Special Agent Sam Nations of the Drug Enforcement Agency regarding the drug bust they had conducted a week ago, and the other was from Agent Quinn Isaacs of the Immigration Enforcement Agency. She'd scheduled a telephone conference with him and Sam at four. Chad knew he needed the help of both the DEA and IEA to deal with some of the criminal behavior that had come into the valley and surrounding hills. However, he was still frustrated that he hadn't heard from Sam in the last week. He'd been relieved to learn that Sam's injuries in the raid had not been life threatening, but he still didn't understand why Sam had rushed into the rental house in the first place.

Chad sighed and redirected his train of thought; he couldn't let anything else interfere at the moment. The interrogation of Bobby Kirk needed to be finished before the conference call. The death of Joe Johnson deserved his undivided attention—and he would see that it got it.

Deputy Thomas met Chad as he walked down the hall toward the holding area.

"Hey, boss. Satisfied with what the DA needs us to do?"

"10-4. Let's step in here and chat a minute." The matron nodded and pointed toward one of the holding cells, indicating she had Bobby Kirk ready for them. Chad returned her nod as they stepped into the small storage room near the matron's desk.

Chad shut the door. "I've watched the previous interviews you and Billy did with this young man. While I'll be a bit different than Billy, I think we can work this pretty easily."

"Don't get me wrong, I respect Detective Williams. But, sir, you're my boss. No problem being deferential to you."

"Well, let's just keep the deference to the interrogation. As lead deputy, I certainly value you as part of the leadership of this organization. Anything you want to share about this young man?"

"Nothing you haven't seen on the tapes. Although he isn't as belligerent as most of the young men we get in here, he does have some bully in him."

"Got it. Let's go do this."

They walked out. Chad nodded to the matron and headed for Room 1. Chad purposely walked ahead of Deputy Thomas to establish himself as having little regard for the woman behind him. He opened the door to the interrogation room and walked in ahead of Susan and Bobby Kirk, who was shuffling with his leg chains. The matron closed the door behind them.

Susan set the recorder on the table and turned it on.

"Deputy Thomas, let's be clear. I'm in charge here. Understood?"

"Sheriff Oliver, with..."

Bobby Kirk's head snapped towards Chad, who had pulled up a chair within inches of the young man. "State your name and date of birth." Chad spoke flatly and didn't even glance at Bobby.

Bobby's voice quivered. "Bobby Kirk, sir." He gave his date of birth.

"Deputy, read Mr. Kirk his Miranda rights."

"Yessir, Sheriff. Mr. Kirk, you have the right to remain silent . . . if you cannot afford an attorney, one will be appointed for you. Do you understand these rights?"

"Yes, ma'am."

"Do you wish to have an attorney present?" Deputy Thomas looked right at Bobby.

"No, I done told you. I ain't got no money, and my pappy said if the police done get you, just say what you know."

"Do you understand that the court will appoint an attorney for you at no cost to you?" Deputy Thomas looked at the sheriff. She acted like she was seeking his approval for saying the right thing.

"Don't matter. I don't want no attorney." Bobby's voice was flat, and he was pumping his knees up and down, causing his ankle chains to rattle.

"Sir, do you think it would be all right if I released Bobby's handcuffs?"

Chad stared at her. His look was not missed by Bobby, who stole a glance at Chad out of the corner of his eye.

"Mollycoddling him, are you? This boy has committed several crimes in our jurisdiction. His comfort is no concern of mine." Susan Thomas looked down the whole time Chad was speaking. Chad's voice was stern but not brutal.

"I know, sir, just thought maybe we could show him a little compassion."

Bobby stared at Susan. He did not look at Chad, who leaned in towards Bobby. The room seemed to vibrate with Chad's words. "Bobby Kirk, look at me."

Bobby turned his head towards Chad, but his eyes remained downcast.

"This *woman* is going to unlock your handcuffs. If I think for one minute that you are not cooperating with this interrogation, you will have those handcuffs back on and be in a cell faster than a hot knife through butter. You got that?"

Bobby had lots of experience kowtowing to an abusive father. He finally glanced up at Chad. "Yessir, I got it. Thank you, sir." There was a slight stutter to his words.

The deputy stood up and asked Bobby to lean forward so she could unlock his cuffs. Very quietly, but loud enough she knew it would be picked up on the recording, she moved away from his back and said, "Just tell the truth."

Chad lifted his right leg, put his ankle on his left knee, crossed his arms, and leaned back in the straight back wooden chair. He looked at Bobby in a way that could not be mistaken for anything other than "I'm in charge."

"Now, from the beginning, tell me what happened when you took your cousin, Jason, for a ride on your Alterra 300 ATV."

Bobby couldn't speak fast enough. "Like I done told the deputy here and that other man, my pappy let me use his ATV. Jason wanted to go for a ride, so we went up in the hills. Then I needed some smokes and Jason done said he needed juice, so we was at the store to get them."

"Tell the sheriff what store, Bobby."

"Deputy, you think I can't ask my own questions?"

"Sorry, Sheriff." She gave a pleading look to Bobby.

"Mr. Joe's store. Ain't no other store here."

Chad dropped his foot to the floor so it made a loud clap when his boot hit the concrete. Deputy Thomas jerked back. Chad felt badly about that; he didn't intend to startle her. But the effect on Bobby meant Chad didn't have to say a word.

"You know, the one they done call the Valley Store." Bobby's voice was fast and trembling.

Chad remained silent.

"Like I told the deputy here and the detective, right, weren't he a detective?" He looked at Susan.

Susan nodded.

"Like I done told them, Jason don't got no money, so I was gonna pay. When Mr. Joe reached under the counter and pulled out the box to get me two packs, I seen how many boxes he had there..." His voice trailed off.

Now Chad spoke. His voice was so quietly demanding that Susan would later tell him she had goosebumps from being worried *she* would say something wrong. "You better speak very clearly, Bobby. Think about exactly how things happened and tell me the truth. You get one time and one time only. This is your last chance, or you're going to be sitting in front of a judge and jury, looking at jail for ten to twelve years. So, tell me the truth. Is that clear?"

Bobby's knees were in motion the whole time, causing his ankle chains to bounce against the legs of the chair. Not for the first time, Susan was glad their chairs were wood and not metal. His head bounced with the rhythm of his feet, but he never took his eyes off of Chad.

"Yes, sir, it's clear. See, I ain't got much money. I seen all those smokes and I knowed he has lots of money. He weren't gonna miss a couple boxes of smokes. I jumped behind the counter and pushed that ole man outta the way. I been thinkin' about it since I first come in here, and I reckon I was pretty mad he had all those smokes and I didn't. I pushed him like I mighta done with a buddy of mine who got in my way from somethin' I wanted." Bobby lowered his head. "I was gonna get those smokes, and he weren't gonna stop me. He tried. I just pushed him harder. He hit his head on the counter when I done that. I reckon it hurt him pretty bad."

Chad stared at him. Deputy Thomas remained motionless, afraid any movement might distract Bobby from his confession.

Bobby nodded at Susan. "She done asked me did I call for help. I didn't. We hightailed it out of there." He jerked his head from Susan to Chad. "I forgot. Jason done took money from the drawer. He gave it to his pappy." His shoulders drooped, and he looked away from Chad.

"I'm only going to ask you this one time, Bobby." Chad's stare was pure steel. "Are you telling me that you pushed Mr. Joe on purpose to get those cigarettes?"

Bobby nodded his head.

"You need to answer me in a voice I can hear." Chad dragged out every syllable, and the heat of his words was not lost on Bobby. The thought of Joe Johnson dying over a carton of cigarettes meant the heat was not an act.

"I didn't care who was there. I was gonna get those smokes." Bobby slumped down in his chair as far as he could without falling off it.

"Deputy, we're going to end this interrogation, and you are going to walk this *boy* back to his cell, then you will report to my office immediately. Do you understand that?"

"Yes, Sheriff." Susan stood and nodded to Bobby to stand, then she cuffed his wrists behind him. "This is Deputy Thomas and..." she looked at Bobby.

"Bobby Kirk," he said.

"Leaving interrogation." She gave the time and opened the door.

Chad stood. "Sheriff Oliver leaving the interrogation of Bobby Kirk." He shut off the recorder and put it in his pocket. He walked past the matron with only a nod then headed directly to the men's room across from his office. He stood and looked in the mirror. *And to think there was once a time when I thought an interrogation was the best part of the job.* He turned on the water at the sink, leaned on his elbows, and let the water run over his hands before splashing it on his face. The roughness of the paper towel wasn't enough to wipe away the worst parts of this work. A kind old man who served his community his entire life was dead, and a young man's life was wasted: all for the want of a cigarette.

What Do You Think?

Joshua looked at Bella, wondering what she was thinking. He knew she thought about things from lots of different perspectives and was often distracted when she did so. However, in this moment he could see that she was giving him her undivided attention.

"Bella, will you stay and go to dinner? Please."

"I can't stay down the mountain too late because of Wizard, so on the way down I was thinking that you and Carla could come up to my place, and I can throw something together. Chad might even be able to join us. What do you think?"

Joshua nodded and moved his eyes up towards the ceiling, which she knew meant he was trying to think of a reason to bypass her plan. "Well, I'd have to see if that works for Carla, and we'd have to call Doug, but . . . What if we ate at The Corral around five? Then I'd be back here before I need to close up and you could head home before it got dark. What about that?"

"That would work for me. I just think I have to be home by seven or soon after. If you can make five o'clock work, then let's do it here."

"Okay, don't get up. I still want to talk to you, but let me go talk to Carla real quick."

Bella settled into the chair but still couldn't imagine what Joshua wanted to talk to her about. Her initial thought that there was a problem with Carla didn't fit with him wanting them to have dinner together.

A few minutes later, Joshua was preceded through the swinging doors by Melody, the high school student who worked for him. Bella saw on her watch it was three thirty already. She stood up.

"Melody, it's great to see you."

"You too, Miss Bella." Melody stood in front of Bella, and they spontaneously hugged each other. Bella knew Joe's death had been hard on Melody, and Bella was glad she and Chad had been able to support her at the funeral. Now, she felt they were friends.

"I just wanted to say, 'hey.'" Melody smiled.

"I'm so glad you did. I hope everything is shaping up for next year. Were you able to get your application submitted for early acceptance at UT Knoxville?"

"Yes, ma'am. With the scholarship from Mr. Joe and Mr. Joshua, I can head to my dream school, if I get accepted."

"You've got this, Melody," Joshua chimed in, beaming.

"Hope so. Gotta get to work now. Take care, Miss Bella."

"You too, Melody. You too."

Joshua and Bella sat down. "Carla is calling Doug. If he can't come help out, we have another person we can call. She said James would put us in the back room at The Corral, so we won't be disturbed." He smiled. "Then I told her it helps to know the owner. She was pretty quick saying, 'It helps that I *am* one of the owners.'" His grin was ear to ear.

"Give me a minute and I'll text Chad, then we can talk." She sent a text. "TC at 5?"

"TC at 5." Chad shot back.

"Okay, we're set. Now what is it you wanted to talk to me about?"

Joshua took a deep breath. "You know I'm not much of a talker, and the two people I talked to the most aren't with us anymore. I was so relieved at how easy it was when I told you I felt you were like a sister. I knew you were the one person I could talk to about this."

Bella waited. She could see he was measuring his thoughts before speaking.

"It's been really great having Carla here every day, and it means I've been able to keep the store open. And for sure she has suggested some changes that have made things work better. There's not one of her ideas that I didn't like. I haven't talked to James, but I believe her when she says they are just fine at The Corral without her there to help out." He took another deep breath. "Her emotional support since my dad died has been more than anyone has the right to expect from another person." Then he went quiet.

CHAPTER 3

In wilderness lies the hope of the world.
John Muir, 1838 – 1914

What's Next?

BACK AT HIS DESK, CHAD SAW A MESSAGE on his computer screen alerting him that Agent Isaacs had changed the meeting from a phone conference to his office. He looked down at his mobile phone and saw there was also a text from her: "Mtg ur ofc @ 4. Hope ok." *Well, Agent Quinn Isaacs, I guess it'll have to be okay.* Chad decided it was just another day in the world of law enforcement. He picked up the phone and spoke to his dispatcher.

"Hey, Cecilia." He had three good dispatchers, but Cecelia was definitely the best. *If I ever decide to have an administrative assistant, I hope she'll apply.* "Please see if you can get the district attorney on the phone for me, then tell the desk deputy that I'll be up to get Agents Isaacs and Nations in the lobby." While he waited to see if Cecelia could reach Peggy, he scanned his emails, catching sight of one from Harold Cooper, the county manager. The message was brief; Harold wanted to talk about "the commission, drugs, and our community." Chad's phone rang.

"Oliver here."

"Sir, I have DA O'Haire on the line."

"Thanks, Cecelia." He waited while she switched the call. "Hey, Peggy."

"Hey, any luck?"

"Bobby Kirk straight up admitted he pushed Joe hard and reckoned it caused him to hit his head. He showed no remorse, even after a week in our fine accommodations."

"You must be giving those folks some pretty cushy cots. I'm guessing it might even beat the peace and quiet of their homes." She paused for a moment. "All kidding aside, Chad, thanks. I haven't received the digital copy of the video yet, but I suspect it will arrive in my inbox shortly. Once I review it, I'll set up a time for the two of us to present the plea deal to him. We'll do his cousin, Jason, at the same time. His charges are pretty straightforward, and he has a prior, so he'll likely take the deal. I'm guessing he'll be more comfortable in state accommodation than his home. I'll get back to you in a day or two. Anything else?"

"I do—on a different topic, though. Do you have a minute?"

"Sure, what's up?"

"Any repercussions on the plea deal with Steve Phillips? Any intervention from his parents?"

"No. None at all. Billy sent him over Friday a week ago; we went before the judge and the plea was signed. Young Mr. Phillips is a guest of Bledsoe for the next six years, out in three if he's a good boy. That wraps up the two survivors of your ATV crimes. Why are you asking?"

"Just trying to piece together some parts of a puzzle involving his stepfather and mother."

"You mean one of your county commissioners?"

"Yes. That one." Chad's tone made his thoughts about this particular commissioner clear.

"Look, Chad, I'll try to get this plea deal worked out and a time on the judge's docket. Maybe we can get Bobby Kirk done tomorrow or the next day. Then you and I should have a visit." Peggy and Chad were smart enough to know that even private lines weren't always private.

"That would be great, Peggy. Just let me know." Chad's voice lightened considerably. He was hoping he could get some insight from her about Zimmerman's activities in Round City. He'd cooperate with the FBI, if they came onboard, but he wasn't leaving the fate of his community to federal government agents.

"I'll be in touch. Later, Chad."

"Thanks, Peggy. Talk to you soon."

Chad saw that it was four o'clock. *I'll let the DEA and IEA agents wait a few minutes. I know these two particular agents are young and have bosses, but I've earned some respect.* He shook his head at the thought. *Mr. Bigshot, if you expect respect you have to give it. Besides, it's only Sam who has you with a thorn in your paw. Get moving.* He reached the front lobby at one minute after four on his watch. It was four o'clock straight up on the lobby clock.

Sam Nations stood and extended his hand. "Sheriff, thanks for the meeting."

"Sure thing, Agent Nations. Glad to see you're up and about." Chad did not see Quinn Isaacs.

The desk deputy, who was a distant cousin of Sam, was trying to figure out the formality. After all, no one else was in the lobby. Chad turned to the deputy.

"Please have someone escort Agent Isaacs back when she arrives." He nodded to Sam and opened the door between the lobby and hallway as his deputy pushed the release mechanism. The two men walked in silence. Chad observed that Sam had a limp after his through-and-through gunshot wound, but otherwise seemed in good health. He opened his office door and, with a swoop of his hand, indicated to Sam that he should go to the round table.

"Coffee? Water?" Chad's inquiry was polite but carried the formality of a sheriff to an agent.

Sam got the message. "I'm good, thanks."

Chad picked up his bottle of water and walked to the round table. He was working hard to tamp down the anger he felt. He sat and looked at Sam.

"I asked Quinn to give me a few minutes. I have some fences to try and mend in my hills, and, honestly, I understand the repair job is going to take more time than you may have to give it right now." Sam stopped and looked Chad square in the eyes.

"I was wrong." Sam stopped for a beat. "I apologize, specifically to you."

His apology hung in the air. Chad did not respond. Sam knew Chad well enough to know that he was not going to speak until he was ready. He watched Chad but plowed ahead.

"I got a text with my marching orders just as we reached the target house. Turns out another team in the DEA had been tailing those two for a while. Higher-ups want the head of the snake, so they weren't willing to sacrifice their goal for your mission. No one had intelligence that guns were part of how these two operated. They were seen as low-level mules, like the kids on the ATVs. SAC McMullen saw I had backup and ordered me to enter the house. I was put on ice afterwards, and I haven't been able to call you." He stopped talking.

Chad slowly sipped his water. He knew Sam meant the DEA Special-Agent-In-Charge McMullen. When he spoke, the words were deliberate and chilly. "I have this round table because I respect the traditions of your tribe. Chief Whitehorse taught me years ago about the value of the talking circle. Lately, my folks have learned the meaning and are perhaps thinking more about it. I saw the circle in action—even before they knew *why* I have a round table. We became a better law enforcement agency because I was no longer the sole decision maker. Everyone here knows I *will* make decisions but better decisions are made because we discuss things."

Sam nodded his head ever so slightly. He knew the power of the talking circle. He also knew he operated every day in a bureaucratic federal agency that claimed to believe in utilizing the brains they hired but was subject to the vagaries of the individuals who owned those brains at every level of the organization.

Chad continued. "Lives are on the line every day in this work:

our citizens and our teams. Your agency, through you as their representative, put the lives of several of my people and an Immigration Enforcement agent literally in the direct line of fire. Added to that, we had no idea if there were others who might make it to 'the house on the hill' and take out two more of your agents, two IEA agents, and a citizen of this community. It's not okay with me. Not then—and not now." His voice remained cold and hard. "Two men died that night. The first one shot directly at me in the backyard. He didn't live to tell his side of it. The second one almost took you out. I went in the back and took that guy out before he could get anyone else. Seems pretty interesting to me that this has turned out to be a DEA operation. Can't help but wonder why no one has been here to interrogate *me* about the death of those two men." Chad leaned in and put his forearms on the table and clasped his hands together. He looked at the man he considered a friend—and someone he had always respected.

"Sam, this is wrong in so many ways. I don't know if I can even count them all. As your friend, I accept your apology. I will work on forgiving you. You are smart, and I suspect you've learned some things about yourself because of this, and I hope to God you've learned something about the bureaucracy you work for." Chad looked at his watch. It was almost four thirty. "Is Quinn coming? Or was this just an excuse to meet with me?"

"She's probably here. I told her I needed to talk to you and would come get her. I suspect she convinced your folks she'd wait."

"I hope you've apologized to her."

"No. You were first on my list."

Chad gave no response. He stood and walked to his desk phone. "Please escort Agent Isaacs back. Thanks." While he waited, he sent Bella a text. "Can u meet me outside TC in 7 mins?" He stood to answer the knock on his door.

"Afternoon, Quinn. Good to see you. Come in."

His phone buzzed with a text. "Cu then."

Quinn smiled and extended her hand to Chad. "Thanks for seeing me." She walked to the round table and ignored Sam, who stood when she entered the office. Quinn sat down without looking at or speaking to Sam.

Chad walked to the table but did not sit. "How long can you be in the valley, Quinn?"

"No rush on my part. I'm actually staying at Joe's house tonight. Joshua has offered it to me whenever I need it. Didn't know how long we'd go tonight, so I planned to stay over."

He didn't bother to ask Sam his plans.

"Then, if it works for you, Quinn, I am going to go meet some friends for dinner, and we can meet back here at seven thirty. If I can make it before that, I'll text you."

"Works for me. It'll give me time to drop my things at Joe's place and grab a salad."

"Will you be part of our meeting at seven thirty, Sam?" Chad's demeanor was far from warm, but it wasn't the coldness Sam was expecting—or believed he deserved.

"Yes, sir. See you then."

"You are welcome to use my office. Just close the door when you leave. I'll see you at seven thirty unless I let you know otherwise. Even if I can be back before then, if you can't, seven thirty is fine with me." He turned and walked out of the office.

He knew Sam had more fence mending to do, and he hoped that Quinn would be receptive. He liked both of these talented young people. He just hated that one of them was having to learn a pretty harsh lesson.

Friends and Dinner

Bella pulled into the side parking lot at The Corral but decided to stay in her Jeep. She was still processing what Joshua had shared with her, and now she was waiting to see what had prompted Chad's text. She rolled her window down and leaned back on the headrest, allowing the cool breeze and bright sun to play on her face and closed eyes.

"I don't want to startle you, but I am going to lean in this window in one second."

Keeping her eyes closed, she turned her head and smiled. "Promises, promises."

She opened her eyes and could see the sparkle in Chad's gray ones as well as the weariness behind them. But all her thoughts flew out the window when he kissed her.

"Thanks for meeting me. Care to go for a little walk? We have about fifteen minutes."

Bella closed her window and stepped out. Chad pulled her into an embrace and a kiss. He couldn't care less who was looking. She certainly didn't care. After a moment, he took her hand, and they walked toward the music stage at the back of The Corral.

"Look up, Chad. The silhouette of the mountains is a picture to behold." She suddenly took off running towards the stage. "Last one there buys dinner."

He had let her win when they ran to her kitchen steps on another occasion, but he decided he would beat her this time. He needed this run to clear his head. "You're on!" The only sound was their shoes striking the ground, then Bella squealed with laughter as Chad caught up with her. It was going to be neck and neck.

A few seconds later they plopped down on the edge of the stage the band used for the jamborees. It was nothing more than a raised platform about eighteen inches off the ground, but it made for a reasonable place to sit and see the mountains.

"Dinner's on me." Bella was winded but not out of breath as she kissed Chad.

"I think *I* owe you. My head was in a really bad place. Seeing you and that little run cleared it right out. Thanks." He gave her a much more serious kiss.

She cocked her head and looked at him. "I'm going to ask you a very personal question, so feel free not to answer it."

He returned her look with a quizzical expression and a raised eyebrow.

"How old are you?"

He began to laugh and couldn't stop. When he finally caught his breath, he put his arm around her shoulder and pulled her toward him. "Oh, my dear Bella, whatever prompted that question?"

"I just realized that at fifty-eight I'm pretty happy I can still run like I just did. Then it occurred to me I have no idea how old you are . . . nothing nefarious on my part."

He kissed the top of her head and then lifted her chin to look her in the eyes. "Bella, Bella, Bella. Where have you been all my life? I love living in these mountains, tucked away from so much of what's wrong in the world. I love the beauty of these hills and the trees and the wildlife. I love my daughter, grandchildren, and son-in-law, but I have never felt as alive in my life as I do when I'm with you." He kissed her.

She returned the kiss, then she pulled back and looked him in the eyes. "And your answer would be?"

He laughed again. "And I love your persistence. I am also fifty-eight, born June fourteenth. And you?"

"June fifth."

"I love being with an older woman!"

"Lots of experience in that regard, have you?"

"Nope. You're the first." His tone became much more serious. "And, maybe, if I had met you when we were in our twenties, you would have been the only woman in my life. Ever."

"That's sweet. I've lived long enough to know that while you might be intrigued with the fifty-eight-year-old me, you might not have been so enamored of the twenty-something me. So, let's just start from where we are." She knew she was a better person because of her life with Matt, and Chad was partly who he was because he had *not* had a good marriage.

"Fair enough, wise Dr. Anderson."

"So, want to share what was on your mind when you sent your text?"

"Just this: being with you and needing some grounding in the good of the world."

"Then I'm glad I could help out."

"Anything special about having dinner with Joshua and Carla?"

Bella smiled and rested her head on his shoulder. She trusted Chad to keep confidences, but she also knew she owed Joshua the same trust that she would keep his. "I think there are four adults in our little corner of the world that just want the pleasure of being with their friends."

They sat without talking for several minutes, her head resting on his shoulder and his head leaning against the top of hers. Bella closed her eyes and drank in the strength of this man and the kindness she knew was the foundation of his being. Chad looked out to the mountains and wondered why the universe had conspired to bring this amazing woman into his life. A loud voice jarred them from their reverie.

"Chad! Bella! Let's eat!" Joshua was standing on the edge of The Corral parking lot, waving at them like a schoolboy calling his friends in from the playground. Bella knew why. She wondered what Chad would think.

Chad stood and took Bella's hand. They headed to the restaurant.

"Thanks, Bella. You may have just saved my life."

She squeezed his hand.

Joshua waited to walk with them.

Agent to Agent

Quinn set her Yeti on the table and looked at Sam. She wondered how much of a thrashing he'd received from Chad but doubted she would ever know. She was prepared to give one of her own.

"Quinn, I appreciate your willingness to let me have a few minutes with the sheriff before our meeting with him. I didn't know it was going to drag out your day like this." He waited to see if she was going to say anything. She didn't.

"I am deeply sorry that I put your life in jeopardy and blew a planned operation. I operated on orders but that doesn't excuse my stupidity in not challenging those orders. I should have."

"And risk losing your job?"

"Not sure I want a job where my assessment on the ground isn't sought and wouldn't have been considered anyway."

"When did you get the order?"

"As we exited my SUV."

"So, we're walking down the road yelling at each other like idiots, and you already knew you were going to storm that house on your own?"

"You didn't see me send a text back?"

"No! I was playing my part—the inconvenienced girlfriend. What woman would look at the man who took her up that godforsaken road and ran out of gas? None!"

"I wrote back. . ." he paused. "Not that it matters."

"Wrote what?!" The fury that she had held in check throughout the week now seemed to radiate off her.

"That DEA backup was not on site." He paused again. He owed Quinn the truth. "SAC McMullen wrote back, 'Use incompetent sheriff and IEA agent!'"

Quinn rose from her chair. She stood glaring at him then began to pace. She walked back to the table, put the palms of her hand on the tabletop, and leaned into Sam's face so they were almost eye to eye.

"Did you tell Chad Oliver this? Is that why he postponed *my* meeting?"

Sam looked down at the table. Quinn backed off and sat down.

"No, I haven't told Chad that part yet."

"So, you intend to tell him? When?"

"Now it will be after your meeting. If he's willing to listen to me."

"Oh no, no, no. You will tell him before the meeting and with me in the room. I am tired of this interagency squabbling, and I am not playing those games. DEA is either in this as an equal partner, playing in the same game, or I will go it alone from the immigration angle with Chad Oliver. At least I know he plays straight."

Sam did not say a word.

"I am going to tell you something friend to friend, not agent to agent. I pray to God that you learned something in this fiasco. The two men who died might have been scum of the earth, but even they deserved a fair trial for their crimes. It's for sure the man whose office we are using accepted us into his jurisdiction with the belief that this place, *your home* I might add, was our priority too. And I promise you I will be mighty careful before I put myself in a situation with you that has the potential to end up as a shootout again. The good news for you is that you and I have a history. Although our romance was not destined to work out, I have always respected you. When I cool down, I'm going to expect an explanation of why you were willing to potentially sacrifice all of us, and yourself, for the likes of SAC Carl McMullen! Even *he* has a boss you could have reached out to. I'll be back at seven thirty." She stood up and walked out.

Sam sat for several minutes, her words replaying over his head and adding to the confusion he already felt. He rose and drove to the home of Chief Whitehorse; he knew he needed the wisdom of his chief.

CHAPTER 4

Dinner and More

Joshua leaned down and kissed Bella on the cheek then shook Chad's hand. Chad smiled at him. They headed towards the banquet room's external door.

"Glad you could break away, Chad."

"Thanks for asking. I always appreciate the chance to sit down to dinner with friends."

"Good. Good. Harold and Julie are joining us as well."

Carla was waiting for them at the doorway. All three of them stopped and stared.

"Carla!" Bella rushed to give her a hug. "You look lovely. Are you a magician? An hour ago you were in jeans like the rest of us."

Carla returned the hug and accepted the kiss on the cheek from Chad.

"I decided I was tired of jeans." She twirled in a circle, causing her layered country skirt to flare out. She had a big grin on her face. "Joshua suggested I put on my dancing shoes. He hinted we might have our own dance here tonight. After all, we have the whole room to ourselves!"

They all laughed. Carla's sense of humor was infectious.

James had a table ready for them, complete with a tablecloth. Through the speakers mounted in the rafters of the log room, Dolly Parton was softly singing "My Tennessee Mountain Home."

Natalia was waiting to take their drink orders.

"Wine, ladies? Beer, Chad?" Joshua asked.

Natalia turned and pointed to a bottle of wine already next to the table. He nodded. Chad looked at Joshua's relaxed face and hated to decline, but he had to go back to work. "Thanks, Joshua. Afraid I'm still on duty. Please have one for both of us!"

Joshua nodded and told Natalia he'd have a Chimay Blue. He turned to the door as Harold and Julie walked in.

"Have a seat, folks, I'll be back in just a minute." Joshua shook hands with Harold and gave Julie a kiss on the cheek. He walked into the main part of The Corral and disappeared.

Natalia took Harold's beer order and Chad pulled out chairs for Bella, Carla, and Julie. He greeted Harold and they all started to talk at once. Chad's more official sounding voice won out.

He looked at Carla. "Enjoying the change of pace at the Valley Store?"

"Chad, you know I've been serving in this restaurant since I was fifteen, except for when I went off to college. Even then I served on summer break. James was always good at the business side of things and worked with our dad before we lost him. Just seemed natural I'd stay with the front of the house. I have to tell you, though, I like the variety of the grocery business. Besides that, Joshua's asked my advice on improving things, and we've done some problem solving to change things around a bit. Not much of that to do here."

"Carla was responsible for the new community bulletin board on the front of the Valley Store. Have any of you seen it?" Bella wanted to give Carla credit for what she had done.

"Saw it in passing last week," Harold said. "I'll make a point to take a closer look."

Chad nodded. "Nora will be happy to have a proper place for her jamboree posters."

Julie turned to Carla. "Are you still thinking about hosting a clogging competition in the spring?"

Natalia came in and set a Chimay Blue in front of Harold and one at Joshua's place. She leaned in to speak to Carla.

"Miss Carla, Mr. Joshua asked me to tell you he would be a few more minutes with Mr. James and to extend his apologies." Natalia stood up and took the wine bottle and asked Bella if she wanted any.

"You can pour me a small amount, Natalia, thanks. When you have a minute, I'll take a glass of tea as well."

Natalia served Carla and Julie and then left the room. Harold and Chad were talking.

Bella looked at Carla. "How old is Natalia? Did you say she's a junior in high school?"

"Afraid I'm breaking the law?" Carla gave a husky laugh. "I'm not about to take on our fine sheriff there." Chad heard her and looked at her. She winked at him.

"Oh, Carla. That's not why I asked." Bella looked embarrassed. "She just seems so mature for a junior."

"She's eighteen. Her parents took her back to Europe for a couple of years while her dad did some kind of post-graduate work. Wherever they were before they came here, they still made her do the grade they said she missed. So, she's older than most of her classmates. I think Dr. Bennett tried to advance her, but she wanted to stay with her class. She seems happy, and I think she does things on her own to learn. Anyway, I'm glad she can work on Saturdays and when we're real busy." She stopped for a minute. "Now that I think of it, I don't know why she's here tonight, though. Front of the house must be busier than normal for a Monday. Have to remember to tell her to thank her mom for letting her come in for a few hours."

Chad spoke up as Joshua entered the room. "Sure glad you clarified that, Carla. I'd hate to have to ruin our dinner by arresting you and James." Joshua turned pale and looked from one guest to the next.

"Come on, Joshua, Chad's teasing. Your beer's getting warm." Carla nodded her head towards his seat. Natalia came in with their dinners. Each plate had a full rainbow trout, hushpuppies, coleslaw, and baked potato.

"Wow."

"Lovely."

"James outdid himself."

Several other comments went around the table.

Joshua spoke softly, "May I ask a blessing?" They all bowed their heads. "Thank you, Lord, for this gathering of friends on this special night in this special place. Amen." The others echoed the "Amen," but the looks around the table were ones of bewilderment at Joshua's unusual prayer.

Chad noticed that Bella did not seem surprised. She smiled when he studied her face, reaching reached around the corner of the table to squeeze his hand.

The confusion was quickly forgotten as everyone began to eat; for a few minutes, the only sound was their knives and forks clinking against the plates. Finally, Harold spoke up. "This fish must have been caught and thrown directly in the frying pan."

Carla shook her head in disbelief. "James must have paid someone to bring it right here in a bucket of river water. We may have to put this on the menu all the time."

"Absolutely!" Bella said. She was happy to see everyone so relaxed and enjoying the meal while talking about normal, everyday things after so much had happened in their community over the past two months. As they finished, Natalia removed their plates without anyone seeming to notice. Bella saw Joshua nod at Natalia.

"When Natalia comes back, I'm going to have her tell James to..." Carla stopped as James came through the door. "Psychic now, are you?" she asked, looking at her brother.

James didn't say a word. The music stopped playing.

Taking Carla's hand, Joshua stood and stepped away from the table.

"I don't have any real experience with this sort of thing, and I think when you're young things get done a bit different. I'm enough of a mountain man that even though I'm trying to come into the twenty-first century, I value traditions." It was so quiet you could hear the breathing of everyone in the room. Joshua looked at Carla, still holding her hand.

"Far as I know, James here is your next of kin. And I know you are a smart, independent woman who can speak for herself, but I talked to him anyway."

Carla had initially turned pale, but color began to rise in her cheeks. Bella wasn't sure if it was happiness because she had figured out what Joshua was about to do, or irritation that he thought he needed her brother's permission. *I think we are about to find out.*

Joshua looked directly at her. "I asked our friends to be here because I think I may need someone to pick me up off the floor no matter what you say." He went down on one knee and said, "Carla Long, will you marry me?"

In the end, Carla was the one who fainted. She slowly melted to the floor like a stick of butter in the summer sun. Joshua caught her, and Chad leapt from his chair to stand behind her to keep her from falling backwards. Bella moved a chair over, and the two men helped her sit. Natalia quickly poured cold water on a cloth napkin and gave it to Chad. James stood not knowing what to do. Carla was soon alert and turned to look at all of them.

In a single voice, almost loud enough to shake the rafters, they all said, "Well?"

Carla looked at Joshua. She smiled. "I never thought you'd ask. Yes, I'll marry you." She leaned toward him as he squatted in front of her and kissed him. The others all started clapping.

Chad leaned over and whispered in Bella's ear. "You knew, didn't you?"

Bella just smiled.

James asked Natalia to go turn up the music, then he went over and hugged his sister. He was the only person besides Carla who had known she'd been in love with Joshua all her life. Dolly Parton started singing "My Mountains." They all swayed to the music as Natalia returned with a tray holding glasses and a bottle of champagne. James opened the champagne and poured it. He raised his glass in the air to make a toast.

"To family and friends! Best wishes for many days of love, health, and happiness!" James hugged Carla and then gave a bear hug to Joshua.

"Best wishes."

"Cheers."

"All the best."

Bella, Chad, Harold, and Julie surrounded the couple to extend their congratulations. "Rocky Top" began to play on the speakers; Carla grabbed Joshua's hand and they moved to the center of the floor. The sound of clogging echoed throughout the wooden walls and rafters. Harold and Julie joined them after the first verse. Bella, Chad, and James clapped as they watched.

Chad leaned close to Bella's ear. "You know I can't do that, right?"

"Makes two of us. Happy for them to have the floor." She looked up and kissed him.

The two couples walked back to the tables from the dance floor. James hugged his sister one more time. "Guess I better go take care of business, or we won't have one. Seems my baby sister has other plans." She hugged him and gave him a kiss.

Bella looked at them and said, "I hate to break up the party, but I have a pup all alone up on the mountain and need to go check on him."

"Duty calls," Chad said. He took Bella's hand after they said their goodnights and headed for the door.

They walked toward their vehicles "That was a nice surprise. I'm happy for both of them."

"It was obvious you figured out I knew. That's why Joshua asked me to come down. He wanted to talk about it because he was worried folks would think it was too soon after losing Jan and his dad."

"Looks like he received some wise counsel from his new sister and did what he wanted to do."

"I just told him to follow his heart and everything else would take care of itself."

Chad stopped, pulling Bella into an embrace and kissed her. "Sage advice."

"Thanks, kind sir. I hate to kiss and run, but I really must get back to Wizard. How much longer will you be on duty?"

"Don't know, unfortunately. There' some federal folks waiting for me at the station. Will you please call me when you get back to Drellag Caban? If I can't answer, at least I'll know you're home safely. I'll call you when I finish, if it's not too late." As Chad was speaking, Bella unlocked the door to her Jeep and slid into the driver's seat.

"Doesn't matter to me how late it is. I'll be up, and, if I'm not, I can always go back to sleep. Fair enough?"

"More than. Thanks, Bella. Drive safely, you have precious cargo onboard."

She looked around for a moment, then it hit her. She laughed and said, "I'll do my best."

He stepped into the open door, leaned down, and kissed her. "Be safe."

"Back atcha." Bella smiled and kissed him once more before he stepped back and closed her door.

Commission of Crimes

It was almost seven when Chad walked in the back door of the sheriff's station. Things seemed quiet as he headed to the front desk to speak to the sergeant on duty.

"Evening, Sheriff."

"Evening, Sergeant Whitehorse. You either work all the time or my random stops up here manage to catch you at the desk."

"Oh, you know, we just like to mix things up."

He laughed. "If Billy was standing here, he would have added, 'to see if you're paying attention.'"

"Likely so, Sheriff. Likely so. How are you tonight?"

"Couldn't be better."

"I imagine." Chad looked at her, puzzled. Sylvia Whitehorse chuckled. "I suspect the word about Carla and Joshua got across the road faster than you. Just me and this fine deputy up here when Walter. . ."

Chad smiled. "Might have known. Did he expect us to put it out on the radio?"

"You know Walter. Waste of a day for him if he doesn't have something to spread around the valley, and nothing else was open except for the Valley Store."

"Well, at least this is true *and* it's good news. Joshua and Carla were both grinning from ear to ear. Glad I could be there for the event."

"Is it usual for other people to be present when a man asks a woman to marry him? In our tribe, the parents make the announcement. Although, now that I think about it, that's when the couple is young."

"Can't say as I know what the traditions are today. To be honest, I didn't really know thirty plus years ago either. I kind of bumbled into mine." He took a breath. "On a happier note, I don't think I've heard Joshua ever talk that much. Happy day in the valley, though, that's what I think."

"I'm happy for both of them too, Sheriff. What are you doing back here, if I may ask?"

"I have a meeting with Sam Nations and Quinn Isaacs. Have time to sit in?"

"Pretty quiet tonight. Happy to do it if you want me there."

"I may need you there to help me keep my focus. I'm still pretty steamed about the way things went down on that operation at 'the house on the hill.'" She just nodded.

IEA Agent Quinn Isaacs walked through the front door followed by DEA Agent Sam Nations. Chad looked at his watch. He didn't realize how long he and Sylvia had been talking.

"Sergeant, I'll ask you to get our guests something to drink, and I'll meet you in my office." He nodded to the two agents and headed down the hall. His personal mobile phone rang, and he saw it was Bella. He stepped into the empty room next to his office to take the call.

"Hey, lovely lady."

"Hey to you. Long time no see."

"Not the kind of joke you want to tell a law enforcement officer who knows how far it is to your cabin and saw you about half an hour ago." He laughed. "Seriously, thanks for calling. I'm glad you're safely home. Is Wizard doing okay?"

"Happy as a tick on a fat dog, although I have to say I hope we don't ever have too many ticks to manage. Wizard was on his blanket on the porch with his tail wagging when I pulled up. Thanks for asking. I'll let you go; I know you have work to do. Glad I got to see you today and that we were part of a great day for Carla and Joshua."

"Me too, on both counts. If I'm finished here before nine, I'll call. Otherwise, I'll talk to you tomorrow. Sleep well, Bella. Dream of me."

"Done and done. Same to you. Call anytime though."

He almost knocked Sam down when he stepped out the door. He realized he was distracted thinking about Bella.

"Sorry, Chad." Sam stepped to the side and waited for Chad to exit.

"I'm the one not paying attention. Did you get something to eat?"

"Decided working on feeding my spiritual self was more important."

Chad just nodded. He wondered if Sam had gone to see Chief Whitehorse. He hoped so.

Sylvia and Quinn were standing at the round table when they entered Chad's office.

"I asked Sylvia to join us. Anything that needs to be said and planned will include her. Have a seat. Thanks for getting coffee, Sylvia." Everyone sat, adjusted their chairs, and waited.

"I believe this is your meeting, Quinn." Chad gestured to her.

"Thanks, Sheriff. Before we discuss the next steps in our plan to get to the source of the business in 'the house on the hill,' as well as figure out who's using land in your jurisdiction for sheltering illegal immigrants, I need us to debrief and clear the air on the recent operation. I think we have some decisions to make going forward about *who* is going to be involved in the current plan." She stopped talking. It was not missed by the others that she watched Sam the entire time.

All four sat without saying anything. Finally, Sam spoke up.

"You don't need me to tell you that the DEA, me in particular, highjacked the joint operation. That I did so under orders explains it, but it doesn't excuse it. As my chief reminded me tonight, you always have choices in any given situation, even when the bullets are flying. I have apologized to you and you." He looked at Chad and Quinn. "I know you weren't there at the moment of my action, Sergeant, but you were impacted by my actions and I apologize."

It registered with Chad that Sam had said "my chief." He knew it meant Chief Whitehorse. Sam would never refer to SAC McMullen that way. He nodded, pleased that Sam had the smarts to go see Tom.

"What I am about to say may well cost me my job..." he paused for a beat, "if I don't resign first." No one said a word. "DEA had been tailing the guys in the house and the assessment was they were just low-level mules. We had no evidence of weapons. At the moment Quinn and I exited my SUV to play our charade of running out of gas, I received a text ordering me to enter the house." He took a really deep breath. "I sent back a text that DEA agents were not on the scene. My boss replied, 'Use the incompetent sheriff and IEA agent!'"

Chad's face turned to granite. It was hard to tell if he was even breathing. Sylvia looked at Sam, her distant cousin, in disbelief that not only was he told that, but that he shared it as well. She gathered he had been up to see her father, the chief of the local tribe. She could see how despondent Sam was, and she hoped her father's advice was enough to keep him from going off the deep end.

"I won't ask why you didn't tell me earlier, or even why you are telling us now, but I am going to need the night to sort out what this means for me and my folks going forward." Chad's words were slow and deliberate. He turned to Quinn. "Agent Isaacs?"

"When working with another law enforcement officer, trust is paramount," she began slowly. "To mount a team, even within your own agency, starts to stretch the boundaries of knowing who has what agenda. To have a multi-agency team, well, that has even greater challenges, as each of us here knows. But without trust it can't work. Sam and I go back a number of years, and I have always respected his integrity, his work ethic, and his judgement. There would be no more discussion if I didn't have that history. However, that said, I need a few minutes with you, Chad, before we go any further."

Chad nodded. Sam and Sylvia stood and headed for the door.

"We'll be in my office, Sheriff," Sylvia told him. She and Sam walked out.

Chad slumped in his chair then leaned his head back and flexed his shoulders.

"One special agent in charge has gone too far this..." Chad stopped himself.

"After you left this afternoon, Sam told *me* what he just shared. He had planned to tell you after our meeting, but I said we wouldn't hold a meeting until he told you—with me present."

"Thanks, Quinn. I needed to hear it, and he needed to say it. Like you, I go way back with Sam, and I know his time in the Marines indoctrinated him well in following orders. But I've seen him making progress on sorting out the gray that surrounds all of us on taking and giving orders. Did he tell you he was considering walking away from the DEA?"

"No. In fact, that stunned me."

"You do realize he meant his tribal chief when he spoke, not his DEA chief?"

"I didn't at first, but then I knew it had to be Chief Whitehorse because of what I believe about Sam Nations. Sam's a good guy. As opposed to what I have to tell you about SAC McMullen, who is *not* a good guy."

"I'm all ears. That is one man I have never liked or respected."

"If I was a betting woman, I'd say it's because you know SAC McMullen epitomizes our ole mountain saying: 'hit dog always hollers.'"

Chad nodded his head. He had the feeling she was about to tell him something specific that would likely confirm the feelings he had about this man.

"Hold on, Quinn." He stood and quickly went to his computer. He pulled up Harold's email. "Commission, drugs, and our community," he read. *Harold wasn't talking about the commission; he was talking about* one *commissioner.* Chad had not wanted to ask Harold about the email earlier to avoid interfering with their dinner as friends, but he made a mental note to follow up with Harold as soon as possible. Chad walked back to the table.

"Thanks. Go on."

"As reluctant as I am to work with Sam, at least for a while, I know him well enough to know he'll be on his full game, and I, for one, owe him that chance. I would be a fool if I didn't say I have my guard up, but for right now I'm willing to consider including him, if you are. Here's the intel we have."

She outlined what Immigration Enforcement knew about a chink in the armor of the DEA. There was credible intelligence reporting that there was someone in the DEA who was involved with some area politician, or politicians, in activities that crossed over multiple jurisdictions. What wasn't known was who was involved and to what extent. She shared what she felt she could without violating her code of ethics because Chad had not yet indicated he was interested in participating or running an operation out of his station.

"Needless to say, IEA is aware of crimes that cross over jurisdictions and agencies, and there is a need to figure out how wide a net can and should be cast. Now you know why I asked Sam to leave."

Chad sat quietly, playing and rewinding conversations in his head like they were on a reel-to-reel tape player: Sam, McMullen, Quinn's boss, Quinn, Harold, Zimmerman. *What does Harold suspect?* Finally, he looked at Quinn.

"I have enough experience with state and federal agencies to know how territorial individuals can be, even when they are supposed to cooperate. I also know that doesn't make them the bad guys. I'm trying to keep my own community safe from others bringing crime here. We have our share of local rabble rousing, domestic abuse, and petty theft, but until the last two months, we've been tucked away here. Not sure we can ever get rid of all crime... too many human beings to make that realistic." He paused for a moment to collect his thoughts. "Sorry, I'm rambling. Since you're staying in the valley tonight, could we meet in the morning? It would help me to have some time to think, give you some time to figure out what you think we can do together, and both of us to decide if we're willing to give Sam another chance and under what conditions."

"Fine with me. I'll get Sam." She stood and walked out the door. They returned in a few minutes and sat down.

Interesting skill set in this young woman. She can take charge and be deferential, but I'm pretty much guessing you better not step on her toes. Chad saw this as Quinn's meeting, so he waited.

"It's almost eight thirty and each of us has had a long day. We'll meet here at..." she looked at Chad.

"I'll be here between six and six thirty, so you decide. I'm good until noon."

"Seven then. Work for you Sam?"

"I'll be here." Sam's voice sounded relieved that he had not been ostracized.

"Seven it is." Quinn stood, shook Chad's hand, ignored Sam's outstretched one, and left.

Chad stood and shook hands with Sam then leaned toward him and said quietly, "Meet me at the tribal grounds in thirty minutes, back building."

Sam nodded.

CHAPTER 5

Come to the woods, for here is rest.
There is no repose like that of the green deep woods.
Sleep in forgetfulness of all ill.
John Muir, 1838 – 1914

Safe and Secure

WIZARD'S WAGGING TAIL AND HIS ABILITY to stay on his blanket until Bella reached him warmed her heart. After a walk to check on the progress of the construction, Bella sat on the porch with Wizard at her feet. She watched with delight as the sun set behind the dark silhouette of the mountains and the sky began to turn the blue-black color that she loved. The sharp cold of late October would soon make these outside evenings fewer and fewer.

She turned her attention to the day's events, and Chad's teasing about how quickly she got home made her smile. *Drellag Caban, we are on the mend—both of us. I have a new man in my life. The shed is almost finished, the new cabin will go up soon, and we have a new companion to keep us both company up on this mountain. I think Wizard likes the security of your hundred plus years surrounding him. I know I do.*

Bella leaned down to pet Wizard then grabbed her notepad and pen. She made a note to talk to Arthur Gillett in the morning. She wanted to discuss a dog run for Wizard that might connect from the house to the shed, and she also wanted him to contact Carl Patrick to arrange a gravel parking pad on the low side of the cabin. She would also need him to add gravel to her road when they finished with all the heavy trucks. *Poor Arthur! I hope he doesn't mind having a client who is constantly making to-do lists!*

She returned the paper and pen to the small table and picked up her book. There were only four more chapters left in Patrick Taylor's *An Irish Country Cottage: An Irish Country Novel*. She was finding this read particularly comforting because, like her, they were rebuilding a cottage—granted, the one in the book was damaged due to a fire. She decided the ATV damage to her shed was probably easier to cope with than a fire, particularly since she didn't lose the whole structure. She was absorbed in the book and enjoyed reading by the glow of the porch lamp, but it didn't take long before the cold air started to make itself felt. Bella stood up and checked the screen door lock. "Come on, Wizard. It's time to move inside. You can warm up on your inside blanket, and I'll take a shower."

Wizard followed her into the living room and waited while she closed and locked the French doors. She had already closed all the windows when she arrived home from dinner, and she was pleased to see the light on her writing desk had clicked on like it was supposed to. Doc Jim, the Vet, had given her the suggestion of putting a timer on it as part of establishing a routine for Wizard, and, as an added bonus, she didn't have to worry about turning lights on as she moved inside from the dark.

Wizard went straight to his blanket. "Good boy, Wizard." She scratched him behind the ears and reached for the jar on the counter beside his blanket. She praised him again and gave him a treat. "I went shopping today, and *you* are the beneficiary."

Her shower was hot and relaxing, and she luxuriated in the coziness of her fleece robe and lambswool lined slippers while she towel dried her hair. As she walked into the kitchen to make a cup of tea, she saw that it was only eight twenty-five. While the kettle boiled, she turned on the remote to the gas logs in the fireplace, smiling at the flames leapt into life at the press of a button. She turned back to the kitchen at the sound of the phone ringing, which was soon joined by the whistling of the tea kettle.

She pulled the long cord on the wall mounted phone so she could turn off the kettle at the same time she answered. "Drellag Caban, may I help you?" She wished her answering machine showed caller ID.

"Is that whistle to wake me up, or put you to sleep?"

"Maybe both, if you're still working. For me, it is definitely for my nighttime cup of tea. This has been a long day for you, Chad. Are you headed home soon?"

"Well, truth be told, I wish I was headed up the mountain to Drellag Caban."

"Come right ahead. I just lit a fire in the fireplace."

"That's tempting in more ways than one, but I have to go meet Sam Nations, and then I have a seven o'clock meeting tomorrow morning. Best if I take a raincheck this time."

"*Mi casa es su casa.*"

"Wait, don't tell me. I know *casa* is house, right? So, I'm going to take a wild stab: My house is your house. Did I get it?"

"Perfect score." She laughed and sat down with her cup of tea at the kitchen table.

"I've planned a break in my day tomorrow around noon. Okay if I run up and see the construction work?"

"Sure, feel free to come up. I'll be in Round City. . ." Bella trailed off, trying to keep from snickering into the phone.

"Oh," his voice dropped in disappointment, but he quickly recovered. "Then I'll change my plans, and I can drive you over." He grinned. *Will I catch you in your teasing?*

"Okay, you win! I could hear a heavy burden in your voice, and I was just checking to see if you were alert enough to drive to meet Sam tonight. I'd hate to have to report the sheriff *to the sheriff* for driving while tired."

"Right, I hear he's a stickler."

She could hear him relaxing a little. "Seriously, Chad, you are welcome anytime. I'll be here."

"Just wanted to hear your voice one more time before your day ends. If all is well up on the mountain, I'll let you enjoy your cup of tea. See you tomorrow, Bella."

"Lord willing." *Matt loved that phrase. I miss him.*

"True that! Sleep well, lovely lady."

"Be safe, Chad. I hope you sleep well, and, who knows, you might even dream of me."

"No doubt about that. Good night."

"Good night, Chad."

After hanging up, she sat in front of the fire and sipped her tea, thinking about the conversation and the events of the day. *I wonder how others over fifty navigate new romance? Expectations are so different than when you are young, but the excitement might be the same.*

She finished her tea, smiling as her thoughts turned to the day ahead. An early morning to write was top of her list of things to do. It had been difficult to concentrate on writing with all the construction taking place, but she was determined to make this part of her new routine. She washed out her teacup and left it in the dish drainer, a habit she was finally comfortable acquiring, then she put the note of things to discuss with Arthur on the small bulletin board by the phone. Arthur was usually there by seven, so she would have several hours to write after speaking with him.

"Come on, Wizard, one quick walk in the yard, and then we're going to have an early night. I might read a bit more, but I'm doing it in bed." She slipped on her boots and clipped the leash to Wizard's collar. By the time they came back, she was shivering and wished she had put a jacket over her robe. She praised Wizard and put him in his crate. He settled in without any fuss, putting his head down on top of his paws. His eyes never left Bella's face. "Good night, Wizard. A new day awaits us on our mountain tomorrow."

Bella realized she had slipped out of her boots and walked into the cabin in her sock feet. Her slippers were still by the kitchen door so she decided to go get them; the floor would be too cold in the morning. The fireplace had gas logs, and she left it burning on low; it would keep the chill from totally invading the cabin. She double checked that she had re-locked the kitchen door.

Once ensconced under the warm comforter, she took a moment to review her day. Not-So-Good List: nothing. She let out a low breath of relaxation knowing there was not one thing for this list. Her Good List was full of things to celebrate: Joshua and Carla's engagement, time with Chad just to relax for a few minutes *and* two phone conversations with him, dinner with friends. *How can I be so fortunate to have so many things for this list?*

Her thoughts drifted closer to home. Arthur Gillett was making quick work of repairing and restoring the shed, the foundation was poured for the new cabin, and he might even get the garage built before winter. Wizard was adapting quickly, and she loved having another beating heart in her home. She rolled on her side and looked at the picture of herself and Matt. *Hello, my love. I know that I am a far better person for having been loved by you. Thank you for telling me to be open to loving someone new. I'm not sure I could open my heart if you hadn't. Who knows, it might just happen.* Bella rolled over on her back and closed her eyes; she was too tired to read. *Sweet dreams, Chad.*

Truth and Consequences

There was a single light on an old telephone pole above the back building on the tribal grounds. This area was used for the annual powwow as well as other events hosted by local tribal members. It was not an area anyone other than a tribal member would generally enter, especially after dark. Chad knew that choosing this location would signal to Sam that this was important—not a meeting be discussed with anyone. Chad pulled up next to Sam's SUV, driver's window to driver's window.

"Well, Agent Nations, we could sit here and talk like two old law enforcement guys passing time on a shift, or we could take a little ride where both of us know we aren't being monitored or overheard."

Sam rolled up his window, stepped out of his SUV, and walked around to the passenger door of Chad's Ford Interceptor.

"Thanks, Chad. Pretty sure I've lost whatever trust Quinn ever had in me, and I was afraid I'd lost yours."

"Jury might still be out for me, and I think you need to give Quinn a little more credit. I'm pretty sure you wouldn't be invited to the meeting in the morning if she had given up on you."

Chad headed out the back road of the tribal grounds, a track not known to most people in the area, and drove up to the lookout area above the grounds.

"I never knew if this was sacred ground. I know the tribe doesn't say anything that we patrol it on our runs. Is there any reason we shouldn't sit here and talk?"

"It's true we don't generally invite Europeans up here, but it's not sacred ground. We can talk here."

"As you're fond of pointing out to me, I'm not as young as I once was, and I need to get some sleep tonight, so I'm going to cut to the chase. You can give me a simple 'yes' or 'no' and I won't push you on details. If you share, it goes no further."

Their eyes had adjusted to the dark once Chad turned off the motor, and Sam knew Chad was watching him.

"We'll take it as an assumption that people in law enforcement take orders from their direct supervisors, some of which are given to them to pass on. That is *not* the question I am about to ask you." Chad paused. "Did you have orders from above SAC McMullen to follow *any* order you were given by the SAC?"

Sam's heart was racing in his chest. He much preferred operations that did not involve his home community—or the man sitting next to him. He thought about what Chief Whitehorse had told him: "You always have choices." Sam knew if he was ever at a fork in the road where he had to make a choice, this was it: his job or his integrity.

Sam's answer was simple. "Yes." The two men sat in silence. Years of trust and mutual respect sat between them.

"I'm going to drive back down this mountain, and I'm going to tell you a little story as we go. When we arrive at your vehicle, I expect you to get out without asking anything. Your response to my little story will tell me if you plan to be fully engaged in our meeting tomorrow as Sam Nations, the man."

Chad started the SUV. Even without talking to Harold yet, he had pieced together some ideas from Harold's email, the events of the past two months, and the shootout a week ago. His gut instinct about DEA Special Agent in Charge McMullen and Commissioner Zimmerman gave him enough of the pieces to know what answer he needed to get from Sam. It would determine Chad's stance in the meeting tomorrow morning.

"Once upon a time, there was a man who grew up in a community steeped in traditions forged for hundreds, maybe thousands of years. His land was invaded by settlers from another land. The two peoples had their differences and even had wars. In the late twentieth century, some of the people from both tribes started figuring out how to respect each other and share the riches of the mountains they now jointly inhabited. This man managed to walk with one foot in his tribe and one foot in the world that had merged. He served his country and his community in many ways. One day he found himself at a crossroads in a field of work he was fully suited for. He learned that even in that work there were people who had their own misguided, or even greedy, reasons for not being as dedicated as he was to the oath they took to uphold the law of the land. This man learned his boss was corrupt, and he took it to higher authorities. The higher authorities wanted to catch the boss in his corruption, so the man was made to choose between his community and his organization. That decision cost people's lives and almost cost the man his."

Chad was driving very slowly while he talked.

"The people protecting his community received information from multiple sources that there was more to the first part of the mission than had been planned by the joint team. However, the overall mission was not completed, and a decision had to be made about whether to include the man in the next phase. The man was given assurances that the others involved in the mission wanted to catch the corrupt boss too. The man was shown how he could be loyal to his oath and his community, but that required a decision on the man's part. The only way the people in his community would agree to the rest of the mission, including the man's participation, was if the *man* committed to the mission, *not* just the employee."

Chad pulled up to the driver's side of Sam's SUV.

"So, my question is simple. Who will show up at our meeting tomorrow morning? The man—or the employee?"

Sam did not hesitate. He reached across to Chad and extended his hand: "The man."

"Good night, Sam. Be safe." Chad shook Sam's hand and drove off as soon as the door closed.

Chad parked his SUV in his garage, left his boots facing out on the kitchen step, and on autopilot removed his service weapon and placed it in the gun safe by the door. He took out a Fat Tire Amber beer from the fridge then walked into the living room and sat down in his recliner. He still had not turned on a light. He slowly sipped his beer, replaying all that this day had brought. This time of quiet was how he processed his day and organized his thoughts for the next.

His determination to catch those bringing crime into his community was his overarching consideration, but he knew that cooperation with Quinn and Sam would cast the widest possible net and have the greatest likelihood of successfully stopping this round of bad actors. He was under no illusion there wouldn't be more in the future. Confident that Sergeant Whitehorse had the day-to-day operations under control, and knowing Quinn was in charge of the meeting in the morning, he took his empty beer bottle into the kitchen, rinsed it out, and put it in the recycling container.

After a very long, hot shower, he settled on his bed, locked his fingers together, and put the back of his hands on his forehead and closed his eyes. *Well, Joshua, my friend, you followed your heart. I wish you and Carla all the happiness in the world. Who knows, the Johnsons and the Longs might just create a business empire right here in the valley.* He smiled at the idea. *Miss Bella, what message can I send to you this night? Do you have any idea how deeply you have lodged in my head and my heart? If I hadn't been afraid you might run the other way, I might have grabbed your hand this evening and made it a double engagement party. Something tells me you are measuring every step of this path we are walking. I'm okay with that. Just don't shut the gate on me. Please. Sweet dreams, my Bella.* He fell fast asleep.

CHAPTER 6

Nature is ever at work building and pulling down,
creating and destroying,
keeping everything whirling and flowing,
allowing no rest but in rhythmical motion,
chasing everything in endless song out of one beautiful
form into another.
John Muir, 1838 – 1914

Awakening

BELLA DRESSED QUICKLY IN JEANS, slipped a silk thermal shell under her plaid shirt, and grabbed her lightweight wool scarf. Even with her lambswool slippers, she was glad to have on socks. She had already heard the construction activity start outside; she wanted to take Wizard for a walk and catch Arthur before he got too busy.

"Morning, Wizard. We'll go for a walk as soon as I heat some water for my tea. That okay with you?" Wizard wagged his tail as she opened his crate and scratched his neck. He went immediately to his blanket, sat down, and looked at her. "Water and some food," she said, pointing to his dishes. Bella was still amazed that Wizard had learned several commands in the space of a week. *Doc Jim is a miracle worker.*

While Wizard saw to his breakfast, Bella poured tea in her Yeti and slipped on her boots and navy blue down-filled jacket. When she looked up from tying her boots, Wizard was sitting at the kitchen door, looking back and forth from the doorknob to her face. She laughed and scratched his head while clipping the leash to his collar. "Let's go see what's happening, Wizard."

They walked over to Arthur who was setting up his tools for the day.

"Morning, Arthur, did you bring this fine morning with you?"

"Morning, Bella. Nope, the good Lord set it down upon us. These are perfect days for our work; it's cool enough in the morning to get your blood flowing, but not so hot in the day to get your blood boiling."

She smiled at him and nodded. "Good point, Arthur. Do you have a few minutes to talk about a couple of things?" Bella's interest in linguistics often caused her to analyze the phrases people used every day, especially mountain phrases. She made a mental note to think about Arthur's use of weather and blood flow.

"Anytime, Bella. My time is your time. What can I do for you and this fine pup of yours?" Arthur had already made friends with Wizard, who eagerly accepted being petted by him.

"Actually, Wizard is one reason I wanted to chat with you. What do you think of installing a run from the wall of the cabin to the shed? It would need to have a roof covering to keep out other animals, right? Should it be wood? Or are there other options you might recommend?" She pointed from the middle of the cabin wall to the end of the shed.

Arthur was clearly listening to Bella, but he was also looking at the location she was considering. He started to walk towards the cabin. He studied the wall and then paced off the distance to the shed. Pulling the pencil from above his ear, he took a small spiral bound notepad from his pocket and wrote down several figures.

"Let me do some thinking on this, and then we'll talk. Right now, I think the best ground surface is going to be concrete. It'll be easier to keep clean, and nowadays we can even put some color in it so it looks like dirt." He paused, looking back towards the foundation for the cabin. "How sure are you that you want to do this?"

"Absolutely sure." Bella did not hesitate. "Do you have a concern about it?"

Arthur chuckled. "Bella, please know I mean no offense by what I'm going to say, but I have not met a woman in these mountains so willing to make decisions so quickly and definitively."

"Blame it on my Grandmother Hazel; she was a determined mountain woman from birth."

"Well, fact of the matter is I have a concrete truck coming up day after tomorrow to pour the foundation for your garage. So, that's a good time to do the run and save some money. We can frame it out today and you can approve it, then we'll be ready to pour. Just so happens I have some PVC pipe on my truck, so we can pour it with a couple of drains so the water runs out underground when you wash it down or it rains. I'm thinking we could frame up a structure and run some trusses across poles and tie it in to the roof lines to give some continuity to joining the shed and the garage. Then I'd suggest putting a coated chain link fence with a couple of gates, one on each side, and running some boards down the side facing your kitchen window. Pretty easy construction. I can have a drawing and some figures for you tomorrow."

"Perfect. Go ahead and do the concrete work, and once you have everything ready, we'll finalize the look." Bella paused. "Sorry I didn't think of this sooner, so you could have it all as part of the original plan."

"No problem, Bella. No problem at all. Anything else?"

"Oh, yes, thanks for reminding me. I was so distracted thinking about the run for Wizard, I almost forgot. Would you please work with Carl Phillips to put a gravel pad on the low side of the new cabin, and be ready to add gravel to the road once the heavy trucks are out?"

"Yes, ma'am, that's a mighty fine idea. We try to be careful, but you're right that there's lots of weight coming up this road right now. I'll work with Carl, sure enough."

Bella extended her hand. "Thanks, Arthur. By the way, I went to the mechanic you recommended, and he's going to work me in next week. He said there's no rush; my Wrangler's in pretty good shape and not beyond the oil change date. Appreciate your advice."

"He'll do right by you. That's for sure." He shook her outstretched hand then turned and walked toward the shed.

Bella walked Wizard around the cabin and checked the trees along the ridgeline to make sure none were likely to uproot and fall towards the cabin. Back inside, she scratched Wizard's ears. "Good boy, Wizard." She could hardly believe her good fortune to save an injured dog and have him turn out to be such a smart animal. Wizard sat down on his blanket. Bella washed her hands and turned on the kettle for more tea. She decided on a piece of toast and an egg for breakfast. She saw on the clock it was only eight, so she had some time to write before Chad came.

New Day, New Plan

Chad had finished a bowl of cereal and was on his second cup of coffee by six. Harold's email was still nagging at him, and he decided he would text Harold to see if they could meet at The Corral. After that, he'd head up to Drellag Caban. He managed to get his dishes in the dishwasher, his weapon and boots on, and himself buckled into the car in under three minutes; not a record, but his target time most days. He was in the lobby at six twenty talking to Eddie Douglas, the night shift sergeant, when Sergeant Whitehorse entered.

"Morning, gentlemen."

"Morning, Sergeant Whitehorse," Sergeant Douglas said.

"Morning, Sergeant. You're here mighty early. Isn't our meeting at seven?" Chad looked at the clock on the wall.

"Yes, Sheriff. Have some things to go over with Deputy Thomas. She's going to cover morning roll call. I'll be at your office by seven."

"Thanks. Appreciate the juggling you had to do to make this work." Chad nodded and made eye contact with her.

"Happy to serve, Sheriff." Sylvia walked down the hall and greeted Susan Thomas, who had come in the back door.

"Anything I need to know, Sarge?" Chad resumed his conversation with Eddie.

"Things are as quiet as we like our mountains to be. Hoping we can keep it that way, Sheriff."

"Me too, Eddie, me too." Chad shook Eddie's hand and walked to the break room to get a cup of coffee. He was pleased the coffee was fresh, not the dregs of the late-night shift. He opted for a paper cup rather than going to get his own mug. He put a dollar bill in the box for the coffee and cup. *Never seem to have a problem with covering the costs for this. Good to have folks working here who do their part. Wish my budget could cover all of it.* As Chad turned to walk out, Jeff Coleman, the detective who had found the connection between Commissioner Zimmerman and the two "by-the-hour" motels in Round City came through the door.

"Morning, Sheriff."

"Morning to you, Detective. You're here mighty early. Something up?"

"No, sir, just helping out our forensic tech while Detective Williams is gone. Alexander has quite a few cases she's trying to analyze. Good to know Billy took a break. It's been a rough couple of months."

Chad extended his hand. "Thanks for chipping in, Jeff. I appreciate it, and all the more for not having to ask. Means a lot. Anything I need to know about in the lab? Any word on the animals from near The Mountain Villages?"

"Happy to be of service, Sheriff. Nothing definitive yet, but Alexander thinks there may be a commonality to what was used to kill those wild critters. Once she gets a hit on the chemical, we can start tracking it down. Hope to know in the next day or two. Other than that, nothing out of the ordinary, just a couple of B and Es in empty cabins. We've got it." He kept walking. "You have a good day now."

"You too, Detective."

Chad walked into his office and sent a text to Harold to see if he could meet at 10:30 a.m. before turning on his computer. He hoped to have a few minutes to review the latest activity report; he still didn't like referring to them as the "police blotter" like big city law enforcement did. Six crime-related deaths in the last two months troubled him deeply. He wanted to make sure the reporting clearly indicated that none of them involved weapons discharged by any of his staff other than him. *Guess I now know why the DEA didn't send someone to talk to me about the two men I killed in the botched raid, no thanks to SAC McMullen. He must have something pretty big he doesn't want disturbed. Wonder how long reports take to get noticed above his paygrade?*

IEA Agent Quinn Isaacs was at the sheriff's office at quarter to seven. She hoped to talk to Chad before they met with Sam and Sylvia. Quinn was glad to have the sergeant involved because she found Sylvia to be bright, deliberative, and, best of all, a good leader among her deputies. The deputy on duty told her to go on back as Chad had indicated he was expecting her. She knocked on Chad's door.

So much for catching up on reports. Chad stood and looked at his phone. "3:30 OK? Or tomorrow, 10:00? The Corral?" Harold had replied. Chad opened the door.

"You're early, Agent Isaacs."

"Couldn't sleep. May I have a few minutes before our meeting?"

"Absolutely. Need any coffee? Water?"

She held up her paper coffee cup. "I reckon I'm fine. Thanks all the same."

"Just give me one minute. Have a seat." He motioned to the table, then quickly typed a reply to Harold—"3:30 OK"—and hit send. *I don't want to be here at three thirty. I want to be at Bella's.* He sighed to himself.

Chad picked up the paper cup with his coffee and started to pour it in his mug but saw the dried remains of yesterday's coffee and thought better of it. He joined Quinn at the round table.

Quinn cleared her throat. "Chad, I've been thinking about Sam's role going forward and what happened a week ago. Something just doesn't fit. I don't know if you're aware, but Sam and I dated in college." Chad didn't say a word or move a muscle, but it was news to him. "We parted as friends and have worked together on a number of interagency projects. What happened the other night at that house just isn't what I know of Sam Nations."

"Tell me your concerns going forward." Chad spoke with little inflection yet conveyed his openness to hearing her out.

"I think he was ordered to go in." She paused. "And one of two things were in play. One, the SAC is out to get Sam and wanted to blame Sam because he expected either Immigration or the local sheriff to raise a stink about the operational changes. Or Sam had orders from higher up to carry out any orders from his SAC, especially if they were unusual."

Chad was very deliberate in his response. "Maybe both, and perhaps a third."

Quinn looked at him. She took several seconds before she spoke. "*Why* would people above the SAC make him obey an order that they knew could get him kill—" She stopped. "They *didn't* know—couldn't know if the SAC kept information from them."

"If I understood Sam yesterday, the intel from the DEA was that the two men in the house were not known to have weapons and were acting as mules, nothing more. Is that what you understood?"

Quinn sat nodding her head. "Oh, sh—" She stopped herself. "Sorry, I don't usually use that kind of language, but..."

"Yeah, I know what you mean. The question now is how do we address the multi-agency crimes in my jurisdiction which could involve SAC McMullen or others at the DEA, and not jeopardize Sam's career or, more importantly, his life?"

"We may need to regroup, given that seven a.m. is upon us. Maybe you and I figure out a part to leave Sam in the dark, so he really doesn't know, and see if that sets a trap for McMullen or whoever at DEA is the rotten apple."

"Are your bosses expecting us to bring in the FBI?" Chad's voice conveyed his conflicted opinion.

"My boss is okay with us trying to wrap up the 'house on the hill' part without the FBI. We can bring them in if we're close to identifying the head of that operation. While your county commissioner looks like the prime suspect, he might be a pawn in a bigger operation. He might know that he's a bit player, and, then again, he might not. Most people don't successfully break into big time human trafficking and drug running on their own. It's clear someone was providing the drugs to the two men who were delivering them to the 'house on the hill,' but it seems unlikely those men were the source. And someone made the connection with the illegal immigrant girls that Zimmerman took to the house. Zimmerman didn't just happen upon a girl and get invited into that trafficking ring."

Chad stared off into the distance. "Did I ever tell you I *like* being sheriff of a small town in a tucked away valley, where we haven't had much more than the normal bad things that go hand in hand with human misery?" He went quiet.

"Well, Sheriff-Who-Likes-His-Quiet-Community, since I asked for this meeting, I hope you'll trust me to propose an operation. Feel free to jump in any time."

The Valley Store

Joshua was at the Valley Store at six to finish stocking shelves for the day. Yesterday was a whirlwind with the normal Monday deliveries and trying to plan dinner with James while not letting Carla hear his conversation. *I'm so happy the dinner turned out great. At sixty-three I am engaged to be married—again! I think James is happy for us.* He began putting cake mix boxes on the shelf, pulling current stock forward so the new went to the back. *I sure was surprised last night after we closed up when Carla told me she had been in love with me her entire life. Could Jan be upset that I would fall in love with a woman who always loved me but never interfered in our marriage? I don't think so. Jan never had a problem that Carla and I were dance partners for so many years. Did Jan know how Carla felt? How come I never figured it out?* Normally he was grateful for the fact that shelving products gave him time to think. He wasn't so sure about that at this moment. The jingle of the silver bell above the front door caused him to look up.

"Morning, Joshua. Just me, your fiancée." Her voice had a lilt, and she was all but singing.

"In the baking section, I'll be there in a minute."

Carla reached him just as he finished putting the last box on the shelf. He stood and gave her a long, lingering kiss as she stood on her tiptoes.

She dropped back on her heels and looked up at him. She seemed to be trying to catch her breath. "Much as I love a good morning kiss, I'm thinking we'd best leave *that kind* of kiss for outside of work." She wiggled her eyebrows at him.

Joshua laughed. "Fair enough. Fair enough." He was struggling as feelings stirred he hadn't felt in a long time. The jingling bell above the door distracted both of them. *Forgot to tell Carla to leave the door locked until seven thirty.*

"I've got it. Have you brought down the cash drawer?"

Joshua nodded. "Been in the habit of bringing it down first thing since my dad..." he trailed off. He didn't want to remember his dad falling on the steps and then dying less than a week later, killed by a couple of kids making a bad decision.

Carla squeezed his hand as he started moving towards the front. "You'll be okay."

She put on a big smile as she moved to the front. "Good morning! Something I can help you find?" Then she saw who it was. "Well, hey, Miss Andrea, Karolina. How're y'all today?"

Karolina looked at Carla and then at her mother. "Miss Carla doesn't work here, Mommy, she works at The Corral."

Carla bent down and was eye level with the blond-haired girl. "I do now, Karolina." Carla looked up and saw the smile on Andrea's face.

"I understand congratulations are in order." Andrea extended her hand to Carla.

Karolina pulled on her mother's hand. "Why, Mommy? How do you order congratulations?'"

Both women started laughing.

"Oh, honey, you were asleep when Natalia came home from The Corral yesterday. I was saying congratulations because Mr. Joshua and Miss Carla are going to be married."

"Really?" Karolina's smile lit up her whole face.

Carla jumped in. "Really!"

Karolina started clapping.

"I saw the front door ajar, so I hope it's okay that we came in. Are you open?" Andrea looked from the door to Carla.

"No problem, Miss Andrea. I was in such a hurry to get in this morning, I didn't close the door all the way and, anyway, it's almost seven thirty. Anything I can help you find?"

"No, we're good. Thanks." She and Karolina started down the aisle towards the fresh vegetables and fruit.

Carla beamed.

CHAPTER 7

There is a love of wild Nature in everybody,
an ancient mother-love ever showing itself whether recognized or no,
and however covered by cares and duties.

John Muir, 1838 – 1914

The Morning Drags On

BY THE TIME SHE LAID OUT A STRATEGY focused on tracking and setting a trap for Commissioner George Zimmerman, Quinn's meeting
lasted almost two hours. Chad noticed Quinn was careful not to mention SAC McMullen. It was not missed by Chad or Quinn that Sam
did not say anything about his actions in the raid that resulted in the
deaths of the two suspected drug runners. Quinn wrapped up the
meeting.

"I appreciate your thoughtful ideas and suggestions. I think we
have a solid plan going forward. As I mentioned, Zimmerman flew
to Michigan on Sunday, but we have agents tailing him to make sure
he doesn't slip across the border into Canada. The anticipated return
flight is on Thursday. That should give us sufficient time to get things
set up. Any questions?"

Sam looked around the table. "I'm not sure there's a role for the
DEA in what you have outlined, Agent Isaacs. Am I missing something?" He looked quickly at Chad and then back at Quinn.

"Agent Nations, this is a direct extension of the operation regarding the transporting of illegal immigrants to the 'house on the hill.'

Do you not see the connection? I just assumed that the DEA would want to follow through as we try to determine the source providing the drugs to the two men who were killed."

Sam nodded his head. His eyes did not seem to focus anywhere in particular. "Of course, Agent Isaacs. Of course it is. I'll do whatever you need me to do."

Chad was trying to figure out if Sam knew Quinn was keeping him in the dark, or if Sam was afraid he was not putting the pieces together. *Careful, Sam, don't overthink this. This community needs you to come through this in one piece, mentally and physically.* Chad looked around the table.

"Quinn, just so Sergeant Whitehorse and I are clear, we expect you to set the trap sometime after Zimmerman returns from Michigan, and Sylvia and I will appear as uninformed interlopers. Do I have that right?"

"Yes, that's correct. The plan, as I outlined it, will work best if you are not the primary lead. Do you have a concern about that?"

"No." Chad dragged out the letter "o" like a train whistle running out of steam. "Not at all."

"Good. Then if you'll excuse me, I have things to do and I'm sure you do too, Sylvia. Chad, I'll be in touch." Quinn stood and shook hands with Sylvia and Chad, ignored Sam, and walked out the door. There was a definite chill in the air as she exited.

Sam stood. "Guess it's time for me to head out too. Call if you need me." Sylvia stood up and surprised Sam by putting her arms around him in a big hug.

"Hang in there, Cuz. Remember, we're the good guys." She smiled at him.

Chad looked on with surprise and admiration. *Sylvia always seems to know what people need.*

Chad walked Sam to the door and lowered his hand, his palm extended behind him to signal for his sergeant to stay behind. "We'll talk soon, Sam. Be safe out there."

Chad slapped Sam on the back and whispered, "Call me tonight."

Sam nodded.

Chad closed the door, and looked at Sylvia, who was staring at the topographical maps on his wall.

"Boss, ever wonder how things might have been different if my tribe, and others like us, had been the victors?"

Chad sat down and waited for her to look away from the maps. "Tell me what you're thinking, Sylvia."

"I'm thinking that there's something going on here that might have my cousin being played as a pawn in a federal interagency chess match. Did I miss something?"

"Can't claim to be an expert on federal interagency cooperation, or lack thereof." Chad stopped for a moment. He wanted to show respect to his sergeant and, at the same time, not reveal what he couldn't tell her yet about SAC McMullen. "Needless to say, the shootout and how it happened has Quinn holding her cards pretty close to the vest. Any concerns for how you see us being involved in her plan?"

"No. If this plan goes off as discussed, I know we'll play the country bumpkins to the Immigration Enforcement knights in shining armor. Can't say it sits well 'cause we're not idiots." She paused. "That said, we've got enough on our plates with the powwow coming up that I guess it's just as well."

Chad jumped in. "Oh my gosh, Sylvia, am I off a week? Is the powwow this weekend? I had it in my head it was the following week."

"Boss, relax. It *is* the following weekend. Remember, the tribe is adding all day Friday so the opening will be Thursday night. Everything is lined up to cover the community with both plainclothes and uniformed deputies. We're in good shape. Do you have a concern about the powwow? Something I need to know?" She could tell he had something on his mind.

"Quite sure you have it all organized. Too many unusual things around here lately not to wonder what might come up with so many folks coming in and out of the valley."

Sylvia nodded her head. "That's why I asked the tribe to up the number of off-duty deputies. They're happy to pay for the security. I want to make sure we have enough eyes and ears. You know how I feel: this is our department, our community, and, for me, my tribe."

"True as a preacher's sermon on Sunday. Thanks for all your work."

Sylvia stood. She was well accustomed to the tone in Chad's voice that signaled the meeting was over.

"Are you on all day, or did you just come in for this meeting?"

"Day shift. Need something?"

"I'm going to be off-duty for a few hours. Going to take a ride up and see the repairs being done to Dr. Anderson's shed. Hope that clears the last item of *that* crime spree."

Sylvia smiled to herself. "Sounds good. Tell her I said 'hey.'" She walked to the door and turned back to him. "Boss, we've got it covered here. Don't rush back." She closed the door silently behind her.

Chad felt some satisfaction in Sylvia being supportive of him having a personal life. *I wish. Seems there's always something to interfere. Have to see Harold at three thirty.* He sighed, out loud this time, and returned to his desk determined to read the activity reports before he headed out.

What to Do

Satisfied that Arthur would find a solution that would provide freedom for Wizard to move between Drellag Caban and the shed, Bella had been pleased with the time to write. *Why am I so focused on writing a novel? Maybe I will just write whatever comes off my fingers and then see if I want to stay with short stories or venture into something else.* Wizard lay on his blanket with his head resting on his crossed paws.

Bella wrote, her fingers flying across the keyboard.

Wizard's whimper startled her. She was so engrossed in writing she had completely lost track of time. She looked at her kitchen wall clock and saw that it was almost eleven. "Wizard, water and food." She pointed to his dishes. Wizard wagged his tail and moved toward the dishes.

"Let me figure out what to fix for lunch, then we'll take a walk. Hopefully Chad will be up here around lunchtime, and we can sit out on the porch and have a meal together. Won't you be happy to see him?" She scratched behind his ears then washed her hands. She pulled out the last of the corn stew in the freezer and put it in a double boiler to start thawing. *Sure don't want it to stick to the bottom of the pot and burn.* She looked in the old recipe box that had belonged to her Grandmother Hazel and pulled out her recipe for cornbread. She set out the ingredients so it wouldn't take much time to mix and bake them. "Okay, Wizard, let's go for a quick walk and see what they've done on digging the foundation for your run."

Wizard ran out as far on his leash as Bella was willing to let him, which, at the moment, wasn't very far. She was aware that the workmen didn't need to be worried about tripping over him, and she didn't want Wizard to get hurt either. The pad on his paw had healed, and he was moving like the pup he was. He headed for his favorite tree and stopped. *You sure picked out that tree on day one. Wonder why?*

She praised him for returning quickly to her side, then started to walk towards the shed. The sound of a heavy vehicle coming up the drive stopped her in her tracks. "Sit, boy! Chad is here. He'll be happy to see you! We'll look at the construction with him."

Chad pulled his Ford Interceptor SUV off to the side so he was not in the way of any construction activity. Bella and Wizard waited close to the porch. She started to walk toward Chad; he put his hand up to stop her but didn't say anything. She stopped. "Sit, Wizard." Chad reached them in several long strides and kissed Bella lightly then leaned down to scratch Wizard's ears.

"Hello, lovely lady."

She thought she heard him give an extended emphasis to the "love" part of lovely—or maybe she just hoped he had.

"Greetings to you! Some reason you needed me to stay here?"

"Just wanted a private moment before we walk the construction." He smiled and kissed her again.

"PDAs an issue for you? Or just when you're on duty?"

"For the record, I'm not on duty for a few hours. And what, pray tell, are PDAs?"

"Public displays of affection. I assumed your mother, like mine, would have drilled that into you."

"She probably did. Except for Nora and my grandchildren, I haven't displayed affection in public for so long I must have for-gotten." They both laughed. "I assure you it wasn't the PDA thing. I was just being selfish and wanted you to myself for a few minutes. Wizard being welcome, of course." He bent down and looked Wiz-ard in the face. "Are you taking care of this fine lady? I'm counting on you." He rubbed Wizard on the scruff of his neck.

"If you'll give me a minute to check the food I have on the stove, I'll show you the construction work."

Bella handed him Wizard's leash.

"What's cooking?"

Bella stopped and smiled. "I reckon you'll just have to wait and find out, won't ya?"

Chad looked at Wizard. "Guess she told me."

Chad was sitting on the kitchen steps with Wizard at his feet when Arthur spotted him.

"Hey, Sheriff. What brings you to this mountain?"

Bella tapped the screen, causing Chad to stand so she could open the door. She walked out. Arthur saw the look on Chad's face soften when he caught sight of Bella; it was all the answer Arthur needed.

"Afternoon, Bella. Want to see the work we've done today?" Arthur was all business.

"Absolutely. Mind if I bring our fine sheriff along?"

With mock seriousness Arthur quipped, "Guess it all depends. You here officially or unofficially, Sheriff?"

"Guess it depends on whether I need to be here officially, Mr. Gillett!" Chad put on an air of officious inquiry. Then he chuckled. "Off-duty, Arthur. My friend here has been telling me what a great job you're doing. The initial incident that caused this pretty major looking project involved a crime on this land. Thought I'd come check it out." *And the fact that I wanted to see Bella is either obvious or it isn't. I'm fine either way.*

The two men were within reaching distance now and shook hands. "Good to see you, Chad."

"Back atcha, Arthur."

"Bella," Arthur turned to her, "if it's all the same to you, I'll show you the work we're doing to get ready for the dog run, and then leave you to show Chad the rest."

"Sounds perfect. Thanks." Bella didn't care about PDAs since Chad was off-duty, so she reached over and took Chad's hand before they started walking towards the area where the workmen were installing the wood frame for the concrete.

Arthur saw the gesture and smiled to himself. Everyone in the valley knew Chad had been alone since his divorce years before, and even though he had met Matt when Bella did the renovations a decade ago, he also knew she'd been alone for years herself. He was glad it meant Bella wasn't completely on her own up here.

"Bella, I was able to do a few rough sketches and work up some figures that I'll show you before I go. Then I can get the final ones to you tomorrow like we discussed. Let me see what you think of the run so far, and I'll tell you my thoughts."

The three of them approached the work area, and the workers all stopped and said hello to Chad. Arthur started explaining that by running the base of the dog run straight off from the cabin and then making a slight turn, he could run it to the far side of the entry door on the shed.

"I can do a simple doggie door on the cabin, or I can do a door that would also let you walk out of the cabin to the shed under a roof. We can add another door on the shed or put a gate in the run just before the existing door. I'd run a short pad of concrete so you'd be out of the mud in the rainy weather. Not much difference in price, but I'll show you the rough figures before I leave. Framing up that short pad, if you want to have it, won't take much."

Bella was picturing the finished run, but she also saw that Chad was listening attentively.

"I had not even considered having a human door off the side of the cabin. It has some appeal to me. I'll think about it before we talk. Thanks for the suggestion."

"Does the door affect where you put the poles I see over there?" Chad looked to see how Bella reacted to him asking. She simply nodded her head.

"Good question, Chad, but no. We had already talked about running open rafters like a pole barn and tying the two roof lines together. Then I got to thinking we could do a regular door and put the doggie door in it, rather than just putting it in the wall."

Bella was surprised to see the large poles, trees stripped of their bark, were already on site. *Guess someone went and got them. I didn't hear a thing. Glad Arthur took me at my word that I wanted this done.*

"Looks like the drainage system you talked about is almost finished." Bella moved away to look at one of the open ditches.

"Yes, ma'am. When I got to thinking about the septic we put in for the new cabin, it was pretty easy to just run the drains down there. You'll have the most efficient cleanup any dog run has ever had. That also got me thinking it would be clean enough to put in a human door."

Chad spoke up. "Looks like some pretty sturdy drainpipes."

"Sure is. With all the high-density polyethylene they use now, these pipes are good fifty to seventy-five years. Sure beats the old clay pipes we used to use. It can stand up to the drastic temperatures that can happen this high up."

"That what you use for the leach field off the septic too?"

"Same material, different pipe."

Bella was fascinated to see Chad's interest in her projects, and she was equally grateful for Arthur's expertise.

"Well, if y'all excuse me, I'll get back and help these boys finish up."

"Thanks, Arthur. We'll talk about those drawings and figures before you leave."

Arthur headed towards his workers, and Chad joined Bella as they walked around to see the repairs to the damaged side of the shed.

"Couldn't help but see when I drove up that the new cabin will sit well where you have it located. Did you plan it so your eye will be drawn to this new siding?"

"Well, the new siding wasn't an option, as you know. No more evidence of an ATV sitting in the middle of it." She went quiet, then she took a breath and continued. "Before the project is finished, it will be stained to look as aged as the other boards. I need to find someone who can do the wall-size painting I want so that I can ask what the best finish will be. Know anyone?"

"Matter of fact, I might. A relative of Sam Nations did the mural on the side of The Corral. What do you think of that work?"

"Oh, I like it. Not sure why I didn't think to ask Carla if she knew someone. I'll check with her to get the contact information. Thanks." She stopped and kissed him on the cheek. He put his arm around her shoulder as they walked towards the foundation for the new cabin.

"Whoa, those are some pretty serious looking footings. Those anchor bolts look like they'd hold in an earthquake."

"Get many of those here?" Bella looked at him out of the corner of her eye.

"We do. These are mountains. That's how they got here in the first place, right?"

"Guess I never really thought about it."

"Good to think about it, no need to worry about it." He kissed her lightly.

"Largest one I know about was a 3.2 quake back in 1979, and it didn't do any real damage. Seems they record 2.0 quakes pretty regularly. We just don't feel them."

"Then I won't worry about it. Thanks for the heads-up. Come around this way." She walked towards the side away from Drellag Caban. "Remember the picture of this cabin model that I showed you with the ferns hanging on the front porch?"

"I do."

"Well, I'm having Arthur do a few modifications to the model."

"What, no ferns?"

"What? Oh, Mr. Funny Guy!" She cocked her head to one side, then winked at him. "Seriously, there will be a porch off this end looking towards the shed and out to the trees. It will wrap around to this side and look out to the northwest. That way I can choose which view of the mountains I want." She chuckled.

"I thought this was a guest cottage?"

"It is. And guess what? I already have my first guests lined up!" She smiled.

"Oh." Chad sounded like he had just lost his last friend. *I don't want to share you.*

"Jealous?" Bella arched her left eyebrow.

"Should I be?"

"Probably."

A smile spread across his face. He suddenly remembered that Nora had been up here recently. He knew she wished her family could live at a higher elevation. He put on his steely look but with a twinkle in his eye.

"It wouldn't happen to be a little boy who keeps trying to steal you away, would it?"

"The very one." She laughed and threw her arms around his neck as she kissed him.

Chad returned the kiss and held her very close. He whispered in her ear. "You make it very difficult for me to keep my promise."

Bella pulled back with a puzzled look on her face. "What promise is that?"

"The one where I said I would respect your need for time to figure out this relationship. Well, what I hope is a relationship."

Bella took his hand and started walking back towards Drellag Caban. "Let's go have lunch."

CHAPTER 8

Our quest, our earth walk, is to look within,
To know who we are, to see that we are connected to all things,
That there is no separation, only in the mind.

Lakota Seer

Sorting Things Out

DEA AGENT SAM NATIONS LEFT THE MEETING at the sheriff's office and headed to the home of Chief Whitehorse. Sam was afraid he was slipping further and further into an abyss; it might prove to be the end of his law enforcement career. He knew Chad would not have asked him to call tonight if he wasn't supportive, but that didn't calm his discomfort with being excluded from the plan Quinn had outlined.

Sam's knock on the door was answered quickly; his tribal chief stood before him.

"Morning, Chief. Thanks for making time to see me again."

"Good morning, Sam. You're always welcome. Come in and have a seat. Coffee?"

"Coffee would be great. Shall I get it?"

"Go right ahead. My beautiful wife is on the back porch, and she'd be disappointed if you didn't open the door and say hello. I'll be right here when you return."

Chief Whitehorse could see that Sam was still troubled, and it caused him concern. Sam was one of the stars of the local native tribe. He smiled as he heard his wife's chair scrape on the porch. She must be getting up to hug Sam; he expected it would be good medicine. He heard the back door close and Sam's footsteps. Sam put his coffee mug on the coaster and sat down on the sofa.

"Chief, I heard your advice about choices, and I've made a couple of major ones in the last two weeks. The first choice I made was as an agent, with a sworn duty that requires me to follow the orders I am given and uphold the Constitution. In retrospect, following the order was not the right choice. The second choice I made was a declaration to a man I deeply respect. I promised him that *Sam Nations* would be present in a meeting today, not just the man who took the oath. Although I was physically present, I was not trusted with the inner workings of the mission. I'm not sure I ever will be again."

The chief was almost always deliberate in his comments. This time was no different. "Perhaps you must first ask if you trust yourself? Was your choice to follow orders a lack of trust in yourself? Or was it a lack of trust in those on your team? If so, did you take the easy way out and follow orders? It seems you now know you succumbed to the fallacy of the false choice in this case. Is that correct?"

Sam sat quietly for several seconds. He studied the face of Tom Whitehorse, respected not only among tribal members, but the local European descendants as well. Sam tried to figure out why he accepted the false choice: the belief that there were only two options. He spoke softly, but with a clarity he had not felt in a long time.

"I did. In that moment I believed my only choices were to obey or disobey my order. There was no known immediate danger. I could have made a choice to trust myself and my team to regroup and make a decision about whether to follow the directive I was given. Yes, I can see that my own lack of trust in my ability to renegotiate the situation led to my distrust in the team. They are right not to trust me. I do not trust myself."

Chief Whitehorse nodded his head slightly. "That, my friend, is the first step to regaining *their* trust. Can you consider that perhaps they are trying to protect you from yourself? Giving you enough information to be informed, but not adding a burden to your journey of discovery?"

Sam simply nodded.

The chief waited several seconds before he spoke again. "If the duties of your work and your health allow it," he gestured to Sam's leg, "I think you must consider making time to take a long walk. Perhaps you have been too long in the city and need to reconnect with the mountains and trees and forest life that feeds our hearts and minds."

Sam did not intend to take more of the chief's time than he needed. "Thank you for your time and wisdom. I will make the time to walk these hills."

"Then go and keep walking forward; there is nothing to be gained in going backward."

Sam shook Tom's hand and headed out. He already had on his boots, so he started up the back road to the mountain from the tribal community center.

The Valley Store

The word had spread quickly through the valley about Joshua and Carla. Each of them went about the work of running the grocery store but delighted in the good wishes and congratulations that poured in throughout the morning.

As the clock behind the register ticked past midday, Carla checked the vegetable soup in the crock pot and decided to call James to send over some biscuits.

"Hey, James. This is your sister calling."

"Really? Think I didn't recognize the number? Not much time to talk these days, what with you working at the Valley Store. Is he paying you more than I do? Is that why you're staying away?"

"Ha! Aren't you the funny one today?"

"Someone needs to take your place. Customers are complaining that there's no one here to give them a bad time. They miss that."

"Ouch! You're on a roll. Do I dare ask if you have someone who could run a half-dozen biscuits over to me? Put it on my tab."

"Oh, it will go on your tab all right. Not letting you cut into *my* profits any more than you are by not being here."

"Get on with you, big brother. That dog won't hunt. I already know that folks love Cheri. Probably means sales are up! I'll be checking *my* profits at the end of the month." They were both laughing now.

"Biscuits are on the way." He stopped. "And, Sis, I'm really happy for you. Joshua is a good man, and I want only the best for you. Gotta run. Stop in some time. You know, like you owned the place. Love you." He hung up.

Carla held her phone away from her head and stared at it. She couldn't remember the last time her brother had been so chatty.

Joshua had told her that Tuesdays were normally a slow day by one o'clock, so she walked halfway up the steps to his office in the loft over the store.

"Have time for some soup?"

"You bet. Give me five minutes and I'll be down. Thanks." Joshua smiled at her.

The little silver bell over the door jingled and the young man who was the dishwasher at The Corral came in and handed her a paper sack.

"Here you are, Miss Carla. Mr. James told me to be quick so they stayed warm."

Carla reached in her pocket to pull out a dollar bill and handed it to him. "Thanks. Thanks a lot. Have a good one, and tell James thanks too, please."

"Yes, ma'am. I will."

Carla headed to the back. She had put place mats and cutlery on the table that now sat beneath the window at the back of the store. She decided that in the spring it would be nice to have a mason jar with fresh flowers, maybe daisies. Not a big fan of artificial flowers, she didn't plan on doing anything before spring. She looked out the window and wondered if she was taking too much for granted. Maybe she should ask Joshua before she made changes in how he was used to doing things. She realized that she had lived alone almost her entire adult life and wasn't accustomed to consulting anyone before doing whatever she wanted to do. With a deep sigh, she wrapped her arms across her chest and smiled; she was going to marry Joshua.

"Hey, how about one of those for me?"

"Did the smell of the biscuits reach the loft?"

"Yes, but I meant one of those hugs."

She turned toward him and gave him a hug. "Happy to oblige."

Lunch on the Mountain

"Water, Wizard." The pup walked over to the bowl and drank. Chad looked at Bella and the dog.

"Wow! You've done that in a little over a week?"

"Can't take credit. Doc Jim already had him trained. I'm just trying to keep it going."

When Wizard moved to his blanket and sat, Chad scratched his ears. "Looks like your owner is preoccupied, boy, so I'll tell you what a good job you did."

Bella glanced over at the pair and smiled. She finished mixing the ingredients for the cornbread and popped it in to bake for thirty minutes. She gave the corn stew a quick stir.

"Okay, muffins are in the oven. What can I get you to drink?"

"A glass of tea would be great, but I can get it. What can I get you?"

"Make it two." She took the glasses out of the cabinet and handed them to him to pour the tea.

Chad handed her a full glass. "Cheers!"

"To good health! Shall we go sit on the porch? I thought we might eat out there. It's nothing fancy, just some corn stew and muffins."

"Sounds perfect." He swept his free hand in a grand gesture toward the living room and out toward the porch. "After you."

Bella sat in her favorite chair.

Chad moved a rocking chair so he was facing her and the mountains. He took a deep breath and let it out slowly. "I could get used to this. A lovely fall day with a good nip in the air, a beautiful view, and the mountains too." He winked at her.

"Flattery will get you nowhere."

"Hmmm… not the version I was hoping for." He laughed. "On a more serious note, you have quite a project going here, or should I say projects? If I'm not being too inquisitive, is the insurance assessment fair value for the work you've had done on the shed?"

"I didn't ask Arthur to separate out what was damage to the shed and what needed to be done anyway. He did tell me that even though the building is over sixty years old, it was built very well. I'm not surprised. My daddy was a fine craftsman." She stopped and stared off towards the mountains in the distance. The trees were almost bare, and a good rain would take what was left of the leaves. "Some lower logs were rotting as the dirt piled up over the years, and I will try to do a better job of keeping it clear. Arthur had a trench dug around the foundation and put in gravel to help with drainage. So, I guess that long-winded answer is my way of saying it was probably fair. Why?"

"Just curious. We see the physical damage done in the crimes we investigate, but rarely have any involvement in the aftermath and the real cost to the owner. I suppose sometimes folks are just glad to get whatever they can and put it behind them. Of course, I know there is no amount of money that can compensate for the violation of your home." *At least I hope you're starting to think of this as your permanent home.*

"I don't remember if I mentioned that I told Gray I had no interest in pursuing punitive damages. It's done, the repairs are now made, and I will move on."

Chad knew that Gray Olson, his own late father's junior law partner—now the senior partner at the valley's only law firm—would have advised Bella on the pros and cons of seeking punitive damages. He also felt pretty certain she knew her own mind.

"Only one of the many things I admire about you, Bella. I'm working on moving on too. Guess the big difference is I didn't commit a crime." He paused then muttered, "Just might have been an unwitting participant in one." He stopped abruptly, thinking of the two men he shot a week ago. He set his glass of tea on the small table and looked at her.

Bella returned his gaze. She ached for the pain she could read in his eyes. Finally, she spoke.

"Chad, this is one of those moments in a new relationship where making a choice to share is just that: a choice. It's not life or death. . ." She stopped abruptly. "Or maybe it is. Or was. I hope you will learn that you can trust me to keep your confidences, for whatever you choose to share. I've already told you I'll let you know if it's something I'd rather not know."

Chad rocked slowly and studied her face. He liked the way the wisps of hair slipped out of her ponytail and curled around her face. He was fighting the demon of distrust from his failed marriage, and the temptation of desire that roared through him whenever he saw Bella, or thought of Bella, or didn't realize he was thinking of Bella. This was a woman worth waiting for, and he was a patient man.

The timer on the stove buzzed. Bella stood to go to the kitchen. She stopped beside him and kissed him on the top of the head. He couldn't remember anyone doing that since he was a child.

"I have no doubt we'll figure this all out." She smiled at him and walked inside.

Chad rocked for a minute then stood and went to help her. She already had bowls of hot corn stew and muffins on two trays, and a pitcher of tea out of the fridge.

"Grab a tray, and I'll go fill our glasses."

"I've got both of the trays. Let's eat!" He smiled at her and headed for the porch.

An Unexpected Phone Call

Detective Billy Williams had just checked into his hotel in Nashville when his phone rang. He was on leave, so he didn't understand a call coming from the sheriff's station.

"Williams here."

"Isaacs here."

Billy almost dropped the phone. He sat down on the bed and tried to recover some composure.

"Good afternoon, Agent Isaacs."

"It's Quinn."

"Well, if it's Quinn, maybe I should give you my personal number and not run through a switchboard."

"Works for me."

He no sooner put away his work phone than his personal phone rang.

"Billy here."

"Quinn here. Where's 'here?'"

"Here is here."

"Oh, I was warned you were like quicksilver with the one-liners." Her laughter was good humored. "Let me try again. Are you in a place you're willing to share with me?"

"Since you ask that way, try Room 343 at the Union Station in Nashville Yards." He waited a beat. "Either way, that's where 'here' is."

"Tempting invitation, but duty calls right now. Maybe a raincheck?"

"Name the day, time, and place."

"Gotcha. I just wanted to check and see how you're doing. I didn't really thank you for your attention at the jamboree. Also, I know some of us are a bit shellshocked from the shootout. I don't like an operation I'm involved in to leave folks troubled. So, I just wanted to see if you're okay."

Billy leaned back on the pillows. He was glad that his normal role as a detective meant he really didn't have any "conflict of interests" with his personal interest in this very smart, very attractive immigration agent.

"I just improved a thousand percent. Miracle what a phone call from a clever and charming woman can do." He let that hang in the air. "And, might I add, one that is so thoughtful as to check on me."

"You're too kind."

"Working on making it a habit. Anyway, I came over to hear some music, clear the muck out of my brain, and regroup. I'm planning to be home on Thursday afternoon. If you can see your way free for dinner any time after that, I'd be pleased as a pig in a poke if you'd let me take you out. Shoot, it wouldn't take any persuasion at all for me to get right back in the car if you're free tonight."

Quinn started laughing. "Relax. I'm interested in dinner, and I'm very interested in spending some time with a rested, recharged detective from that amazing little valley in the hills. So, call me when you get back. Assuming you know how to save a number in your phone, you have my personal number."

"Ouch!" Billy let out a yelp. "Already saved it. Thanks, Quinn. Thanks for checking on me. Are *you* doing okay?"

"Managing. Haven't encountered a situation like this before, and I don't care to encounter anything like it again. Still lots of pieces of the puzzle to put together, but I'm confident we'll work it out. But I digress. You're on leave; go enjoy it. Call me when you get back. Later, Billy."

"Later." He barely got it out before the phone line went silent. He put his feet up on the bed and closed his eyes. *This was not a call I expected in any way, shape, or form. But I'll take it in any way, shape, or form.* The exhaustion of the last six weeks took over, and he fell asleep.

CHAPTER 9

Taking a Walk

WHEN SAM WAS DISCHARGED FROM THE HOSPITAL, Doc Fred had given him detailed instructions for rehabilitating his leg while the gunshot wound healed. He had ignored most of the instructions, and the doc's words about exercise in moderation were forgotten as Sam parked his truck on the pullout at the plateau above the tribal grounds. He grabbed his water bottle, locked his truck, and headed up the mountain on foot. The ache in his leg was easy to ignore compared to the turmoil in his head and heart.

He understood the chief's wisdom in suggesting he needed to reconnect his spiritual, emotional, physical, and mental states to regain balance. He softly chanted as he walked, clearing his mind of the intrusive everyday world and the most recent events from work. The jagged peaks of the mountains above and around him were interrupted by the majesty of the evergreens intermingling with the twisted bare limbs of the deciduous trees. Although their brightly colored autumnal foliage had fallen, Sam was reminded of the possibility for growth and rebirth that would come with the spring.

He took in deep breaths to smell Mother Earth—to connect the smells to the earth beneath his feet. He listened for the sounds of the animals going about their lives: the ever-present eastern towhee, the soon-to-be-gone katydids, the red and gray squirrels scurrying to hoard their final few nuts for the winter ahead. The sounds of the larger animals—the deer, the coyotes, the bobcats, and the black bears—would be unmistakable.

Sam's goal was to move among them without intruding so as to take the energy of their lives into his own. The point of the walk was with purpose and without destination. The soft chant Sam repeated would take time to push the thoughts of his work out of his mind. *Why did McMullen isolate me from other DEA agents after I left the hospital? What did he tell his superiors? Anything? How widespread is the knowledge of the deaths at the rental cabin? Who were those guys?* His chanting increased and his steps moved him skyward. He knew the intrusive thoughts would move away, although it could take the rest of the day and most of the night. This isolation from day-to-day living and the challenges of his job would allow him to start healing— if he was open to it. He continued his walk.

Taking in the Mountains

"Great muffins, Bella. Family recipe?"

"Glad you like them. An old Oliver recipe, in fact. I still have the index cards on which Grandmother Hazel wrote all her recipes. There's more corn stew and muffins. Want some?"

"Let me get it. What can I get you?"

"Nothing, thanks. Help yourself."

Chad took his tray into the kitchen. Bella looked out towards the mountains. So many changes were happening, and not just on her land. She wondered what Chad meant when he said he might have been an unwitting participant in a crime. Her thoughts then drifted to Joshua and Carla. She did not hear Chad return to the porch.

"Hope that smile on your face is backed up by some nice thoughts."

She turned her head to look at him. "Didn't realize I was smiling. Just then I was thinking about Joshua and Carla."

"Well, that's a nice thought for sure. Never ceases to amaze me, even in the middle of all that I deal with day-to-day, that some of the changes in our community are ones we can really be happy to celebrate."

Bella nodded her head. "Chad, you'll find out that random things pop into my head and I'm prone to say them without context. At some point, I usually figure out that it was something I'd been thinking about somewhere in the recesses of my brain."

"Nice to think about friends. After all, he's your brother now, right?"

She laughed. "Yes. Yes, he is."

Chad saw the serious look in her eyes.

She smiled gently. "I mentioned I'm prone to random comments because it relates to my earlier thoughts which were about you. I'm not asking you to tell me anything you don't feel comfortable saying, but I do want you to know I'm concerned that you're carrying a pretty heavy burden, more than you usually seem to have. Can you take some time off?"

"You may find this hard to believe, but taking several hours off in the middle of the day to come here is the best thing I could do for myself right now. I don't think I've ever done that, and I'm very sure I've never had such a good reason to do it."

"Then I'm glad I could be a distraction."

Chad interrupted her, "Oh, my dear Bella, you have no idea how much of a distraction you are—in the best possible way!"

She wasn't quite sure how to respond to that.

Chad finished his second helping of lunch and pushed the small table aside. With his glass of tea in his hand, he started rocking slowly and turned his gaze from the mountains to Bella. He would be careful what he said, but he absolutely believed he could trust her.

"I have about an hour before I have to go back for a meeting. Care to take a walk?"

"Certainly. We can just set the trays on the counter, and I'll clean up later. Let me grab my jacket and scarf then I'm ready to go. Anyplace in particular?"

"I have enough in my work life that has to run on a schedule, let's just wander."

They headed down the road towards the gate. Arthur Gillett watched them walk hand in hand, and he decided all was right with the world when a man as good as Chad Oliver could find happiness at his age.

Without any fanfare, Chad said, "Bella, it's going to take me time to figure out what I'm willing to put on your shoulders."

"Chad, maybe you shouldn't think about it so much. I don't have any experience in law enforcement, but I think I'm smart enough to know that if you don't feel you can trust me to keep your confidences then we don't have much chance of a relationship over time."

"No, no, no, Bella." He stopped suddenly and turned towards her, twisting the curl that had fallen loose from her ponytail around his finger then tucking it behind her ear. He leaned his forehead against hers. "It's not *you* that I don't trust; it's me. I could tell you every minute detail, and I know it wouldn't go any further." He paused. "I'm afraid I'll scare you off."

Bella straightened up, looked him in the eyes, and said, "Chad, I'm not going anywhere, other than back to North Carolina..." She saw the look in his eyes and started laughing. "You silly man; quit fretting. I have to go back and get my winter clothes, make sure Victoria is good to stay another semester, and I've decided to talk to a realtor."

He pulled her into a tight embrace, kissed her, and held her. He whispered, "I haven't heard the expression 'quit fretting,' in more years than I can remember. My grandmother on the Oliver side loved that expression."

Bella backed away, took his hand again, and started walking. "Come on, I know a place we can sit by Bella's Creek. Want to race?"

"You're on!" He watched her take off and just decided to enjoy the picture unfolding before him: a beautiful woman running down the hill toward the water. In fact, a woman he had already figured out he was in love with—he just hoped she would feel the same. Just before she reached the gate he called out, "Okay, I gave you a head start, better claim your ground soon or I'll beat you."

She turned the corner just beyond the gate and disappeared behind the new fence amongst the tall grasses. He caught up with her just as she sat down on a big rock jutting out into the creek.

"You win. Want to gloat?" He wasn't out of breath, but he was sucking in air.

"I was always going to win. You had no idea where I would say I was headed!"

They both laughed. Catching their breaths, she leaned over and cupped her hand in the creek. "No water better than fresh mountain streams." She drank the water. He reached down and did the same.

"Bella, I want to tell you what's troubling me, but not now. I need this time just to be with you... like this. Is that okay?"

"Anytime, Chad. Anytime."

"Great! So, tell me what you've decided to do with the new cabin."

"I haven't made any definite plans, but I'm leaning more and more towards having a writing retreat up here. I need time to plan and advertise and screen potential writers. Winter won't be the time to have retreats, so I have several months to sort it all out."

"You'd need to screen people who attend a workshop?"

"No," she chuckled. "I've also considered doing a writer-in-residence program, which would mean having someone stay in the new cabin for an extended time. For that, I think I'd have to do a background check, don't you?"

"Absolutely. Glad you've thought of it. Have you talked to Gray Olson about setting up a company so you can protect yourself financially?"

"I know I need to do that, just haven't gotten that far yet. I'm not sure of the etiquette around what I'm about to say, but you already know I just plow ahead."

He looked at her quizzically.

"Both my parents were only children, and I'm an only child. My daddy was pretty successful in business, and my mother was a financial wizard. Matt and I didn't have any children. What I'm trying to say is that I don't have to worry about money, and, in fact, I have to do some serious planning for this land since I have no one to inherit it. I did tell Gray that I wanted to discuss the land with him. I'm thinking about putting it into either a conservation trust or establishing a trust for this place as a writer's retreat."

"Whoa, you've worn me out. How on earth have you had time to process all that with everything that has happened since you arrived last month?"

She smiled. "Not all of it is new thinking. I admit the writer's retreat is, but my earlier idea had been a conservation trust. Anyway, nothing has to be decided right away. Although the conservation trust hasn't been established, it is included in my will. So, if I don't make a decision and something were to happen..."

He interrupted her by pulling her into a kiss. "Shhh with that talk. I am counting on lots and lots and lots of years of growing old with you."

She returned the kiss and nestled her head on his shoulder. "I'm fine with shhh..."

Suddenly a jarring ring startled them both. Chad reached for the phone on his belt. He saw that it was 2:45 p.m. He'd forgotten he had set an alarm so he could be back in the valley in time for his meeting with Harold.

"Sorry about that. Should have told you I had set an alarm." He stood and reached his hand out to her as she stood up. "I hate to go, but I must." Bella didn't say a word, she just took his hand and started up the road. They reached his SUV.

"Mind if I call this evening?" He searched her eyes.

"If you *ask* me again, the answer will be a polite 'yes.'"

"Good." Then what she said dawned on him. "Wait a minute. That 'yes' really means 'no, I can't call' doesn't it?"

She just nodded her head. "Try this, Sheriff Oliver: 'Bella, unless something unexpected comes up, I'll call you this evening.'"

"Ouch. Fair enough. I appreciate the reminder." He kissed her lightly. "Bella, unless something unexpected comes up, I'll call you this evening. Hope to chat with you then."

"It would be my pleasure, Sheriff." She gave him a more passionate kiss.

He got into his SUV and rolled the window down. "Thanks, Bella." She saw him reach over and turn on the radio. "I can't sing, but my lovely daughter can. I leave you with this." She heard Elvis' "Can't Help Falling in Love." Nora's voice carried through the window, "Wise men say, only fools rush in. . ."

Bella smiled, threw him a kiss, and waved as he drove down the mountain toward the county road.

More Than He Was Expecting

Chad pulled into the side parking lot at The Corral with one minute to spare. He didn't see Harold's car in the parking lot, so he took a moment to check in at the station.

"Sheriff, how may I direct your call?"

"Hey, Cecelia, fine afternoon. Sergeant Whitehorse, please."

"Yes, sir. And, sir, you're right, it *is* a fine afternoon in our hills." Cecelia knew the sheriff had been up the mountain seeing Dr. Anderson. She was happy for him.

"Sheriff, good afternoon." Sergeant Whitehorse picked up the call.

"Hey, Sylvia. Just letting you know that I'm back in the valley and meeting up with Harold at The Corral. Anything I need to know?"

"Nothing requiring your attention, but I will let you know we had a four-car wreck on Route 54 just before it drops back towards

Round City. Highway patrol was there before we were, so they've got it covered. Looks like one of our locals might not make it though."

"Who?" Chad's voice was all business now.

"Mrs. King. She was coming home from a doctor's appointment in Knoxville. She was medevacked to UT hospital."

"Wife of Mr. King, the groundskeeper at the Presbyterian Church?"

"Yes. He was notified and Pastor Fisk took him to Knoxville. The two kids, both high school students, were picked up by the pastor's wife after school. Everything that can be done is being done."

"Sorry to hear this. Let me know by text if anything develops. Any other locals involved?"

"No. Well, not local, local. Looks like the wife of Commissioner Zimmerman caused the accident but that hasn't been confirmed yet. The highway patrol captain said he'd let me know."

Great, just great. Anything else going to happen with that family? "Okay, thanks. Not sure how long I'll be with Harold. Call if you need me. Appreciate your work, Sergeant."

"Here to serve, Sheriff."

Chad hung up the phone just as Harold drove into the parking lot. He beat Harold to the door and held it open. "Afternoon, Harold."

"Afternoon, Sheriff."

"Do I need to back up and start over, Mr. Cooper?"

"No, sorry. Just got word that our favorite commissioner has another family member misbehaving."

"Oh?" Chad assumed he meant Mrs. Zimmerman. He waited for Harold to continue.

Both men walked toward the back corner booth. Cheri had water in front of them before they sat down. "Coffee, gentlemen?" Both nodded. She turned over their mugs and walked away to get a fresh pot.

"Chad, what do you know about the wreck out of town on Route 54?"

"I've been out of the office for several hours, and it sounds like you have something you need to say." Chad never ceased to be amazed at how fast word traveled through such a small, spread-out community. He was aware several folks probably had police scanners and just waited for an opportunity to be the first to share anything that crossed the airwaves. He knew Harold was not one of these people.

Harold reiterated what Sylvia had told him, but added the community perspective. "Fine folks, the Kings are. Raising two fine kids and as dedicated to the Presbyterian Church as the pastor and his wife. I just pray she makes it."

"Me too, Harold. Me too."

"Well, I guess it shouldn't be a surprise that the word on the street is that Zimmerman's wife caused it. Did you know that?" Harold barreled ahead without waiting for a reply. "I wanted to talk to you. . ." Chad interrupted him as Cheri headed to the table. Chad realized that Harold had not seen her and he didn't want Harold to say anything he'd later regret.

"Thanks, Cheri. Harold, need something to eat?" Chad waited to see if he needed food.

"Not right now, thanks."

Chad nodded to Cheri. She walked off.

Harold didn't seem to be able to stop himself. "Now where was I? Oh, yeah. Zimmerman is getting pretty brazen in his demands about the county endorsing his road expansion. He threatened my job verbally last week, and now that he's out of town, he's sending me emails telling me how to word things on the agenda so the rest of the commissioners will agree to his plan and not even know it. Ha! That's what he thinks! Except for one of them, the others are on to him."

"Slow down, Harold. I can hear you're pretty upset about the wreck, and we'll all pitch in and help out where we can. You know that's how our community works. Let's start back at the reason for us having this little off-the-books meeting." Chad hesitated. "Unless you need it to be on the books?"

Harold shook his head.

Chad knew the fact that Mrs. King had been taken to Knoxville generally meant the injuries were life-threatening. No surprise Harold had been agitated. He'd try to help Harold refocus. "You sent me a pretty vague message that read, 'commission, drugs, and our community.' How about telling me what's behind it?"

"You know I don't know any of this directly. The word that got passed to me by one of our long-time commissioners is that the two men killed in the drug bust-up on the hill were actually DEA agents."

Chad stopped his coffee mug halfway to his mouth and had to catch himself from spilling it. He set down his mug and studied Harold's face.

Harold nodded his head. "Yep, and the word is that Zimmerman left town because he maneuvered things to make it happen." Harold stopped and sipped his coffee.

Chad was in full sheriff mode now, his resolve to get to the bottom of the case growing with every word Harold spoke. The one thing he knew for sure; there were no leaks in his department.

"That's it, Chad. That's all I've heard. I don't know if it's true. You did know there was a drug bust, right?"

Oh yeah, buddy, I knew. If there is one word of truth to this, I am going to own the head of SAC McMullen on a stake. Not one muscle in Chad's faced changed to reveal his thoughts.

"Listen, Harold. We're not used to the kind of activity that's found its way into our hills, and we're sure not accustomed to having federal agencies in here on a regular basis. But I'm afraid that's how it's likely to be from now on." He measured his next words carefully. He knew that Harold wasn't a gossip, but Chad also knew how he carried himself when there were problems in the community would be a signal to others. "I promise you that my department will do everything we can to stop the influx of drugs, prostitution, and any other illegal activity. And I will not hesitate to call in the DEA, Immigration, FBI, and any other agency if I need help to stop it. But, make no mistake, *we're* in charge of our community. Questions?"

"Nope. That's what I needed to hear. Sorry the accident with Mrs. King set me off earlier. I hate it when any member of our community is hurt or injured on our roads, no matter how it happens. Thanks for bringing me back to earth."

"No problem, Harold. Thanks for the information and keep me informed if you hear anything else. Call me anytime, and I mean *anytime*. If I don't answer, dispatch will know how to reach me. Fair enough?"

"You got it, Chad. Might help if you could drop in on the next county meeting."

"I'll try. I'll sure try. Now, let's end this friendly little talk on the good news of the day. How about that Joshua?!"

Harold slapped his knee and said, "Surprised even me. We've been like brothers most of our lives, and I sure thought he was interested in Bella Anderson."

For the second time Chad had to stop his coffee mug before he got it to his mouth. *Did Harold not see me with Bella at dinner last night? I thought it was obvious we were a little more than just friends.* Then he considered it. The engagement itself, Carla fainting, and the dancing probably distracted everyone. He set his mug down again.

"Well, I for one am happy as can be for Joshua and Carla." *And for me!*

Harold nodded in agreement. "Guess we'll be getting word on a wedding before too long. I'm thinking Joshua won't drag it out, and I doubt Carla will want to either."

Chad agreed. "They should do whatever they want to do. We'll all support them in whatever decision they make."

"Hate to be Harold the downer, but any word on those boys that caused Joe's..."

"I suspect we'll hear from the DA in the next week about final charges and whether she's going to convene the grand jury. Between us and Round City, she's got her hands full these days. Besides, I think it's good to let a little time settle for Joshua before he has to face all that. Don't you?"

"Yeah, you're right. Good point. Well, thanks, Chad. Glad we had time to get together. I'll let you know if I learn anything else."

"Counting on it, Harold. Thanks." Chad saw Harold pick up the check. "Let me leave the tip, that should about make it even."

"Fair enough, Chad. Fair enough."

The two men stood and exited The Corral then shook hands and walked to their respective vehicles, the needs of the community weighing heavily on the minds of each. Chad was no sooner in his SUV than he took his secure phone and dialed Agent Quinn Isaacs. He wanted answers—*now*.

CHAPTER 10

Things to Do

With Wizard at her feet, Bella sat on the steps outside Drellag Caban enjoying the warmth of the sun against her face. She wondered if the warmth was more about the music Chad was playing as he pulled away than the sun. *Are fifty-eight-year-old men really that romantic? Maybe it's more about him hearing Nora sing than being sentimental?* She shook her head in an attempt to clear her mind. She started a mental list of the things she needed to do: call Mr. Edwards to check the well pump, Carla about the painter for the shed, and finalize the plans Arthur suggested for the dog run. She reached her hands up over her head and stretched. "Wizard, I'm not sure a day can get much better than this." She stood up. "Come on, boy, let's clean up the kitchen and then get to my to-do list." She opened the screen door, walked inside, and held it open for Wizard. He trotted in behind her.

The cord on her wall phone stretched all the way around the kitchen so she called the Valley Store as she filled the sink to wash the lunch dishes.

"The Valley Store, Carla speaking, may I help you?"

"Hey, Carla. It's Bella."

"Hey, Bella, what's up? You okay?"

"I'm fine, thanks. Wondering if you have time to answer a couple of questions for me."

"Fire away. We're slower than molasses running uphill in the wintertime."

"Guess that's a change for you, isn't it? Is it a change you like?"

"Bella, I don't mind being busy or slow, comes with living in these hills. What I can tell you is that I am as happy as a hog wallowing in mud to be working with Joshua every day. Thinking I may need to give my notice as a server at The Corral." She was cackling like a hen.

"Oh my! It never occurred to me that you'd stop being a server. Of course, you would want to help Joshua. Don't envy you the decision."

"No decision to be made, really. Bella, can I tell you a secret?"

"Sure, Carla."

"I never imagined I would get to spend every day with a man I have loved, well, forever. I am so happy."

"Aww, Carla. I'm happy for you *and* for Joshua. I wish you all the joy of knowing the love of a good man."

"Yeah, pretty clear you know about that. From a distance it sure looked like you and Matt knew love, and, from where I sit now, I'm pretty sure you might be feeling that from our good sheriff."

Bella's voice caught in her throat. "I think you're a pretty good observer of folks, Carla. Not sure I deserve to know the love of *two* good men in my life."

"From what I can see and hear, I'm pretty sure that you do. Besides that, take advantage of it. Loneliness *is* all it's cracked up to be."

"Thanks, Carla. I'll tell you I'm equally glad to have a new friend in you."

"Back atcha, Bella. Now, I'm guessing we should save chatting about our love lives for a porch rocker and a glass of wine. What do you need?"

"Well, I *have* needed a friend with a good sense of humor for a long time, but you're right, I called to ask about the person who painted the mural on The Corral. I need someone to do the side of my shed, and Chad said a cousin of Sam Nations did yours."

"She's the best, I tell you. It's beyond me how someone has the talent for showing perspective to make you feel like you're right there in the scene. She'll do a great job for you. Give me a minute to pull out my phone."

Bella set the last of the dishes in the hot soapy water to soak, grabbed her pen and paper, and waited for Carla.

"Here you go, Bella. Her name is Paula. She is very talented and can help you finalize your ideas too. Her phone number is 555-431-9595. If you'll give me a few minutes, I'll reach out to her and let her know that I've shared her number."

"Sure, that would be great. Feel free to give her my house phone and she can call me when it's convenient for her. Do you have that number?"

"Yeah, Joshua made sure I know how to reach you." Bella could hear the bell above the door at the Valley Store jingle.

"Carla, it sounds like you have a customer, so I'll let you go. Give my love to Joshua. Talk to you soon."

"Catch you later. Come down the hill sometime!"

"I will. We'll get together soon. Bye."

Bella looked up Mr. Edwards' number. The call went to his messages. "Mr. Edwards, this is Bella Anderson. I'm going to be staying at Drellag Caban through the winter, and I would appreciate it if you could schedule a visit to check my well pump at your earliest convenience. Thanks so much."

She hung up and saw that Arthur was standing at the back door, about to knock on the frame of the screen door.

"Come in, Arthur. Can I get you something to drink?"

"A glass of tea would be great, if it isn't too much trouble."

"No trouble at all. Help yourself to the facilities." She pointed to the bathroom.

"Might wash my hands, if you don't mind." He set his pad of paper on the table and headed down the hall.

She poured them both a glass of tea, took out the bowl of lemons she kept sliced in the fridge, and put them with the sugar bowl and a teaspoon on the kitchen table.

Bella gestured for him to sit at the kitchen table. "Sugar? Lemon?"

"I'm guessing more of us drink tea without sugar these days than used to be the case. I'll pass, thanks."

"I've considered making a batch of sweet and unsweet tea, but everyone who has been up this fall drinks it without sugar. So, I decided each person could choose... no offense to the memory of my very proper mother." She glanced at him.

Arthur smiled. "Know what you mean. Not always so easy to sort out what of our upbringing is still a good thing, and which we can improve upon."

"Why, Arthur, what a great way to express it. I tend to let my mountain guilt creep in, but if I think about improving our ways, then it's not so bad. Thanks!"

"No credit to me. My missus helped me see the difference."

"Lucky you!"

"Indeed. Now, let me show you the drawings with and without the people door." He flipped the pages on his pad of paper, and she marveled at his artistic skill. The drawings looked like the rendering of an existing structure.

"I like the look of the people door, and I especially like the continuity of the roof lines. It will look like the door has always been there... the walkway, too." She studied the drawings, including the one which added a door to the shed. "Want to talk me through the options?"

Arthur gave her the pros and cons, as he saw them, for each of the options. "One idea that occurred to me might be more extravagant than you want to get, but I feel I should tell you. Since we haven't poured the concrete yet, we could put radiant heat in which would keep the concrete walk warm enough to prevent ice and make it safer for you and the pup. It would add about two thousand dollars."

Bella studied the different drawings. "What is this bump out here?"

"It looks like you have his pup pretty well trained already. We could put that little area there and come off it with a shed roof. You could teach him to use that particular spot and keep your pathway clear. It was just a thought."

"Arthur, that's a great thought. Any problem having that organized for pouring concrete tomorrow?"

"None whatsoever. Held one of my boys back this afternoon. He and I can dig out and frame that small space in no time. In the meantime, any questions about the rough figures for the overall cost?"

"The figures look more than fair. Let's do this." Her enthusiasm was evident. "I really like the bump out, so let's do the people door on the shed and the house."

"Just need to confirm what you want for the doors. I'd recommend either solid core wood doors or steel. Steel runs about a hundred more, but they're much more secure, especially with a dog going in and out."

"Can you paint the steel to match up with the log siding?"

"No problem at all. I was hoping you'd agree to the steel door. They come with the doggie door already installed, which makes them even stronger."

"That sounds like a good thing. Thanks, Arthur. Any problem matching the metal roofs that you put on the cabin and shed years ago?"

"Nope, none whatsoever. Those metal roofs will save you a lot of headaches over the years with the winter snows we get up here. Well, I think that about wraps up my questions. Anything else you need?"

"Not at all. I like the look, and I appreciate your thoughtful ideas about all the things I should consider. I'm hopeful you'll let me keep these drawings when you're finished."

"Yes, ma'am. The drawings are yours. I'll stop by the county of-fices and Abigail will add the final plans for the dog run to the permit. So, we'll be good to go." He tore off the drawings and the page with the rough costs and handed them to Bella. He reached out shake hands. "Pleasure working for you, Bella. Wish everyone was so as-tute and easy going."

"The pleasure is mine, I assure you. Thanks, Arthur." She walked him to the door.

"Well, Wizard, you're going to be one happy pup with so many choices about where you hang out." She scratched behind his ears. The sun was slowly moving toward the ridgeline of the mountains, so she latched the screen and closed the door, making sure the lock clicked into place. She then moved throughout the cabin, closing the windows and preparing for the evening.

Wanting the Truth

The sheriff listened to the ringing of Agent Isaacs' phone. He had decided to return to his office before calling her just to make sure he had settled his thoughts about the possibility that the two men killed—that *he* killed—in the rental house were DEA agents. *Wouldn't they have responded when Sam called out that he was DEA? I can't imagine that anyone who was a sworn law officer would come running out the back door and aim at me without giving a verbal warn-ing before he pulled the trigger.* Waiting to call Quinn had given him time to think.

"Isaacs here. Oh, hey, Sheriff."

"Hey! Any chance you're still in the valley?" He didn't really expect her to be, but it was worth the chance to ask.

"No, I headed back after our meeting this morning. I could be in twenty-five minutes... less if I act like a cop."

"I think we need to talk face-to-face as soon as possible. I can come to you."

"On my way." She hung up without any further comment.

Chad could have sworn he heard a siren start as she ended the call. However, he knew she would not break the law herself; she might use her lights though. He walked down the hall to the break room to get coffee, glad that he remembered to take his mug and wash it out. Cecelia was getting coffee too.

"Hey, Sheriff. Haven't seen you in a while. Life treating you okay?"

"You know something? Life quit treating me; I had to learn to pay my own way."

She laughed. "Now, there's some truth, for sure. Headed back to the headset. Have a good rest of the day, sir."

"You too, Cecelia. Thanks for all you do for our community."

"Any time." She smiled at him and walked out the door.

Chad dried his mug with a paper towel to make sure he got rid of all the residual oils from the coffee, rinsed it again with fresh water, and filled it with fresh coffee. *I think it was actually Cecelia who taught me the trick of getting that brown paper towel taste out of a mug by rinsing it with cold water. Hope I thanked her.*

Back at his desk, Chad opened his email to try and address as many messages as he could before Quinn arrived. Most were updates of ongoing cases, and some, thankfully, were final dispositions. Two of the cases caused him to sit for a moment and think about the notes. Elizabeth Alexander, his top-notch forensic tech, had isolated the poison that was common across the wild animals whose carcasses seemed to be piling up outside of The Mountain Villages. He'd talk with her about it in a few minutes. The other was the district attorney confirming that she was going to offer Bobby Kirk a plea deal, and only take it to the grand jury if Kirk refused. His cousin, Jason, had already been in juvenile detention, so he would probably jump at the chance for a deal and turn state's evidence. *Even Bobby Kirk admitted that Jason had nothing to do with Joe's death. What a waste!* The DA said she was trying to get over on Wednesday to offer him the deal. Chad made a note on his calendar. He picked up his phone to call Elizabeth, but then he decided to walk down to the lab.

Chad scanned his card and the door unlocked. She looked up at the sound of the click. "Afternoon, Alexander."

"Afternoon, Sheriff. Missing Billy... uh, Detective Williams?"

"Actually, I think we're all enjoying the peace and quiet." It was impossible to miss the humor in his voice. "Seriously, I'm glad he took some R and R. It was long overdue. I'm thinking you're long overdue too."

"Sir, no disrespect, but the peace and quiet of this lab is its own kind of rest and recuperation. But my powerful skills in deductive reasoning aside, I assume you're here about the poison?"

"Very good, Alexander. Very good." He smiled at her. "What do you have?"

"The carcasses we have include a young bear, a coyote, several rabbits and raccoons, and two cats. Neither had collars but they looked domesticated rather than feral. All died from cyanide poisoning. As a matter of fact, the detectives are out right now to see if they can find evidence of M-44 devices and to map the distance of the animals found from the road and the housing development." She waited to see if the sheriff would say anything.

"Orange particles or yellow?" Chad asked her without missing a beat.

She smiled. She liked working for a sheriff who stayed informed and learned what he didn't already know. "Yellow for all but the bear. The bear might have been able to make it further from the source of the M-44 device. That could explain why it found one used by the Wildlife Service. But the yellow ones are definitely bought by someone on a mission."

Chad nodded his head. "Good work, Alexander. I'll follow up with the detectives. I'm guessing there were no legal markers indicating the devices were there?"

"Likely not. You know something, Sheriff? Seems to me if you don't want the wildlife that comes with living in these mountains, you should stay in the city. Right?"

"You've got a point, Alexander. Keep up the good work." Chad turned and headed back to his office. Agent Quinn Isaacs was coming through the front door as he reached the hallway. He spoke to the deputy on desk duty and motioned Quinn to come to the door. The deputy buzzed it open, and she joined him in the hallway.

"Need something to drink?"

Quinn held up her Yeti. "I'm good. Thanks."

"Do I need to check the contents of that?" Chad chided her.

"I'm sure this water is not as pure as your mountain streams over here, but it's relatively harmless." She held out her Yeti. "But, by all means, be my guest." He chuckled and pointed to the round table as they walked into his office. Chad picked up his coffee mug and joined her. He took a deep breath.

"That sounds like some heavy thoughts must be about to find their way into the air." She wondered what could have made him want to talk in person.

"Quinn," he studied her face as he spoke, "who were the two men I shot at the rental house up above 'the house on the hill?'"

She remained impassive and looked at him in return. She trusted Sheriff Chad Oliver, maybe more than any other law enforcement officer she worked with, but she had to figure out why he had suspicions. She knew she had not shared any of the information she had received through channels at Immigration Enforcement. She weighed her words carefully.

"Well, Chad... That's an interesting question, and one for which I have no clear answer. There are no prints on file for either man, and facial recognition normally takes a long time. It can take even longer when dealing with photographs of a corpse."

"Quinn, I am not as sophisticated in the machinations of federal agencies as you and Sam, but I am also very well read, stay informed and up-to-date, and I'm fairly smart, if I do say so myself."

She simply nodded her head in agreement.

"Therefore, I am going to posit two hypothetical explanations. These men have never actually been arrested before, which I think is unlikely, or they could be employees of a federal or state law enforcement agency, thus blocking their prints. So, let's start with the easy one. They've never been arrested."

"Not having an arrest record could track in both of your hypotheticals. Government agencies have from time to time, for their own reasons, hired known criminals and expunged their records, although it is rare." She stopped, her eyes never leaving his.

Chad nodded. He liked Quinn. She was sharp, professional, and didn't play games.

She looked away as she picked up her Yeti and took a drink. "In this day and age, while there are actually some serious efforts being made at interagency cooperation, it's not perfect. Trust takes a long time to earn, and, as you well know, can break faster than fine crystal hitting the edge of a table. So, it is unlikely that any agency will admit to having two agents in that house, much less shot by the local sheriff. I can tell you, unequivocally, those two men did not work for Immigration. Beyond that, your guess as to who they are is as good as mine. Since the DEA is in charge of their remains, and cooperation is really low in the local regional office at the moment, we may never know if they're from their agency."

"We'll know." Chad's determined gaze gave her no doubt. "Maybe not anytime soon. But we *will* know before I'm willing to let go of this case."

She nodded.

"Thank you for your perspective and for driving across the mountain to meet with me. The least I can do is buy you an early supper at The Corral. Do you have time?"

"Wow! That's the second offer of dinner I've had out of this fine law enforcement agency today. Declined the first, so how could I turn down another one?"

Chad tried for a moment to figure out what her comment was about, then let it go. "I'll meet you there. That will put you a few minutes closer to home than leaving from here."

Quinn stood without a word and headed out the door.

Chad sat for a moment, trying to decide how much he was willing to tell her in a more informal setting. He walked out the back door to his SUV and called dispatch on his way to say that he was going to supper and then home. He was hoping to meet up with Sam before the night was over.

CHAPTER 11

When one is alone at night in the depths of these woods, the stillness is at once awful and sublime. Every leaf seems to speak.

John Muir, 1838 – 1914

Strengthen My Spirit

SAM WALKED HIGHER AND HIGHER ON A TRAIL etched in the grasses of the upper reaches of the mountain. The thinner air made him grateful he stayed in shape and had mastered the lessons he received as a young child on regulating his breathing to accommodate the altitude. He slowed his pace and matched his breaths with his footsteps while he focused on breathing from his diaphragm. He knew that these were not the highest mountains in the country, but they brought their own evidence of outwitting man.

A rock outcropping ahead was his goal. From there, he could take in the ridgelines across the Smoky Mountains. This was not the Spirit Walk known to many native tribes, but any walk reconnecting with the very roots of one's spirit would provide the opportunity to regain balance; it was this balance that Sam wanted—and knew he needed.

The quiet chant he maintained throughout his walk was beginning to push out the negative thoughts and fears he carried when he went to Chief Whitehorse earlier. As he stepped up over what he knew was the last crest before the outcropping, his eyes took in the greatness of the hills and valleys that constituted the Smoky Mountains. He stopped and slowly scanned from left to right. Then he slowly scanned back to the left. He did not look back onto the trail that had brought him here. He wanted to walk forward, to leave behind the poor decisions, the betrayals, and the disloyalty he knew he had shown to Quinn and Chad. He walked onto the outcropping and sat. During the day, the heat of the sun permeated the stone, and it now rose through his body in a way that helped him feel he was literally and figuratively connected to Mother Earth. Sam knew the requirements of his job would not allow the three or four days that would bring the most meaningful changes from his walk, but he decided that staying through the night would be as close as he could get right now. He completely forgot that he was going to call Chad.

Building Trust

Chad realized that Billy must have told Quinn that the locals park on the side of The Corral; she was getting out of her SUV on the far back side. Chad smiled. *It would be good to have you as a local, Agent Isaacs.* He pulled into a parking space and hopped out of his own SUV, arriving at the door a few steps before Quinn. As he opened it for her, he was amused her face mirrored Bella's when a door was held open for her.

"Before you say anything, I know you're perfectly capable of opening a door. I'm not opening it for you because you're a woman, I'm opening it because you're my guest." *Wonder if that will fly? Good to try it out on her before I use it on Bella.*

Quinn looked curiously at the smile—or was it a smirk—on his face? "Sure, Sheriff, whatever you choose to believe." She walked through the door and stopped, not sure where in the restaurant he would want to sit.

"I know you've been to the music grounds out back, but have you been inside before?" Chad raised an eyebrow as he asked her.

"No."

"Then here's the insider scoop. Locals enter by the side door and sit as close to the back as possible. So, pick a table."

Quinn headed for the back corner booth. Chad nodded approval and turned to the head server. "Hey, Cheri, we have a newcomer. So, if you'd grab a menu, I'd appreciate it."

"Good as done, Sheriff." Cheri put a menu in front of Quinn and the other next to Chad, filled up their water glasses, and asked what she could get them to drink.

"Agent Isaacs?" Chad wanted to make a point of using her title so that when she came in here alone, which he hoped she would, Cheri would be aware of her law enforcement connections, if not her agency.

"Unsweet tea, please."

"Same here. Thanks, Cheri."

"Although I haven't been in the restaurant, I've eaten food from here, so I'm guessing you can't go wrong with most anything."

"That's the gospel truth, Quinn." Chad's back was to the wall, so he saw Walter walking towards them. "Don't turn around, but you're about to meet one of the valley's finest citizens."

"Evening, Chad. Ma'am," Walter said as he reached the table. He nodded his head towards Quinn, a gesture more like a bow that some mountain men did when greeting a woman. "Haven't seen you since the big announcement about Joshua and Carla. They got a wedding date yet?"

"Walter, I'd like you to meet Agent Isaacs. She's a federal officer visiting our fine hills."

Walter's eyes grew as big as saucers. He nodded again, this time almost bowing his waist. "Well, I'm honored, ma'am, uh, Agent. Welcome."

Quinn put on her best mountain twang when she spoke. "Why, Mr. Walter, it's my personal pleasure to make your acquaintance." She nodded her head in acknowledgement of his greeting.

It took every ounce of Chad's self-control to keep a straight face. He doubted that Walter would push any further… and was honestly relieved when he didn't.

"Well, I'm mighty sorry to intrude on what must be a highly official meeting. Evening, ma'am. Evening, Sheriff." With that, Walter turned and walked away.

Quinn all but burst out laughing when she was sure Walter was out of earshot. She rolled her eyes and gave Chad a quizzical look. "Local source of gossip?"

"Astute young woman. Joshua proposed to Carla last night in a back room in front of a group of us friends. Walter was at a table out here. As soon as the word spread into the restaurant, he took off and went to my station to share the news. There was nowhere else open in our fair valley that he could go and pretend he was the town crier. Thought you'd enjoy the local color."

"Indeed. Good to get better acquainted with the players in this part of the mountains."

"He's harmless. He sold his gas station, the only one here in the valley, a couple of years ago, so he lost his audience. Mostly he tells the truth, at least as he believes it to be."

"Every community needs one of those, right?"

"Maybe." Chad looked around and was relieved that there was no one else sitting near them. "The talk that hit me here earlier today was the reason for my call. And, for the record, Walter was not the source."

Quinn sat sipping her tea. She leaned the front edge of the glass toward him as a kind of toast, acknowledging she understood.

Cheri came over to take their order. Both ordered the special: meatloaf, mashed potatoes, and green beans. Chad was surprised that Quinn would eat such a big meal but realized she might not have grown up with the clean plate rule that he did.

"Now, Chad, you were saying?"

"You already know I don't spread gossip, and I don't talk about things I shouldn't. This talk, not gossip, was from someone I trust, and who has direct knowledge of some of the actions of Zimmerman."

Quinn looked at him. "Is there verification that his wife caused the pileup on the road today? The one investigated by HP?"

"Word does travel fast in some circles, doesn't it?"

"We try to stay well connected in our agency. Happens that one of the cars was driven by the girlfriend of one of my colleagues. Her aunt lives over here, and she had been visiting."

Chad jumped in quickly. "Is she okay? Was she hurt?"

"No. No, she's fine. Pretty shook up though. She drives these roads enough to know the edges pretty well and apparently managed to only get her fender bent. Her boyfriend is one of our techie guys, and he called me because he knew I'd done some work over here. That's all I know."

"Well, one of our residents was medevacked to UT Knoxville hospital. Don't know her status at this point. However, directly to your question, I don't have verification yet, but apparently Zimmerman's wife was in one of the vehicles. Her responsibility is unknown to me."

"I'll text you if I hear anything."

"Thanks, Quinn. I hope the young woman is okay. Returning to my earlier comments, I was informed that the two men in that house were DEA agents, and Zimmerman was involved in having them there. Know anything about that?" Chad hoped that Quinn would see the nature of their conversation in this environment as unofficial, and he hoped she trusted him enough to tell him what she knew.

Cheri arrived at the table with their food and placed their plates in front of them, serving Quinn first. "Thanks, Cheri. Separate checks, please," Quinn said, her voice expressionless.

Chad suddenly got worried. He had specifically invited her to dinner. Now he was concerned that her request for separate checks meant she saw herself as on the clock. *Guess I misjudged the level of trust between us. Hope I haven't screwed up by telling her about the DEA.* Cheri nodded and walked away from the table.

"In case you're trying to figure out why I asked for separate checks, relax. Might as well let my earlier meeting count as work, since it was, and put it on my expense account. Nothing personal.

Saves me from explaining why I didn't have a receipt for supper when my log shows I came over to meet with you, and it will be noted I returned well after suppertime." She smiled and lifted her tea glass in another mock toast.

Chad liked and respected her even more. *She is one smart cookie. Hmmm, guess I need to ask Bella what word I can use since I'm pretty sure calling her a smart cookie will be way outdated, and likely sexist.*

"This meatloaf's almost as good as my grandmother's. Local cook, I take it?"

"The cook grew up in this very kitchen at her mother's knee. Her mother was the cook before her. Can't beat recipes passing down the generations."

"That's the truth." She paused a second. "Whether the identity of those men is the truth, I don't know. We've heard the same talk. We both know the DEA controls the remains, so we may never know. I promise you this, though, if Zimmerman's involved, DEA agents or not, I'll take him down. If there's a way to find out who was in that house, I will."

"Oh, Quinn, there's a way." Chad's voice was flat and hard. She just raised her eyebrow.

"There's always a way. And I promise you that I will not stop until I know the true identity of those two men, even if it takes me years."

They ate in silence for several minutes, and Chad dropped the subject. Each now knew what the other knew, and he planned on talking to Sam tonight. He'd see what Sam had to say.

"I see you're not eating your green beans." Chad held up a forkful.

"Hmm... not a fan."

"Of green beans, or just overcooked green beans?"

"The latter."

"Ah, see, when you've lived alone as long as I have, you aren't as picky." He put the beans in his mouth and his eyes smiled at her.

Quinn just nodded.

"I enjoyed the jamboree, and it was nice to see the community come together for Mr. Johnson. I appreciate Joshua letting me use Joe's home. By the way, Billy was a gracious host. Maybe I'll show him the big city one of these days. Knoxville, not Round City." She laughed.

Chad was chewing his food. *Guess that's who invited her to dinner from my agency. Good. I like both these young people.* "Do him some good to see Knoxville through the eyes of a native. I'm pretty sure his university years there weren't exactly spent learning about the culture of the city."

They finished eating without much further talk, then Quinn spoke. "None of my business, but I couldn't help but notice that Miss Bella had your attention at the jamboree. Anything serious?"

"Did you get a chance to meet my daughter?"

"The singer?" Quinn wondered why he didn't address her question.

"Yes, the very fine singer, if I do say so myself. Her name is Nora."

"I agree. She is a very fine singer. I hope to meet Nora one of these days."

"I'd like that. I think you two would like each other. You're probably about the same age. She and Sam were in the same class at the high school, but Nora went to MTSU." He noticed Quinn flinched when he said Sam's name.

"Yeah, then I guess we are. What's that got to do with Miss Bella?"

"Well, I'm learning that young people are a lot more open about expressing their observations and opinions on the lives of others than my generation." She started to interrupt him. "Hold on, I'm not saying it's bad, just different. I've been lectured for weeks by my daughter that I better treat Bella right and not 'mess this up.' I've been divorced for almost fifteen years, and my lovely daughter likes to remind me I need to step up my game."

Quinn roared with laughter. Cheri was approaching the table with their checks and stopped until Chad waved her over. She set the checks beside each of them. "Coffee, Sheriff? Agent?"

"Yes, Cheri, I will. May I have it in a to-go cup? I have to drive back over the mountain this evening. You, Sheriff?"

"I'm good. Hoping for an early night." He paused. "Now, what's so funny about what I said?"

"Chad, I am quite sure I will like your daughter. I like a woman who is confident enough to tell her father not to mess up a good thing. You see, I like Miss Bella myself."

"That makes two of us. And, believe you me, I am trying to make sure I don't mess it up."

"Good. Then I'm sure you won't." Quinn lifted her check to Cheri and pointed to the coffee cup, indicating it should be added to the total. Cheri smiled and walked off.

"Cheri knows you're law enforcement. The Long family has owned this restaurant since the doors opened. Carla and her brother, James, inherited it when their parents were killed in an accident out where the one was today." He paused, thinking about the community member now in the hospital from the current wreck. "Well, anyway, Carla and James own this fine establishment now." Quinn nodded as if she were building a mental dossier on the members of the community. He realized she probably was. "They have never charged a law enforcement officer for coffee. Mr. Long, the father, used to say, 'no different than giving the deputy a glass of water, just has some flavoring to it.'"

Quinn smiled. "The more I learn about your part of our mountains, the more I like it. Thanks for the company, Chad, and I hope I didn't offend you by asking for separate checks. Folks in my agency's accounting department do know how to match travel times to mealtimes. Just makes it easier and cleaner. But, for my part, the meal was two friends. I hope it was for you too." She left money for her check and picked up her coffee cup. "I'll head out and get the last of the daylight on the upside going over the mountain, if it's all the same to you."

Chad put his money on his check and stood. "I'll walk you out."

When they got outside, Chad said, "Quinn, Thanks. I appreciate you coming back over the mountain. Thanks, too, for being a friend and a very fine agent. You give me hope for our federal agencies."

"Get on with you, Sheriff," Quinn said with her best mountain twang. "We'll talk in the next couple of days."

"Anytime. Oh, and Quinn, call me old-fashioned, but I worry about my friends driving these hills at night, so would you text me when you get home?"

"Sure, thanks for caring that I get there. Night, Chad."

"Night, Quinn." They each turned and walked towards their respective SUVs. As soon as Chad was in his vehicle, he looked to see if Sam had sent him a text. He had not. Chad decided to go home, and if he hadn't heard from Sam by then, he'd call him.

Once home, he put his weapon in the gun safe and headed for the shower. As he toweled off afterwards, Chad realized it was early enough that Sam might be at his folks for dinner, so he decided to get the one beer he allowed himself each night and sit down in his recliner to drink it.

Fat Tire Ale in hand, Chad leaned back in his recliner with the lights out. He dialed Sam's number. It went immediately to voice mail. "Sam, this is Chad. It's a bit after eight. I'll be up for another couple of hours. Call me."

He put his phone down on the table beside his recliner and thought through his day. He liked the young IEA agent and felt a tinge of guilt for having her come back over the mountain today. Then he remembered when he was young, he wouldn't have thought twice about driving it himself. He let it go. *Glad we're on the same page about trying to find out who was killed in that house. I didn't miss her point that former criminals end up in various roles with federal agencies where they can be of benefit. So, maybe they weren't DEA agents but DEA informants.* That analysis didn't make the fact that he had killed two men sit any easier, but it made more sense to him that there was misinformation. However, either way, SAC McMullen had to be involved. He was sure of that.

The ringing of his phone startled him. He grabbed it without looking at the screen. "Sam?"

"Sorry to disappoint you, Daddy. It's not Sam."

"Oh, hey, sweet girl of mine. Apologies for not checking. Everything okay?"

"Something have to be wrong to call my daddy?"

"Not at all. Glad to hear from you. I need lessons on being a better father and calling you instead of you always being the one to call."

"In our next lives." She giggled just like she used to do when she was a little girl. "Not a problem, Daddy. I'm just glad I caught you. All's good here, the kids seem to be growing every day. I really called to tell you what Lilly asked me when I tucked her in—are you ready?"

"Ready!" He grinned thinking of his little granddaughter.

"Where Ga-pa?" Nora spoke in a little girl voice.

Chad was amused. *Guess all those voice lessons paid off for her.* Then he had to keep himself from catching his breath hearing Lilly's question. He hoped his smile came through the phone. "You tell her that Grandpa is always with her, even when she can't see me."

"Think I didn't?" Nora teased him.

"Thanks, Nora. I know it can't be easy to have me tied up so much of the time they're growing up. Hope Fred and the kids are well."

"Daddy, the kids are young. I'll make more demands on you when they get a few years older. Fred and kids are doing great, but speaking of demands on your time, I'd be one happy daughter if you told me that you were making some time to see Bella."

"Are you sitting down?"

"Yes," Nora said tentatively. She wondered what was coming next.

"I actually took a ride up there at midday, saw the construction she's having done, and ate lunch with her." He pulled the phone away from his head while she whooped loudly. "Young lady, you will ruin that lovely singing voice of yours, to say nothing of bursting my eardrums. I take it you're happy about that."

"Daddy, I'm so proud of you. How's her new cabin coming along?"

"Footings are poured and the logs will be there the end of the week. And guess what?"

"What?"

"She told me she already has reservations for her first guests in the cottage."

"Did she now. Someone I want to be?"

"Not sure what that means, but she had the nerve to tell me it was that little four-year grandson of mine. I'm telling you; he and I may have to have a real heart to heart so I can explain that he needs to back off. She's mine." He said it with such sincerity and affection that Nora caught her breath.

"Oh, Daddy, you have just made me the happiest daughter on earth. You deserve to have a nice lady in your life, and I know from thirty plus years as your daughter that she's getting a great guy," she sputtered, and he could hear she wasn't able to hold back tears.

"Hey, come on now. It's Joshua and Carla walking down the aisle. Right now, I'm grateful for her company, and I'll admit to you that it will be all good with me if we end up growing old together."

"Good, Daddy. I'm happy for you, for Bella, and for Joshua and Carla. That was great news to hear today. It was actually another reason I called, just to find out if the word on the street was true. Glad to know it is."

"Nora, thanks for being the amazing daughter you are. I'm glad you like Bella and I hope that the six of us get to spend a lot of time together going forward."

"Me too, Daddy. Let's make that happen soon. I hear Mac calling me, so I need to run. Love you to the moon and back."

"Love you more."

"Love you more than you love me."

"It cannot be, my dear daughter. Thanks for loving me. Good night." He ended the call and set his phone down again. A moment later, a text popped up on his screen. It was Quinn. She was back in Round City. It read simply: "Tks, Sheriff." He replied: "All good. Tks."

No text or call from Sam. *I pray he didn't do something stupid. I should have scheduled a time with him. Where are you, Sam?* He picked up the phone and hit redial. It went straight to voicemail. "Sam, no matter what time you get this message. Call me. I don't care if it's two a.m." He saw that it was now 9:20 p.m. He could use an early night, but first he was going to tell a very special lady good night. He dialed Bella's number.

CHAPTER 12

Close to a Perfect Day

BELLA DECIDED TO TAKE THE RISK of letting Wizard out while standing in the doorway. He ran to the tree and came straight back. "Good boy!" She nuzzled him and gave him a treat, then pointed to his blanket. He went straight to it.

She took a shower and layered her lightweight wool robe over her nightgown. She knew she was going to either have to buy some warmer clothes or go to North Carolina soon and get her winter clothes. The fireplace was not the best source of heat. *Wonder why I didn't put in a wood-burning stove with the renovations a decade ago? Guess I never really believed I would have time to be here for more than a day or two in the winter.*

She sat in front of the fireplace in what she always thought of as Matt's chair, a glass of her favorite Kim Crawford Sauvignon Blanc within easy reach. She opened *An Irish Country Cottage: An Irish Country Novel* and began to read. Wizard rested his head on her feet. It was after nine when she turned the last page.

She stood up and stretched, smiling over the joy she always felt when she finished a good book. *In some ways, these hills remind me of the community of Ballybucklebo in Taylor's Ireland.* She loved the picture Patrick Taylor painted of the tight-knit community and the realities of day-to-day living. She found herself thinking about her interest in mysteries and wondered if she might think of a new focus for her own writing.

"Come on, Wizard, I don't think you'll need your crate at night much longer. What do you think? Maybe you'll like sleeping at the side of my bed in a few more nights, boy." She headed for the kitchen, and he leaned against her leg while she washed her wine glass. After setting the clean glass on the side of the sink to dry, she flipped off the light switch.

After ensuring Wizard had settled in for the night, Bella prepared herself for bed. She was just about to climb under the covers when the phone rang. She hoped it was Chad. She hurried into the kitchen, pulling her robe around her against the chill in the cabin.

"Drellag Caban, may I help you?"

"You just did. The only thing more a tired man could ask at this hour of the night is to hear that beautiful voice in person."

"Well, aren't you the charmer?"

"Rarely, but I'm working on getting better at it. How am I doing so far?"

Bella chuckled. "Did I ever tell you that I love the old TV series *MASH*? To make a long story short, there's a line from one of the new nurses to the MASH unit who likes the company clerk, Radar. He's a shy, naïve young man who wants to impress her but keeps stumbling over his words and his own two feet. He finally quits trying to impress her and tells her so. Her response was, 'You don't need to try and impress me. I like you when you're unimpressive.'"

"Nice reminder about that series. Never been much of a TV watcher, but I remember seeing several episodes. Works for me if I don't have to try and impress you."

"Thanks for coming to visit today. How was the rest of your day?"

"Ninety-nine percent of it was work. The good news is that I am also working on keeping my promise—to you and to me. The other one percent is that Nora called tonight."

"How is she? Fred? The children?"

"They all seem to be doing well. She whooped in my ear when I told her I took time off to head up to see you. Believe me when I tell you that is not a normal reaction from my daughter."

"I'm glad they're all doing well, and I'm pleased that she's happy for you. I am too."

It took him a moment to process her comment. "Does that mean you're happy for you, too?"

"It does. I'm very fond of you, Chad Oliver, and I'm deeply grateful to you for your patience in understanding my need to sort out all the emotions that have surrounded me during the last six weeks or so."

"Easy to do, Miss Bella, very easy. Now, I didn't have the courtesy to ask if I woke you."

"You did not. I had just put Wizard in his crate and pulled down the quilt. Are you headed to bed?"

"Yes. I'm still hoping to hear from Sam tonight. I've asked him to call me no matter the hour."

"Oh, it sounds like you have an important case. Do you need to go?"

"No, but I need to let *you* go. My call to Sam was to check on him. He's been having a rough week. I'm sure I'll hear from him before too long." He paused. "Thanks for lunch, and I loved seeing all that you're doing to Drellag Caban. Can't wait to see the finished work. I could talk to you all night, but we both had a very long day. I'll check in with you tomorrow. Sleep well and dream of me."

"I will. I hope you can rest. Thanks, again, for coming up to the mountain today. Sweet dreams."

"Sweet dreams, Bella." *I hope you know I'm in love with you.*

Bella hung up the phone and saw that Wizard was sound asleep. She headed for bed, hoping she would be able to follow suit as she pulled the covers up to her neck. With such a full day, she wondered if there was anything that made her Not-So-Good List. She realized there was nothing directly related to her, but she *was* concerned for Chad. Something that clearly happened in the past few weeks that was troubling him, but he hadn't revealed anything about his work lately.

Her concern for him made it important to also start her Good List with him at the top. They had a wonderful visit over lunch, and she appreciated his interest in her construction projects and the thoughtful questions he asked. *It reminded me of Matt, who always felt comfortable giving his opinion but never tried to take over something I was managing. Could I have that with Chad too?* She added to her list the joy she felt over Wizard and his quick adaptation to his new home. She decided they would go on a hike tomorrow so he could start to learn his land. Another important item on her Good List was the attention to detail and ideas that Arthur brought to the projects. She added the memories she had throughout the day about her mother, daddy, grandmother, and Matt—her life loves. Satisfied with her attention to her lists, she rolled onto her side, closed her eyes, and wondered if Chad Oliver would be added to the list of life loves. *I think I'd like that.*

Sleep Won't Come

Chad hung up the phone and sipped his beer. *Yeah, the only thing better than talking to you on the phone, Bella, would be that you were sitting here with me. I hope that day will come.* Chad looked at his phone, absently wondering why he had not heard from Sam. It wasn't like him. Chad normally used this time at night to ponder the cases and his community, but tonight his mind could only focus on one thing: something was eating at Sam. Chad knew it—he just didn't know what it was.

What is Special Agent Carl McMullen up to? Are he and Zimmerman collaborating? Why did Zimmerman head off to Michigan? Chad

had no doubts about Zimmerman's involvement in the "house on the hill," but he also knew they had to identify all the possible pieces. If they moved in too quickly, they would run the risk of getting him on some minor charge that he would likely weasel out of. He took the last swallow of his beer, then took the bottle to the kitchen to rinse out and put in the recycle bin. He walked to his bedroom at the end of the hall, the hall he hoped to have Bella walk down with him one of these days.

Stretched out on the bed, Chad locked his fingers and put the back of his hands against his eyes. *I wonder why I do this? Is it from so many nights of going to bed exhausted? Or too many years of going to bed alone?* He took a deep breath, let it out slowly, and hoped for sleep. Between thinking about Bella and Sam, he wasn't sure it would come easily.

Cold Night

The warmth Sam had enjoyed when he first sat on the large, flat slab of rock, called Mantle Rock by his tribe, was rapidly disappearing. The modern comforts to which he had become accustomed pushed through the edges, begging him to go back to his SUV and sleep in a warm bed at his parents' home. They would not question his arrival at such a late hour. He knew, though, that giving in to that desire was the very reason he was here; it was the easy way out of facing himself—finding himself.

He stared out across the darkness and imagined he was looking into the darkness that was taking over his soul. He wondered when his idealism gave way to blind obedience. He had been a passionate believer in the rule of law, and it made sense to join the Drug Enforcement Agency to help rid the nation of the drugs that were destroying young people. But now—were his recent actions really just following orders? He started thinking about the senior administrator from the DEA divisional office in Louisville who approached him about SAC McMullen. *Who is really being tested? Me or McMullen?*

Did I accept the directive to gather evidence on McMullen, including to follow his instructions, with no consideration for the risk to others? Should I have known who was inside that house? How is it they had guns when I'd been told surveillance had them pegged them as unarmed drug runners?

For the first time in days, Sam began to feel his mind clear and his thoughts become more coherent. He was determined to sit on the rock, enveloped by the cold air, and totally shut off from the world—at least until morning. He continued to chant under his breath, hoping to further clear his mind and open himself to regaining balance.

In the Middle of the Night

Bella was sleeping soundly when she heard the phone ring. At first, she thought she was dreaming; the incessant ring was not unlike dreams she had had of falling. She finally woke up enough to realize it was the kitchen phone. She looked at her watch on the nightstand and saw it was four o'clock. She grabbed her robe and ran to the kitchen, fearing a call at that hour meant someone needed her. The answering machine had already kicked in and was blinking by the time she turned on the light under the overhead kitchen cabinet. She pushed the button to listen to the message, hoping whoever it was would call back.

"You better tell your boyfriend to back off, or things could get real ugly." The call ended with a loud click. *Who would have left me such a message? Why? My boyfriend? What?* She reached for the button to replay the message, but she really didn't want to hear it again. Instead, she found herself pulling out a kitchen chair to sit down.

There wasn't much to go on. It was a male voice, but it wasn't familiar. She couldn't even place the accent or the age. *Of course, it could have been a wrong number. That was it, a wrong number.* Disappointed it wasn't Chad, she was determined not to let the call spook her. She sat shivering, trying to force herself to get up and go back to bed. She couldn't move.

A New Dawn

Around five o'clock, Sam Nations was startled awake as the sensation of falling overtook him. His feet were slowly sliding down the great rock, causing his head to jerk up off his arms and snap back so he was looking straight up into the star-laden sky. He repositioned himself and gazed into the abyss. The stark darkness of the valley below and the melodic waltz playing out overhead in the twinkling of millions and millions of stars drew him in. He took a deep breath and felt the cold air reach far into his lungs, a cleansing he felt was long overdue. Piece by piece, the puzzle of the past several weeks was no longer obscured. There were clear lines allowing him to fit the pieces together: his obligation to the DEA, his loyalty to his community in general and Chad in particular, and the deep realization that he had betrayed Quinn in ways he could never likely repair.

By 6:00 a.m., the pale light of early dawn hovered just below the ridgeline of the mountains. He decided to wait a little longer to walk back with natural light, not the light of man he could have from his phone. As he thought about his phone, he felt like he had been punched in the gut. He was supposed to have called Chad. With no signal at his elevation, he couldn't, and he had no way of knowing if Chad had tried to call him. Determined not to engage in one more betrayal of Chad's trust, he stood quickly and turned to head down the mountain. It was too much for his injured leg; he collapsed, his head striking the rock.

Alarm

The internal alarm Chad relied on to start his day came on with a jolt he was not expecting. He opened his eyes, shook his head, and reached over to look at his watch. The luminous numbers on the dial stood out in the darkened room: 5:17 a.m. *Why today? I could use another half hour of sleep.* He picked up his phone to see if he had been mistaken; perhaps it wasn't his *internal* alarm. *Maybe the phone rang.*

Did Sam try to call? He was disappointed to see no messages and no calls. He felt a foreboding to the morning that was not usual for him. Twenty minutes later he was dressed, his bed made, and his first cup of coffee downed. *Where's Sam? It makes no sense.* He removed his gun from the safe and holstered it then stepped into his boots. With any luck, he'd catch Sylvia Whitehorse and see if she knew anything about Sam.

CHAPTER 13

Nevertheless, again and again, in season and out of season, the question comes up, "What are rattlesnakes good for?"
John Muir 1838 – 1914

Drellag Cabin

SLEEP DID NOT RETURN FOR BELLA. She thought perhaps she had snoozed a bit in Matt's chair, but she knew restful sleep had not come. Looking at the clock, she was a bit surprised to see that it was already 7:00 a.m., and the first light was already creeping over the mountains. She heard Wizard whimper. "Okay, boy, you've probably not rested much either. Let me bundle up and we'll do an early walk and then try to get in a hike later today." *Arthur and his men will be here in an hour, so we should enjoy the solitude.*

Bella and Wizard were almost down to the gate when she heard the sound of a car engine. She expected it to be Arthur coming up early since the concrete truck was coming to pour her garage floor and the run for Wizard. She stopped walking when she saw the SUV was from the sheriff's department, but it wasn't Chad's. She waited for the driver to pull up and get out of the car.

"Morning, Dr. Anderson. Sure didn't expect to see you out so early. Everything all right?"

"I'm fine, Deputy Bennett. Last check up our way on your shift?"

"Yep. This road is in my sector all this week. When I saw the silhouette of someone on the road, I thought I'd stop and make sure it was you." He sounded as casual as if it were a conversation over a cup of tea.

"Why, thanks, Deputy Bennett, I appreciate it."

"Any unusual happenings lately?"

"No. Unless, of course, you're referring to all the construction up here."

"Great, we like to make sure our citizens are safe and secure."

"It's all good. Nothing out of the ordinary at all." She debated if she should mention the phone message. "I do have a question, though. Do boys make prank calls to another boy's girlfriend? Like if they're mad about something?"

Ken chuckled. "Ma'am, for my money, robocalls are prank calls. As far as kids calling other kids, likely so. Some reason you're asking?"

"Well, I do think it's just that, a prank call." She hesitated. "I had a strange call in the middle of the night. Someone left a message on my answering machine. I'm sure it's nothing."

"Do you still have the message on the machine, ma'am?"

"Yes. Yes, I do. Do you think I should be concerned?"

"Better safe than sorry. Mind if I have a listen?"

"No, not at all. We'll meet you up at Drellag Caban." She and Wizard turned and started walking up the road. Bella noticed the deputy took his time walking back to his SUV and seemed to be looking around the gate area.

Deputy Bennett pulled up and parked. "Wow, Dr. Anderson, you weren't kidding about the construction! Did you get the shed repaired?"

"Yes, the shed is repaired, and that," she pointed down the hill, "is going to be a guest cabin." The phone in the kitchen started to ring. "Please, may I get that? Do come in."

Ken followed her to the kitchen and stood by the door.

"Drellag Caban, may I help you?" Bella asked, a bit winded from hurrying to answer before her machine did. The caller hung up. Bella saw there was another message on her answering machine.

"Deputy—"

The word was barely out of her mouth when the phone began to ring again. She couldn't decide whether she should be worried or annoyed.

"Ma'am, let it go to your machine," the deputy spoke sternly. She did.

"Drellag Caban, please leave a message," the recording could be heard by both of them. "This is not a joke. Tell your boyfriend, the hack sheriff, to back off, or it's going to get real ugly."

She stared at Ken for a moment, then she pulled out a chair and sat down.

"Mind if I listen to that message again?"

"Go ahead. There's one before it too." Bella got up and busied herself making coffee.

Ken rewound the messages and heard the hang-ups and the first call. He looked up at her and asked, "Is this a digital or tape recording?" He only remembered answering machines from his grandparents' home.

"I think it's digital."

He pressed play again and listened to the messages again.

"Ma'am, I need to call the sheriff. May I use your phone?"

"Yes, go ahead." She walked out to the front porch and closed the French doors behind her, grateful she still had on her jacket.

"Bennett here. I'm at Dr. Anderson's place. I need to talk to the sheriff. If he's not in, patch me through. It's important."

The dispatcher said she thought he was behind closed doors.

"Interrupt him."

"Oliver here."

Ken told him what had happened. He repeated the messages verbatim.

"I want you to stay there until I get there, please. Let me speak to Dr. Anderson."

Bennett walked as far as the phone cord would stretch and called out, "Ma'am, Sheriff Oliver would like to speak to you."

She rushed toward him and took the phone. "Chad? Are you in danger?"

"Whoa, Bella. I'm fine. I need to know how *you* are."

"I was fine, but the second call has kind of spooked me." She felt calm, but her voice was shaking. She heard it but attributed it to getting chilled on the porch.

"I can imagine. Listen, I'm going to call the State Bureau of Investigation. They'll help sort out what we can do to trace the call. In the meantime, I'll have Ken stay with you. Also, I'm asking you to come down off the mountain."

"Chad," she said, glancing at the deputy. He heard the familiarity in her voice, and he walked out the kitchen door. "I've told you before, I will not be run off of my property. Besides, we don't even know that they are threatening me. They could just be sending you a message. Either way, I don't like it, but I'd rather know what we're dealing with before I put my tail between my legs and run."

Chad sighed. The very strength of this woman was one thing he found so attractive, but, at the same time, made him concerned he couldn't keep her safe. "Okay, maybe we could agree to hold that decision until I talk to the state guys and then get up there myself. Can we do that?"

"Okay," she said, drawing out the word as she thought about it.

"Thanks. I'll be up there as soon as I can. Meantime, you and the fine deputy have a cup of tea or coffee on that splendid porch of yours, deal?"

"Deal," she said. "And, Chad, please be careful."

"You too. See you shortly." He hoped his voice did not contain the worry he felt.

More Than One

Chad was on the phone with the SBI, waiting on the Assistant Director for the Knoxville region. He had worked with Elliott Nelson before; he said a silent prayer of gratitude that Elliott had given him his personal number and would take his call no matter the time of day.

"Sheriff Oliver, to what do I owe this unexpected pleasure?" Director Nelson's tone was even and pleasant.

"Wish it was a social call." Chad gave him a thumbnail sketch on what had been happening in his jurisdiction recently and the candid statement that he didn't know how pervasive the drugs or prostitution might be. "I'm much more concerned that this new twist could involve a local county commissioner." He explained the phone messages and said he needed assistance.

"Yes. Yes, you do," Elliott said. "This directly involves you, so you already know you can't investigate it. So, from this moment on, do not do anything, I mean *anything*, to jeopardize things. Clear?"

"Clear. How soon can you have someone here?"

"Just need to run it through channels, but I'd say within two hours, outside. *Is* this woman your girlfriend?"

Chad sat there for a minute. "At fifty-eight, I'm not sure girlfriend is the right word, but we have been out a few times and, to be fair, I'm more than a little interested in her."

"Well, on that one, I say good for you. Hope she's worthy of you, but let's keep this clean. Okay?"

"Of course."

Elliott waited a beat. "Where will you be?"

"I'll be at Dr. Anderson's—" Chad was interrupted by Elliott.

"Not a good idea, at least until we've spoken with her. And I'd prefer you don't call her. If she's expecting you, just have someone in your shop call and tell her you'll be delayed. Our agent will meet you at your office as soon as I can make it happen."

"Thanks, Elliott, I can follow orders."

"We're on it. Hang tight." Elliott hung up.

I hope so, Elliott. I hope so. If anything happens to Bella. . . he was distracted by a text.

"Call me. ASAP. NOS." When his daughter, Nora Sara Oliver-Smith, wanted to tease him, she would use her middle initial and write SOS. The use of her first and last initials meant it was serious.

He dialed her number from his speed dial.

"Daddy, sorry to bother you. There was a strange message on my house phone..."

"Hey, favorite daughter of mine. Where are you?"

"At this hour? I'm at home. Why? Is this something I should be worried about?"

"Don't think so, but please don't erase the message. I can't explain right now, but I don't want you to tell me what it says. It could just be a prank call, but until I know otherwise, I'm going to send someone over to be with you. Are the kids home? Fred?"

"Fred's already at the hospital. Daddy, are we safe?"

He could hear the anxiety rising in her voice since he had asked about the kids. "I have always told you I will do everything I can to keep you safe, right? So, that's all I'm trying to do. We're on top of this, and I'll be able to talk more with you later today. Okay?"

"Okay, Daddy, but please be careful too. Promise me."

"I promise. I'll have someone there shortly. Gotta run. Love you to the moon and back."

"Love you more than you love me," she said. He could hear the angst in her voice.

"It cannot be."

He called dispatch and asked to speak to his senior deputy, Susan Thomas.

"Susan?" Chad surprised even himself when he used her first name.

"Yes, sir?" she answered with the last word drawn out. She knew his use of her first name was unusual.

"I can't give you any details right now, and I don't really have many anyway. The SBI is headed here. In the meantime, I need you to go stay with Nora and the kids. Can you do that?"

"Out the door, sir. Don't worry. Be there in less than ten minutes."

Chad asked dispatch to call Dr. Anderson's home and tell Deputy Bennett that he had been delayed and to sit tight for the time being.

"Yes, sir, good as done."

Chad looked at the screen of his computer and saw a note from Sergeant Whitehorse; it was sent with a notification code that signified it was important, but not urgent. It was timestamped 5:16 a.m. *Not sure about psychic phenomenon, but it's pretty bizarre that this message reached my inbox about the same time I was jolted awake.* He read it carefully: "DEA SUV located on side of building at tribal grounds. Sam Nations? I'm sending some folks up. Have our backup ready if needed." It was signed Sylvia. Chad knew that meant she was handling this personally and sending tribal members, not deputies. He was relieved to see that she had deputy backup ready to go. Technically they couldn't go on tribal land without invitation, unless in pursuit of a crime. He sure hoped they weren't going to be needed.

Voices

Sam slowly opened his eyes and saw the first light of day was easing over the far eastern ridge of the mountains. His head hurt and he was having trouble moving his leg. Voices sounded faint and distant. He wondered if he was hallucinating as he reached up to rub his head and felt a large knot above his ear. A deep low moan escaped his lips as he tenderly probed the swelling. Slowly, Sam began to realize he was in fact conscious and not dreaming.

He reached down to touch his leg, but it was twisted back between him and the outer edges of the large boulder on which he had been sitting through the night. He didn't have the strength to move it, and he wasn't even sure it would move. He leaned his head back gently, looking up at the stars as they faded against the early morning light. He could hear the sounds getting louder and recognized it wasn't voices, but the gentle whistling call his tribe had used for generations when in search of a lost tribal member.

After an initial attempt to return the tribal call failed, he realized he needed to wet his parched throat. He hoped the increasing daylight would let him see a glint from his stainless-steel water bottle; he carefully scanned the area around him as best he could from his prone position. For the first few moments, he could see nothing, then a quick flash drew his eye to the bottle. It had rolled down the hill and rested just below his outstretched good leg. Sam closed his eyes to figure out the logistics of retrieving it—if he could.

What Now?

Deputy Bennett walked back into the living room and picked up his mug of coffee. "Thanks, again, ma'am, for the coffee. Probably need to give you a double thanks since I see you drink tea, not coffee."

"Never got the habit."

"Right. Well, ma'am, since I let that call go to the machine, I'm sure you heard dispatch say that the sheriff has been delayed."

"I heard."

The rumbling of vehicles outside brought the deputy to his feet.

"Relax, Deputy. It will be Arthur Gillett and his crew. They're pouring concrete today."

"If you don't mind, I'll just go have a look." Ken Bennett knew the landline was the only communication from up here, so he wasn't willing to go too far astray. He also didn't want another threatening call to occur with Dr. Anderson in the house by herself. Standing at the kitchen door, he recognized the logo for Gillett Construction on the first truck. He opened the screen door but went no further than the steps.

"Morning, Arthur."

"Morning, Ken. What brings you up here so early in the morning? Problems?"

"Nah, nothing serious. Just waiting on the sheriff to give me a call back. You know how it is, no signal up this high."

"That's as much truth as grits with butter is the best way to start the day."

"Amen to that. Looks like you've got a pretty big project going on here."

"Sure do. Glad Miss Bella asked us to do this work for her. It's been an interesting project, and my crew is grateful for the work going into winter."

"Everybody in these parts know there's no better crew than you and your boys. I'm waiting on that call, so I can't come out right now, but I'm looking forward to seeing the repair on that shed, for sure. It was a real shame that boy ran an ATV into the side of it. Nice old structure."

"Yeah, I understand Miss Bella's going to have the repairs aged with stain, so it should match right up. Well, gotta run. We need to do a final check on our frames before the concrete truck gets up here."

The phone began to ring as Ken waved farewell to Arthur. He turned and caught Bella's eye. She stayed where she was, allowing the call to go to her answering machine. The recording clicked on.

"Drellag Caban, please leave a message."

Bella held her breath.

"You're not listening, lady. Tell the sheriff to back off." The phone slammed down. It was a different voice from the previous messages.

Bella started to slide down the wall. Bennett took two long strides, reaching her before she could fall. Supporting her with one hand, he grabbed a chair and put it under her so she could sit. Wizard stood beside her, the hem of Bella's vest in his mouth.

"Dr. Anderson, that's one smart dog you have. He had hold of your vest and was going to keep you from falling."

Bella turned beet red from embarrassment. She had no idea what had just happened to her. *Was I about to faint? Did I faint? Why did Deputy Bennett and Wizard reach for me?*

"I'm fine, Deputy, honest. Thanks for the chair though." She put her hands in her lap and even she could see they were shaking. Wizard sat beside her. She bent down and put her cheek on his head and scratched his neck. "Good boy, Wizard."

Bennett walked into the living room to get their drinks and give her a moment of privacy to recover. This message sounded more threatening than the others. The dispatcher had told him that Deputy Thomas was sent to Nora's home because of a message on her machine, and he assumed it was similar. He knew not to mention Nora's call.

"Thank you, Deputy. I'll just get some warm water to heat up my tea." She started to stand.

"I'll get it, ma'am." He turned on the kettle to reheat the water. "Would you like another tea bag as well?"

She smiled. "No, just a little warm water will be fine. Please help yourself to more coffee. If you'll give me a couple of minutes, I'll be happy to make you some breakfast. You've been on duty all night, right?"

"No need, ma'am." Hoping to keep her distracted until he heard back from the sheriff, he continued. "I believe you were a professor, right?"

"Yes, I was. I taught English at a high school and then college."

"I think you know my wife is the principal of our joint middle and high school. We often joke that being in education and law enforcement means meals don't run on a clock." He was pleased when he heard her laugh.

"That's the gospel truth, Deputy. I'll admit it was a little easier at the university than at the high school level, but you'd be amazed how many meetings faculty members have to attend." She stopped. *Why am I going on about that? I'm retired. It doesn't matter anymore. But it is nice that this man understands the realities of our chosen professions.* "Well, enough of that."

She stood and walked toward the fridge.

He watched to make sure she was okay.

She pulled a bag of frozen biscuits out of the freezer then turned on the oven. "I have to confess that I've been known to take modern shortcuts. But you'll promise not to say anything out loud about it, okay?" She smiled. "The truth of the matter is I can make biscuits in about the same time it takes to bake these, but there are times I either don't want to clean up the mess, or I'm the only one and it just isn't worth the effort." Bella knew she was talking to hear herself talk, as her daddy used to say.

"Yes, ma'am. My wife and I do the same thing. Between our jobs and two children, shortcuts are just a way of life nowadays."

Their heads turned in unison as the phone began to ring.

CHAPTER 14

Higher Ground

WHEN SAM TRIED TO MOVE HIS HEAD, it hurt even more. He didn't think trying to lean down was an option. Scanning the earth around him, Sam looked for a way to retrieve the water bottle. He spotted a stick just below the edge of the rock. Staring at it, he tried to calculate how far he would have to lean over to reach it. Just as he stretched out his hand, the stick slithered down the hill.

Sam dropped his arm against the rock and blinked his eyes repeatedly; he was shocked he failed to recognize the snake. The whistling sound of the call was getting louder. His Army training kicked in and he went into full survival mode. *I can pull myself with my arms. I will pull myself with my arms. No one is firing at me. I will do this.* He grabbed his pants leg with both arms to give himself something to hold onto while he turned his body. Slowly he pulled his shoulder toward his knee. Then he started rolling. He had not realized how steep the incline was. He thought he heard running feet as he toppled down the hill.

Keeping Busy

Chad knew he had plenty of reports to catch up on, and thoughts to gather, ahead of the meeting he expected today or tomorrow about the Kirk boys. *I promise you, Joe, I will do what you would have expected of me.* The knock on the door brought a sigh of relief. Human distraction would help get through this morning. He stood and opened the door. "Morning, Sergeant. Come in."

Sergeant Sylvia Whitehorse entered, handed him a cup of coffee, and carried a paper sack towards the round table. "Figured you could stand to eat something. I know I'm ready." Chad savored the smell as Sylvia took out four biscuits; she handed him two and put a container with blackberry preserves in the center of the table.

"Sergeant Whitehorse, you are a saint." Chad opened the heavier biscuit. It was filled with a fried egg and country ham. His mouth began to water. "I'm sure glad you got some for yourself because I might not have been generous enough to share." He gave an almost maniacal laugh; it was a laugh she had never heard from Chad—nor, he realized, had he.

Recognizing it as the sound of someone trying to protect his family, Sylvia simply said, "Chad, food is universal across cultures. We use it for nourishment, comfort, and for building family and community. Just enjoy." They both took a bite of their biscuits and sat in companionable silence.

Chad was grateful that Sylvia was coming off the night shift because at this moment he needed her as his friend, and a woman of very wise counsel. Another sergeant would pick up the morning shift, so Chad knew he could count on her to stick around.

"Sylvia," his voice was low and now in total control. "I get mighty territorial when someone messes with my community, but *no one* has seen what will come out of me if they mess with my family... and Bella."

Sylvia continued to eat without saying a word. Chad finished his ham-and-egg biscuit and unwrapped the other. He took the blackberry preserves and slathered it across the surface of each half of the biscuit. He sat back and looked at the woman across the round table from him. She was tall, wore the russet skin of her tribe like the burnish on a bronze statue, and had straight, jet-black hair. The poise of this woman never ceased to amaze him. Her piercing black eyes were unwavering as she looked back at him. She finished the last bite of her ham biscuit and took a sip of coffee.

"Sheriff. Chad. I am here as your employee and your friend. We both go back a long way in these hills and our roots are solid. I am going to give you the counsel I know you would give me, if our places were reversed." He continued to look at her. "You are capable of the objectivity to protect your family and our community, if you keep your mind clear and your thoughts focused on the problem. You will not be in charge of some of this, and you have to accept that. We know when we take on the badge that not only do we serve, so do our families. What none of us ever want to face is the reality of how vulnerable our families are due to our choices."

She went quiet and drank her coffee. Chad looked past her to the topographical maps on the wall. He stood and walked over to them. "Where's Sam, Sylvia?" Chad's voice was flat, but she knew that Chad considered Sam family too.

"Under normal circumstances I would not divulge what I learned just before coming in here, but these are not normal circumstances. I have spoken with my father and I was assured that Sam is on a walk. What I am not sure about is his condition. Our members will find him." She moved to stand next to Chad, pointing to the elevation of the tribal grounds. "His SUV is roughly here. There are four two-person teams headed to the most popular healing places on our collective land. All we can do right now is wait for news."

Chad turned and looked at her. She saw the concern that was deep in his gray eyes. They both turned at the knock on the door.

Sylvia moved towards the door, but Quinn Isaacs walked in before Sylvia could open it. She went directly to Chad.

"Elliott Nelson called my boss, who called me. Some reason *you* didn't call me?" Anger hung on the edge of her tone.

"Don't get your Irish up with me, young lady." Chad sounded like the young woman's father, not the sheriff.

"I'm not Irish. I already told you: Spanish, Scottish and Welsh, and cut the boss role. I left you at The Corral last night making pretty clear that I consider you a friend. You know perfectly well these calls have something to do with our case."

"Quinn," his eyes softened as he spoke. "*Please*. I can't talk about it. Sergeant Whitehorse can take you out of here and tell you what we know officially at this moment. But I can't say a word."

Quinn's shoulders slumped. "Of course, you're right. I've had twenty-three minutes from Round City to here being steamed at you."

"Twenty-three minutes!" Chad and Sylvia reacted at the same time, their voices overlapping.

Chad stared at her. "At this hour of the morning?!" He turned to Sylvia. "Sergeant, please take Agent Isaacs to the conference room. I expect company from the SBI, likely in less than an hour. Please have someone order a variety of biscuits to have available. I will join you when the SBI invites me." He walked to his desk, sat down, and opened the next message in his inbox.

Stir Crazy

Bella was not hungry at all. In fact, the thought of food made her nauseous. She went through the motions of fixing the biscuits, cooking some ham in the iron skillet, and taking out the butter and blackberry preserves to keep herself occupied and to feed the deputy. When she saw she had put a dozen biscuits on the cookie sheet, she realized she was hoping she'd be feeding Chad as well.

"You didn't need to do this, Dr. Anderson, but it sure smells good."

"Deputy Bennett, I have tried, really I have, to respect the responsibility you have as a law enforcement officer in this particular moment, but it would certainly help me relax if you would call me

Bella. I promise I will not think less of you for it, and I can still be compliant if you need to direct me to do something."

Ken Bennett started laughing. She turned and looked at him quizzically. "And that's funny, why?" Even she heard her professor voice when she asked.

"Sorry, ma'am, uh, Bella. Before you came back to our hills, my wife was the only female with a doctorate of any kind in these parts. It has taken a lot of reminding folks that they would never call Dr. Smith, Mr. Smith. And, in his case, mostly everyone calls him Doc. She earned her Ph.D. last year, so it's still pretty fresh and I'm proud as punch that she went after her dream. So, forgive me, but my use of your well-earned title is out of respect for you and the degree. And, please, call me Ken."

Her whole face lit up. "Ken, thank you. I totally forgot that you would understand the challenges of having a degree that carries a title." She sat down across from him. "I would very much like to meet your wife."

"I know she wants to meet you. She was an English teacher too. We'll try to make it happen sooner rather than later." His voice got louder as the roar of the concrete truck started up outside. Bella shut the inner kitchen door.

"That won't stop all of the noise, and none of the vibration, but if we sit in the living room, it will be easier." She turned off the heat under the iron skillet and saw there were fifteen minutes left on the biscuits. She was glad she had set the timer and not relied on watching the clock. *Too many distractions to trust my memory. Where is Chad?* Bella felt her heart skip a beat in her concern for him.

She and Ken settled in on the L-shaped sofa, the piece of furniture farthest from the noise. Bella tucked her knees up under her and sipped her tea. As much as she loved it, she wasn't sure how much longer she could take being confined to the cabin.

Daily Life Goes On

The tingling of the silver bell above the door of the Valley Store just past seven signaled to Joshua that Carla had arrived. He wanted a few minutes with her to talk about the day ahead. Their dinner on his deck the previous night reassured him he had made the right decision in asking her to marry him. It also left him wondering what he had missed by being satisfied with his dad taking on the role of customer service in the store.

"Good morning, Joshua. Did you miss me?"

"More than you know, Miss Carla Long. Soon, I hope, to be Mrs. Carla Johnson." He heard her stop on the stairs. He rolled his chair over to look down. "Something wrong? You okay?"

She stared up at him, turned, and sat on the bottom step. He hurried down to check on her, having visions of his father the day he fell down the stairs. He knelt in front of her and took her hands in his. "Carla?" He saw the tears on her face. "Are you hurt? Where? Do I need to call 9-1-1?"

She leaned towards him and kissed him gently on the cheek, then she rested her head on his shoulder and wept. He put his arms around her and pulled her to him, totally bewildered. Gently taking her hand, he walked her over to the stool by the register and had her sit on it. The tears were drying up.

"Are you hurt?" She shook her head. "Did I say something to hurt you?"

Choking a little as she tried to speak, she looked up at him. "You have no idea how many years I dreamed of being Mrs. Joshua Johnson, Carla Johnson. A dream I never ever expected to come true. I feel so guilty because I loved Jan; she was always one of the most beloved teachers and community members here." She turned her eyes away from him, and hiccupped. They both started laughing.

"Well, seems to me neither of us asked for Jan to become sick and pass away. I always loved dancing with you, but I never knew you were in love with me. I don't think we are betraying Jan. She wanted me to remarry." He squatted in front of her and looked her in the eyes. "I'm sixty-three years old. I married my high school sweetheart, and I have been faithful to her, and her memory, every day. I can't explain how quickly I knew I had fallen in love with you. But this I do know: I want to get married as soon as you're ready."

She smiled at him. "Joshua Johnson, you will come to find out how crazy I can be at times. Those tears were both joy that you *want* to marry me, and the stark realization that I never thought of my last name being anything other than Long." She looked at him and could see the worry in his eyes.

"I am working on becoming a thoroughly modern man. Bella has been a big influence in a very short time. Although, to be honest, Jan tried and did get me on the path. If you want to keep your last name, I'm fine with that." He kissed her lightly on the nose. "Or, hey, if you want me to take your name, I might even be able to become that modern." They both started laughing so hard they barely heard the knock at the front door of the store.

Carla jumped up and ran to the door. "Welcome. Oh, hey, Harold. Come on in." She saw it was almost time to open.

Joshua jumped to his feet and shook Harold's hand. "Hello, my friend. Whatcha need this fine morning?"

"Sorry, it looks like I interrupted something."

"Not at all," Carla said. "Joshua was just trying to calm the jittery nerves of a not-so-blushing bride-to-be."

"Well, that's a good job for him. If you're sure I'm not interrupting, I'd like a couple of minutes with you, Joshua."

Joshua looked at Carla. She nodded her head towards the back. "Go have some coffee. I'll just put my purse upstairs and we'll be open for business."

Lifted Out of the Roots

Sam's head was throbbing now, but he was relieved that the tactic he had learned in basic training had worked. He just hadn't calculated the steepness of the hill accurately. Blinking his eyes, he hoped the inability to identify the snake and calculate the angle of the hill was just from the pressure of the knot on his head, not something more threatening to his vision.

He reached out and touched his water bottle, imagining how many times he had seen a man lost in a desert depicted reaching for water. Even if the water bottle had not been close, he now saw there were still some green leaves he could pick from the ground cover and chew to get some moisture. He opened the bottle and sipped slowly to give the inside of his mouth and throat a thorough soaking. He also didn't want to upset his stomach by drinking too quickly; he suspected this knot on his head might cause nausea.

He grabbed a root on the tree he had rolled next to and pulled himself up. He tried the call he knew would help the searchers locate him. He was relieved to hear the call come out, and he heard it returned from two different angles. Someone knew he was here, and, for whatever reason, they were looking for him. He leaned back against the tree and waited while he counted to fifty before he repeated the call.

"Nations? Nations?" The call of his name was clear and closing in.

"Here! Mantle Rock."

The sound of boots crushing the fallen leaves, crisp at this hour from the cold, allowed Sam to close his eyes, relax, and try to imagine how he could thank whoever sent help.

"Hello, Cousin." He opened his eyes. Standing in front of him was Fire Chief Mike Smallwood, husband of Sergeant Sylvia Whitehorse. "My wife said you might be needing some help. Nothing better to do than get yourself all banged up?" Behind Mike, Sam saw a younger tribal member who he had heard was on the fire squad.

"Thanks, Mike. And, in case my brain goes completely, thank Sylvia for me too."

A man and a woman arrived next. One of them was carrying two poles with a canvas that would serve as a stretcher to carry Sam out. All four looked at his leg and knew they would need it.

Sam spoke to them in their native language. "Your kindness passes through to me and I am eternally in your debt." He didn't know the youngest member of the group had never learned their language.

They carefully eased Sam onto the stretcher and began down the hill. As the path widened, they were able to put one person on each corner and move fairly quickly.

Mike Smallwood passed off his corner to his colleague as they reached a level where he knew he would have a phone signal. He pointed for them to go on down, he wanted privacy for this call.

"Sylvia."

"Hey. Please tell me you found him." She and Quinn were still the only ones in the conference room at the sheriff's office, so she didn't leave. She listened intently. "Do you have an ambulance there? Okay, I'll call. Thanks, Mike. I love you."

"Love you too." Mike hung up and walked quickly to catch up with the others.

Sylvia picked up the desk phone in the conference room and told dispatch to send an ambulance to the tribal grounds immediately. "Yes, it's Sam," she replied to the dispatcher.

She hung up the phone. Then she saw the look on Quinn's face. "Oh my, Quinn. I'm so sorry I didn't tell you sooner." She explained about Sam's SUV being spotted behind the buildings at the tribal grounds. Concerned about him, she had sent her husband and others out to check on him before she learned from her father that Sam was on a walk of restoration and balance. Quinn went pale.

"Then why does he need an ambulance?"

"Sam's able to talk but was almost asleep by the time they got to a low enough elevation for Mike to call… Mike's my husband and the fire chief, by the way. I don't think you've met." Quinn shook her head. "They were trying to keep him awake in case he has a concussion. Nora told me earlier that Doc Smith is at the hospital, so he'll get the best care."

"What if they don't have what they need to treat him?"

"Doc Smith would never take a chance. He'll medevac Sam to Knoxville if he's at all concerned. Let's just wait and see."

Quinn went silent, disappearing into her thoughts. She had ignored Sam in their last meeting and verbally attacked Chad. She regretted her attack on Chad, who she knew was a good man and a by-the-book LEO. Her attack was wrong on so many levels, not the least of which was Chad's worry for his daughter, who she now knew had received a call similar to Bella's. And, of course, he would be worried about Sam. She stared off to the far wall of the conference room.

"If you'll excuse me, Quinn, I need to tell the sheriff that we have Sam and check to see if we have an updated ETA for the State Bureau folks."

CHAPTER 15

Don't let yesterday use up too much of today.
Old Cherokee Saying

Who's First?

CHAD OPENED HIS DOOR TO A SOFT KNOCK; Sylvia stepped inside and closed the door. She looked at Chad and saw worry in his eyes for the first time in all the years she had known him.

"Mike found Sam. He was up at Mantle Rock but had fallen and injured the same leg where he was shot. Mike said the leg doesn't look good, but Sam is conscious. He's on his way in an ambulance to the hospital and Doc Smith knows he's coming." She stopped and watched him.

Chad sat back in his chair and pointed to one nearby for Sylvia. He tightened his fist and hit the arm of his chair. "I knew I should have followed up sooner to check on him."

"You cannot be responsible for another man's journey. You can try to show the way, make suggestions, and be a friend, but, in the end, each of us walks our own path. Sam was on a walk to restore balance in his life. This is part of the journey."

Chad stared at her. Sylvia had been on the force almost as long as he had. *I always knew she was smart and kind, but I should have taken advantage of her wisdom a long time ago. Why didn't I ever take the time to hear her?*

"Sheriff, I suspect this is going to be a very long day. Right now, everyone is safe, and it is our job to keep them that way. Sam will get the care he needs. We need to be ready to do whatever the SBI recommends to protect everyone else."

With a weary sadness he had never expressed at work, Chad said, "You're right—"

Sylvia interrupted him, something she had never done. "Chad, at this moment, as far as we know, it is Nora and Bella who have received calls. We don't know who might be next."

Chad jerked his head towards her; it looked like someone had just flipped the switch that returned him to being sheriff.

"Okay, I was wrong. You are *absolutely* right. This is not just about me. It's *our* case: our team, Immigration, and DEA. I was just the natural first line of attack in the valley. Whoever called Nora and Bella had resources, at least in Nora's case. Her home number is private because Fred is a physician."

Sylvia smiled. The sheriff was back. "I'm going back to the conference room. Read your reports. It'll be good for you to see how well the team you've assembled works. This case is not the only show in town." Without another word, she stood and walked out. As she walked down the hall, her secure phone buzzed.

"Whitehorse here."

"Sarge, the SBI agents are here."

"On my way."

Under Observation

The ambulance pulled into the emergency room entrance at the small rural hospital and the doors opened immediately. Mike had kept Sam awake by talking to him during the time it took to get him in the ambulance and throughout the ride from the tribal grounds down the mountain. Mike saw Dr. Fred Smith walking towards them.

"Hey, Doc. Found this boy up in the hills and thought you might want to take a look at him."

"Did ya now? Guess the clear sky made it a good night for a walk."

"Hey, Doc." Sam all but moaned out the greeting. "Think I'll ever be able to straighten out this leg?"

"I'm still trying to figure out how these folks managed to get you down the mountain and over here with that leg still folded behind your rear end. I know you've missed us since you checked out of our fine hospital recently, but is this the best act you've got?" Fred was good at trying to ease a patient's fears, which he knew even this tough young man had. He was well aware Sam had seen combat in Afghanistan and worked for the DEA—and had likely seen some pretty gruesome things there too. He knew that did not lessen the concerns an injured person felt.

Sam started laughing. "Ouch. Isn't it bad enough my leg and head hurt? Do you have insult me on top of it?"

"Oh, you hit your head? *That* explains this nonsense." While they were bantering, Fred was listening for anything that would indicate Sam was affected by the head injury. He looked Sam over while the nurse took Sam's vitals and started to wash the dirt off his head. "Okay, Agent Nations, I'm due for a coffee break…" Sam looked at him and rolled his eyes. "And your reaction tells me it's time to go take it." Fred laughed.

"So glad I can start your day with a side show. By all means, don't let me distract you from your coffee break. Biscuits and gravy to go with that?"

Mike smiled. Sam might have some recovery and rehab ahead of him, but he was okay. "Guess I'll join Doc here and leave you to the care of this excellent nurse." Mike turned to walk away.

"Hey, Mike. Thank everyone for me, please. I'll do it personally later."

"You've got it, Cuz. Now shut up and follow orders. You know how to do that, right?"

"When I should." Sam felt a huge wave of relief flow over him.

"I'll be back after they do some x-rays and a scan. Need to be sure your brain is still in there." Fred patted Sam's shoulder and walked out behind Mike.

Sam let out a long breath and looked at the nurse. He didn't know her well, but knew she was from one of the tribal families. He saw her name badge and said, "Marie, I'm in your hands now. Don't be too rough on me." He closed his eyes but knew he should not sleep.

The Conference Room

Sylvia walked back into the conference room long enough to tell Quinn the SBI agents had arrived.

Quinn stood. "I'm going to step out to the restroom and will be right back."

Sylvia nodded and headed for the front of the station. The desk deputy clicked the lock to the waiting area and Sylvia opened the door walked up to the first agent who came towards here. "Welcome, I'm Sergeant Sylvia Whitehorse. Thank you for coming." She realized the man behind the lead person was in a suit, not a windbreaker. She greeted the three agents—two men and a woman—then reached the man in the suit. "Sir."

"Morning, Sergeant."

"Thank you for coming. Wish you were here to enjoy our pow-wow."

"Hope to come back for that. Next weekend, right?"

"Yes, sir. In the meantime, if y'all will follow me, we'll go to the conference room."

Elliott Nelson nodded. "Sheriff here?"

"Yes, sir. In his office. He'll be available when you want him."

"Good. Good." The doublespeak fell as naturally from Elliott's mouth as honey from a wooden dipper stick. Sylvia knew he was originally from Round City and that his brother was police chief over there. They were mountain folks.

Quinn was standing as the five entered the conference room.

"Agent Isaacs, glad you could make it."

"Morning, Director Nelson. Thanks for the call."

Introductions were made and the six law enforcement officers fixed themselves coffee; several took a biscuit from the tray on the counter.

"Sir," Sylvia started, "this is your operation. We are at your disposal. Just to brief you, we have a deputy at the home of Sheriff Oliver's friend, Dr. Bella Anderson, and our head deputy with the sheriff's daughter, Nora Oliver-Smith, and her two children. Dr. Smith, her husband, is at the hospital and there is security there." She wanted to make sure the agents were aware of the connections.

"Thank you, Sergeant. I would first like us to hear from Agent Isaacs about the criminal operations leading up to today. If you could then send someone out with my agents to Ms. Oliver-Smith and Dr. Anderson, Agent Jones and I will interview the sheriff. Then we'll regroup."

"Yes, sir. Quinn, the floor is yours."

Drellag Caban

The timer rang on the stove and Bella went to the kitchen. She pulled the biscuits out of the oven, spread melted butter over the top of them, and turned the iron skillet back on to warm the ham.

"Ken, how do you like your eggs?" She almost shouted it to get above the concrete machine.

He joined her in the kitchen. "I'm good with a biscuit and ham. Thanks." He saw it was late enough to call his wife. "May I use your phone?"

"Certainly. You don't need to ask."

He dialed his wife's personal cell phone, knowing she would answer unless she was dealing with a crisis at the school. "Hey, Amanda. I'm fine, just wanted you to know I won't be home for a while. My day got extended." He listened for a minute. "Good, thanks for taking care of the kids. Hope you have a great day. Love you."

Bella heard him put the handset back in the cradle of the wall phone. She had struggled with whether to leave the room but was in the middle of scrambling an egg for herself when he picked up the phone. The endearments Ken shared with his wife warmed her heart. She put the scrambled eggs and ham slices on a platter and hoped he would eat some of the eggs. After settling four biscuits in a basket, she placed the others back in the oven to stay warm until the oven finally cooled off. They sat down at the kitchen table and started to eat.

"Did you say you had two children?"

"Yes, a boy, thirteen, and a girl, eleven. Now that they're in middle school, they go in with Amanda. It was a bit more challenging when she needed to be at work so early and they were in the elementary building. Shift work doesn't always make it easy for me to help. One of the things we love about being in these hills is that folks help each other out. No amount of money can pay for the support of a community."

"Or the love of a family," Bella said quietly.

The ringing of the phone stopped them both. The deputy moved towards the phone to pick up if it was anyone other than another threatening call. If it was a threat, he'd let it go to the machine to record.

"Deputy Bennett, could you please pick up?" They both heard the voice of the dispatcher as the machine started to record.

"Bennett here." Ken picked up the handset and listened for a moment before he hung up the phone and sat down again.

"Bella, the sheriff sent word that he is fine and will talk to you as soon as he can. In the meantime, an agent from the State Bureau of Investigation is on her way up here with one of our deputies. She will want to talk to you about the recordings and how they will handle them going forward. Just so you know, when they SBI agent is finished, I will take her back down to the station and the deputy who comes up will stay with you."

"It's really not necessary."

"I suspect you can imagine that our sheriff would offer this service for any citizen until we have a handle on what's going on here.

For you, he's pretty much going to insist on it." Ken smiled. "And, by the way, Bella, it's none of my business, but I'm happy for both of you."

She smiled at him and stayed quiet. She was struggling between her concern for yet another crime that involved her through no fault of her own, her concern for Chad, and her downright irritation that she had not been consulted in decisions on how to protect her.

Friend to Friend

Joshua poured coffee for Harold and himself then sat down opposite Harold at the table in the storeroom.

"Must say, ole boy, I like the table here by the window. Guess it took a take-charge woman working here to help you see the light."

"Well, aren't you the comedian, Harold? I thought you wanted to talk to me, not harass me." Both men laughed. "Yes, Carla has helped me see a lot of things I haven't paid attention to for far too many years. I'll tell you; I'm feeling like one pretty lucky man right now. At sixty-three I've known the love of a great woman in Jan, and, since I asked Carla to marry me, I found out she claims to have been in love with me all her life."

"What?" Harold looked stunned. "What are you saying?"

"Yeah, can you believe it? She told me she fell in love with me when she was quite young and came back here after college to work in the restaurant to be near me, and never dated or had interest in any other man. The only person who ever knew was James."

"And you didn't know that until after you asked her to marry you?"

"That's right. Feels pretty strange, I'll tell you."

Harold reached over and slapped Joshua on the back. "I'd say that makes her a pretty special woman. I'm happy for both of you."

"Thanks. Means a lot coming from you. Now, what's up? You didn't come to talk about my love life."

"No. No, I didn't. I need some advice."

"If I can help, I will."

"I just got a call from Commissioner Zimmerman. He told me he had an unexpected family matter that required him to go to Michigan. Said his wife was in an accident yesterday and she had called the highway patrol since she doesn't trust our sheriff. He wants me, as county manager, to make sure that the sheriff does not get involved in the investigation." Harold stopped and took a sip of coffee.

"Whoa. Let me think about that a minute." Joshua sat quietly and then nodded his head.

"Then he made this comment, which is why I need some advice. He said, 'And I mean you *better* get the sheriff to back off if you want to keep your job.'"

Joshua waited a few seconds before he spoke, but he thought there was only one clear option. "You have to tell Chad. No question. Remember when we talked about the ATVs? Now that we know what caused all that ATV noise, it's clear that Chad was putting all the pieces of a puzzle together. I wouldn't be a bit surprised to find out down the road that this is part of something too. Do you want me to call him to come over?"

Harold nodded his head slowly. "Yeah, this is probably the best place for us to meet. Except in the movies, who would suspect anything out of the ordinary from three men talking in the grocery store?"

"Only men who send their wives to do the shopping." Joshua chuckled.

"Hey! Are you coming into the twenty-first century? Julie won't believe you said that."

"Of course not, her husband has bought the groceries for their whole marriage."

"Yeah, buddy, take lessons. You're about to marry a modern woman!"

"Let's call Chad," Joshua said and pulled out his phone.

While he waited for Chad to answer, Joshua realized he was not offended that Harold's comment might suggest Jan had not been a modern woman. Joshua knew she had lived with one foot firmly in the twenty-first century while retaining the charms and customs of the mountains. He was okay with that.

Mommy

Deputy Susan Thomas received a text that an SBI agent was on his way over with a deputy, and she walked into the kitchen to tell Nora.

"Mac, please take Lilly into your playroom. Mommy will be there in just a minute."

"Okay, Mommy. Let's go Lilly."

Susan noticed that he took his little sister's hand and immediately started telling her the fun things they would do in the playroom. "Your children are so sweet, Nora. Nice job you and Fred are doing with them."

"Thanks, Susan. It's a full-time job, that's for sure. What's up? Is my daddy okay?"

"Yes, he's fine. One of our deputies is bringing over an agent from the SBI." She saw the look on Nora's face. "Hang on, it's okay. Your dad called for them to come."

Nora's face muscles relaxed. "If he called *them,* then they aren't investigating *him*. They're here because it involves him?"

"Never thought much got past you, Nora. That's right. They'll want to hear the recording and tell you what they'll do regarding that tape and any other calls that might occur. Just tell them what happened. You've got this."

The doorbell rang and Mac called out, "Mommy, do you want me to answer the door?"

She nodded to Susan to get the door and hurried to the playroom. "Mac, there are some folks from Grandpa's office that need to talk to me for a few minutes. You could help me out the most by playing with Lilly. I know I can count on you. Any questions?"

"No, Mommy. We'll be fine. See, we're already building a fort. I guess I'll let her put her dollies in it." She knew he meant to reassure her with his most serious concession to let the dolls be in the fort.

"Thanks, Mac. I'll be back as soon as I can. We'll be in Mommy and Daddy's office if you need us. Deputy Thomas is here too."

"Okay, Mommy." He turned back to building with his Lincoln Logs. Lilly took down one log for every four he placed. Susan Thomas watched from the doorway, amazed that he didn't seem to mind the log removal. He just picked up another one and put it on.

Nora looked at Susan. "They'll be fine. Will you be with us in the meeting?"

"No, it will just be you and the SBI agent for now. He will want to record you, is that okay with you? Do you want to call Gray?"

"I don't think I need a lawyer, and I hope I never do." She walked toward her living room. Susan stayed in the doorway of the play-room.

"Good afternoon, I'm Nora Oliver-Smith. Welcome. Thank you for coming. May I get you some tea?" Both men declined.

The agent and the deputy introduced themselves. The deputy stood by the door in a fairly formal "at rest" position. Nora invited him to sit but knew he wouldn't.

"Agent, if you'd like to come to my office, we can talk there and you can also hear the recording." He followed her into the office, and she pointed to a chair, closed the door, and sat opposite him.

"Ma'am, I assume you know that this is a routine inquiry based on the fact that you may have evidence that is pertinent to an ongoing case. I will ask you some questions to document who you are, how you might be connected to the case, and I will ask you to describe for me everything that has happened since the phone call came in. I may then have some further clarifying questions. Are you okay with that?"

"Of course." Nora's reply was what the agent expected the adult child of a sheriff would be: short, sweet, and to the point.

CHAPTER 16

Gathering Evidence

DEPUTY AMY MURPHY WAS NOT PREPARED for all the construction going on at the top of the mountain. She had been glad she was the one on the inside of the turns on the switchbacks as a concrete truck passed her. A quick glance at the pale SBI agent clutching the armrest suggested *she* was even happier about it.

"Not so many switchbacks near Knoxville, are there?"

"Whew, I'd say not. Let's add to that I'm a city gal from Memphis, and I much prefer city streets to these roads. Sure glad you're driving."

Amy laughed. "You'd get used to it. I grew up here, and my first nighttime fast pursuit was more than a little unsettling. I made a decision to remedy it: I went out at night and practiced in my own car. I was fine. One time, though, one of our deputies stopped me. Boy, was he surprised to see I was the one doing some high-speed shenanigans on a back road."

The SBI agent couldn't stop laughing. "What happened?"

"We buddied up and went out and practiced together when we both had a night off. I decided he was right that I shouldn't be up on that mountain by myself doing crazy turns."

"Must make for a pretty special place to work."

"Yeah, only ever wanted to do rural policework. We have a great shop, and I wouldn't trade my job for any other."

"That's the sign of a good boss."

"Oh, he's a good boss, all right. But he expects each and every one of us to speak up on our operations and cases. Seems he learned about the talking circle some of the Native American tribes use. Anytime we're discussing a case, we sit at a round table. I think it makes for good teamwork. Well, here we are." They pulled through the gate and up over the crest onto Bella's land.

"Wow! What a view! How many people live up here?"

"Just one as far as I know." Amy parked the car out of the way of the work crew and got out. "You'll like Dr. Anderson."

Bella was relieved to see it was Amy Murphy. She had the screen door open and called to them. "Hey, Deputy Murphy. Come in this way."

Amy remembered the comment Bella made last month that folks rarely used her front door. She led the way and the SBI Agent followed her.

Bella stepped back as they came in on the porch. She shook hands with Amy, who introduced SBI Agent Davis. Bella shook her hand as well.

"Welcome to Drellag Caban, Agent Davis. I am Bella Anderson. Come in. Come in."

The women started across the porch as Bella locked the screen. The SBI agent found that curious. Wanting to put Bella at ease, Agent Davis asked, "Worried we'll escape?"

Bella looked at her, trying to figure out what she meant. "Oh, that. Force of habit. You don't want to walk out to discover that some of our mountain wildlife has found its way on to your porch."

For the second time in less than thirty minutes, the SBI agent went pale. "You mean like bears?"

"Oh no." Bella shook her head.

Davis smiled as color returned to her face.

"This screen will hardly keep out a bear who thinks there might be food here. I try to be very careful about not leaving crumbs."

Amy was actually amused; she never expected an SBI agent to blanch about wild animals. Then again, she was probably more used to the human kind.

Deputy Bennett was standing in the living room when they came in through the French doors. He introduced himself and asked to speak privately to Amy. They returned from the kitchen a few minutes later.

"Kitchen door okay to exit? I'll wait outside. Looking forward to seeing all this construction work," Ken said.

"Of course." She reached out to shake his hand. "Thank you so much for your concern and stopping when you saw me this morning." Bella saw that Wizard, who had been on his blanket since they had entered the house, was up and looking at everyone.

"Wizard, it's okay. This is Deputy Murphy, she's from here. And this nice lady is from the State Bureau of Investigation. Don't worry though, you and I are not in trouble." The women and Ken looked at Bella and then at the dog, who had kept his eyes on Bella the whole time.

"Deputy Murphy, Agent, meet Dex the Wizard."

"He's beautiful. He looks like he's part German shepherd and part Lab," the agent said as she extended the back of her hand toward Wizard. Murphy decided the agent was more comfortable with domesticated animals.

"Yes, he's a sheprador. It's a relatively new breed. He wandered onto my land with a hurt paw..." Bella looked up from petting Wizard and resumed, "Sorry, you didn't come here to visit, although you are welcome. Thanks again, Deputy Bennett. I look forward to meeting Dr. Bennett." Ken nodded and headed out the door, pulling it closed behind him.

"Looks like the shed is repaired. Boy, you have a lot going on up here," Deputy Murphy said.

The agent asked, "Who's doing all this work for you?"

"Arthur Gillett. He's a local contractor and does excellent work. Are you from around here?" It seemed a casual question to Bella, but she wondered if the agent suspected Arthur of something.

"No, ma'am. I'm from Memphis originally and posted to Knoxville."

"Welcome to our hills then. May I get you coffee? Tea?" She looked at both women.

They both said, "Coffee."

"I have some warm biscuits that I just made. Interest you?"

The agent declined.

"I already told you LEOs will eat you out of house and home. I had to get up before breakfast this morning. I'm not shy. I'll have one. How can I help?" Amy moved forward.

Deputy Murphy put some ham on a biscuit and grabbed her coffee before excusing herself to head outside. There was really nowhere in the cabin not to hear what was being said, so she left them to the job the agent came to do.

"Dr. Anderson, I assume you know that this is a routine inquiry based on the fact that you may have evidence pertinent to an ongoing case. I will ask you some questions to document who you are, how you might be connected to the case, and I will ask you to describe for me everything that has happened since the first phone call came in. I may then have some further clarifying questions. Are you okay with that? Do you wish to have someone with you?" The agent rattled through her introduction as if she had memorized it from a textbook.

"Agent, please call me Bella. I know the formalities maintained and why, but I assure you I will tell you what I know, and I can follow directions should you need to give me any. I don't need someone else present." Bella was formal but not unkind.

"Thanks, Bella. I'm Sandy Davis. However, for the recording I will use titles, just so you know." Bella nodded.

Sandy started the recorder with a test, making sure there was no problem with the small device. After giving her professional information, the agent said, "Please state your name, legal address, and date of birth."

"I am Bella Anderson, my legal address is 1444 Hillcrest Lane. . ." Bella continued to give her legal residence in North Carolina, her location in the mountains, and her post office box address, along with all three of her phone numbers. "My date of birth is June 5th. . ."

"Dr. Anderson, you have been advised that this is simply an interview to gather any information you may have related to a potential crime and that you are not being charged with a crime nor identified as a suspect at this time."

Her last words caused Bella's head to jerk back from looking out the kitchen window at the sky. "I don't expect to be a suspect at any time, Agent Davis. I have done nothing wrong, and I am fully cooperating with your questioning. I am ready when you are." She was terse this time.

Sandy knew Dr. Anderson was a professor and was quickly reminded of some of her professors at university: no nonsense. She liked that.

"Please describe your understanding of why I am here today."

Bella began without hesitation. "I was awakened around four o'clock this morning when my wall phone rang. My mobile phone does not work at this elevation." She described in detail the message, which she offered to play for the agent. "I took my dog, Wizard, out for a walk and Deputy Bennett saw us near the gate. He stopped to verify it was I—and to see if I was okay." She realized she was speaking with very formal language. She continued, explaining about their return to the cabin for him to hear the message, his subsequent call to the sheriff, the next call hang-up, and then the subsequent message. "Then we ate breakfast while we waited on your arrival."

"Have you spoken to Sheriff Chad Oliver today?"

"Yes, Deputy Bennett told me Chad, uh, Sheriff Oliver, wanted to speak to me when he called in the report on the phone message. I would say that was around seven o'clock this morning. Sheriff Oliver checked to make sure I was safe, and I asked if he was. He told me he would come up here as soon as he could."

"Has Sheriff Oliver been here or spoken to you since that call?"

"No. He told me he was going to call the State Bureau of Investigation and then he would be up. I'm assuming he was advised not to make the trip. I can understand that." Even though it was cold, Bella picked up her cup of tea and took a sip.

"What is the nature of your relationship with Sheriff Oliver?"

Bella looked at Sandy and thought about Chad; she knew he was going to be asked the same question about her. *What is the nature of our relationship?* She took a breath and looked straight at the SBI agent.

"I met Sheriff Oliver last month when several ATVs were using my property as a crossing between a meth lab out in the mountains and wherever they took the drugs when they headed back to the valley. Since then, the sheriff and I have become better acquainted and have friends in common. I guess you would say we have a mutual attraction, but nothing serious."

Agent Davis had read the reports about the recent ATV case and meth lab explosion during the drive to the valley; everything Bella said seemed to match up with the official documentation.

"*Is* he your boyfriend?" Sandy asked. She was professional without being intrusive.

"At my age, I'm not sure that the term boyfriend is appropriate, but if you want to know if I am interested in him romantically, then the answer is yes. I don't know what the future holds."

The SBI agent asked the last of her questions and then asked to hear the recordings, which she added to her official record. She had already determined that the machine was digital, which meant there was no tape to retrieve and take with her. They also needed to record any other incoming calls, so she didn't want to take the machine. "Please do not erase any messages. If our technicians need the original of these recordings, we will be in touch. This concludes our interview at this time. Thank you for your cooperation." Sandy turned off the recorder.

"May I ask what your profession is?"

"Was. I was an English professor. Why?"

"Good with words."

"Accurate with words," Bella said and smiled.

Sandy opened the kitchen door and signaled Deputy Murphy to return. "Thank you, again, Dr. Ander... Bella. You have a lovely place here. I believe Deputy Bennett is going to take me back to the station, so I'll leave you now. You're in good hands."

"Unless you're superstitious and want to use the porch door, you are welcome to go out the kitchen door."

Sandy looked at her and realized she had a lot to learn about real mountain folks. "This door is fine. Thanks." Amy shook hands with Sandy and entered the kitchen.

"More coffee, Deputy Murphy?"

"Amy is fine. And, yes, please. That air is a lot colder than I thought."

Bella boiled water for her tea and made a new pot of coffee for Amy. When it was ready, the two women went to the living room and sat by the fire. Bella stared into the flames. *Please let Chad be safe.* She called Wizard to come off of his blanket. He sat at her feet and put his head across them. She reached down and scratched behind his ears.

"Nice dog. Lucky you found him. Did Doc Jim fix him up?"

"Yes. Yes, he did."

Bella said nothing more, and Amy kept quiet.

The Boss' Turn

Chad's personal cell phone rang just as he answered the knock on his door. He hesitated about taking it when he saw it was Joshua, but he was determined to keep his pledge to be a more available friend. He motioned to the round table and the two SBI men walked to it. He saw they already had coffee. "Excuse me, gentlemen."

"Chad here." He wanted the SBI men to know it was a personal call. "Hey, Joshua. What's up?" He listened intently as Joshua said that he and Harold needed to talk to him right away. "I'll call you back in twenty minutes or less, will that work?" He hung up the phone and walked to the table.

He shook hands with both men, meeting the younger agent for the first time. "Nice to meet you. Sorry it's under these circumstances. Thanks for coming, Elliott. Didn't expect to get you over these mountains today. Before we start officially, I don't know the nature of that call I just received, and I am assuming that IEA Agent Isaacs has informed you about the possibility of some involvement on the part of a local commissioner. That said, Joshua Johnson, owner of the Valley Store, asked to meet with me and the county manager, his best friend, about a call from the commissioner to Harold. I'm quite sure Joshua told him they needed to relay whatever had been said him. You obviously heard me tell him I'd call back in twenty minutes or less. These are upstanding men in our community, and if I call and tell them to come here, they will come." He stopped without another word.

"Is there a possibility it's related or could be tied into the calls that have been made?"

"Absolutely. They didn't call to invite me for a beer!" He looked at Assistant Director Nelson. "I'm sorry, Elliott. Long morning already and I don't need to tell you my concerns are real."

"Chad, if we've learned nothing else over the last several decades in this profession, the reality of the vulnerability of our loved ones is *our* greatest vulnerability. I wouldn't be here if I didn't believe this was serious and wasn't able and willing to help out. Call the men, ask them to meet you for lunch here at, say, eleven thirty? I'm assuming we can order in and do it in your conference room. Unless, of course, you think this will rise to the level of a formal interview?"

"I don't know what it will rise to, honestly. But I think starting out over lunch is a good plan, and you can call the shots. If you want to shift gears, all you have to do is say so." Chad hit redial. "Hey, Joshua. I'm kind of tied up at the moment. How about you and Harold come over here for lunch? My treat. About 11:30?" Chad nodded his head. "Good, see you then."

He hit another button on his phone. "Sergeant, please ask dispatch to order lunch for five in the conference room at eleven thirty, and three more for you and the other two SBI agents. Can you find a decent place to eat with them?" He saw Elliott nod his head. "Okay, thanks."

He turned back to the two men. "Well, might as well get one more mountain question out of the way. More coffee?" The two SBI men laughed and shook their heads. Chad picked up his water bottle from his desk and sat down.

"Prefer to keep this informal for now, Chad. If you think we need to record anything, then say so."

"Your call. I just want it as clean as possible. I don't ever want to be part of a case going south because of a technicality."

"We're good. There are two of us, and if you want Sergeant Whitehorse here, I'm fine with that too." Elliott Nelson didn't bat an eye.

"Hadn't expected that, Elliott. She's been on the case, or cases, and is one of the most objective LEOs you'll ever meet. She also knows more about my personal life than anyone in the department. Might be good for you, in case I lose objectivity." Elliott nodded. Chad took out his secure phone and dialed Sylvia's number.

"Please join us, if you have time. Bring something to drink, it might be a while. Thanks."

There was a soft knock on the door and all three men rose. Sylvia walked in and took a seat at the table. The men all sat.

"We've reviewed the reports to the SBI on the recent uptick in activity here. I have to tell you, it's pretty impressive that you've managed these cases as cleanly as you have. It's not routine stuff for a department your size." Elliott watched Chad's face. Not a muscle moved. He expected nothing different given what he knew of the man. Elliott also noticed that Sergeant Whitehorse had not taken her eyes off of him or his agent.

The agent, who they both now knew was the agent in charge for the Knoxville office of the SBI, asked, "Have calls like those received by Dr. Anderson and Ms. Oliver-Smith happened in this department at any time in your tenure here?"

Chad had not expected that question; he mentally chastised himself that he should have. He and Sylvia looked at each other, both raised their eyebrows, and shook their heads.

"No. Never, as far as I'm aware. You, Sergeant?"

"No, sir, not in all my years in the department." The AIC just nodded his head.

"Sergeant," the AIC continued, "how would you describe the relationship between Dr. Bella Anderson and members of this department?"

Sylvia didn't hesitate. "Dr. Anderson... Bella... is from these mountains. Although she hasn't spent all of her time here as the sheriff and I have, her roots go back more than a hundred and twenty years. Like most folks in these hills, we'd say, 'She never meets a stranger.'"

The AIC had moved to Tennessee thirty years ago, but it was to Memphis. He knew he had no idea what she meant. "You mean she doesn't talk to strangers? That's always good advice these days."

Sylvia looked at Director Nelson before turning to the AIC. She tried to keep her smile from becoming a smirk. She thought Elliott might be doing the same. "No, sir, that means she's friendly to everyone. If I drove you up there right now, even though we're in the middle of a potentially dangerous situation, she'd offer you something to drink and eat."

"And her relationship with Sheriff Oliver?" The AIC looked from Sylvia to Chad and back.

"Sir, to my own personal knowledge, the sheriff met Dr. Anderson at the time of the ATV traffic on her property. I can't speak to the circumstances. As a long-time law enforcement officer, and pretty good observer of people, I would say that Sheriff Oliver and Dr. Anderson were cordial throughout the events that took place on her property and the subsequent investigation and closure of that case."

"And since the case closed?" the AIC asked without missing a beat.

"We recently lost the oldest European descendant in our community. I think it's fair to say that during the time when the sheriff and Dr. Anderson were supporting Joshua Johnson, the son of the victim, they developed a mutual interest in each other. Beyond that, I am not privy to the sheriff's personal life, and I don't inquire. Although I may, from time to time, give him unsolicited advice." She smiled.

"Is the advice heeded?" Elliott asked casually.

"My general unsolicited professional advice is always taken into consideration. As for any comments I may have made about the opportunity to change his personal life, time will tell." She smiled again.

Elliott turned to the AIC. "So, you see, we mountain folks live in each other's kitchen, and there are always a lot of cooks."

Chad remained expressionless. As did the AIC.

CHAPTER 17

Hospital Visit

QUINN LEFT THE SHERIFF'S STATION as the SBI agents went to interview Bella, Nora, and Chad. She drove to the hospital in the center of the valley and was stunned by the beauty of the view as she approached the ER. She stopped to take in the bare trees and evergreens as they drew her eyes up to the ridgeline of the mountains. With the early morning light, she imagined it would be difficult not to feel the presence of God as you entered this place of healing. She nodded at the guard and walked directly to the small reception desk and pulled out her badge. A woman slid back the glass partition and looked at the badge.

"Good morning, I am Agent Isaacs, and I'm here to check on the condition of Agent Sam Nations." Quinn quickly read the ID badge and saw the woman was an RN named Angela.

Angela smiled and nodded at her. She was accustomed to law enforcement officers, but she had not been expecting anyone to check on Sam. She glanced at the badge but did not notice the specific agency. "Please wait here, Agent Isaacs." She closed the glass partition and walked towards Dr. Smith's area.

Quinn decided she wouldn't push the federal officer routine unless she needed it. She also knew in today's world it might not work anyway. She stood relaxed but maintaining an official posture. To her surprise, the side door opened and Angela said, "Right this way, Agent Isaacs."

Quinn realized she almost clicked her heels as she turned to walk towards the nurse.

"Thank you." She smiled at Angela but maintained her formal stance. Quinn saw Dr. Smith standing in the hallway. They had been introduced at the jamboree, but the Celebration of Life for Joe Johnson had been the focus of attention that night. She extended her hand, "Dr. Smith. Nice to see you again. Sorry it's under these circumstances."

"Nice to see you, Agent Isaacs. Did someone send for you?" He knew about the threatening call to his wife at home. He wondered if it was related to Sam being here as a patient. He hoped not.

"I assume you have some knowledge of the matter that brought me to the valley. I need to talk to Sam if he is able to speak." Her voice was calm, reassuring, and professional. Gone was the ire she had extended to Sam at their meeting two days ago. Sam was hurt. Sam, her college lover and her colleague on more than one cross-agency case. Sam, who she had finally figured out was struggling with something much bigger than he had let on.

"Sorry," she said, turning her distracted attention back to Dr. Smith. "I missed that."

"I have spoken with Sam, and he is willing to see you. I must warn you that his leg is causing him a great deal of pain and, if this is an official visit, I will not allow it."

"Not official, Dr. Smith. Colleague to colleague, friend to friend. That's all. Thanks for understanding." She followed Fred as he walked down the hall to the last bed. He stopped and pulled back the curtain. "Thanks," she said, smiling as she looked Dr. Smith in the eyes and shook his hand.

Sam turned his head to look at her. "Hey," he said quietly. The nurse walked out past Quinn.

"Hey, yourself. I would have brought you breakfast but wasn't sure what part of you put you in the ER."

He tried to stifle a laugh. "Stop, it hurts to laugh. I have one splitting headache." Then he got very serious. "Does my agency know I'm here?"

"Not from me. Doubt if Chad told them either. Are you on duty or leave?"

"Still on leave, even though I attended your meeting the other day." He looked at her carefully. "Should I have declared that?"

"Not to me. Have they given you pain meds?"

"Do you think I'd look this miserable if they had?"

"I think if they had, I would *have* to call your agency. Who knows what you might say under the influence?" She winked at him. "On second thought, maybe I should tell the Doc I'll officially stand guard so he can give you some relief. I might learn something." She said it playfully, but not without sending a message they both knew was the truth: they were federal agents. He was walking a fine line regarding his obligation to report to his agency.

She placed her hand on his arm. She felt the need to touch him, to assure herself and him that everything was going to be okay. She didn't love him as she did in college, when he was her first love, but he would always be a personal friend.

He reached awkwardly across his chest and put his other hand on top of hers. "Thanks for coming, Quinn. I'm really sorry for my bad decisions recently. I want to talk to you about them. However, today is not the day, and this is not the place."

"No, today is not the day." She stepped back when they came to take him for his scans. "I'll be here when you come back." She gave him the Quinn smile she knew would tell him their friendship was intact.

Waiting

Bella needed to walk Wizard and, personally, she felt like she needed to get outside. It was a crisp, clear October morning and the cool air was giving way to a beautiful day. She liked this deputy and hoped she would want to have a look around too.

"Amy, there is a bell I can turn on to hear the phone outside. Want to look around?"

"Love too. I walked around with Deputy Bennett, but I'd love to hear from you what you're doing up here. I suppose this boy is ready for a walk too."

"More than. Wizard, water." The dog stood and walked to his water bowl and started lapping it up.

"How long have you had him?"

"A little over a week. If you're impressed at his response to commands, that's all Doc Jim. I'm just good at following instructions."

"Well, so is Wizard." Wizard looked up at Amy when she said his name.

Both women slipped on their jackets. Bella flipped the switch on the outside bell for the wall phone, put Wizard's leash on him, and picked up her mobile phone. Amy looked at her quizzically.

"No, there's no signal up here. I learned to take my phone with me to take pictures during the last episode that brought you here. And, surprisingly enough, I've enjoyed getting pictures of the various stages of the construction. Well, at least it's surprising to me."

"Do you wish you had a signal up here?"

"For many years I've been glad I didn't, but you can imagine that recent events make me think otherwise." As they stepped off the kitchen steps, Bella stopped suddenly, looking from Drellag Caban to the new cabin. "Oh my, I didn't think about a phone for the new cabin." She walked hurriedly towards Arthur, waving her mobile.

"What's up Bella? Phone call for me?" He laughed. He knew there was no signal up here.

"No, Arthur, silly man. I totally forgot about a phone for the cabin. Is it too late?"

"Now, Bella, you know that worrying never did any good." He chuckled. "I'm kinda taking to a phrase I heard in an Australian movie recently. 'No worries.' I wonder if they really say that. Anyway, since it didn't cost any more than the wire, and I had some of that..." He stopped and looked at Amy. "Might be one of the last places in this country still needs phone wire." He looked back at Bella. "Now, as I was about to say, I went ahead and ran that wire when we were laying conduit anyway."

Bella ran toward him and gave him a big bear hug. "Arthur, you're finer than the china in the cabinet. Thank you. Thank you." She backed off, turning red, and wondered if it had been inappropriate to hug him. Wizard nuzzled Arthur's leg.

Amy could understand why the sheriff was taken with this woman. Although Amy was a couple of years older than Nora, they had gone to school together and she was not a fan of Chad's ex-wife, Mary. She had long thought he deserved a good woman; she just hoped Bella was interested in *him*.

Any Questions for the Sheriff?

Chad wondered if the SBI AIC was going to ask him any questions. He didn't mind Sylvia answering and knew she was saying what she knew. *I hope Bella is okay. If these two guys are here, someone is up with Bella. And Nora. Sorry, ladies. I'll make it up to both of you. Has the DA tried to call me? I want to wrap up the Kirk case. Any word on...*

"Sheriff?" The AIC was clearly trying to get Chad's attention.

"Sorry. Too many active cases in my head. I apologize for being distracted. Did you have a question for me?"

"Yes. What is the nature of your relationship with Dr. Bella Anderson?"

Chad expected the question but had purposely not come up with an answer. He had wondered how he would answer it.

"Promising."

Sylvia and Elliott smiled, but the AIC looked perplexed. "I beg your pardon?"

"This is a very small community and there aren't many opportunities to meet women that won't present a potential problem on the job. As Sylvia and Elliott know, I have been divorced for fifteen years and alone for most of the last thirty. By that, I mean my ex-wife and I stayed in the marriage until our daughter, Nora, left for college. Then we divorced and she moved to Knoxville. It's for the best. So, yes, when I met Bella... Dr. Anderson... while working the meth lab case, I was, as we say in these hills, happier than 'ole Blue laying on the porch chewing a bone'."

He watched the face of the agent. Leaning in, he said, "Sir, I am fifty-eight years old, and I've been in law enforcement since I returned from university. I love my family, my community, and the law. As for my family... my daughter, grandchildren, and son-in-law... they are my heart and soul, and I will defend and protect them at all costs. And I will tell you I am well on my way to hoping I can add Bella Anderson to the level of protection I afford my family." He leaned back in his chair. "I will also tell you I am a patient man." He thought Elliott Nelson was about to clap.

"Good to know. And, please, call me Ralph."

"Ralph, it would be my pleasure. What else can I tell you? I need your help to protect my family, Bella, and this community. I am hopeful that you already have some background on Commissioner Zimmerman that will help us sort out whatever else he is involved in."

"What do you know for a *fact* that he is involved in?"

"One of my detectives has identified him as the owner of two new pay-by-the-hour' motels in Round City." Chad noticed Elliott did not seem surprised; Elliott's brother was the police chief in Round City, and Chad suspected that there was a strong line of communication between Chief Nelson and the SBI.

"And how did he do that?"

"He tracked him through multiple shell companies. We have the complete web that I'll share with you." Ralph looked both surprised and impressed.

"By himself?"

"Does he own them by himself?"

"No, did your detective do the work by himself?"

"He did, and I want him to have credit for it. Although saying it out loud makes me realize you might try to steal him away from me. Please don't try."

"Sheriff, I would think you would want any employee to have an opportunity at a better, uh, employment in a larger agency, if she or he wanted."

The glint in Chad's steel gray eyes sparked, but he held his temper. "Ralph, this might come as a shock to you, but there are actually people who like living in paradise, no matter how far back in the hills it is." He waited a beat. "Now, as for the ownership of those motels, the ties go directly to Zimmerman. The challenge for us is that he may be unaware, or could at least plead ignorance, of how these motels are being used. However, we also have proof that he delivered two illegal immigrants to a house of prostitution in our community. He also brought in another woman who he thought was an illegal immigrant, but she was an Immigration Enforcement agent."

"I see." Ralph looked at his boss and waited for direction.

Chad's secure phone buzzed. It was a phone he answered no matter who was with him.

"Oliver here." His face hardened as he listened. "Show them to the conference room and tell Joshua I'll be there in a few minutes."

"Problems?" Elliott asked.

"Nora has received two more messages. Now they're threatening my grandchildren." He took a very deep breath and gripped the arms on his chair. "Joshua Johnson and Harold Cooper are here."

"Agent," Sylvia said, "I think that Ms. Oliver-Smith will likely tell the agent who went to interview her, but in case it doesn't come up, it's important to know that Nora's husband is a physician here in the valley and their phone number is private."

Both Elliott and Ralph blanched

Elliott stood up. "Chad, I think we're good here. If you can direct us to the men's room, we'll leave you to check on your daughter and Dr. Anderson. We'll wait at the—"

"I can take you out, Director," Sylvia said, then turned to Chad. "We'll wait in my office until you have time to inform Joshua and Harold that we have guests."

Chad stood and shook hands, but no one missed the look of resolve on his face.

Checking

As soon as his door was closed, Chad dialed Nora's mobile phone. "Hey, favorite daughter of mine."

"Daddy, is something wrong? Are you okay? Are you safe?" The words gushed out of her.

"I'm fine, and I'm just checking to see how you are. Is one of my deputies with you?"

"Yes, Daddy. I'm well protected. Now, what's up?"

He already knew that she didn't know the content of the messages, or she would have called him no matter who was there. *Unless, of course, they were threatening her life. I am so stupid! I can't just assume she can always call me if she's in trouble.* Then an idea occurred to him.

"Honey, I'm going to tell you that I'm more rattled about the call you received than I realized."

"Calls, Daddy. More than one. I'm not listening to them, and I don't plan to do so."

"Good girl. Tell you what. I'm about to meet with Harold and Joshua, then I'll take a run over there and let my granddaughter know that Grandpa is here. Okay with that?"

"Better than butter on a biscuit. See you soon, Daddy. And Daddy … thanks. I love you."

"I love you more than you love me."

"It cannot be."

"See you soon, Nora." He held the phone to his ear as she hung up. He took a drink of water and dialed Drellag Caban. It went to the answering machine.

"Deputy, please pick up the phone."

"Hey, Sheriff. Murphy here." She sounded out of breath. He visibly relaxed. He knew he was fortunate to have so many good deputies, but some just rose to the top, like cream on churned milk.

"Hey, Murphy. Everything okay up there?"

"Sorry, took a minute, we were outside." She took a breath. "Two more calls, but the language is basically the same as before. I'm guessing the SBI agent is back in the station by now, right?"

"Guess so. Been behind closed doors for a while. Anything I need to know?"

"No, sir. I think we're good up here."

"Glad to hear it. May I speak to Bella, please?" It did not escape his deputy that he called Dr. Anderson by her first name.

"It's for you." She handed the phone to Bella, who had run in behind her and heard Chad's voice on the machine.

"Chad, are you all right?" She saw Amy walk out the kitchen door.

"The far more important question is whether *you* are all right."

"I'm fine. Please tell me how you are."

"I'm feeling a bit shell-shocked at the moment. The two most important women in my life are being harassed and there is nothing I can do about it."

"Oh no, Chad! Nora has received calls too? Is she okay?"

"Yes. Yes, she's fine, and so are the kids. Fred's at work and there's a deputy at their home. Listen, I have to go into another meeting. We're trying to get to the bottom of this. But I just had a hairbrained idea. Promise me you'll say no if there is any concern on your part at all."

"I hope by now you know I will always tell you the truth. Even when you don't want to hear it." The control and softness in her voice almost undid him.

"We'll have the big guns, all the way to the FBI if necessary on this. In the meantime, I need to protect you, Nora, and the kids. At first, I was going to ask you to go to her place so I can keep you all under one roof. I know you don't have your guest cottage finished, but how much of a hassle would it be if Nora and the kids came up there for a couple days, maybe through the weekend? Do you have room?"

She did not hesitate. "What a great idea! I have a small second bedroom for the kids, and Nora can have my bed, and I'll sleep on the sofa. It would be good for me to have the distraction, and I can see that having us all in one place will make it easier for you. It will be fun." She stopped. "Okay, a strange choice of words, but yes. By all means, yes!"

"You're isolated enough that my deputies won't have to be in your cabin. They can patrol the perimeter. Your house phone will be rerouted through a secure SBI connection, and they will give you a signal that will let you know they asked a personal caller to call back so you can answer. It also means anything you say on your phone will be recorded. I suspect they are working on that now, or soon will be." He stopped talking. "Bella, I think you know you are very special and important to me. I need to have my head in what's going on, and I can't even do what they'll let me do if I have to worry about the four of you. I'm going to ask you to think about it and make sure..."

"Chad, stop. There is nothing for me to think about. Just get them up here as soon as you can." She paused. "And, in case you haven't noticed, you are very special to me, too. I want this behind us and all of us safe. We deserve to have some fun. So, let's focus on getting this done and moving on. Okay?"

"Dear, dear Bella. Isn't there a line in a song from a movie I used to watch with Nora that says, 'somewhere in my youth or childhood, I must have done something good'?"

She smiled and he could hear her voice brighten. "Yes, from *The Sound of Music*, one of my all-time favorites. Any idea when I can expect Nora and the kids?"

"I'd say mid-afternoon. I need to go to one more meeting, then I want to go talk to Nora in person about this. I'll call you from there. Okay?"

"More than."

"Thanks, Bella. I miss you and I need you… to be safe. Talk to you soon."

"Be safe, Chad. I hope to see you soon."

CHAPTER 18

The sun shines not on us but in us.
. . . and every bird song, wind song, and tremendous storm song
of the rocks in the heart of the mountains
is our song, our very own, and sings our love.
John Muir 1838 – 1914

Community

CARLA WAS PLEASED THAT JOSHUA AND HAROLD were going to have lunch with Chad at the sheriff's station. A number of the longtime residents were talking about the changes in their community, and she wanted to see more people involved in managing growth in the area. James, her brother, kept saying he was going to attend the county meetings, but something always seemed to come up at The Corral. Her thoughts turned from the valley to her own situation. *Guess I'm going to have to make a decision about my involvement in the restaurant now. Maybe it's time I put that college degree to use and move more to the management side. Then I can be with Joshua in his business and help James too.*

Carla leaned back against the divider between the two registers and surveyed the store. She had never shopped anywhere else for groceries; it was how she had made sure she got to see Joshua every week over the years.

The jingling of the silver bell above the door broke into her thoughts.

"Hey, Miss Andrea. How are you today? Where's Karolina? Oh, it's a school day, isn't it?"

"Yes, it is. I just needed a couple of things, and sometimes it's helpful to walk the aisles and see what else I might need or didn't know was here before."

"I'll tell you, we sure do like having Natalia at The Corral. She is always so polite, and the customers appreciate that. So do I."

"Natalia likes interacting with the customers, for sure. She's also fascinated with the things that Melody does here at the store. They talk about their jobs when they finish their schoolwork."

"Both smart young women. We're going to miss Melody when she goes to university next year."

"Natalia told me that Mr. Joe and his late wife set up a scholarship, and Melody will be the first to receive it. That's such a wonderful legacy, to invest in our young people."

"He did, and..." Carla paused to make sure the other customer in the store was not nearby, "it's designated for the top girl student." She winked at Andrea, knowing she couldn't say that Natalia was likely to get it next year.

"Well, that's very nice of them. I'm happy for Melody, and all to come after her." Andrea picked up a shopping basket from the stack by the register. "I'll just have a look around. Be back in a little bit."

"Take your time. We have some new products from a deli in Gatlinburg over in the refrigerated section."

"Thanks." Andrea smiled and headed down the nearest aisle.

Sharing Her Plans

Bella and Amy went back outside after Chad's call.

"Amy, I apologize for interrupting our walk with that business about a phone. I have no idea how I could have forgotten the need for a landline in the cabin. Guess I've been more distracted than I thought. Anyway, come let me show you the new wall on the shed."

They stopped for a moment to take in a panoramic view of the mountains. The various shades of blue, muted by the ever-present haze that defined the mountains as the Smokies, were breathtaking.

"It's so beautiful up here, Bella. Do you know why your great-grandfather picked this particular piece of land, or did he inherit it?"

"No, and I honestly don't know how he acquired it. Grandmother Hazel only ever told me that out of the eighty acres, he picked this spot to build the cabin. He even cleared the road that later became the county road." Bella liked talking with Amy about her family and their ties to the land and the mountains. "My daddy built this shed in the 1950s to replace an old shed that had collapsed."

"Shed? I think this would qualify as a barn."

Bella laughed, "I agree. I have an old drawing of the property that is so fragile I don't look at it very often, but it really was a shed early on. I suspect my daddy had big plans for making a woodworking shop in there one day."

"Why didn't he?"

"Never had the chance. He passed away in the 1960s; he wasn't even forty yet." Bella hoped she didn't sound too melancholy answering the question.

"I'm so sorry. I didn't know."

"No apologies needed. I've lived long enough to understand the warnings, even the subtle ones, that we get when we are children that you live and then you don't. I'm just so grateful that my family have all been hard-working, loving people. That's a pretty good feeling to have as you age."

"Now that's the God's honest truth." Amy wanted to switch topics to distract Bella from the concern she had for the sheriff. "I like how you see this wall when you come up over the rise from the gate. It draws your eyes out to the mountains."

"It does. My daddy was going to paint a mural on it, but I never knew what he had planned."

"You should do that," Amy said excitedly. "I know a local woman, Paula, who is a fantastic artist. She did the mural on The Corral. I can get you her number."

"Thank you for endorsing her. I just got her name from Carla, and I need to reach out to her so we know what kind of stain will make this wall look like the rest of the barn, but she'll still be able to paint on it."

"I'll remind you when we go inside. Now, willing to share what you might put on this wall?"

"Don't know exactly. I've been thinking about it and I want it to look like you're actually seeing part of the trees here, but I want it to draw your eyes out to that amazing view toward the northwest. Please come up and see it when it's finally painted. I suspect it won't be until spring though."

The women were headed towards the foundation for the new cabin. "I think the logs are coming tomorrow or Friday. Arthur made it sound like it was no more difficult than building a model with Lincoln Logs. It will be fun to watch it go up."

"Is this a guest cottage?"

"Yes." Bella hesitated. "And I'm thinking about ways to use it for writing retreats."

"That would be awesome. My best friend is a writer. Well, not a full-time writer, but she loves to write, and I love to read her stories. I'll have to introduce you."

"I would like that very much. It would be nice to connect with another writer up here."

Amy knew how easy it was for someone being protected to feel smothered, so she took her time walking around the foundation of the new cabin while Bella looked out over the mountains with Wizard sprawled at her feet. When she rejoined Bella, Amy was about to ask a question when the clanging of the bell that signaled a phone call pealed out across the property. Bella jumped and turned towards the noise so quickly she almost fell down. The deputy gently took her elbow.

"Let it ring. We can walk back and see if it's for you or me, but we'll let it go to your answering machine."

Bella stepped off toward the house and Amy unobtrusively dropped her hand from Bella's elbow.

"Thanks, Amy. I might have fallen. I haven't turned that bell on since I've been back up here, and now I remember why! Are you up for a dash to the house? I could use some exercise." Bella unclipped Wizard's lead and took off running; he galloped after her. Amy laughed and followed them to the house.

They stopped at the kitchen steps and Bella sat down and undid her boots. "These have been on long enough. Back to my inside autumn footwear." She looked up at Amy. "Socks!"

"That's my kind of footwear!"

"Be my guest." Bella's shoulders sagged. She realized this woman was not here as a visiting friend; she was on duty—guard duty. Boots in hand, she opened the screen door and ushered Amy inside, set her boots by the door, and walked to the sink.

"I don't want to hear the message, so I'm going to the bathroom to wash my hands. Then I'll make us a cup of tea, or coffee for you if you prefer." She turned to Wizard and gave a command: "Water and food, Wizard." She knew he would then go to his blanket. She headed towards the other end of Drellag Caban.

Amy had already turned the volume down on the message playback. She washed her hands in the kitchen sink, giving Bella time to reach the bathroom, then she hit play.

"Hey, you dumb broad. Tell your dumb sheriff to stay put." The caller hung up.

Amy picked up the wall phone and called the dispatcher. "Murphy here."

"Yes, Deputy, I recognized the number. Who do you need?"

"Sergeant Whitehorse or Deputy Thomas, Cecelia. Thanks."

"Thomas here."

"Hey, it's Amy. Just got another message at Dr. Anderson's."

"Any different than the others?"

"Different words, and a different voice, but maybe it was altered. The directives seem to be the same tenor. 'Tell your boyfriend to back off.' Nothing directed at her."

"Thanks, Amy. The sheriff is with the SBI folks right now, so I'll let them know when they're available. Anything else of concern?"

"Nothing out of the ordinary. Usual stress that comes from these things. She's a strong woman, though, so I think her concern is much more for the sheriff than herself. Let me know if you need me to do anything."

"We'll sort out the next shift and let you know."

"I'm good for whatever time you need me to be up here."

"Thanks. Always glad you're on our team."

"Yeah, me too. We'll be inside now for a while if you need me."

"Okay. Someone will be in touch."

Amy liked Susan Thomas as a person and as the senior deputy. She was clear headed, fair, and, as far as Amy knew, all the deputies liked her. She turned to see Bella standing there.

Bella stepped toward the sink. The look on her face showed she heard at last some of the conversation. "Okay, hot water for tea is the next order of the day. Then we need to have some lunch. Any dietary concerns?"

"For my money, I'll eat one of those biscuits and some of that ham you put away earlier. But, please, eat whatever you would normally eat." She pointed to the biscuits in the plastic container Bella had left on the counter.

"Need mustard for lunch?"

"I beg your pardon?"

"Most of us don't eat anything but the biscuit and ham for breakfast, but any other time in the day we put mustard on it."

"Bella, you are my kind of woman! Bring on the mustard." Amy started laughing so hard she stomped her boot on the floor without realizing it.

Bella saw Wizard stand; he was on full alert at Amy's foot stomping. "Good boy, Wizard. The deputy is our friend. Sit." Wizard sat.

Bella took the ham and mustard out of the fridge and put them on the table. Amy took the container with the biscuits to the kitchen table, and asked, "Plates or napkins?"

"I'm good with napkins if you don't tell the spirits of Drellag Caban, my mother's especially, and please do *not* mention the way I served the mustard."

"I had that same mother. We'll keep it our secret. No condiment jars will ever be mentioned." Now both women were laughing. Amy looked at Bella out of the corner of her eye. She thought Bella might be relaxing again. "Oh, and let's remember to call Paula after we eat. I'm sure she'll be interested in painting that wall."

Look, Mommy

After hanging up from Chad, Nora sat looking around the large country kitchen and knew she needed to make lunch for her children. She had purposely not walked back into the home office she shared with Fred, a place where each could have some solitude when paperwork or preparation for their jobs needed attention. Most of all, she liked the office when the children had gone to bed and they could be in there together. That office now held messages threatening her father—and she didn't know why. There were people in her community, like all communities, who skirted and even broke the law; she knew that. *Why now? Why Daddy? What is he investigating? Why does he need the SBI?*

She felt the hand of her two-year-old daughter pulling at her pantleg. She leaned over to pick her up and hug her. "Hey, Lilly. How's Mommy's precious girl? I bet you're hungry, aren't you?" Lilly snuggled her head against Nora's neck and nodded. "Where's that brother of yours? Is he still playing?"

The house phone rang. She automatically reached for it with her other hand before remembering she wasn't to answer it. Letting her arm drop back to her side, she was reminded why she had put the answering machine in the office in the first place. She didn't normally want to hear messages if she couldn't answer the phone. Now, she didn't want to hear them at all. Grateful they were low enough in the mountains to have a cell signal, she knew Fred and her daddy would call on her mobile phone. Kissing Lilly's forehead, she put her in her highchair and turned to open refrigerator. She stopped. *That phone number is private. How did they get it?* Now she knew why the SBI was involved.

"Mommy, I'm hungry. Let's eat, please." Mac climbed up onto a stool at the counter. "Can I have some vegetable soup?"

Nora kissed her son on the top of his head, tousled his hair, and asked, "I don't know, are you able?"

Mac giggled as only a four-year-old can. "Yes, I am able. I can hold a spoon, and I know how to eat soup without spilling it." He was matter-of-fact and not at all disrespectful in his reply.

"How true. How true, my special boy. Can you heat and serve from the pot on the stove?"

"No, Mommy, not yet. When I'm bigger, I'll help you fix lunch. Okay?"

Nora chuckled, looked over the heads of her children, and saw the deputy in the doorway. "Please join us for some vegetable soup and a grilled cheese sandwich."

Deputy Young, a handsome man in his late twenties, smiled. He was hoping she had not heard the latest message threatening to kidnap her children. He had been directed to let all messages go to the machine and *not* leave Ms. Oliver-Smith and her children at any time.

"I'd be delighted, ma'am. How may I help?"

"Mommy, listen. The depudee knows the magic word!"

Deputy Young stood next to Mac and asked, "What word would that be, little Mac?"

With a very serious look on his face, Mac looked at the deputy. "Depudee, I'm not little. I'm the big brother."

"That you are, Mac. That you are!"

Mac pulled on the sleeve of the deputy's shirt. "But I didn't tell you the magic word. It's really two words: may I!" Mac grinned from ear to ear.

Nora laughed and stroked her son's cheek, then looked at the deputy. "It's a full-time job trying to teach manners. I see you learned yours well."

"No choice, ma'am. My momma was as strict as a warden..." he trailed off. There were children present.

Nora made three grilled cheese sandwiches on the griddle of her cooktop. She was thankful the deputy had pulled up the stool between her children and was keeping them entertained by talking to Mac and tickling Lilly. She put some soup in bowls to cool for the children then served the deputy.

"Thanks, Mommy. You're supposed to serve our guest first." Nora's heart flipflopped; she just never knew when a lesson she was trying to teach her son would connect. She watched Deputy Young tousle Mac's hair. She smiled.

"What would you like to drink, Deputy?"

"Looks like you're having tea. That would be just fine, ma'am. Thank you."

She knew this young man worked for her daddy, but she had figured out long ago that you either had manners and used them, or you didn't—even with the boss' daughter.

"Mommy, may I say grace?"

"By all means, Mac. Let me sit down first, please."

"Sure, Mommy." He waited while she poured tea for the deputy and took a stool at the end of the counter next to Lilly. She nodded at him and smiled.

"Thank you, God, for our food and our family, and protect us all and specially my grandpa. Oh, yeah, and the depudee. Amen."

"Amen," the deputy said.

"Amen," Nora said, holding her daughter's hand. "Now, Mac, tell us what you were building in the playroom with your Lincoln Logs."

CHAPTER 19

More to Come

THE CONFERENCE ROOM DOOR WAS AJAR, and Chad almost hit the wall slinging it open. He slammed it closed. He walked to Joshua and Harold and shook their hands. "Have a seat, guys. Food will be here shortly."

"Chad, Harold has something really important to tell you."

Chad put his hand up in a signal to stop. "Hold that thought, Joshua. Apologies for slamming the door. Sit, please. I need to ask you to understand that I can't tell you all that's going on, but I have some folks here from the State Bureau of Investigation and I need them to hear whatever you have to say if it involves Commissioner Zimmerman."

Joshua and Harold looked at each other, wondering how Chad could have known. "Chad, my friend, are you okay? This sounds really serious, and you look like... well, you look like what's left of a possum after a hunting dog got hold of it... save the physical injuries."

Chad laughed and slapped Joshua on the back. "I can always count on you to lighten the load and remind me why I live in these hills. Thanks, Joshua. I probably do look that bad; I have too many things on my mind. Anyway, these boys from Knoxville are okay, and I need their help to deal with what's going on. This is just a talk. Nothing official. You okay with that?"

Harold nodded. "Sure. Glad you have some big guns to help out."

Joshua nodded. "I'm here for moral support—whatever you two need."

Chad nodded and walked to the door. The two SBI agents were waiting.

"Joshua Johnson, Harold Cooper, this is the Assistant Director in charge of the Knoxville office of the SBI, Elliott Nelson. This is Agent in Charge Ralph..." Chad realized he had not even bothered to get the man's last name.

"Ralph Jackson. Pleased to meet you."

There was a knock on the door, followed by Sergeant Whitehorse bringing in the box lunches for the five men. Water and tea had already been put on top of the cabinet at the end of the room. Sylvia told Chad she had the other two agents in the small office next to his and would have lunch with them there. He nodded. "Thanks, Sergeant."

"The valley's finest restaurant food, gentlemen." He saw that Joshua was handing drinks to the others. He lifted a bottle of iced tea towards Chad, who nodded.

Chad looked around the table. "Mind if we eat and talk?" All of them nodded their assent.

AIC Ralph Jackson started without preamble. "Joshua, Harold, this is a routine inquiry based on the fact that you may have evidence pertinent in an ongoing case. With your permission, I will record the discussion."

"Whoa," Joshua's voice was low and slow. "We came here to tell a friend, our sheriff, something that was said to Harold. Are you saying this could end up in court?"

"Mr. Johnson... Joshua... there are a number of serious things happening at this moment that may involve multiple crimes, across multiple jurisdictions, including threats of bodily harm. If you have information that is material to this investigation, you would be right to tell us. Recording the first telling of the concern makes sure we have the information as detailed and accurate as possible. We are trying to solve these crimes. It is part of an investigation, not an arrest or trial testimony."

Chad felt sorry for Joshua and Harold. They were good mountain men who had done right by their community all their lives. They weren't accustomed to the methods or intricacies of trying to solve a case.

Chad spoke up. "For reasons I can't explain, this has to be handled by Ralph and Elliott. I trust them, and I promise you I need their assistance. Anything you have to say that may be important could help. That said, you don't have to say anything. You need to know that."

Ralph almost came out of his seat. Elliott touched his elbow, getting his attention; he settled. Ralph wasn't accustomed to mountain ways.

Joshua looked at Harold. "I'm the one who said we had to bring this to Chad. It's up to you."

"Gentlemen, I want to help in any way I can. You may record what I have to tell you. Only Joshua knows what I'm about to tell you, and he's not directly involved. He's my best friend, and well, frankly I've never experienced anything like this."

"Very well." Ralph turned on the recorder and gave the date and time. "This is AIC Ralph Jackson, in the conference room of Sheriff Chad Oliver, with..."

"Assistant Director Elliott Nelson of the Knoxville office of the SBI..."

"Chad Oliver, county sheriff..."

"Harold Cooper, county manager..."

"Joshua Johnson, owner of the Valley Store."

Ralph nodded approval. "Mr. Cooper?"

"I got a call early this morning from Commissioner Zimmerman. He told me he had an unexpected family matter that required him to go to Michigan. Said his wife was in an accident and she had called the highway patrol since 'they don't trust our sheriff.'" Harold put air quotes around the Zimmerman's words. "He wants me, as county manager, to make sure that the sheriff does not get involved in the investigation. I tried to tell him I am not the sheriff's supervisor—he's elected. Guess it's different up north where he comes from. Anyway, that was bad enough, but this is the part that spooked me. He said, 'And I mean you *better* get the sheriff to back off if you want to keep your job.'" Harold's hand was shaking as he took a drink from his bottle of tea.

Given the phone calls Nora and Bella had received, Chad was not surprised by what Zimmerman had said to Harold.

Elliott and Ralph looked from Harold to Joshua then to Chad.

Elliott looked at Joshua. "Mr. Johnson..."

"Please, it's Joshua."

"Joshua," Elliott continued, "have you ever known any of the commissioners to make threats to Mr. Cooper or any other member of this community?"

"No, sir. Can't imagine any that would. Even this one surprised me."

"Are you involved in county politics?"

The local men started laughing—even Chad. "No disrespect, Mr. Director, but I own a grocery store and have worked there since I graduated from UT more than forty years ago. I think most folks here would tell you that I work seven days week, including after church on Sundays, and... well, I just lost my wife after several years of serious illness. I used to attend the county commission meetings as a concerned citizen, but the last thing I want to do is be involved in politics." Joshua paused for a moment.

"Oh, and one more thing. Don't mistake my lack of involvement in politics as a lack of concern for my community. I have very deep roots here and my family has served this community for more than sixty years." Joshua sat back with a look of satisfaction on his face.

Ralph looked at each of the men, trying to figure out if he was in a time warp. He was accustomed to the thrust and parry of city folks. The difference was they learned survival in the midst of large crowds and on the streets, not in the woods of the mountains. He had never experienced anything like this. He waited to see if the Assistant Director was going to continue. He did not.

Ralph nodded and then spoke. "Thank you, Joshua. Harold is there anything else you want to add?"

"Well..." he hesitated. "I don't know if it matters, but about a month back Commissioner Zimmerman, who has been trying to get the folks in Nashville to widen Route 54, made a comment at a county commission meeting that he had some business opportunities for this valley that he thought the men were really going to like."

"Did you tell anyone about that?"

"Well, sir, our meetings are broadcast on the internet if anyone wants to watch them. I did talk to Joshua about how strange I thought it sounded, and later I told Chad... uh, the sheriff... about it. Chad never says if one thing he hears lines up with something else, so I just let it go."

"Thanks, Harold." Ralph handed him his card. "Call me if you think of anything else. This is my direct number."

"Sure. Sure, I'll do that, but what should I do about what the commissioner said about my job?" His hand was no longer shaking as it gripped the bottle of iced tea, but it was clear that dealing with Zimmerman made him nervous.

"I'm going to have one of the other agents talk to you about recording any future calls from Zimmerman. As far as I'm concerned, you have reported the threat to the authorities..." Harold saw Chad and Elliott nod in agreement. "At this point, I would appreciate it if you would cooperate with our agents and not share this information with anyone else at this time. We will do everything we can to resolve the concerns you have and any potential threats to your community. That work for you?"

"Yes, sir. It helps."

All of the men seemed to relax and went back to eating their lunches. Casually, the AIC asked, "So, you've pretty much figured out I'm a city boy. What's so important about living in these hills, lovely as they are, in an isolated community?"

Joshua, Harold, and Chad started talking at once. They stopped, laughed, and looked at each other. Harold spoke first.

"Ralph, besides the fact that each of us have roots here going back more than a hundred years, and the fact that you would be hard pressed to find a more beautiful place to watch the seasons change in these Great Smoky Mountains, and the fact we have the freshest water and air for miles around, it's the people. Folks care about their families and each other. We've even managed over the last thirty or so years to show respect to our native residents. Hey, you should come to the powwow next weekend. Then you'll see."

Joshua waited a beat, thought about not saying anything, but then spoke. "Sir, this man is our county manager so you would expect him to sell the quality of life here. It's his job, in a sense. But the part he didn't say was that we trust each other to have enough rules and laws to make life fair for everybody, but not so many as to keep you from living life for fear of breaking one of them. And speaking of the law, we have a fine sheriff and department that lives the motto of 'serve and protect.'"

"Yeah, folks in other places could learn some lessons from them, seems to me." Harold nodded as he spoke.

"Okay! I hear you. I might just try to meander over here next weekend. Someplace I can get information on it?"

"On our county website. We'd be pleased to have you." Harold stood. "Now, if you don't need anything else, I need to get back to the county off—oh, should I talk to your agent first?"

"Yes, please. He won't take long, and he'll be your official contact. Come with me, I'll introduce you."

Joshua stood and shook hands with Elliott and Chad. "Sounds like there might be a lot going on in our little corner of the world. Glad you came to help, Elliott. Let me know if you need anything, Chad." Both men just nodded. "Catch you later."

Joshua shut the door behind him.

Chad looked at Elliott. "Did you need the city boy to get a lesson in rural Tennessee living?"

Elliott just smiled. "Might have to admit I've learned a thing or two today too. Now, let's talk about a plan."

The Patient

Quinn caught up on emails while waiting for Sam to return. She was grateful for the presence of a signal; she knew they weren't a guarantee in this area.

"Hey, I'm back." Sam tried to sound cheerful as he was wheeled back from the scans.

"Do you have a brain?"

"Jury's still out. I'm sure Doc Fred will be filling us in shortly." He chuckled and looked at Quinn as the nurse turned his bed and locked it in place.

"Well, then let's just wait and see." Her eyes showed a tenderness he remembered and missed from days gone by.

"Will you stay with me for a while?"

"I can stay until Chad lets me know I'm needed back at his shop. Okay?"

"Anything I can know about?"

"You can know, but let's leave it 'til we get you patched up. Things are heating up with our prime 'el jefe.'" She purposely chose the name they had been told the guys selling illegal immigrants used: the boss. He would know she meant Zimmerman.

"How uncomfortable is that leg screwed up behind your back?"

"Hurts. I just hope nothing is broken."

"Me too. What was it like up on top of that mountain? Sylvia said you were at a place called Mantle Rock."

"There is a stillness, a quiet, that forces you to listen. When you do, you can hear the abundance of life in these mountains. And, you know, Quinn, it's not just the animals moving about, it's the movement of the trees, the grasses, water running in the distance, and the drops of moisture in the air. I swear even the rocks must creak. I need longer out there." He looked up at her. "I've lost my way—forgotten my roots. I'm on the path back. Last night helped, but I need longer."

"Then take it, Sam. You're a good guy, a great agent, and we need you. But we need you whole."

He noted that she said "we" need you. Not "I" need you. He knew better anyway. *They* knew better; they'd figured out their junior year at UT that there would be no "we."

"Nice of you to say, Quinn. Nice of you to say."

"Am I interrupting?" Doc Fred walked through the curtain and looked at both of them. He could tell by the look on their faces that the conversation was more personal than work related, but he didn't pry. "I need to talk to you about the scans."

"Quinn can stay if she has the time and the stomach for it."

"Ouch! Need I remind you I'm a field agent with the Immigration Enforcement Agency, not a pencil pusher?"

Sam laughed. "Real easy to get her goat, Doc. What's the word?"

"The good news is that there are no broken bones."

"Then what hurts so blooming bad?"

"That's why I did a scan as well as the x-ray. Needed to see that soft tissue. You've managed to do a nice rip on the inside of your leg where the bullet passed through. It's going to hurt when I straighten that leg out, but then *if* you do what I tell you, it should heal nicely and you'll be fine."

Quinn visibly relaxed.

Doc Fred grinned. "So, shall we straighten that leg?"

"Quinn, will you hold my hand?"

"Only because I hate to hear a grown man cry and your ego will keep you from that with me here. Besides, I hate the thought you might punch out Doc Fred."

"Ha ha! Thanks for nothing." Sam managed to wink at her, then held the side of the bed with one hand and Quinn's hand with the other. "Let's get this over with."

Dr. Fred Smith quickly straightened the leg and pulled it next to the other as Sam rolled over on his back. "Now, since you didn't listen to me the first time, I'm going to give instructions to Quinn. We'll see if she can have whoever is in charge of you this week make you do them."

"I know, Doc. RICE!"

"Rice?" Quinn looked quizzically at Sam and then the physician.

"I'll let him tell you. Be a good chance for me to see if he *knows* what to do, even if he didn't do it." He smiled.

"Rest, ice, compression, elevation. RICE."

"Ahhh..." Quinn nodded her head. "Let me guess. He did exactly...what? None of them?"

"My turn to say 'ouch!' Need I remind you that I am a field agent with the Drug Enforcement Agency?" He smiled at her. "She's right, though, Doc. I've not been very good at this whole 'following directions' thing: when I should and when I shouldn't. I'll do what you say."

"Good. Then we'll get you processed and out of here. Quinn, can you get him home, or do I need to..."

"I've got it, Doc. Thanks. Does he need a walker?"

Sam just rolled his eyes.

"No, but I'm going to have him use crutches or a cane for the next two days."

Sam started to protest, but Quinn was still holding his hand and she squeezed it tightly. He stopped, looked at her, and said, "Cane. Please. Thanks, Doc. Tell Nora and the kids I said 'hey!'"

"Will do. Someone will be with you shortly." Doc Fred left the room.

"Will you go to your parents?"

Sam looked at her. "No, I need to get my head in this case. Thought I might ask Chad if I could stay with him for a few days. My medical leave is through next week. I'm good."

"Okay. We'll head over to the sheriff's office, find out what's going on now, and go from there."

"Great. Thanks, Quinn. Thanks for everything."

"Anytime, Sam."

CHAPTER 20

Man must be made conscious of his origin as a child of Nature.
Brought into right relationship with the wilderness,
he would see that he was not a separate entity
endowed with a divine right to subdue his fellow creatures
and destroy the common heritage,
but rather an integral part of a harmonious whole.
John Muir, 1838 – 1944

Now What?

THE WALL PHONE RANG JUST as Bella and Amy were finishing their lunch. Bella's eyes searched the room. Amy knew the look: the anticipation of something bad to come.

"You might want to turn off the outside bell. I think it sounds even louder in here." Amy wanted to distract Bella as they waited for a message to begin.

"Drellag Caban. Please leave a message."

"Dr. Anderson, it's Victoria."

Bella jumped up and grabbed the phone. "Victoria, hey! What's up?"

"Hey! How are you? You sound winded. Did you run in from the mountaintop?"

"No. No, I was just... I was just trying to get to the phone before you hung up. Everything okay there?"

"Yes. Everything is fine at the house. It's probably nothing, but there was a weird message on your house phone."

"Stop, Victoria. Does it include a threat? Involving a boyfriend? Does it?" The words rushed out in a torrent. Amy stood up from the table and moved toward Bella.

"It does. Sorry if I scared you. Do you know about it? I thought it was a prank."

"Victoria, are you calling on your mobile or my house phone?"

"My mobile."

"Okay, hold on one minute." She turned and looked at Amy.

Amy whispered, "Have her play the message so you can hear it."

"Listen, Victoria. It's nothing to worry about, but could you play the message so I can hear it?"

"Sure. It is a prank, right? Hold on."

The voice was the same as the first two calls at Drellag Caban: "Tell your boyfriend to back off. NOW!"

"The time is seven forty a.m.," the machine announced.

Amy nodded. She had heard it all. She whispered, "Don't erase."

"Listen, Victoria. Don't erase any of the messages from now on. And, hey, I should have told you I found my password to retrieve the messages, so I'll just check them from here. In fact, you don't need to answer that phone, just let it go to voicemail. There's nothing to worry about. I agree, it's just a prank. So, how's the thesis coming along?"

Amy watched as Bella went from acting like a deer caught in the headlights to a calm, directive individual with no coaching at all. She found it fascinating.

"Okay, well that's great. Just keep up your good work and remember if Dr. Carlsen gives you problems, let me know." Bella laughed. "Yes. I know he's a great guy. Just always saw it as part of my job to give him a hard time. Okay, you take care. Thanks for the call." She hung up the phone.

Amy picked up the phone and looked at Bella. "You did great, Bella. Who was that?"

"Victoria is a graduate student at the university where I taught. She's housesitting for me."

Amy dialed the number for the sheriff's station while Bella spoke. She nodded and smiled at Bella.

"Yeah, hey, Cecelia. I need Sergeant Whitehorse. It's urgent."

"Whitehorse here."

"Murphy here. Dr. Anderson just received a call from her house sitter in North Carolina." She raised her eyebrows in a questioning look to Bella. She nodded. Amy gave all the details to her sergeant.

"Okay, Murphy. May I speak to Dr. Anderson?" Amy handed the phone to Bella.

"Bella here."

"Hey, Dr. Ander… Bella. It's Sylvia Whitehorse. How are you holding up?"

"I'm worried about Chad." The weariness and concern she had been feeling all day came across in her voice.

"He's fine, and he's going to be fine. So are you. Listen, Bella, we have the State Bureau of Investigation here. I'm with some agents now. I'm going to talk with them and then we'll be back in touch. You're in good hands with Deputy Murphy."

Bella started to speak. There was a knock at the door. Amy opened it when she saw it was Arthur.

"Ma'am, there's a drone flying up above. Just thought Bella might want to know."

"Okay, thanks." She held up a finger to Bella indicating to wait a minute.

"Hold on, Sergeant… Sylvia. Sylvia, *is* he okay? Really?"

Sylvia wasn't sure if Bella knew about Nora receiving calls too. "I'm sure he'll call you soon. He's fine. Something up?" Sylvia could hear a commotion in the background.

"I think Amy wants to talk to you." Bella suddenly was aware she was using their first names. *Why am I okay using the first name for women, but was reluctant with Detective Williams?*

"Bella? Bella?" Amy was looking at her saying her name.

"Oh, sorry. My mind wandered. Here, talk to Sergeant White-horse."

"Sarge? There's a drone overhead."

"I'm going to talk to the SBI agents... What?"

"The contractor on Dr. Anderson's property just told me there's a drone overhead."

"I'll call you back." The phone went dead.

Time to Make Plans

Using her secure phone, Sylvia called Chad. "Sir, I need to speak to you and the SBI folks."

"Come down."

"Yes, sir." She turned to the two SBI agents eating with her. "Duty calls. Let's go."

Chad already had the door open when the trio arrived. "What's up, Sergeant?"

"Sir, you might want to sit down." Chad sat, and Sylvia and the SBI agents followed suit.

Sylvia told them of the phone call to Bella's house in North Carolina and the drone. She watched the color drain from Chad's face.

"Who's with Bella?"

"Murphy, sir. She's fine. I just spoke with both of them."

Elliott took charge. "Jackson, see if the drone's ours. Sergeant, get this man up to Dr. Anderson's home." He pointed to the young agent who had interviewed Nora. Sergeant Whitehorse and the agent left the room. He turned to the female agent who had interviewed Bella. "Do you have any concern about Dr. Anderson's ability to handle this current situation?"

"No, sir. She was direct, detailed, and calm."

"Good. Get the liaison officer on the phone and tell him we need cooperation from the North Carolina SBI and a contact. No action yet, just get me a name and a number. Also, I need him to get hold of my contact at the FBI. He'll know who it is. Explain what's going on and see if the FBI can get somebody over here ASAP. Then see if you can find out where Agent Isaacs of Immigration went and ask her to get back here. Questions?"

"No, sir. On it. I'll be in the room next to the sheriff's office." She exited the room.

"Chad, you are officially *off* this case. I want you and your family, and Dr. Anderson, in protective custody."

"Whoa, Elliott. Let's talk."

"Chad, it looks to me like Sergeant Whitehorse can..." He stopped and looked at Chad.

"Elliott, I need your help, and I appreciate you taking charge and getting folks moving. I know I can't, without your authorization, direct your folks. I want Nora, her family, and Bella protected. The best way to do that is to get them all together in a safe place."

"Right, that's what I said. You too."

"I have already talked to Bella about having Nora and the kids go up to her place, where we can easily patrol it."

"How?"

"Well, with any luck that UAV is yours. Were you expecting one?"

"Yes, it's probably ours. We have a full complement of unmanned aerial vehicles, and I ordered one for Dr. Anderson's home. I like the word drone myself." He smiled hoping to lighten Chad's load.

"Me too, but the Feds who have been here recently insist on UAV." He chuckled. "I have other cases going on right now and need to be involved. I will step back on the Zimmerman aspects, reluctantly, but I can't put Sergeant Whitehorse on the local stuff *and* have her available to you. Besides that, we both know that teamwork is most likely to yield the best results. Each of us has some knowledge and experience that is going to make this work."

There was a knock on the door. Chad reached back from his chair and opened it. It was Quinn. "Give us two minutes, Agent?"

"At your service." She stepped back and walked away from the door. Chad closed it gently.

"I need to go talk to my daughter and make arrangements to get her up to Drellag Caban."

"Where? Drellag Caban?"

"Yes, that's the name of Dr. Anderson's cabin." Elliott nodded. "I doubt my son-in-law will leave; he's the primary physician in these parts with a couple of part-timers. He can stay at the hospital, and they have security there. He'll want Nora and the kids up at Bella's. I promise you that at the first sign they are *not* safe up there, we'll go to Plan B... once we have Plan B."

"Can we secure Dr. Anderson's place?"

"There's probably nowhere else in these hills that we could secure as well as her family's homestead. She owns 80 acres; the cabin sits on top of a mountain with only one very winding county road up, and that ends at her property. Between whatever forces you can bring in and my own, we can cover it. Do we have an understanding?"

"Yes. I have enough respect for you to trust your judgement."

"Thanks. I'll be back in twenty minutes. Sylvia can set up a meeting in my office where we have everything we might need to access. We can move to another room as we add deputies and agents. While I'm gone, please listen *very carefully* to Quinn about our concerns on DEA SAC Carl McMullen." Chad saw a flicker of interest in Elliott's eyes, which he read as prior awareness that something was amiss with the DEA SAC.

"We'll be ready when you get back. Take my agent with you, I'll let you know about the drone as soon as I hear. Ralph will have the information I need for the North Carolina SBI and FBI by the time you get back." He stood and extended his hand. "We'll come through this, Chad. All of us."

"Thanks, Elliott. I owe you."

"Wait 'til we're done, then you can decide. Let me get with Agent Isaacs and you get with my agent. Let's do this."

Going to Drellag Caban

"Sir, come in." The deputy opened the door for Chad.

"Afternoon." He heard the small footsteps at the same time he heard the voice.

"Grandpa, Grandpa, Grandpa." Mac was almost airborne by the time he ran across the large open living room and flew into Chad's outstretched arms. He could see Lilly standing in the archway into the kitchen, her Raggedy Ann doll hanging from her hand. He took long strides towards her, carrying Mac. She had her arms in the air as he arrived, and Chad scooped her up.

"Look, Mommy, Grandpa can hold us both at one time."

"So he can. It's nice to see that he is *able* to do that. Hey, Daddy." She leaned in between her two children and kissed him on the forehead.

Mac pretended he was whispering to Chad. "Grandpa, Mommy and I are working on manners. Did you know that 'can' means you are able? Sometimes I say that when I mean I need permission." He leaned into whisper. "You know. . . may I?"

Chad pulled him into a tight hug and whispered in his ear. "That's my smart boy." He set him down but kept Lilly on his hip.

Mac pulled on his pant leg. "Grandpa, I'm sorry but I can't be your boy. I'm Daddy and Mommy's boy. I can be your grandboy."

Chad tousled his hair. "Then so you shall be."

"Mommy, does that mean okay?"

Nora laughed. "It does. Now please take your sister and go play with your Lincoln Logs." They both saw the disappointment on Mac's face.

Chad jumped in. "Hey, Mac. Miss Bella is going to have some full-sized Lincoln Logs in a couple of days. How would you like to go watch the men put them together at her cabin?"

"Can. . . May I? Please, Mommy, may I? Miss Bella!"

"We'll see. Now please do as I asked."

"Sure, Mommy. Come on, Lilly."

Before he lowered Lilly to the floor, Chad whispered to her, so that Nora could hear. "And to you, my very smart Lilly, I am always with you—even when you can't see me. I love you."

"Lub, Ga-pa." He put her on the floor. She took Mac's hand and ran off.

"Okay, my very special daughter, I need a hug."

"Happy to oblige."

"Thanks. I needed that."

"Me too. Been one of the stranger days of my life. I'm just glad you're okay."

"Speaking of okay." He looked his daughter in the eyes. "Nora, we need to make this happen really fast, and I need to ask you to trust me. I called Fred on the way here and he knows the plan. He was headed into surgery but said to tell you he'd call as soon as he finishes."

"Plan, Daddy, what plan? Any chance you intend to bring me into the plan?" He could hear the Irish temper rise in her voice. He also knew it was exacerbated by fear.

His eyes showed sympathy and urgency. "Right this minute, Nora, I just need things to happen quickly."

His secure phone rang. He answered it.

"Okay, Elliott. Thanks. Glad the UAV is friendly. See you shortly." He hung up, turning his full attention back to Nora.

"We're on top of what's going on. The Assistant Director of the State Bureau of Investigation is leading a team at my office. But *I* need to protect you and the children and Bella." He saw her eyes darting around. "You're fine. We're fine. I just want to keep it that way. I know it would be easier for you if Bella came here, but I... *we* can protect you better if you're up on the mountain. I asked Bella if it was doable, and she jumped right on it."

A dark look came across Nora's face. He remembered that look well from her mother. Then she softened. "Oh no, Daddy! Have they been calling Bella too?" He nodded. "She can't be by herself." Nora was emphatic. "Of course we'll go. Fred and I had been talking about going to the zoo in Knoxville this weekend, so I had already started putting together some things. Can you give me forty-five minutes?"

"Thirty?" The pleading look in his eyes told her this was more serious than she had even imagined.

"Thirty."

He walked back to the archway and signaled the agent from the SBI. "Nora, this is Agent Davis with the SBI. Agent Davis, this is my daughter, Nora Oliver-Smith." The two women exchanged greetings.

"Agent Davis has offered to help the kids pack up some toys, under whatever directions you give, and get them ready to go. I have a deputy waiting outside, and he will drive me back to the station. Your deputy has instructions to take you by the hospital if you want to see Fred, then it's up to Bella's. Thirty minutes, though, from the time I walk out the door. Please."

"Sure, Daddy. I love you." She kissed Chad and hugged him. Agent Davis stepped back into the other room.

"I love you more than you can ever know, and we're going to be fine. It will just help me not to have to worry about you and the children. Thanks."

"Sure, Daddy. Will you come up?"

"As soon as I can. Now we're at thirty and counting. See you soon."

"See you soon, Daddy." She stood and watched him walk to the door. Her heart skipped a beat wondering if she would see him again. She prayed she would.

Chad got in the passenger side of his SUV as he took out his secure phone and called Bella. He hated knowing that it would go to the answering machine. "Murphy, pick up, please."

"Sheriff." Amy saw the look of relief on Bella's face.

"Everything okay up there?"

"Right as rain on a summer afternoon. We're playing gin rummy. Dr. Anderson's pretty much whipping that state agent you sent up here though."

"And you, Murphy? She's beating you too, I take it?"

Amy laughed. "Yes, sir. That she is. I'm assuming you called to talk to her."

"Please."

Bella was already at the phone. The SBI agent and Murphy headed out the kitchen door at the same time.

"Chad, please tell me you're okay."

"I'm fine. How are you? Other than embarrassing a couple of LEOs at gin rummy?"

She laughed. "Did I tell you I love to play cards, board games. . ." she trailed off. "No, and now isn't the time either. Have you spoken with Nora?"

"Yes. They are packing a few things, and we will have folks bring them up. They should be there in an hour or so. Nora will bring some food with her, but do you need anything? I will have someone go to the store. . . better yet, would you call Carla and tell her what you need? I'll catch up with them and pay. Joshua will be fine with that."

"That's a good plan. Cut out the middleman, so to speak." Bella smiled at how much she admired Chad's ability to problem solve on the fly.

"Thanks, Bella. Oh, I got word that the drone belongs to the SBI, so you have aerial surveillance. They will not be close over Drellag Caban again, they were just getting the lay of the land. Sorry, I didn't know to alert you."

"It's fine, Chad. Will you come up too?"

"I'm going to try and make it later today. I have some things to do before that. Bella, I want you to know that the SBI Assistant Director has already reached out to the North Carolina SBI, and they will monitor things around your home there. They will also watch out for Victoria. They'll keep their distance unless this becomes more than the threats. We think that's all it is." He stopped to let that sink in for her.

"Chad, does Nora know about the calls?"

"She heard the first two at her home but has not listened to any-more. We're working on a way to intercept your machine so you won't hear anymore up there. I want the four of you to relax and have fun. And, most of all, I want you to be safe."

"Thanks, Chad. I'll enjoy getting to know Nora and the children. Oh, isn't Fred coming? He's welcome too."

"No, he's our only full-time doctor, and he's safe at the hospital. He wouldn't have it any other way. Nora knows that."

"Okay. I'm so relieved to hear your voice. Please take care of you for me."

Chad almost dropped the phone. He had waited a long time for someone who would say that.

"I promise. Oh, and before I get off the phone, I have a question to ask."

"Okay," she dragged out the word while trying to figure out how on earth he could think of anything else right now. "What is it?"

"Well, I was very impressed with something Agent Quinn Isaacs said today and found myself thinking, 'She's one smart cookie.' Then I realized 'cookie' is probably not the right word. So, what is?"

Bella started laughing so hard she pulled the phone away from her mouth and held her side as she doubled over. Tears started running down her face. "Chad Oliver, that was the last thing I expected you to ask me." She laughed again. "Honestly, you could have had a worse thought."

"What? How? That was pretty sexist, right?"

"Yes, it was. But at least you didn't think she was one smart chick or a sexy gal!"

"Okay, I'll ask for the lesson another time. I'm glad I could amuse you with my efforts to stop being a Neanderthal."

"Oh, Chad, precious Chad. You are far from a Neanderthal. I love… that you asked. And, the short answer is, just think 'she's smart.'"

Chad stopped listening at "love." *I am living for the day that sentence will be "I love you."*

"Chad? Are you there?"

"Oh, yes, dear Bella. I am. However, I have to go now and save the world so that we can enjoy it together. Thanks for having Nora and kids come up. I'll call later. Take care of you for me."

"Back atcha." She lowered the phone as she heard him click off. She set it in the cradle on the wall box and went to the bathroom to wash the tears off her face; tears of joy for this man in her life and tears of dread for the danger he might face.

224

CHAPTER 21

*The deeper the solitude the less the sense of loneliness,
and the nearer our friends.*

John Muir 1838 – 1914

Order to Go

CARLA TURNED HER HEAD AS THE SILVER BELL JINGLED. It still startled her every time the door opened, but she wondered if Joshua even heard it anymore. "Oh, hey, Melody. Wow! Is it three thirty already?"

"Hey, Miss Carla. No, it's two thirty. I didn't need to go home and help my mama today, so I came straight from school."

"Well, whatever time it is, I'm glad to see you, and we can sure use your help."

"Of course, what do you need?"

"I'll let you get the items on this list, and I'll find some boxes to put them in."

"I'm on it." Melody put her purse under the register and took the list from Carla.

Joshua heard the conversation and wondered what on earth Carla was doing. *Did I hear right? Melody is getting groceries for someone? Carla's in the...?* He stood up and hurried down the stairs. He caught up with Carla by the time she reached the doors to the storeroom. "Hey, long time no see." He leaned in and kissed her as the doors shut behind them.

She kissed him back. "Hey, yourself. Bookwork going okay?"

"No problem. It's ready for Melody to do her part. What are you looking for? Need help?"

"Just some boxes. Bella called with a list of things she needs and said that one of the deputies would stop and pick them up. She said Chad would try to pay but don't let him. She'll pay next time she's down the mountain. Oh, she offered to give me a credit card, but I said it wasn't necessary. Hope that's okay."

"What's going on?" He shook his head. "Sure, no problem, but all of this is strange. I mean, I don't have any problem with us getting what Bella needs or who pays when, but this has never happened."

"I don't know. I didn't think she sounded like herself, but I didn't question her. Just said we'd have it ready."

"Good. Good. I can help." He walked over to a stack of boxes he was planning to break down for recycling, picked several that would not be too heavy to lift if full, and headed to the front. "These should work just fine."

"I found everything. Do you want me to ring these up, Miss Carla?"

"That'll be just fine, Melody. I'll help put them in the boxes."

The bell jingled and they all turned to see Deputy Bennett. "Howdy, folks."

"Hey, Ken." Carla and Joshua said at the same time.

"Here to pick up some supplies for Dr. Anderson. Hey, Melody, how're ya'll doing?"

"I'm fine, Deputy Bennett. How are you?"

"Better than a hound dog stretched out on a front porch in summer. Stopped to pick—"

Joshua lifted the first box. "Got it all right here. Need help? I could have taken these up to Bella. What's going on?"

The deputy opted for an explanation that he thought might be plausible. "I think Nora and the kids are going up to spend a few days with Dr. Anderson. Something about seeing real Lincoln Logs."

"Oh, sure," Carla said. "She told me they were putting up her new cabin tomorrow or Friday. What little boy wouldn't want to see that? Heck, what grown woman doesn't want to see that?"

"Guess we'll have to wait for the movie to come out." Ken winked at Carla. He took the box from Joshua and saw that there were three more. "Best get this loaded up. Appreciate the help to my SUV, Joshua." The two men each took two boxes and headed out.

Carla stopped Joshua as he headed back up the stairs to his office. "Is that a service you've considered offering?"

"What? Boxes? Carry out?"

"No, silly, delivery!"

Joshua looked first at Carla then Melody, whose head was nodding in agreement. He leaned against the wall. "You know, I never thought about it. We've delivered a few times, like when someone was sick, but I never considered making it a service."

"Mr. Joshua, it would sure help my mama when I go to college. You know she has MS and without me here to help her out, it'll be pretty hard for her to carry groceries home."

"Melody, I never… I'm sorry. It never occurred to me we could make things easier for her." He turned to Carla. "Let's figure out how to do this. What do you say?"

Carla felt her pulse accelerate. This man she had loved for so long not only wanted to marry her, he also wanted her to be part of the decisions in his life. She said, "We'll make it happen. And, Melody, we'll be sure to help out with your mama when you're away. Don't you worry your pretty little head about that."

Joshua looked at Carla and wondered if it was sexist when a woman used that phrase with a younger woman. He knew he wasn't about to use it ever again.

Marching Orders

Quinn had made arrangements with Joshua to stay at Joe's house for a few days, and she took Sam there when he was released from the hospital. She did not tell him she was going to a meeting at the sheriff's station.

Chad walked into his office to find it bursting at the seams: Sylvia, Quinn, Elliott, Ralph, and a man he assumed was FBI were waiting for him. He walked directly to him, extended his hand, and said, "Chad Oliver. Welcome to our valley."

"Bill Michaels, FBI. Pleased to meet you, Sheriff. Sorry it's under these circumstances."

"Have you been briefed? Wait, how'd you get here so fast?"

"You just never know who's driving the highway and close enough to swing over on Routh 54." Agent Michaels grinned from ear to ear.

"That's the truth if I ever heard it," Quinn said.

Chad looked around the room and the alphabet soup of agencies: SBI, FBI, IEA, County Sheriff's Office. *Hmmm... haven't thought of us as the CSO in years. Where's our DEA agent?* "Seems to me we're missing an agency here."

Quinn did not miss a beat. "Agent Nations," she turned to the Agent Michaels, "of the DEA, has just been released from the hospital. He'll join us later today."

Chad nodded slightly but looked at Quinn. She turned her eyes toward Chad, smiled, and gave him a slight nod in return. Chad couldn't help but wonder what she and Elliott might have decided while he was gone. *I have no control over that. Just need to get a plan in place to protect my family and Bella—and hope they catch Zimmerman and whoever else is in on... what are they in on?*

"Sheriff?" Elliott was trying to get Chad's attention. Chad snapped back, knowing he needed to get his head in the game.

"With you, Elliott. Just counting heads and making sure there was no one else who needed to join us."

"May I begin?" Elliott asked.

"By all means." Chad nodded. *Like I would stop you?*

"Agent Isaacs, Quinn, has brought us up to speed on the current status of the recent shootings, the 'house on the hill,' and the known actions of Mr. Zimmerman. I asked to have Agent Nations join us for a later session so that he could rest, but this also gives us the opportunity to discuss his boss."

Chad relaxed. It finally occurred to him there could be things Sam shouldn't know about his own boss, but once the team had a plan, they would need Sam. *Could I stay objective enough to run this operation?*

"While the political machinations of concern to the local residents about the expansion of Route 54 are understood, for our purposes the underlying issue is the manner in which Zimmerman may be operating to achieve his goals. Here's what we currently know about Carl McMullen, the Senior Agent in Charge of the DEA, who appears to be operating in tandem with the junior legislator in Nashville from this region and Commissioner George Zimmerman on the political side and..." he hesitated, "dare I say, social front?"

Elliott outlined the information that the various agencies had amassed and the actions each was prepared to take. Chad took it all in. He was satisfied that the basics were being shared to bring a case against Zimmerman and, most likely, McMullen too. Right now, his concern was primarily Zimmerman because he believed the commissioner was behind the phone calls, although he likely had help. He was also quite confident that not everything each agency knew was being divulged.

"Now, to the immediate issue at hand, the phone calls. For our purposes, there is a great benefit to having landlines as they are easier to tap and monitor. We also have the technology to reroute the calls so that Dr. Anderson and others in the cabin... what did you call it?"

"Drellag Caban," Chad answered.

"Yes, Drellag Caban. So, no one will have to hear the calls should any more come in. We have already placed an agent at the home of Dr. Smith and Mrs. Oliver-Smith, and yours, Sheriff Oliver, to ensure the properties are protected should there be any attempt to enter the homes. The calls to the Oliver-Smith landline are being redirected to us as well. We also..." He did not look at Chad while he spoke.

"Excuse me, Director." Agent Michaels looked at Elliott. "I believe that Sheriff Oliver should be aware that the FBI has its own information that is being compiled, and we are already seeking a warrant to tap the phones of Zimmerman and McMullen."

Well, well. There is something on both of those men. How long were you boys willing to let my community be guinea pigs before acting? The smirk on Chad's face was so subtle only Sylvia saw it. She had years of watching his iron face and was keenly aware of Chad's ability to give nothing away. She *knew* there was a smirk in the corners of his mouth, but what she wanted to know was *why*.

"Thanks for the update, Agent Michaels. And, please, call me Chad. Now, ladies and gentlemen, I need to hear a plan for protecting my family and Dr. Anderson. Once I am satisfied that it is operational, I will leave you to get the big city criminals, and I will go back to trying to solve and resolve the smaller ones we have here. Sergeant Whitehorse will be my representative with you, and she is authorized to provide whatever resources are needed from our end. If I find the need for more information than Sergeant Whitehorse can give me, I will ask. Now, let's look at the topographical maps on that wall. Sergeant, would you please point out the area of Dr. Anderson's property and home, and what you recommend for surveillance?"

Sylvia stood and walked to the map. "The good news is that there is only one road in and out, which is easy to cover. As we learned in a recent case, the potential paths for ATVs are another matter. Fortunately, the cabin itself sits on a fairly flat mountain top, which will allow us to monitor the vulnerable areas. The SBI has a drone in the area, and we can add to that as needed. The DEA had a helicopter in that area as part of our recent operation, so we know it is possible to navigate the trees around the property. It also means that anyone making a serious threat to the sheriff's family and Dr. Anderson could come in by air. I suggest. . ."

Chad did not miss one thing being said while he scanned the faces of the agents. He had confidence in Sylvia and knew she would set high standards. She would also be very determined to cover every possible point of entry to Bella's land. He was relieved every face in the room was totally focused on the topo map. That was a start.

Comments, suggestions, and discussion by each person in the room contributed to a plan for protection on the high mountain, a plan to get the family off the mountaintop if necessary, and plans to protect the sheriff.

"Whoa, whoa, whoa. I appreciate it folks, but the only protection *I* need is for the people on the Anderson property. As soon as I meet with our local district attorney on a case, I am going up there for a visit. I will determine for myself if I'm satisfied with the plan in place, and then I will return to the valley. I will sleep at the station so I am readily available to *you*, but it will reduce access for anyone else. Does that work to your satisfaction?"

Elliott nodded slowly. "Depending on where we are with all this, I'd like to take a ride with you. Would be good for me to see the property."

And you want to check out Bella Anderson, don't you?

"Happy to have you along for the ride. I need thirty to forty minutes and then I'll be ready to roll."

"See you then." Elliott paused, and Chad could tell he was thinking through the plan of attack for the afternoon. "Wait a minute, Chad. Better if I stay here with this team."

Chad nodded. It was clear the meeting was over. He made sure his computer was off then shook everyone's hand as he headed for the door. "I suspect I don't need to remind you this is my family and my... my very special lady." He walked out and closed the door.

That went better than I expected with all the high-level folks in the room. What's that old saying? "Too many cooks spoil the broth?" Maybe not this time. Maybe not this time.

Order of the Day

Deputy Ken Bennett arrived at Drellag Caban and was about to knock at the kitchen door when Amy opened it. "Someone ordered groceries?" He smiled at her.

"This is the place. Pretty high-powered delivery service, I'd say. Need help?"

"Three more boxes." He handed the first one to her and headed back to his SUV. The SBI agent stepped out the door to help him. They introduced themselves and walked back to the cabin.

"Oh, thanks so much. Here let me take one of those." Bella reached for a box. Ken handed her the lighter of the two boxes. "Thank you for making that trip twice today."

"Well, ma'am, the first one was on the job. This one is community service."

Bella laughed. "Whatever it is, thank you. Do you know when Nora and the children will arrive?"

"I think they're about ten minutes behind me. So be ready. I suspect Mac will go crazy when he meets Wizard."

"Amy," Ken Bennett nodded to Deputy Murphy. "Head on back. Sergeant Whitehorse would like to talk to you before you go off duty. I'm good up here for a while."

"Deputy, I'll be here." The young SBI agent stared hard at him.

"Good. That makes two of us." Ken Bennett was not about to leave Bella without local protection, even if she hadn't been the sheriff's lady friend. He looked over to the kitchen table. "Good! Cards... I'm a shark."

Amy started laughing. "Yeah, go right on believing that one, Bennett." She walked over to Bella. "You okay for me to go?"

"I'll miss your company, but I think you've had a long day of duty, just like Ken. Thanks for everything, Amy. You've made this bearable and made me feel secure. I appreciate it. You didn't give me the name of the writer friend of yours."

"Oh, it's Dona. She works at the lib—"

"Library. Of course! Why didn't I ever think to ask Dona if she was a writer?"

"Of course, you would know her as the librarian. Didn't think of that. I think she mostly writes short stories, but may do some poetry, too. Hope you two can get a writing group going. Okay, I'm headed down the mountain. Nice to meet you, Agent, thanks for coming. Later, Bennett. See you soon, Bella. You'll be fine."

Bella walked over to the door and touched Amy's arm. "Thanks again." She smiled and waved as she walked out the door. Bella saw Arthur walking towards the door. "Hey, Arthur, have we caused too much disturbance for you to do the work you need to do?"

"Nope, not at all. Came over for two reasons. First, the logs will be here bright and early in the morning. We'll start setting them by ten. Thought you'd want to see that. It means we won't be working on the garage or dog run 'til next week at the earliest."

"That's perfect. The sheriff's grandchildren are coming up to stay with me for a few days, and they are going to be happy for a ring-side seat. I have plenty of lawn chairs in the shed, and we'll be sure to stay far enough away. Is that a problem for you?"

"Wouldn't deny a kid the chance to see a cabin go up any day. Don't know if Nora's ever seen one go up herself."

"I don't know either, but I haven't. What was the other thing you needed?"

"Just want to make sure you're okay. I don't think the number of law folks that have been here today is a social event. If it's none of my business, just say so."

"I'm sure Chad's going to want to have a talk with you, and he'll be able to clear everything up. May I call you to the phone the next time he calls?"

"Yes, ma'am. No problem. No problem at all. You be safe, now."

"I will, Arthur. Thanks. I'll get you as soon as he calls."

Two SUVs came up the hill as Arthur headed back to the work. Bella stayed in the doorway to welcome her guests. She glanced back at the kitchen to see that Ken was taking the last of the groceries out of the boxes and the SBI agent was putting food in the fridge. She shook her head in amazement. *Thanks for helping me to see that there are fewer... what did Chad call himself? Neanderthals. You're all good men.*

The vehicles came to a stop. Nora stepped out and waved to Bella, then she turned her attention to getting Mac out of the child safety seat in the back. She lifted him to the ground and whispered something in his ear while the agents started to remove their luggage from the trunk.

"Miss Bella! Miss Bella!" Mac called to her while doing his fast walk to avoid getting in trouble for running. She quickly walked down the steps and squatted down to greet him. He went right into her arms.

"Welcome to Drellag Caban, Mac. I'm so happy you're here."

"Dwel... What?"

"Oh, the name of my cabin is Drel-lag. Say that for me."

"Dwel-log." He was very deliberate and did not seem to mind that his "r" sounded like a "w." Bella didn't either.

"Drellag is the Scottish word for dragonfly. Caban is a Welsh word. It means Cabin. It just sounds different. Listen. 'CAh-bahn.' You say it."

"Caw-bawn."

"Perfect, Mac." She loved that his version sounded like "cow barn." Bella took Mac's hand and welcomed Nora and Lilly, who was riding on her mother's hip. The agents seemed to have everything in hand, and Bella decided to accept that she was not needed to help unload. "Come on, I'll show you to your rooms."

Inside the cabin, Bella walked straight to the master bedroom. "Nora, this will be the room for you and Lilly. Let me know if you need anything. And this," she walked to the second bedroom, "this will be your room, Mac."

"Oh, Bella, both children can sleep with me. Let us take that room and you stay in yours."

"The bed in that room is over a hundred years old, although the mattress is more modern," she chuckled, "and it is too small for three people. I'm fine to sleep on the sofa, and I have already moved my things out here." She motioned toward the living area. "Deputy Murphy helped me pull the small dresser out and my clothes are here.

So, you do whatever is comfortable for you, but I'm fine on the sofa. Been known to sleep there more than once." She smiled at Nora.

"Okay, no need to sort that out right now." Nora noticed how high off the floor the bed was in the second bedroom. She flipped on the light and was surprised to see side rails. "How is it that you have side rails for this bed?"

"Oh, that. One of my young colleagues came up with me several years ago and brought her four-year-old. I went online to figure out how I could make the bed safe. And, voilà, bed rails! Maybe I shouldn't tell you I slept on it as a child and never had bed rails."

"You are one clever lady. Thanks, Bella. I'm sure she thanked you too."

Both women noticed Mac had not moved. He was staring at Wizard, who sat on his blanket with his head cocked to the side. Each seemed to be eyeing the other up.

"Mac, I am so sorry. I forgot to introduce you to Wizard. Mac, this is Wizard. Wizard, this is Mac." She smiled at Mac while she rubbed Wizard's neck. "Good boy, Wizard." She squatted down and put her arm around Mac so that Wizard would see he was their friend. "If you put your hand out with your palm down, like this, and hold it out without putting it right in his face, he will nudge it and then you can pet him. Once you've petted him, he'll know you're a friend."

"Be gentle, Mac. You know how to greet a dog. Go ahead," Nora encouraged him.

Mac put out his hand, and Wizard pushed it up with his snout. Mac giggled. "It tickles."

Bella took Mac's hand in hers and scratched Wizard's neck and behind his ear.

"He has nice fur, Miss Bella. I like Wizard."

Lilly said, "Dug, dug."

Bella reached up and took her from Nora. "Come on, Lilly, meet Wizard." She helped her pet him and Wizard rubbed his snout against Lilly's arm. She giggled.

Nora smiled. "Nothing like making new friends, is there?"

CHAPTER 22

Wrapping Things Up

CHAD WALKED TO THE CONFERENCE ROOM where his deputy had seated District Attorney Peggy O'Haire. The prisoners would be ready in holding. He hoped each of the Kirk boys would admit their part in robbing and killing Joe Johnson and take the plea deal. Then it would be up to him to tell Joshua… and hope the community would see that not having a trial was the best route for Joshua to start to heal.

"Peggy, I appreciate the notification that you're ready to deal, let's hope these boys are. Thanks for coming on short notice."

"Of course, Chad. I'd like to do Jason first. He already knows that he can benefit from a deal from his time at juvie. If he takes it and we can then have them pass safely in the hall, Bobby will be more likely to take the deal."

"Sounds like a plan. I have them ready, and our new cameras and sound system are operational."

"No live streaming yet?" She meant it as a bit of ribbing.

"Got folks working on that. The signals in these hills, or lack thereof, make it a bit challenging."

"Okay, I hear you. Let's get this done."

Two deputies brought Jason to the door.

"Sir, reporting with Jason Kirk." Chad nodded for them to enter the room. The deputies took Jason to the far side of the table, opposite the DA, and stepped back but stayed on either side of him. Chad closed the door and sat down.

Chad spoke first. "This is a recording of the meeting between the district attorney and Jason Kirk." He gave the time and date. "Present are..." he nodded to each of the deputies, the DA, and Kirk. Finally, he said, "I am Sheriff Oliver of the CSO." The old abbreviation slipped out of his mouth automatically, but it was his title that caused Jason to turn his head. He had never seen the sheriff before, but he knew his name.

"Jason Kirk, please give your date of birth."

Jason spoke clearly but quietly.

"I will now read you your Miranda rights." Chad looked directly at Jason the entire time. "Do you understand these rights and responsibilities?"

"Yes, sir."

"Do you wish to have an attorney present?"

"No, sir. No need. I took the money. I done give it to my pappy, so it's long gone. I'll have to repay it." He kept his eyes downcast and focused on the tabletop as he waited for the next question.

Peggy spoke. "Jason Kirk, you have admitted to taking money from the cash drawer at the Valley Store. Is that correct?"

"Yes, ma'am. That's all I done though. Oh, and I didn't call for an ambulance when Bobby pushed Mr. Joe down." A tear fell on the table.

Chad believed it was remorse, not a show.

"Are you willing to testify in court, should you be called, to your statement that Bobby Kirk pushed Mr. Joe Johnson?" The DA was always very clear and concise in her questions.

His voice grew softer. "Yes, ma'am. He did. I couldn't stop him. It all happened real fast. I'm sorry. I liked Mr. Joe."

"Mr. Kirk, I am here today to offer you a plea deal. You have declined to have an attorney present. Do you wish to change that decision?"

"No, ma'am."

"Your case has not been taken to the grand jury since you have cooperated with this investigation and are not considered the prime suspect in the death of Mr. Johnson. However, you are aware that you have a prior conviction, and you are not one year past that time, so your juvenile record is not yet sealed. Did your probation officer explain that to you?"

"Yes, ma'am."

"The punishment for a theft of less than a thousand dollars is up to eleven months and twenty-nine days of incarceration and a fine of twenty-five hundred dollars. The amount you stole was four hundred and fifty. I am prepared to offer you a sentence of six months in detention and a five-hundred-dollar fine, plus repayment of the four hundred and fifty dollars you stole."

"Okay." Jason could barely be heard.

"Mr. Kirk, I need to know if you wish to accept this deal?"

"Yes, ma'am." He hung his head and tears continued to fall on the table.

"We have to go before the judge. He will want to make sure you freely made the decision to accept the plea deal and were in no way coerced or offered other incentives to make a plea. Do you wish to go forward?"

"Yes, ma'am." Chad sent the text he had written on his phone.

"You will be taken to Round City for the first opening on the judge's docket. This concludes the plea offer to Jason Kirk. I am District Attorney Peggy O'Haire. Please state your name."

"Jason Kirk."

Chad and the two deputies gave their names.

"This session is ended." Chad gave the time and turned off the recorder. He knew the wall-mounted video camera would continue to record Jason's exit from the room. He nodded to the deputies, and they pulled back Jason's chair. Jason stood and started to walk out but stopped.

"Ma'am, I'm real sorry Mr. Joe died. I wish I had never asked Bobby for juice." He shuffled out of the room.

Peggy looked at Chad. "There are some days I can feel satisfaction in doing my job, mostly when a crime is heinous and the perpetrators are out-and-out criminals. It's actually a little easier when I have a grand jury indictment and the case goes to trial. Feels like someone else is responsible for the recommendation. Then there are some days when the absolute tragedy of what has happened to a child, through no choice of his own, is too much to think about."

"I know, Peggy. I'm working here to get a whole lot better at prevention. I've always had that perspective, but I have recently figured out I haven't done a very good job of uniting our community around a prevention plan—it's *high* on my list to address now. Thanks for all you do." There was a knock on the door.

"Sir, reporting with Bobby Kirk." The deputies entered with Bobby. He sat, everyone stated their names, and Bobby gave his date of birth for the record. Chad read him his Miranda rights and Bobby declined to have an attorney.

"Mr. Kirk, do you understand the role of the grand jury in an arrest?"

"No, ma'am. Ain't got no idea."

"Following an arrest, particularly with grievous bodily harm... that's harm where someone is permanently disabled or killed." She stopped to let that sink in. "The grand jury is available to hear the evidence I present and determine if an indictment is in order. Do you know what an indictment is?"

"No, ma'am."

"An indictment means the people, citizens of our community, believe there is enough evidence to present your case to a judge and jury and find you guilty of reckless aggravated assault resulting in the death of a person." She looked straight at Bobby; he glanced at her, but would not look her in the eyes. "Do you understand?"

"I think so. Don't it mean that 'cause I pushed the old man and he died, I have to go to jail?"

"Did you plan to push him?"

"No, ma'am. I just done it when he wouldn't get out of the way. Made me mad. He could afford those cigarettes and wasn't gonna miss 'em. I didn't do it to hurt him, just to move him."

"That is why we are here now, Bobby. The evidence shows that you didn't go in the store meaning to hurt Mr. Joe Johnson. However, you did. You took his life. The people of the state of Tennessee have laws that require you to be punished for that."

"I know." His voice was low and his broad southern drawl unmistakable.

"If I take this case to the grand jury, I believe they will find there is enough evidence for you to go to trial. If you go to trial, whether with the judge or with a jury, the sentence for aggravated assault is two to twelve years and up to a five-thousand-dollar fine. You also stole two cartons of cigarettes, which is a Class A misdemeanor. The sentence for that is up to eleven months and twenty-nine days incarceration and a twenty-five-hundred-dollar fine."

"Wait, ma'am. I don't got no more than about seventy-five dollars. I done give everything I get at the gas station to my ma. Helps pay the groceries."

"The court will work out how you will pay the fine and repay the cost of the cigarettes you stole. Now, since you have no previous criminal history, and the evidence supports reckless aggravated assault resulting in death, I am offering you five years in prison with the possibility of parole in three years, with repayment of the cigarettes, and a two-thousand-dollar fine for both offenses."

Chad wondered how much of this the boy actually understood. There were times he wished you could force someone to have an attorney.

"Okay. I accept. Is that what I have to tell you?"

Peggy hated her job at this moment. There was nothing that would be fair for the death of Mr. Joe Johnson, and there was nothing that putting this boy in prison for twelve years would accomplish except pretty much assure he'd go back not long after getting out. She was hopeful someone might increase the boy's skills as a mechanic, and, with an early parole hearing, he could get out, be monitored, and do honest work.

"Yes. That's what you have to tell me. Now, you will have to go before the judge, and he will want to make sure you understand what your sentence is and that you weren't forced in any way to take this plea deal."

"No, ma'am. You were real nice. Ma'am, I'm sorry Mr. Joe died."

Chad shook inside. This boy never had a fair chance in life.

"This is District Attorney Peggy O'Haire terminating this meeting, please state your name."

"Bobby Kirk."

"...returning him to holding to be delivered to Round City at the first available opening on the judge's docket."

Each of the deputies and Chad said their name for the record. Chad turned off the recording as the deputies took Bobby back to a holding cell. "Thanks, Peggy. I know there will be folks in these parts who will have wanted blood from these boys, but I think you were fair. I also appreciate the effort to wrap this up so Joshua can put it behind him. He will not second guess your recommendation on the plea. Thank you."

"I think we'll get it wrapped up pretty quickly and have those boys off to Bledsoe. Hopefully they can learn a trade and do something worthwhile when they get out."

They both stood and walked to the door. Chad said, "Got a couple of minutes?"

"Sure. Shall we get coffee at The Corral?"

"Great, see you at The Corral in ten minutes, then you can get back to bringing justice to our community."

"See you there."

With everything going on, Chad wasn't sure where Sylvia would be, but he headed to her office as a starting point. To his surprise, she was in it.

"Anything I need to know?" His eyes begged for any information.

"Not at this moment. How about on your end?"

"Kirk boys took the plea. I'm going to The Corral to have a cup of coffee with Peggy O'Haire, then I'll go up to Drellag Caban. My goal is to be back in the valley to see Joshua at closing. I'll call and ask him to wait. Don't want him to know I'm sleeping here tonight."

"Clean sheets on the bunk for you. Need anything in particular?"

"No, Sylvia. Just need our lives to get back to something close to normal. Oh, yes, there is one thing. Any word on Sam?"

"We're having another meeting at seven tonight and Quinn said he'd be here."

"Make sure that meeting lasts long enough for me get back here, please. I want to talk to him."

"I'll do my best. But should you talk to him? He'll be part of the task force and I know you want to keep it at arm's length."

Chad nodded his head. "And that, Sergeant Whitehorse, is why you are lead sergeant *and* on the task force. Thanks for reminding me to let other people do their jobs. Tell Sam I asked after him, please."

"I will, Sheriff. Tell Bella and Nora and the kids hello from me. Please tell them I look forward to seeing them all at the powwow."

"You bet." He smiled at her and walked out.

Even though she wasn't truly a local, Peggy was parked on the side and walking in the side door when he pulled in the lot. He found her at a back corner booth.

"This work for you, Chad?"

"Yes, ma'am. Hey, Cheri."

"Coffee and a glass of water, please." Peggy said it before Chad could ask.

"My usual."

"Sounds like a mid-afternoon drink is a good idea. Too bad I have to drive over the mountain."

"My mid-afternoon usual is iced tea. Sorry to disappoint." He looked at her with compassion for the difficulty it must be day in and day out to deal with only the worst situations in the community. *At least I get to participate in trying to improve our community, and I am determined to focus on prevention.*

Cheri placed their drinks in front of them and returned to the front of the restaurant. "Thanks again, Peggy, for making this happen. Joshua is not a vindictive man, and he wants to remember all the good years in his dad's life. I'll go see him when he closes up the store to tell him they took the deal."

"When I talked with him, he told me pretty much the same thing. Hey, did I hear that he and Carla are engaged?"

"Best news in this valley in a while. Seems like a good thing for both of them."

"And how about these rumors I hear about you? Most eligible bachelor in these parts and there's a woman who has finally caught his fancy? Expecting an earthquake any day."

Chad laughed. "Most eligible bachelor, eh? Didn't know I'd been branded. Well, whether I am or not, the rumor is true. A lady has caught my fancy, and right now I'm doing everything I can, without being able to do a blessed thing, to protect her, my daughter, and my grandkids."

"Run that by me again real slow. What?"

"For the record, I'm speaking to you off the record, but as a law enforcement officer."

"Got it."

"We're not sure what's actually going on, but Bella and Nora have received threatening calls telling them to have me back off."

"Back off of what?"

"That's the million-dollar question. On top of this, it seems our county manager was threatened directly by a certain commissioner. Harold was told he'd lose his job if he didn't keep me from interfering in the accident involving the commissioner's wife."

"And have you interfered?"

"Not even so much as a phone call. Guess they took you straight to the conference room and you didn't see all our guests. FBI, SBI, IEA, DEA, now I know my..." His voice had the singsong lilt of the alphabet song.

"Have to admit I did see more than one official looking sedan. Just thought maybe lottery money was upping your fleet."

"Ha! Not even taxpayers' money from the state or feds. Anyway, while I am not actively working the case—Sylvia is."

Peggy nodded and smiled. "Good choice. Guess I should call her and tell her what I know." She watched as his gray eyes took on a steely look. Most everyone who worked with him knew it meant to be your best professional self. "Relax, Chad. Just checking the temperature of the water."

"At this moment, it's pretty hot. I have every reason to believe that the commissioner is involved in the threats and whatever else is going on."

"Then be safe, Chad. That's what matters right now. You couldn't have any more help working it than you have. Have you talked to Elliott Nelson?"

"Talked to him? He's here!"

She raised her eyebrows. "Really? Well, welcome home, Elliott. Glad you had the smarts to come yourself."

"So...?"

"All I have is innuendo from folks we've had arraignment hearings on. They talk about 'el jefe,' but no one ever seems to be willing to put a name to him. Needless to say, Police Chief Nelson follows every single case we have trying to get a link to Zimmerman." She stopped as Cheri approached the table.

"More coffee, ma'am?"

"Half a cup, please."

"Sheriff?"

"I'm good, thanks."

He and Peggy each put a five-dollar bill on the table.

"No need, folks. Mr. James follows his daddy's tradition. 'Ain't no different than water, just a little coloring in it.' Enjoy your day, folks." They left the money on the table.

"Listen, Chad. If I find out anything that can help, I'll call Sylvia. Meantime, I think you need to go check on those women in your life. And you can tell Dr. Anderson for me that she'd be a fool to walk away from you. Catch you next time." She slapped him on the shoulder as she walked past him to the exit.

Chad sat thinking for a moment then headed out himself. He pulled out his phone and dialed the Valley Store as he walked to his SUV. "Hey, Carla. Chad here. Joshua available?"

"Hey, Chad. Sure." Joshua picked up the line and Carla hung up. "Hey, Chad. What's up?"

"Just checking to see if I might have a few minutes with you at the close of business today? I should be there around quarter to seven. I can wait until you're finished up."

"No problem at all, Chad. Got a few questions of my own. See you then."

"Sure, Joshua. Later."

A few questions of his own? Guess I'll find out soon enough.

Beating the Clock

Bella rushed the children and Nora onto the front porch when she heard the phone ring. She did not want the children to hear it. The SBI agent and Deputy Bennett stood at the ready, treating the answering machine as if it were a hand grenade that could explode at any moment. Bella quickly closed the French doors.

"I'm so glad you still have your coats on. Let's sit out here for a couple of minutes and then I'll fix us a snack."

Nora spoke quietly and focused her gaze on her children. "Miss Bella will let us use her kitchen. Isn't that nice?"

"Yes, Mommy. Miss Bella is always nice." Mac had a serious look on his face. "Aren't you, Miss Bella?"

"Well," she said word out slowly, considering how best to answer. "Mac, I would like to always be nice, but sometimes I mess up. Do you ever do that?"

"Miss Bella, sometimes I mess up too. Mommy says that it's okay to mess up if you learn from it and try really hard not to do it again. Is that what you do?"

Bella scooped up Mac and sat down with him on her lap. She looked him in the eyes. "Mac, I think you have a very special mommy, and she has a very special boy. I'm glad you're my friends."

"I am too. But could you and Grandpa get married so you could be my grandma?"

Bella almost dropped him. Nora stifled a laugh.

The French doors opened. Detective Bennett motioned to Bella. "How about you and Lilly look out there to see if you can find any birds? I need to talk to the deputy, and I'll be right back." She looked at Nora, raised her eyebrows, and shrugged her shoulders.

"Ma'am, that call was another threat. It's recorded. No different than the others. Then there was a second call immediately after, don't know if you heard the phone ring."

"Why no, no, I didn't. Another threat?"

"Not unless you're worried about the sheriff coming up here."

"Oh, Ken, is it safe for him to come? I mean, of course, I want him to come up, but I want him safe more than that."

"He'll be fine, ma'am. Said he'd be here in twenty minutes or less."

She looked at her watch. It was already 4:30 p.m. She walked back out to the porch. "Anyone here like chili with hotdogs?"

"Me, me." Mac danced around. "Lilly will eat the hotdog, but not the chili. Is that okay?"

"Absolutely. Nora, if you think the children can hold on for thirty minutes, I already have the chili heating, and I'll put the hotdogs on and warm up the buns. I made some coleslaw and..." She mouthed the word brownies.

Nora nodded and smiled. "Of course, they are pretty good eaters."

Mac came over and pulled on the leg of Bella's jeans. "Miss Bella, may I help?"

"You bet! Do you think you could go with Deputy Bennett to walk Wizard while I fix us some supper?"

"Yes, ma'am!" He looked at Nora. "May I, Mommy?"

"Absolutely. How may I help, Bella?" She was holding, Lilly who was trying hard to keep her eyes open. "I'll lay her on the sofa in the living room, if that's okay, and be right there."

Bella leaned in and quietly said, "Your dad will be her in twenty minutes. I'd like us to eat together. Then we can talk about your normal schedule; is that all right with you?"

Nora spontaneously leaned over and kissed her on the cheek. "We're adaptable!"

After ensuring that Lilly was sound asleep on the sofa, Nora and Bella began to prepare the meal. They kept their conversation light, chatting about the beautiful fall weather and the kids, while carefully sidestepping the topic that brought them under one roof.

"Ken must have taken Wizard and Mac on quite a walk. I hear a vehicle coming up the road. Must be your dad already."

"Oh, I can just imagine he might have pushed some limits to get here." She grinned.

They heard a horn honking and walked to the door. Mac was jumping up and down, and Ken Bennett was doing all he could to hold on to Mac with one hand and Wizard's leash with the other.

"Grandpa! Grandpa! Look, depudee, it's my grandpa. Did you know he's the sheriff?"

"Indeed, I do, Mac. Indeed, I do."

"My mommy says things twice too. I think I do it sometimes. I don't know why."

"Doesn't matter why, Mac, it's part of our mountain ways. Good thing to learn."

Chad stepped out of the SUV and Ken let go of Mac's hand. He ran this time—right into Chad's arms. Chad scooped him up and kissed him then walked over and scratched Wizard's ears. He was glad Elliott Nelson had decided to stay at the station and spend time on getting the officers from these different agencies working as a team. Chad needed this time with the people he loved.

He greeted Ken, "Hey, have they worked out a relief for you? Seems to me you were up here this morning."

"Yes, sir. I was. That was work. This is community service. Think I'd leave Miss Bella, Nora, and the kids alone with an SBI guy who's still wet behind the ears? Sarge told me she'd have an official schedule before dark. I'm good. How are you?"

"Not easy to let go of the reins, but bigger guns than ours are running the show. So, I pretty much figure all this is about teaching me a lesson."

"Sir, not wanting to overstep my bounds, but you'd be crazy not to back off, spread the work around, and take advantage of time with a fine lady like Dr. Anderson."

"I'll take that as advice from a friend. Thanks, Ken. Just help me keep to it."

"Any way I can, sir." They were at the door.

Chad leaned in with Mac on his hip to kiss Bella. and winked at Nora. "Where's my *little* girl?"

"Shhh... Grandpa, she's taking a nap."

"Got it. Thanks, Mac."

"Grandpa, I have a question."

Nora and Bella looked at each other. *Is this going to be a repeat of what he asked on the porch?*

"Sure, Mac. What's your question?"

"Did you come to see the Lincoln Logs go up like a cabin tomorrow?"

Bella and Nora smiled and stepped back into the kitchen. Chad walked in and kissed his daughter, then set Mac on the floor. "That's right, Mac. How about you go play? Do you have some toys here?"

"Yes, Grandpa. Miss Bella put them in the living room by the fireplace. See you later."

Chad pulled Bella into a hug and then he saw the SBI agent. "Afternoon. I see you've met my family."

"Yes, sir. Pleasure's mine." He was standing by the phone.

"Something going on?"

"Just had another call, Sheriff."

"Any progress on getting them rerouted so they don't come in here?"

"Last word I had was they had the permissions needed and would have it done by five o'clock. That's not too long now. Then I'll be able to tell Dr. Anderson how we'll handle her calls."

"Good. Good. Now, something smells mighty fine in here."

"Supper will be ready in about ten minutes. Can you stay and eat with us?" Chad saw the plea in her eyes.

"Add a plate. I'm hungry. If you'll excuse me, I need to go talk with Arthur, then I'll be in to wash up for supper. Work for you, ladies?" Both of them nodded. "How about you come with me?" He nodded his head toward the door while looking at the SBI agent.

"But, sir, the phone?"

"Agent, I'm going to instruct my daughter to answer any calls by picking up the handset and putting it right back down. And I'm going to ask Dr. Anderson to turn off the volume on her answering machine. Then we will all have a peaceful supper and regroup afterwards. This way?" Chad pointed his head toward the kitchen door.

Ken had come in and handed Wizard off to Bella. "You too, Deputy Bennett. It's going to be dark soon." The three men went out the door.

CHAPTER 23

The Task Force

THE TASK FORCE MET IN THE CONFERENCE ROOM at five to have supper prior to their scheduled meeting. Sylvia was the only local law enforcement officer present. She had made arrangements with The Corral to bring over fried chicken, coleslaw, baked beans, cornbread, baked potatoes, and chocolate chip cookies.

Elliott Nelson looked at the spread and shook his head. "This, Ralph, is how these mountain folks stay so trim."

"Beg your pardon, sir?" Elliott's agent in charge stared at him. "How on earth could they stay trim eating like this all the time?"

"In Knoxville, we just walk from one desk to another and from our offices to our cars. Out here, they hike our lovely mountains, chase their kids up and down them, and generally live their lives appreciating the nature we've tried to obliterate in our cities."

"I get your point. I might be a city man born and raised, but I get the point."

"Good. Good. Then fill up that plate. It's going to be a long night."

"Exactly, and a full plate will have us all sleeping."

Elliott looked at Sylvia and winked. "Did I fail to mention to the group that we're going for a hike before the meeting?"

"Sir, I believe you made it perfectly clear when you said we'd eat and then step out for a bit." Sylvia was happy to play along.

"Director, I thought 'step out' meant to get a bit of fresh air."

"Exactly. Get some fresh air while stepping out onto a mountain trail. Don't worry, we'll do it before dark and the bears usually wait until after sunset to search for food." He slapped Ralph on the back. "Relax, Ralph. Just having a bit of mountain fun at your expense. You might find you like the outdoors if you stay here long enough."

"Too quiet for me, sir. Too quiet."

"Director, he's already getting the hang of this place." Sylvia looked from one man to another. "He just used our double speak."

"Your what? I did what?"

"You said 'too quiet' twice. You didn't learn that in the city. Story goes over here that we grow up hearing the echoes in the mountains, so we just naturally say things twice. Anyway, I'm not being a very good host as our local agency representative. Please get some food."

Quinn Isaacs came in about ten minutes later. Sam was behind her. Everyone stood, made introductions, and went back to eating.

"Nice to have some real food." Sam grinned as he picked up a chicken leg.

"Agent Nations, aren't you based in Knoxville with the DEA?" Ralph looked confused.

"Yessir, that's my duty post, but I am a local boy born and raised. Went to Knoxville when I went to UT. Recently had some not-so-subtle reminders that these are my roots. I am grateful to be reconnected to them."

"Roots are important, that's for sure. I'm grateful for my city roots. So, I guess it's each to his own."

They finished eating and Elliott looked around the table. "Okay, let's go take a walk."

"Sir, do you have any place in mind?" Sam looked around the table.

"How about you choose one? Sunsets about 6:30. We need to be back here by six fifty."

"We have a small park near the valley that has a view back over the mountains, and it's worth every step to get to it. We can easily do it in that time."

"Then let's go," Elliott said.

Sylvia nodded and they split up into two vehicles: Elliott drove Sam, Quinn, and Sandy. Sylvia drove Bill Michaels and Ralph Jackson. Sylvia knew that Elliott was doing this to strengthen the team through a shared experience.

Strategizing on the Mountain

As Chad, Ken, and the SBI agent walked out of Drellag Caban, Arthur headed towards them. His crew was already headed down the mountain. "Evening, Sheriff."

"Evening, Arthur. Didn't expect to see you again so soon. You've met these two gentlemen I believe."

"Yes, I know Ken, of course. Made this young man's acquaintance earlier."

"I wanted to tell you personally that some folks seem to think a form of entertainment is threatening the sheriff to get him to back off on a case. Unfortunately, those threats didn't come directly to me, they came to Bella and Nora. Since it directly involves me, I am not handling the matter. Know Elliott Nelson from over in Round City?"

"Yep. Know both the Nelson boys. Both in law enforcement for a long time. Not sure what Elliott is doing these days though."

"He's the Assistant Director of the State Bureau of Investigation and heads up the Knoxville office, overseeing the eastern region of the state. We're fortunate to have him there. But, right now, he's here heading up this investigation. They'll get to the bottom of it."

"Yessir, I believe they will. Are Bella and Nora okay?"

"They are and they will be. Starting tonight when these two men leave, there will be round the clock protection up on this mountain until we get... until it's settled. What I need to know is if you would be more comfortable delaying your work until it is."

"Nope. Not afraid of anyone... except maybe you if you were after me for a legitimate reason. Since we both know I'm not going to do anything to invite that kind of attention, we'll be fine. All my crew are good, clean, honest folks, and they'll be fine."

"Can they handle it if an SBI or FBI agent stops them and talks with them?" Chad was trying to let Arthur know that if anyone on his crew had problems they were trying to hide, they might not be able to withstand the questioning that could, and likely would, come for anyone coming up this mountain.

"Clean as a baby's bottom after splashing in the washtub."

Chad raised an eyebrow. That particular saying didn't necessarily mean the baby was the first one in the washtub.

"Now, Sheriff, you know the baby these days gets first dip in the clean water." Arthur smiled. "Seriously, though, Pastor Fisk would vouch for every one of them. Not worried about it all."

"Good. Glad to hear it; I expected nothing less. Might want to give them a call tonight and tell them they might get some questioning on their way up tomorrow. It would help if you gave Deputy Bennett the names of whoever will be here so he can get a jump on clearing them. Don't want to make it too tough on the SBI and FBI boys. We want to be accommodating, right?"

"Sure enough. I'm not worried at all. This will be the safest place in these hills outside your offices, to be sure."

Chad slapped Arthur on the back. "Good point, Arthur. Good point. I'd appreciate it if you tell your crew we're doing a joint training exercise with these folks. No need getting the whole community riled up."

"Perfect. I was going to ask you what would be best to say. You know I'll keep your confidence."

"Goes without saying, Arthur. Thanks. Now you get on home because my grandson is pretty excited about seeing Lincoln Logs go up tomorrow. I think he's building a replica in Bella's living room right now."

"Then I'll let you go help him. Ken, I'll give you those names. Good night, gentlemen."

"Night." Chad and the SBI agent said in unison.

Chad looked at the SBI agent, trying to figure out how old he was. He suspected he was older than he looked, which had lots of advantages in state and federal law enforcement. "What do you say we go wash up and have some supper?"

"Be mighty fine, Sheriff. Thanks."

"Don't thank me, thank Dr. Anderson." They chatted as they walked towards Drellag Caban.

The Valley Store

"Does Chad need something I can get together for him?" Carla called up to Joshua. There was no one in the store.

"No. He just wanted to know if he could stop by just before closing. Has something to tell me."

"Sure seems there's something amiss. Did you ever know Bella to call and ask to have an order ready for pickup, by her or anyone else?"

"Never. In fact, she might have the farthest to travel in this region to get here, well, of the locals, and she always comes to do her shopping."

"I thought what she ordered was pretty curious."

"What was it? I didn't see the items, just saw there was lots of it."

"Hot dogs. Can you picture Bella ordering hot dogs?"

"Maybe she's having a cookout?"

"Could be. She also got marshmallows, graham crackers, and chocolate bars."

"Well, see, then she *is* having a cookout."

"She also got enough grits to feed a schoolroom of children and those icicles you can freeze."

"Maybe she has friends coming from North Carolina. I'm sure she'll tell us if she wants us to know. Now, I'll let you take care of those customers coming up the steps, and I'm going to start stocking the shelves." He kissed her and headed to the back.

Carla smiled and then shrugged. *Maybe I'm going to miss the chatter among the servers at The Corral after all.*

Soups On!

Chad and the young SBI agent walked into the cabin, and Bella encouraged them to wash up for supper. Chad looked at the agent. "Down the hall, straight ahead. Soups on!" He was hoping for a moment with Bella.

"Yessir."

Chad pulled Bella into a hug and kissed her. It was a lingering kiss, but the hug was almost possessive. He stepped back, keeping his arms around her, and looked at her. "You, lovely lady, are a sight for sore eyes. I never imagined that my work would bring this into your life."

"Our lives." Bella said it matter-of-factly.

He hugged her again. "I don't remember the word for a word that carries two meanings at once, but I'm sure hoping that 'our' is one of them."

Bella started laughing so hard his hands slipped off her shoulders. "What's so funny?"

"Oh, Chad. You're not going to let me forget my roots as an English professor, are you?"

"I'm just trying to impress the teacher."

"Didn't I tell you I like you even when you're unimpressive?"

Chad saw the SBI agent standing awkwardly in the dining room. "I think our guest is ready for supper. Let me go wash my hands and see if my lovely daughter has her little munchkins ready to eat."

Bella moved the crock pot full of chili to the kitchen table. "By the time I get things out of the fridge, the hot dog buns will be warm. What are you drinking?" She looked at the SBI agent.

"Tea is fine, ma'am. I can help."

"I think all the adults will have tea, so it would be great if you could grab that bucket of ice out of the freezer and put some in each glass. Thanks."

As he returned from the bathroom, Chad scooped up his grand-daughter from the floor. "Grandpa's got you."

"Ga-pa. Ga-pa." She leaned against his neck.

Chad looked at Nora. "Is there any better feeling than the head of a little angel?"

"Oh, I think the big angel in the kitchen is doing a mighty fine job for you."

"Yeah, well, that's as true as a preacher's sermon on Sunday."

"But much more fun." She smiled at her daddy. "I, for one, could not be happier for you."

"Thanks, Nora. Means the world to me to have you on my side. How's Fred?"

"I called him a little while ago. Normal day for him. I dropped off some clothes for him, and he'll stay at the hospital. It makes me feel better to know he's there."

"Good. I'm glad. Now let's wash up these kiddos and eat."

Chad handed Lilly to Nora. "Come on, Mac. Miss Bella has supper ready. We need to go wash your hands."

"Grandpa, I can wash my hands. Remember, 'can' means I am able. Want to come see?"

"Absolutely. I do a pretty good inspection of hands. I check under the fingernails."

Mac looked at his nails. "Why, Grandpa?"

"To make sure you washed all the dirt away."

"Okay. You can look. Let's go."

Hands and face washed, they settled in at the dining table. Mac was seated on a cushion in one of the two dining room armchairs, and Nora had remembered to bring Lilly's booster seat. "Thanks for letting me put plastic on the seat covers, Bella. The kids are pretty careful eaters, but I would hate it if we damaged anything in your home."

"Nora, please don't worry. I don't necessarily want my things damaged, but you and your family are far more important to me than the things I have. So, let's relax and enjoy each other's company. Deal?"

Nora smiled. "Deal. May I ask Mac to say grace?"

Bella and Chad both nodded.

"Me, Mommy? Now?"

"Yes, please, Mac."

"Dear God, thank you for our food, our family, our neighbors, and all the earth. Amen."

Amen was echoed around the table.

Bella looked from Nora to Lilly to the SBI agent and then to Chad at one end of the table and Ken Bennett, who sat next to him. She sat between Ken and Mac. "I am humbled to have all of you gathered around my table. It has been many, many years since this table was full."

Chad saw the tears well up in her eyes.

"Grandpa, may I say something?"

"Yes, Mac. What is it?" He hoped it would take the eyes off of Bella.

"I get to sit in the daddy place. You know, the end of the table."

"Then am I in the mommy place?"

"No." He stated it with great authority. "You are in the grandpa place." He picked up his spoon and ate some chili. The adults all chuckled.

"Nothing like a child to give you perspective, is there?" Ken Bennett asked with a smile.

"Andrew," Bella addressed the young SBI agent, "where is home for you?"

"In Knoxville now, ma'am. I'm originally from Franklin, Tennessee, in the middle of the state. My family's been there for five generations. My dad's a farmer and trying to hold onto his land. Development from Nashville is moving out our way, so it's not easy."

Chad looked at Andrew. "Sounds like our hills aren't the only place changing. I was in Franklin years ago. Now I mostly get to Nashville, but I must admit only when I have to be there."

"Daddy, you wouldn't go to Knoxville if you didn't have to. Tell the truth. You're a mountain boy to your core."

"Lot of truth in that, Nora, but I hope I'm here because I want to be here, not because I can't go anywhere else. There's a difference when you live somewhere by choice, even when it's your homeplace." He saw that Mac was eating quietly and looking around at the adults. Chad was proud of his grandson and of Nora and Fred for taking the time to make sure their children had good manners.

"Hey, Mac. Good job down there."

"It's not a job, Grandpa. It's supper."

Nora tried not to laugh. "Mac, Grandpa spends most of his time with adults. When you tell an adult 'good job' they know it means you approve of something they are doing or have done."

"But, Mommy, I don't have a job except to clean my room and put away my toys, help with Lilly, and read. Right?"

"That's absolutely right, Mac." She chuckled. "You know all those jobs and you do them well. Maybe Grandpa will be a little more explicit about what he meant."

On cue, Chad said, "I noticed that you are eating with your spoon and fork and sitting quietly while people talk. That's what I meant by 'good job.'"

"Okay, thanks, Grandpa. I'll keep doing it."

Andrew finished eating and turned to Bella, "Ma'am, thank you for supper. If I may be excused, I'll go check around outside."

"Please, by all means. Thank you for joining us for supper."

"My pleasure, ma'am." He stood and took his dishes to the kitchen; she heard him rinsing them off.

"If I may be excused," Ken Bennett said, "I need to check in with Sergeant Whitehorse."

"Thanks, Ken. Glad you could eat with us. Still want to meet your wife one of these days."

"Miss Bella."

"Yes, Mac." Bella reached over and touched Mac's arm.

"Do you know that he's a depudee and my grandpa is the sheriff?"

"Why, yes, Mac, I do know that. It means we're very lucky they protect us, doesn't it?"

He had just taken a bite of his hot dog, so he just nodded.

Nora watched Chad, who was moving his eyes between Bella and Mac as they chatted. He caught her looking at him and winked. She was trying to picture her own mother talking with Mac like Bella was. She imagined her daddy was thinking the same thing.

"May I get you anything else, Bella?" Chad stood.

"No, I was about to get up and see if any of you need anything."

"Nora, Mac, Lilly... may Miss Bella and I be excused from the table? I need to talk to her and then I have to get back to the station."

"It's okay, Grandpa. Right, Mommy?"

"Please. We have enjoyed our dinner with you. We'll finish up and then clear the table."

Bella was already picking up her plate when Chad reached and took it from her.

"Thank you very much, Chad. Let me go put some water in the sink and the dishes can soak."

They walked into the kitchen, put the dishes in the sink, and the cold food back in the fridge. "The chili will be fine, and I see we made short work of the hotdogs. That's good. I can clean up the rest later."

Chad took her hand and took her jacket off the hook behind the door. "Let's go for a little walk. Shall we?"

"Sounds fine to me."

As they walked down the road away from the two men already outside, Chad had his arm around Bella. "More than anything, I wish this was an end of the day walk with you where we could talk about our day, you could tell me how your writing is going, and I could tell you that everything in our hills is normal. It isn't. I don't know who's behind these calls and, worse yet, I don't know what they might try to do to carry out those threats. There's a good plan to keep you and Nora and the children safe up here. And, after this meal, you will barely know they are up here. There will be my folks, SBI, and FBI. You will likely be the safest place in the whole state outside of the Capitol building, and I suspect these folks will be more diligent because they aren't bored."

Bella slipped her arm around his waist and leaned into him as they walked. "And you, Chad? Who's protecting you?"

"When I leave here, I'll be headed to the station; I'm staying there. I always have a change of clothes there, so I'm good. The SBI has agents on my house and Nora's just to avoid any property damage. Fred is staying at the hospital. So, we're covered. I just need to know that you feel safe."

"We'll be fine, Chad. I just hope Nora can feel comfortable up here." They turned and headed back towards Drellag Caban.

"She'll be fine. The kids are good. She trusts me to keep them safe, and she knows Mac is very excited about your cabin going up tomorrow. I'll talk with her before I go. But I need to go."

They reached the steps and he stopped her. "Bella, I never expected something like this to happen to you because of me. Please let us keep you safe, and then if you want to tell me you never want to see me again. I'll understand. I won't be happy about it, but I'll understand."

She leaned into him and kissed him passionately. She said, "You best take care of you for me. Do you understand that?"

He kissed her back. "With armor on, I promise. In one minute, I am going back in that cabin to talk to Nora and tell all three of them that I love them and that I am protecting them. I am not asking you to respond in any way, but I am now going to tell you what I have wanted to say for weeks." He looked deep into her eyes. "I love you and I am going to protect you too."

She kissed him again and said, "I know."

They went inside. Nora was getting Lilly ready for bed in her pack-and-play, and Chad saw that Mac was playing with his Lincoln Logs again. "Nora, got a minute?"

"Sure, Daddy. Play with your animals, Lilly. Mommy will be right back."

He and Nora stepped into the second bedroom. "Look at me, my beautiful, smart, talented daughter. I'm sorry. I'm sorry that my work brought this into your life. I know you worry for me, but I never thought I'd have to worry like this for you and Fred and the kids. Forgive me."

She glared at him. "You did not ask these people to do what they're doing. I will not accept an apology from you, and you are not to say that ever again. I know what you do for work; I'm proud you keep us all safe. Right now, I'm happier than a clam that you have an amazing woman in your life. Let's focus on all that, and this will be behind us soon. Understood?"

"Well, I guess that was made perfectly clear!" He said each word deliberately. "If I didn't look in the mirror to shave each morning, I'd wonder where you learned to be so determined." He hugged her. "Nora, I love you more than anything. I love your children and your husband. And I just told the woman who I hope I will be with for the rest of my life that I love her."

"Daddy! Did you? I'm so proud of you. I love her too. We're going to have many good times ahead." She hugged him tight. "I'm so happy for all of us. Good for you." She pulled back. "Do you need me to give you specific behaviors to explain that?" They both roared with laughter.

Mac used his fast walk to reach them. "Mommy, Grandpa, please... Lilly is trying to rest."

Nora and Chad looked at each other and tried not to laugh even harder.

Chad scooped Mac up. "Hey, my favorite grandson. I have to go back to work. You have fun, and I'll try to be here tomorrow when they start putting the big Lincoln Logs up for Miss Bella's new cabin. But, if I don't make it, you pay close attention so you can tell me."

"Okay, Grandpa. I will. Good night. I love you."

"Love you more than you love me. The end. I win."

Chad kissed and hugged Lilly and told her he loved her. After he gave Nora one more kiss, he went into the kitchen. Chad didn't care that Ken Bennett was there. He kissed Bella and whispered in her ear, "I love you."

As he left, a tear ran down Bella's face. *Dear God, please keep him safe.*

Ken told Bella that there would be shifts starting at eight that would involve multiple people from multiple agencies. "You might hear a drone overhead, but it's a friendly. They will try not to disturb you. Andrew is going to come and tell you when you should answer the phone. You can call out anytime you want. Just know that there will be people listening."

"I'll just imagine it's like my childhood when we had a party line. Someone was always listening." She laughed.

Chad was careful as he drove down the mountain. He navigated the switchbacks with ease while listening to Nora's CD. She sang, ". . . but I can't help falling in love with you." He reached the bottom of the road and stopped at the intersection with Route 54. As he was about to turn right to go to the Valley Store, three vehicles boxed him.

CHAPTER 24

Few places in this world are more dangerous than home.
Fear not, therefore, to try the mountain passes.

John Muir 1838 – 1914

Stepping Out

SAM GAVE DIRECTIONS TO ELLIOTT as he drove up to the mountain park. They pulled onto the flat, and Sam turned to Sandy, the female SBI agent. "This rock was a place where the members of the native tribe and the European descendants came together about seventy years ago in a celebration of community. Mind you, not all members of either community were willing to participate in the first public powwow, but enough came that over the years it has grown so large we can no longer hold it here. It's a county park now, but for the members of my tribe, we still consider this rock a sacred place, and we are grateful it has served as a meeting place for our community."

"Do you still have powwows?"

"Yes, we do. In fact, this year's will start at the end of next week. Hope you can come."

Sandy nodded. "If I'm off, I will. Thanks."

Elliott got out of the SUV and opened the door for Quinn. "Have you been up here, Quinn?"

"No. I'm always happy to learn about a new place to take in the world around me."

Bill Michaels, the FBI agent, stepped out and turned around in a circle. "Wow, this is like being *on top* of the world. I mostly see the mountains driving on I-40."

Elliott half-sang, half-said, "On top of Old Smoky, all covered . . ."

Sam looked around the group. "Welcome to the land before it was America."

Everyone nodded and clustered around Elliott. "I'm asking each of you to walk away from the rest of the group. With your back to the center of this rock, look out, think about what we are here to do, and discard any notions you have of the exclusivity of your agency. We are all sworn to uphold the Constitution and the laws of this nation. That is what we are here to do. I will come and invite you to return to the SUVs, and we will drive back to the station in silence. Please disperse."

Each of the six walked away from Elliott in a different direction. The rock, which was above the park area, was about forty feet in diameter and fairly flat. The silence was deafening once the footfalls stopped.

Sam wondered how much of the silence the city folks could take. Minutes ticking by can be an eternity if you're not accustomed to the silence of the mountains. It can take a long time to begin to take in the unique sounds of nature, such as the rustle of the last leaves of autumn hitting the ground and crunching under the feet of the many animals that called this wilderness home: the white-tailed deer, the black bear, the red and gray fox, and the ever-present birds, including the eastern towhee singing their lovely call of "drink-your-tea, drink-your-tea."

Sam knew that he, Sylvia, and Elliott would bask in it. He also felt grateful to be included. He wondered if Elliott knew that he was officially on medical leave from the DEA.

Ralph looked out over the expanse of the mountain range. He was proud to be the special agent in charge for the Knoxville branch of the SBI. Normally, he was the one in charge of operations, but he realized now that Assistant Director Elliott Nelson, as chief administrative officer, was here because it was home for him. He also knew they had been closing in on Zimmerman, and it was clear the other agencies were on the same mission. He hoped they could snare him and put him out of operation, but he wondered why it took a threat to a small-town sheriff—he chuckled, realizing you couldn't really call the valley a town—to bring agencies together.

Quinn picked a spot where she could see the valley. She wanted to remind herself that the lives that had been lived in these hills for hundreds of years were hers to protect just as much as the more visible ones in the cities and towns across the country. *And that includes the ones who arrived here illegally.* Although her input related solely to the immigration violations, she knew the ultimate goal was to get Zimmerman and anyone else who was involved. She wondered how much overlapping information each agency had, and what might be missing that could prove to the linchpin to this case.

Sylvia was at home on this rock, in this land of mountains shrouded in haze, covered in the evergreens that gave them color year-round, as well as the sugar maple, majestic oaks, and towering ash. She wept for the fir trees that were being eradicated by an insect brought by Europeans in the early 1900s. She wondered when people would learn that the earth is theirs to protect. Chad Oliver and his family, along with Bella, were hers to protect at this moment. She had a renewed respect for Elliott Nelson. That he would make the time to bring this little team of people from across local, state, and national agencies together in this way was impressive. It gave her hope for a swift resolution to the immediate menace, and perhaps it would be the first step towards sharing information across all of the agencies.

Sandy had felt a connection to Dr. Anderson as soon as she met her. As an SBI agent, she admired Bella's matter-of-fact way of dealing with the questions she had needed to ask. On the way back to the station from Drellag Caban, she realized Bella reminded her of her favorite professor in college. They were both smart women who knew their stuff and didn't hide it, but they didn't flaunt it either.

That's who she wanted to be. This case might just be her opportunity to show the Assistant Director of the SBI what she could do. She struck a yoga pose without realizing she was doing it. She had lifted her leg behind her in the Natarajasana—Lord of the Dance—pose when she heard Elliott speak to her softly. She was embarrassed and almost fell when she heard his voice.

"Agent, I picked you for this team, and I need your help to wrap up this case. I am counting on your ability to bring a hyperfocus to the not-so-obvious things that others miss. Please return to the SUV." She nodded her head and walked to the SUV.

Elliott went to each of the people on the rock and highlighted their contribution: to Ralph—his organizational skills, to Sylvia—her knowledge of Chad and the community, to Sam—his knowledge of the inner workings of the local DEA and the potential of SAC Mc-Mullen's involvement with Zimmerman, to Bill Michaels—his extensive knowledge of all the FBI had on Zimmerman, to Quinn—her well-earned reputation for being a team player and understanding the power of uniting a team. Elliott was actually excited to see if they could pull this off—Chad's life might depend on it.

Drellag Caban

Nora had just finished monitoring Mac's bath, and he went to pick out which book he wanted to read. "Bella, it's so nice to have him at this age and have his bath be something more than a time for getting clean. He loves to splash in the water with his toys. I hope he didn't make too big a mess in your bathroom."

"Don't worry about it. I'm so thrilled that we can be together, and somehow..." She stopped and looked at Nora. "Somehow it makes this time more intimate for the mutual concern we have for your dad."

"Daddy will be fine. If my family wasn't motivation enough for him to be safe, you certainly are."

Bella flushed then stepped over to Nora and hugged her. The

two women stood clinging to each other until Mac tugged on Nora's jeans.

"Mommy, don't you want Miss Bella to be your mommy?"

"What?" Nora wasn't sure she heard him correctly.

"You know, if Grandpa marries Miss Bella and is my grandma, then she's your mommy like my grandpa is your daddy."

The two women stared at the four-year-old, then they looked at each other.

Bella picked up Mac. "Precious Mac, if only the adult world were so simple. Do you remember at the jamboree when we first met?"

"Yes. I remember meeting you, Miss Bella."

"Do you remember your grandpa telling you we are friends?"

"Yes." His head was cocked to the side as he looked at her.

"Then you told us that your mommy and daddy are married and best friends."

"They are. Aren't you, Mommy?"

"We are, Mac."

Bella smiled. "So, adults become friends first, and then sometimes they become really good friends, and then sometimes they decide they want to spend the rest of their lives with that friend. But people can be friends and not be married. Do you understand that?"

"Sure, I have a best friend, but I don't think I will marry him."

Nora hugged the two of them, and the threesome stood rocking while the two women chuckled.

"My very special son, it's time to read your book, say your prayers, and get to sleep. What book did you choose?"

Bella walked Mac into the bedroom and put him on the bed. "May I read your book to you tonight, Mac?"

"Please, Miss Bella. It'll be fun." He handed her one of his favorite books, *On the Day You Were Born* by Debra Frasier.

Bella sat on the side of the bed. "Do you say your prayers first?"

"Yes. It's okay, right, Mommy?"

"Yes, Mac."

"God bless Mommy and Daddy and Lilly and Grandpa and Grandmother Mary and Miss Bella and all the people on the earth. Send Jesus to watch over us. Amen."

"Amen," the two women said.

"On the eve of your birth. . ." Bella began reading.

Nora watched her son as he curled up and put his hand on Bella's leg. Nora had tears in her eyes. Her own mother, Mac's Grandmother Mary, had never read him a story. Yet here was a woman who welcomed them into her home, wanted them to be safe, and, most of all, offered them unconditional love. She understood why her daddy had fallen in love with Bella. It was easy.

"We are so glad you've come!" Bella read the last line of the book with enthusiasm. She saw that Mac was sound asleep. She leaned over, kissed his cheek, and tucked his arm under the covers. "I'm glad you've come to my home, Mac." She turned to see Nora wiping tears from her eyes.

Bella pulled up the side rails carefully to avoid waking Mac. The second one clicked into place without him stirring. She walked over to hug Nora and whispered, "Time for a glass of wine, my friend."

"Time for a glass of wine." Nora looked at Bella and hoped that she would be another mother for her. They walked into the kitchen.

"Thanks for cleaning up, Nora. Let's go sit by the fire."

Closing Up

"Joshua? Are you upstairs?" He didn't answer. It was almost seven and they had been quite busy for a Wednesday night, but she could have sworn that Joshua went to his office. She didn't see any cars in the parking lot, so she locked the front door and took the cash drawers upstairs to start closing them out. He wasn't there.

"Ouch. Stupid box cutter." There was a clatter as he dropped the cutter on the floor.

Carla grabbed the first aid kit and hurried downstairs. She found him in the canned goods aisle trying to stanch the flow of blood.

She took a rubber band she had grabbed off the desk and quickly wrapped it around the base of his finger as a makeshift tourniquet. "Let's get to the back."

He held his hand up as they quickly walked to the storeroom sink. After stopping the blood, she wrapped his finger in gauze and taped it tightly.

"That should do it, Carla. Thanks. I haven't done something that stupid in a month of Sundays."

"Accidents happen. Just wish it hadn't happened to you. Did your hand slip?"

"No. I was distracted. I glanced at my watch and saw it was almost seven and Chad hadn't stopped by yet."

"Oh, yeah. We got so busy I completely forgot he was coming. Should you call him?"

"I think we'll wrap up things here and see if he shows up. He may have gotten detained on some case. His life is a lot less predictable than ours."

"Well, I for one like an adventure, but I like predictability more."

He leaned against the wall and put his arm around Carla. "Shall we have pizza at my place?"

"Works for me. How about you gather what you want, and I'll finish that box you were working on. I'll come in early tomorrow and help you stock. I think that finger is going to hurt a lot more than you realize. But wait, what about Chad?"

"If we're not here, he'll call or come by. I always know I can count on him to do what he says he will, even when he can't always make the time on the dot. Although I have to say, I can't ever remember a time he didn't call if he was going to be late."

By 7:15 p.m., Joshua finished with the cash drawer and had food ready to take home for their dinner. He dialed Chad's personal mobile phone number, but there was no answer. Carla was waiting for him at the door. "I don't call his work number when it's personal. And since I don't know what he wanted, let's just go. He knows where to find me."

"Fine with me, my soon-to-be husband."

He stopped and looked at her. "Did you say 'soon-to-be?' Does that mean you've made a decision about when we'll get married?"

She stood on her tiptoes and kissed him. "Time enough for that talk over pizza and a beer. Let's go home." Carla had spent a lot of time thinking about where they would live; she had a plan in mind but hadn't talked to him about it yet. She found she liked calling Joshua's cabin "home."

Joshua grinned from ear to ear. He did not miss Carla's comment: *Let's go home.* He liked the sound of that.

They walked out to their cars. After closing Carla's driver door behind her and watching her pull out, Joshua walked to his own car, looking forward to the day they would go home in one vehicle. The drive to his cabin was short; he pulled in the garage and Carla parked on the apron. As he waited on her to walk into the kitchen ahead of him, he was surprised by what she said.

"Oh, I forgot to tell you that the ad you put in the Round City Gazette got three calls today for people wanting to see Jan's car. They're coming tomorrow, so you can drive it to the store and I'll bring you home. Will that work?"

"Thanks, Carla. Thanks for handling that. I appreciate it."

"Happy to help." She smiled up at him. He put down the food and beer and pulled her into a passionate kiss. His mobile phone rang. They ignored it for a moment.

Carla pulled away. "Oh, my goodness. See if it's Chad."

He saw that the number was the sheriff's station. "Let me call back."

"Listen to the message first. Maybe he said what time he'd be by."

"Joshua, this is Sylvia Whitehorse. The sheriff said he was stopping to see you. Is he there?"

"That's odd." Joshua and Carla looked at each other. Joshua's eyes showed concern. "It's not like Chad for no one to know where he is. I'll call Bella."

"Good idea."

He dialed the phone at Drellag Caban, and the answering machine clicked on immediately. "Drellag Caban, please leave a message."

"Bella, this is Joshua. Have you seen Chad? He was supposed to come see me at six forty-five and didn't show up. Apparently, they're looking for him at the station too. Call me back as soon as you get this." He had no way of knowing that his call was not being answered in Drellag Caban.

CHAPTER 25

Split Second Decisions

Chad slowed but did not take his foot off the gas pedal as he assessed the situation. His Ford Interceptor would hit sixty miles an hour in 5.7 seconds, and he could hit speeds of 150 mph, although Route 54 was not the place to do that. As sheriff, his car had special glass even beyond the others in their fleet. It would take a rocket launcher to take him out. Of course, the trucks could have one for all he knew. All three were black and modern, likely with their own special equipment.

A bullhorn sounded. "Stop the vehicle, now."

Chad continued to roll, tap the brakes, roll. He scanned the SUVs, trying to see through his own darkened glass into their darkened glass.

"Stop the vehicle now. This is the DEA. You are commanded to stop."

Well, well, well. Welcome to my valley, boys. What misinformation did SAC McMullen give you that brings three of you to call on me? You must have a junior agent on my left flank because I can push through him faster than a bullet headed for quail. Chad had the advantage because he knew the roads like the back of his hand. He knew exactly how long it would take him to get to his station and that's where he was headed.

He pushed the button for his secure phone to dial the station.

"Boss, where are you?"

"Open gate: ETA two minutes. Only let one vehicle chase me through if they can make it happen. SWAT to back lot, code 207a. Starting now."

Cecelia responded with a 10-69: message received. She was already talking to the gate guards and announcing the code for an officer in trouble—code 999 rang throughout the station. She knew a 207a was a kidnapping in progress, but she couldn't imagine anyone trying to kidnap Sheriff Oliver. "SWAT to yard, SWAT to yard." Boots could be heard running through the building.

Sweet Dreams

Bella had listened attentively to Andrew when he explained the FBI were monitoring her answering machine and would call her phone if she had a personal call. They were the only ones who could now get through, so she should pick up if her phone rang. More than anything, she wanted to call Chad before she went to sleep. But she decided he would call her if he could. "Another glass of wine, Nora?"

"No, thank you. One is my limit tonight. I want to be able to hear Mac if he calls for me. With Lilly's pack-and-play next to your bed, I will hear her with no problem. Bella, I could sleep with Mac, and you could have your own bed."

Bella leaned over and touched Nora's hand. "I'll be fine. I like sleeping on the sofa. Let's see how Mac does. If he needs you to share a bed, we'll sort it out tomorrow. Fair enough?"

"Fair enough. I'm pretty tired. How about you?"

"I think I need a shower before I fall asleep. Between the wine, the fireplace, and the great conversation, I'm ready to sleep. You go ahead."

"Then I'll tell you what. You go shower, I'll clean up these glasses and call Fred, then we can sing a song to Mac and Lilly before we go to sleep."

Bella took a quick shower and towel dried her hair. After putting on her gown and robe, she paused for a moment and looked in the mirror. It wasn't something she did often. *Where are you, Chad? Please be safe for your precious family... and for me.*

"Wizard, crate." Bella was so relieved that Ken Bennett had offered to walk Wizard while they put the children to bed. Wizard stood up from his blanket, stretched, and walked to his crate. He curled up on his blanket and looked up at Bella. She reached in to scratch his ears then closed the gate. "Good night, Wizard. You're a good dog."

Nora was standing in the door to the second bedroom and turned to look at her. "Bella," she said quietly. "I like to stand in the door to Mac's room and sing. Come join me."

Bella walked over. Nora put her arm around Bella's shoulders. "Do you know 'All Through the Night?'"

"Hmmm... the Welsh lullaby?"

Nora nodded.

"My Grandmother Hazel used to sing it to me at night in that very bed."

"Sleep my child and peace attend thee, all through the night..." Nora sang softly. Bella hummed through the first stanza with her. They sang two more stanzas together and Nora returned to the first stanza. "... Soft the drowsy hours are creeping, Hill and dale in slumber sleeping, I my loved ones' watch am keeping, All through the night."

Nora dropped her arm from Bella's shoulder and walked in to kiss her son on the forehead. She appreciated that Bella had a night light for him. "I am watching over you, Mac. Love you forever."

Bella stood at the door. She hugged Nora. "Make yourself at home. My home is your home."

"Thanks, Bella. Thanks for welcoming us to Drellag Caban. I'm grateful the men and women protecting us are all outside now, but I also like knowing they're here. Daddy will make sure we're safe."

"I just pray he is."

"So do I. Every minute of every day. Sweet dreams, Bella. Thanks for coming into our lives."

"Thank you, Nora. It is you who have given me a gift. Sweet dreams. Oh, did you reach Fred?"

"Yes, he knew we were being recorded so we kept it short. This will pass soon. He's fine. Good night, Bella." She walked into Bella's bedroom and leaned into the pack-and-play to kiss Lilly. "I am watching over you, my sweet Lilly."

Bella walked back into the living room and sat on the sofa. After taking her slippers off, she tucked her feet under her and looked into the low flames of the fire. *I think this is one of the most difficult nights for my Not-So-Good List.* At the top of the list were the threatening phone calls and her worry for Chad's safety. She leaned her head against the back of the sofa as she tried to think of anything else on her Not-So-Good List. *Matt, I put my picture of our anniversary in a drawer to get the bedroom ready for Nora. Is that a bad thing?* Then she decided Matt would understand; she didn't want anything else on her Not-So-Good list tonight.

Her Good List was overflowing. Nora and the kids were here, and tomorrow they would watch her cabin go up. They were surrounded by law enforcement, so they were safe. Wizard had been a really good dog with all the changes and people in the house. She had thought of Matt when Chad told her he loved her. *Did you send him to me? He's kind and gentle like you, Matt. But he's different too. I need a sign that you're okay with what I think is happening to me.*

She thought of Chad's comments about Mac learning the difference between "may" and "can." *May I fall in love with Chad, Matt? I'm pretty sure I* can. She put her head down on her pillow. *Is there more to add to my Good List?* Deciding she could think of nothing else, she prayed that Chad was safe. It was just past eight and seemed far too early to go to bed, but she was emotionally exhausted. Her eyes drooped closed, and she was sound asleep.

Teamwork

The team drove back to the sheriff's station in silence, then they gathered in the conference room to establish ground rules for their strategy session. Each person would present information they had on County Commissioner George Zimmerman. Elliott passed around a paper bag that rustled with slips of paper. "Each of you draw a number. That is the order in which you will share your information."

"We have agreed on our ground rules. There will be no comment during the initial presentation. Discussion and clarification will only occur after the first round of information has been presented from each agency. Correct?" Elliott looked at each member of the team. Each gave a response:

"Yes."

"Yo."

"Agreed."

Ralph asked, "What if any of our evidence duplicates or corroborates another agency?"

"Present it anyway." Elliott was direct in his reply without being dogmatic.

"Who begins?" Each member of the group looked at his or her number.

"Surprise. I have number one." Elliott turned the piece of paper around for them to see. He had not planned it this way, but he was grateful he could model his expectations. He had considered telling them he'd go first, but then realized it would negate them seeing themselves as a team. He had, in fact, been the last to draw a number.

"At the executive level of the SBI, we have the following corroborated evidence specific to Zimmerman. These include multiple documented incidents of sales tax evasion as well as encroachment on endangered species habitats in the Smoky Mountains, including the northern flying squirrel, red-cockaded woodpecker, Indiana bat, and spruce-fir moss spider." He looked around the group. "Ralph will have additional evidence when it is his turn."

"I have number two." All eyes turned to Quinn. "There will be some overlap between my evidence and Sergeant Whitehorse's as part of our work involved a joint sting on the prostitution ring. I will focus on the evidence we have involving human trafficking and Zimmerman taking custody of young immigrant women who were transported across the US. We have documented evidence of multiple violations of the federal Victims of Trafficking and Violence Protection Act of 2000. Additionally, two IEA agents posing as immigrants were picked up by Zimmerman and brought to this community and the house being used." Quinn outlined additional incidents where Zimmerman was connected to two motels used for illegal purposes.

"Number three?" Elliott asked.

Bill Michaels of the FBI raised his piece of paper. "I am at liberty to present evidence we have of tax evasion, fraud, and attempted fraud across state lines involving the sale and purchase of equipment and goods for the construction of three housing developments in two states."

"I have number four." Suddenly they heard the all-call throughout the sheriff's station.

Sergeant Sylvia Whitehorse put the paper with the number 4 on the table and asked the agents to remain seated. She told them someone would come and give them directions, if needed. She left the conference room and moved quickly to the desk deputy.

"Sheriff called in a code 207a and should be coming through the back gate right about... NOW!" They both stood and watched the sheriff speed through the gate, trailing three black trucks in his wake. Right behind the second truck, the gate slid closed faster than either of them had ever seen. "Sarge, SWAT has the back and front covered, and Sergeant Eddie is at the back." He told her the directions dispatch had been given by the sheriff.

"Don't let anyone in the front door." Her voice was firm and clear.

"Yes, ma'am."

Sylvia returned to the conference room. "The sheriff called in a 207a along with instructions to open the gate to the back and close it immediately after one truck. To be honest, I didn't even know the gate could move that fast. We have vehicles blocking the other two cars in. It is my considered opinion that the sheriff is in control at the moment."

Elliott stood. "Sylvia, please go monitor the situation. We'll take a ten-minute break. If you step out of the room, please stay clear of any part of the operation being run by members of this department."

Don't Push Me

Chad knew the gate was capable of a fast closure, which was not normally used for two reasons: one, it wasn't necessary, and two, he didn't want it known that the gate could close that fast. *I guess folks now know how fast that gate can close. Good job getting just one of them through.* He was proud of his gate guard. He glimpsed the first of his SWAT team as he purposely put his SUV into a spin to be nose to nose with the incoming truck. The SWAT moved in on the truck. He thought the truck that came through was the one to his left. The one he had calculated he could get by. He couldn't wait to see how old this agent was, if he was an agent. He saw something fly out of the driver's window. He saw one SWAT member cover another as it was picked up. The object was handed off to Sergeant Eddie Douglas, who moved around the back of Chad's SUV and came up on the driver's side.

Chad rolled his window down. "Good maneuver. What did he give us?"

The sergeant handed him a plastic-coated card. Chad read: Agent Chuck Dixon, Drug Enforcement Agency, U.S. Justice Department.

"Invite him to step out of his truck."

"Put him on the ground, Sheriff?"

"Not if he follows directions. But otherwise don't hesitate."

The deputy ran back around Chad's SUV and took the bullhorn. He called out, "Exit your truck with your hands locked behind your head. Exit now."

Chad saw enough headlights on the other side of the gate to know that his deputies had the trucks boxed in between them and the closed gate. *My folks will be talking about this for the rest of their lives. I pray this is the worst emergency situation we ever have.*

The truck door eased open, and the man put his hands up over the truck door. As he exited, he called out. "I am Agent Chuck Dixon of the DEA in the lawful execution of a warrant for the arrest of Sheriff Chad Oliver."

"Hands behind your head, NOW!"

The agent complied. Two deputies moved in quickly and had the man's hands behind his back and cuffed within seconds. It wasn't until he was cuffed that Chad stepped out of his SUV. He saw the other two agents remained in their trucks outside the gate. *That's just fine, boys. We're going in the building and then my folks will invite you to park your trucks and join us.*

He told one of the deputies to open the walk-through gate for the other agents once he was inside the building. Once he was about six feet from the agent inside the gate, Chad spoke. "Welcome to our valley, Agent. Please come into our station, and I will be happy to discuss what your needs are at this moment." Chad said nothing more. He walked toward the back of the sheriff's station and scanned his card. He buzzed the desk. "Please admit our guest and the two to follow."

What's Your Pleasure?

Joshua had turned on the oven as soon as they entered the kitchen and put the pizza stone in to warm up. When he turned, Carla was standing directly behind him.

She threw her arms around his neck, although they barely reached. She measured in at five foot eight, but his six-foot-four-inch frame was tall even for her. She gave him a passionate kiss. "I've waited all day to do that."

"Then do it again," Joshua encouraged. They stood holding each other until Carla stepped back and looked up at him.

"Let's get married."

"Tonight?"

"Okay, maybe we can't do it tonight, but let's not put it off."

"What do you want for a wedding?"

"You." She looked at him with so much love in her eyes, he almost fell back against the counter.

"I meant what kind of wedding do you want to have?"

"Let's just ask Pastor Fisk to marry us, and then we can celebrate at a jamboree. I've waited all my life for you. I don't wait to plan some fancy something. We can have whoever you want there. The one person I care about being there besides you is James."

Joshua hugged her and said, "Carla, Carla, Carla. We can go get married tomorrow morning as far as I'm concerned."

"Good. Then it's settled. Let's put on the pizza, grab a beer, and light the fireplace. Then we can make the final decisions."

He smiled at her. "Yes, ma'am. You've got it."

Your Choice

Chad walked to the conference room where he knew the team was meeting. The young DEA agent followed him. Suddenly Chad stopped. He didn't know if Sam was in the room and he didn't want to disclose him to this man. Sylvia was walking towards them.

"Sergeant Whitehorse..."

"Evening, Sheriff. Visitors?"

"Yes. I believe this is Agent Dixon of the DEA. Seems he has a warrant for my arrest."

"That so?"

"We're going down to my office. Please ask Elliott to join us." Chad doubted that Agent Dixon knew who Elliott was. That's just how he wanted it at the moment.

"Agent Dixon, anything our sergeant can get you to drink?" Chad wished he had a photo of the bewildered look on the agent's face as he shook his head. "No? Okay. We try to be hospitable around here. Please follow me." Chad opened his office door, turned on the light, and pointed to the round table. "Two more with you, are there? Just want to make sure we have enough seats."

The DEA agent stared at Chad. He had never even imagined such a scenario, much less expected to be in one. "Yes, there are two more."

"Good. We'll wait for them to join us." He turned as Elliott walked in. "Elliott, sorry it took me a while to get back here. Elliott, this is Agent Dixon of the DEA. Agent Dixon, this is Elliott."

"Pleased to meet you." Elliott extended his hand as he moved toward a chair. The agent shook it, but the look on his face made Chad think he might need a camera in his office just for the sheer entertainment of times like these. Then he realized he never wanted another time like this... this was not about him. It was about what was being done to his family... and Bella.

"Sheriff," Sylvia Whitehorse appeared in the door. "Here are our other guests. They have been offered water or coffee; both declined."

"Thank you, Sergeant. Please join us."

He looked at the man and woman who entered as Sylvia stepped back. "Welcome. If you'd be so kind, I'd like to see your identification." Both showed their IDs, indicating they were DEA agents. "Fine, fine. Have a seat." He and Sylvia sat.

"We are here in the execution of a lawful warrant for your arrest, Chad Oliver." The female agent stated.

"That's Sheriff Oliver." Chad's voice was flat, his gray eyes as hard as steel, and his face like granite. Chad extended his hand. Finally, the woman, who Chad assumed was the lead agent, handed him the warrant. He was familiar with warrants, so he went immediately to the name of the judge. As Chad expected, it was a federal judge.

With no introduction of Elliott, Chad looked at him. "Elliott, do you know this judge?"

Elliott looked at the warrant. He nodded.

"Mind giving her a call? Before I surrender on this warrant, I just want to make sure it's legitimate."

The lead agent sputtered, "You can't do that."

Chad ignored her. "Feel free to use the phone on my desk."

"Thanks, Sheriff. I'll use my own. I can put it on speaker if needed." Elliott dialed a number that was clearly stored in his phone. "Judge Warren. Hey, it's Elliott. Sorry to call so late. May I have a minute?"

The three DEA agents stared at him.

"I'm with Sheriff Chad Oliver and three DEA agents who have presented us with a warrant for Sheriff Oliver's arrest showing your name and signature. Just need to verify it before I turn this fine man over to them." Elliott listened. He raised his eyebrows and his eyes feigned shock. He said, "Really? You never issued such a warrant? Why, Judge, I think these agents might want to verify that directly with you. How would you suggest we do that? Yes, ma'am!"

He handed his phone to the lead agent. She took it.

"Agent Perry, DEA, speaking." The woman listened. "ID 7493251, ma'am. Yes, ma'am." She listened again. "Special Agent in Charge McMullen, ma'am." Her eyes narrowed at whatever the judge told her.

Chad watched her the entire time. *So, the penny dropped. She now knows her boss is a crook.*

"Yes, ma'am. Here he is." She handed the phone back to Elliott and sat stone-faced.

"Judge, how may I be of service? Uh-huh, yes. Well, actually I have an FBI agent in the next room. I'm sure he can make a call and have that happen. Will do. Thank you, Judge. Sorry to interrupt your evening." He hung up the phone then turned to Chad and said, "She and my wife are sorority sisters." He smiled at the agents.

"Agents, may I introduce Assistant Director Elliott Nelson, head of the Knoxville office of the State Bureau of Investigation. Sergeant, will you please get the FBI agent?" Sylvia stood and walked out.

Chad's secure phone rang. He always answered it. "Oliver here." He hung up. "Agent Isaacs will accompany Agent Michaels." The three DEA agents looked at each other.

Sylvia came through the door first and handed Elliott a fax. Quinn and the FBI agent, Bill Michaels, followed. Introductions were made and everyone sat. Chad noticed the perplexed look on Agent Perry's face that an Immigration Enforcement agent was here. Elliott passed the fax across to the lead DEA agent.

"Please read it aloud, if you don't mind, Agent Perry."

In a voice trembling with rage—at least Chad assumed it had to be rage—she started reading from the top. Her tone was icy as she read, "...for the arrest of SAC Carl McMullen of the DEA on charges of perpetrating a false arrest, forging the signature of a federal judge, and other charges yet to be named."

When she finished, she turned to Chad. "Sir, it is with deep regret that we assumed the legitimacy of this warrant and, I might add to all those present, followed the directions of SAC McMullen to execute said warrant away from your station to ensure success in said false arrest." Her shoulders stayed rigid and her gaze firm.

Chad actually felt sorry for her. "Agent Perry, you are free to make whatever calls you need to make to verify the copy of the warrant you have just seen."

"It's not necessary, sir. The judge gave me information that satisfies me she was who she said she was."

"Really? How?" Chad realized he sounded like a curious small-town sheriff but didn't care. It might be a skill he needed someday.

"After I gave her my ID, she told me to wait. I could hear her on a keyboard. She immediately listed five cases in which I had been before her as the primary arresting agent. She's who she said she was."

FBI Agent Michaels spoke at last. "Prior to entering this room, I spoke with my boss, and he had just received the warrant and FBI agents are on their way to arrest SAC McMullen. As soon as we're notified he's in custody, you'll be free to go." The three agents nodded.

"Sergeant, would you please take our guests to the conference room and see what you can do to make them comfortable while they wait?"

"Yessir." The agents rose and followed Sylvia out without a word.

As soon as the door closed, Quinn spoke. "I received word just before we came in that Zimmerman was arrested by our agents who were following him as he tried to cross into Canada from Michigan. We have enough to hold him on immigration violation charges and, from what I've heard so far, I'm sure there will be more charges from the FBI's work. So, for my part, gentlemen, I think we should let this fine man get back to taking care of his family and Dr. Anderson and this amazing community where he keeps getting re-elected as sheriff."

"May it remain true for years to come," Elliott chimed in.

"I'm new to the area," Michaels said, "but you have my vote… if I could." He smiled. They all stood, shook hands with Chad, and walked out. Chad sat in his office chair and picked up his phone.

Bella's phone went to the answering machine. He knew who was listening. "Agents, this is Sheriff Oliver. Please put me through to Dr. Anderson."

CHAPTER 26

Teach us love, compassion, and honor
that we may heal the Earth and heal each other.
Ojibwe Proverb

The Phone Call

THE RINGING PHONE STARTLED BELLA AND NORA awake at the same time. Wizard sat up in his crate as Bella hurried to answer it, hoping the noise wouldn't wake the children. "Bella Anderson speaking." Nora hovered at the edge of the kitchen, waiting to see what the call would bring.

"I don't think I've ever heard you answer the phone with your name before."

"Chad! Are you all right? Where are you?" Bella was shaking, more from her concern for Chad than the chill that had settled on the kitchen.

"Hello, lovely lady. I'm at the station and I'm fine. You and Nora and the kids are fine now too."

Bella looked at Nora, smiled, and motioned her over.

"I'm so glad you're okay. Nora is standing right here with me. No speaker phone so we're both listening on the handset." Nora put her arm around Bella.

"Too much to tell you on the phone. Big break in the case and we're all going to be fine. I have a number of things to wrap up here at the station, so I'll get that done. You will still have protection through the night, and we'll make final decisions tomorrow."

"Oh, Daddy, I'm so glad you're okay. We're fine here too. Bella has been amazing."

"I know she is. Hope she's still listening." There was cheerfulness in his voice. "Kids okay?"

"Sound asleep. They even got a duet for their sleep lullaby."

"That's great, sweetheart. That's great! I'll talk to you tomorrow, Nora. Okay?"

"Okay, Daddy. Here's Bella." She could tell he wanted a private word with Bella.

"Chad, I'm so relieved to know you're safe. I can hear it in your voice. We're fine."

"I can hear it in your voice too. What time is that Lincoln Log show in the morning?"

It took Bella a moment to realize he meant the new cabin. "Oh, Arthur said they would begin about ten o'clock. Can you come?"

"Count on it. What time's breakfast up on that mountain?"

"Any time you want."

"I'll be there by eight thirty." He sounded like a schoolboy on a first date. "And, dear Bella, I meant what I said. I love you."

"I love you too, Chad." She felt the goosebumps rising on her arms; she knew she meant it.

Nora had sat down on the arm of the living room sofa trying not to intrude, but the truth was you could hear anywhere in the cabin. She started clapping. "Woohoo!"

Bella turned and looked at Nora and grinned.

"I can hear my daughter. I think that she's saying she loves you too. Sweet dreams, my Bella. See you in the morning."

"Stay safe, Chad. We'll see you in the morning. Love you."

"Love you more than you love me."

"It cannot be."

Bella hung up the phone and turned to see Nora with tears running down her face. She reached out and embraced Bella. They stood hugging.

Bella stepped back. "Let's have a cup of tea by the fire." Bella moved towards the stove.

Nora moved towards the fridge. "Oh no, special lady. A glass of wine."

The two women sat on the sofa, pulled their feet up under them, and Nora made a toast. "Here's to all of us being safe and with enough love to heal all that ails us. Cheers."

"Cheers to that!"

Clearing the Sheriff's Station

Sylvia was walking towards Chad as he exited his office. Chad turned around and walked right back in. He saw it was already 9:00 p.m. Sylvia stopped at the door, and Chad gestured her in but held up a finger for her to wait a moment. He tapped out a text to Joshua: "Too late to run by?" He put his phone down and looked up at his sergeant.

"What's up, Sylvia?"

"All of our visitors are in the conference room waiting for you. Before we go, though, I had word from the highway patrol on the four-car accident on Route 54."

A text popped up from Joshua. "Anytime."

"And?" Chad returned to full sheriff mode.

"Mrs. King is going to make it."

"Thank God."

"Indeed, sir. They also shared their preliminary report based on the vehicles' positions, braking distance, et cetera, as well as the background checks on everyone involved. Long story short, they have enough evidence to arrest one of the drivers."

"Mrs. Zimmerman?"

"No. A male from Michigan who has a rap sheet including attempted vehicular homicide and crash-for-cash scams. They are on a lead that may well tie this man back to *Mr.* Zimmerman. Apparently, there is a sizable accidental death insurance policy on Mrs. Zimmerman payable to Mr. Zimmerman. I'm not sure what else they have, but I've informed the SBI and FBI agents in our conference room."

He looked at her. "Thanks for the update. I want a meeting of our leadership team on Monday morning of next week. Would you please organize it? We need to be ready for the powwow. I also plan to make some changes around here with your help." His gaze was warm and sincere.

"I'll organize the meeting. Anything else?"

"Well, let's not keep our guests waiting." He put his hand out and gave her a strong handshake. They walked down the hall side by side.

He walked in the room and everyone stood. "Please, we only do formal when it makes things more efficient." He looked around the table and everyone had something to drink. He grabbed a bottle of water and sat. The first thing he did was look straight at Sam and nod. Sam nodded back.

Elliott began. "Chad, we will take this multi-agency case back to the city and leave you to this unique community in our hills. We will leave the agents in place for tonight. Agent Michaels heard from the FBI, and they expect to arrest the person who made the calls anytime now. He was on a list of suspects linked to Zimmerman. Once he's in custody, we'll remove the agents at your homes, and the ones on Dr. Anderson's home in North Carolina and her house sitter. That should occur tomorrow morning. The DEA agents here with us are all now aware of the arrest of SAC McMullen, which occurred about five minutes ago. I have given these agents my assurance that I'll be available to speak to their superiors regarding their actions in carrying out a directive from a direct supervisor."

"Me too!" It was echoed by Sylvia, Bill Michaels, and Quinn Isaacs. Sam sat silently.

Chad nodded. "I would like to commend all three of you for the lawful execution of a directive, and I would be honored to speak to your professionalism, even though I was the target. Thank you for not drawing your weapons on me."

Agent Perry looked at him. "Sir, we appreciate your offer. We'd also like to convey our admiration; your actions in getting us into your station were slick. We'd like lessons."

Everyone at the table laughed.

"Anytime, Agent Perry."

He looked at the group.

"If the actions of all here are any indication, I have hope that you will become a model for interagency cooperation. Thank you."

"Right!"

"For sure!"

Assurances were heard around the table.

"If that's all you need from me, you're welcome to our conference room. I'm the sheriff of a small community, and I'm already late in delivering a plea deal acceptance to the victim's son. Please excuse me."

They all stood and reached out their hands to shake with Chad.

Elliott said, "I'll talk to you soon."

Then Chad reached Sam. He saw the relief in Sam's eyes.

"I'm going to talk to Joshua. Then, if you have time, I'd like to meet you at my home. I'm still waiting on that phone call from last night." He winked. "I need something to eat and a beer."

"I'll be waiting at your place."

"Good night, folks."

Chad stopped on his way out to commend his dispatcher.

"Cecelia, good job! You may have saved my life. I have a leadership team meeting on Monday morning at eight thirty and I'd like you there. If you're scheduled to be on, please arrange for someone else to cover."

"Yessir." She smiled as she looked up at him and answered a call. "Nine-one-one, what is your emergency?"

Clearing the Path

Chad walked out the back door, got in his SUV, and drove through the now open gate. As he pulled into Joshua's driveway, he saw Carla's car. He took the front steps two at a time, and the front door opened before he hit the porch.

"Sorry, Joshua. Evening, Carla. Had a little unexpected activity tonight and couldn't call. Hope it's not too late."

"Never. Get you something to drink?"

"I'm good, Joshua. Thanks." Chad sat on the armchair that flanked the end of the sofa where Carla and Joshua sat. He leaned in towards Joshua. "Peggy O'Haire spoke with you before we met with the Kirk boys, right?"

"Yes. She told me about the deal she was going to offer them. She told me my rights, but they don't really matter to me. There is nothing that's going to bring back my dad. He would want me and the community to heal. I know now those boys didn't go there with the intention of hurting us; that helps a little."

"I'm not here to defend their actions, Joshua. They committed multiple crimes, including aggravated assault resulting in the loss of your father." He did not want to drag this out.

"Peggy explained all that." Joshua was somber and soft-spoken.

"We met with each of the boys earlier today, and each accepted the plea deal. They have left our county and will held in Round City until the judge has an opening on the docket to hear their plea."

"Will they get help, Chad?"

Chad looked at Carla who, until now, had been sitting quietly and holding Joshua's hand.

"I assume they will be sent to Bledsoe. The folks there have programs to teach them a trade, and we can hope they will take advantage of it. I want you to know that the boys expressed remorse. I believe them."

"Then it's done. Now Carla and I have something to ask."

"Sure, anything." Chad looked from one to the other.

"We're going to get married as soon as Pastor Fisk can do it. We'd like you and Bella to be there with James, Harold, and Julie."

"Wouldn't miss it for the world. Tell me where and when. I think I can speak for Bella that she wouldn't miss it either." Chad stood and hugged Carla, then turned and gave Joshua a bear hug. "I'm happy for both of you. I'll leave you to your evening. Talk to you soon." He walked to the door.

Carla and Joshua followed him and stood in the doorway with their arms around each other, waving as Chad drove away. He was home in seven minutes. He hit the button for his garage door, then saw Sam leaning on a cane and talking with a woman who he assumed was the SBI agent guarding his house. He stepped out and walked toward them.

"Chad Oliver. Welcome to our community."

The agent introduced herself. "Director Elliott called and said to leave once you were home. I'll wish you a good evening, Sheriff."

"Same to you. Thanks for protecting my home. Drive safely."

"Come in, Sam." Chad headed toward the kitchen door. "Something to drink?"

"Iced tea, if you have it."

"Two iced teas, coming up. Too chilly for you on my back deck?"

"I'd welcome the view of the mountains and some crisp air to clear my head."

Chad grabbed one the veggie trays he kept in the fridge, and they walked out to the deck.

After discussing Sam's wound and the latest threat to it from the fall on the mountain, Sam turned to look at Chad. "I'm not excusing myself for following orders without talking to you and Quinn. I should have told you my orders and then you could decide. . . . no, we could have decided the best course of action. I now suspect that Carl McMullen had a hand in arming those men."

"Were they DEA agents?" There was angst in Chad's voice. He was the one who had killed both of them.

"No, they were informants, clearly being used by McMullen. That said, I know the weight of carrying a life you have taken, criminal or not. I carry the weight with you and pray you will forgive me."

"You have my forgiveness. What I need is for you to forgive yourself. You're one of the finest minds I know in law enforcement, and it has become pretty clear to me that I can't wish away the drugs that will find their way into our valley and hills. So, I need you and a good DEA SAC to work with me."

"Hate to tell you, but I have some intel that we're going to be facing some real risk of drugs moving through at the powwow next week. I need you too."

Chad stared at him. "I need twenty-four to forty-eight hours to make up some important time to Nora, Fred, and the kids. And, most of all, to Bella. I also expect I'll be at a wedding before our jamboree on Friday night."

Sam whooped. "Yippee! Yours?"

"Whoa, boy. Slow down. Not saying I'm not interested, but this is Joshua and Carla."

"Good for them."

"Can the information I need on the drug intel wait a couple of days? If you can talk to Sylvia and get her up to speed, I'll catch up by Saturday."

"Fair enough. Now, I need to go make amends with Quinn." Sam looked apologetic.

"Someday you'll have to tell me how you let her go. Any chance for reconciliation?"

"Nope, the chemistry just isn't there. Friends for life, I hope. But... well, I've got a pretty good idea she might have her sights on your lead detective."

"Billy? Well, that would be fine with me too. He's due back in town tomorrow."

"Pretty sure he's here."

"What?"

"I don't think Quinn meant to use his name when she took the call while we were waiting for you in the conference room, but she did. I'm good with it. I like him. Now, I'm going to leave you to your family and Bella, and I'll talk to you in a few days." Sam stood, using the cane for support. "Thanks, Chad. More than you know. And, in case I never told you, I want to be just like you when I grow up."

Chad slapped him on the back. "Afraid that's not possible, but you can take any good I may have passed on and make it your own. Glad you're my friend."

"Me too." Chad watched Sam take the stairs carefully then drive off in his SUV.

Chad walked straight to the bathroom, stripped down, and took a shower. When he stepped out, he realized how chilly the cabin had become. He saw he had left the doors open to the deck. After closing them, he grabbed a beer and walked into the living room. He sank into his recliner.

Normally his thoughts would go to pending cases; he still had to figure out what was happening with the poisoned wildlife and make sure to check on the King family. He was glad Mrs. King was going to make it. Then he'd have to deal with the information Sam had about drugs at next week's powwow. But he would not dwell on them tonight. He was going to bask in the four simple words from Bella. "I love you too." He leaned his head back, sipped his Fat Tire ale, and let out a contented sigh.

Morning Brings a Cabin

Nora heard Mac calling her. Bella beat her to the door. "Morning, Nora. Please, go ahead. I was hoping to get to him so you could sleep."

"You go, Bella. I think he will be thrilled to see you first thing in the morning."

Bella walked in the room. "Morning, Mac. Did you sleep well?"

"Snug as a bug in a rug, Miss Bella." He stretched his arms up to her and yawned. "Sorry. I yawned in your face."

"Apology accepted. Ready to get up?" As she reached over to lower the railings to the bed, he leaned towards her and gave her a hug. She almost melted. She had never known the joy of a child waking and giving her a hug. She hugged him tightly and set him down on the floor. "Big day today."

"I know. I know. Lincoln Logs making your cabin." He saw his mother standing in the doorway. "Mommy." He fast walked over to her. She bent down and picked him up.

"Morning, my special boy."

"Mommy, I'm your only boy."

She chuckled as she set Mac back on the ground. She knew he heard her tell her daddy the same thing about being his only child. "That you are. Let's get your face washed and get dressed. Grandpa and Daddy are coming up to watch the cabin logs go up."

He jumped up and down. "Really, Mommy? Really?"

"Really. Now let's see if we can let Lilly—" Too late.

"Ma-ma." Lilly's sweet voice called.

There was a knock at the back door. Bella turned, expecting Arthur, but saw Chad instead. She ran to the door, unlocked it, and flung it open. Chad went through the doorway and enveloped Bella in a bear hug. Mac came running to the door.

"Grandpa, Grandpa." Chad kissed Bella and they kept one arm around each other and turned to welcome Mac into a group hug. Fred knocked on the kitchen door.

"Morning, folks." Nora went right to him, and they hugged each other. Mac and Lilly joined in.

Forty-five minutes later they had finished breakfast, and Mac and Lilly were playing in front of the fire. The adults stayed at the kitchen table. Chad gave them a thumbnail sketch of the arrests of the DEA SAC McMullen, Zimmerman, and the man who made the threatening calls. "I still don't know how Mrs. Zimmerman's accident may play into this—and that happened in my jurisdiction. Handled by the highway patrol, yes, but still my jurisdiction. It isn't over yet."

"What I don't understand, Daddy, is if the SBI, FBI, DEA, and whatever other agencies knew so much, why hadn't they already arrested Zimmerman and these others?"

"The Feds get many cases referred to them, Nora. Some could, and probably should, be filed at the state level. However, the federal agencies have far more resources than state agencies, and they also have much broader powers than the states. They try to get as much information to support a case as they can. I don't like it any more than you do, and today less than ever. But, if the little bit I saw happen with a team of agents across all those agencies, I have hope they will become a model for how agencies could work together. For now, let's just be grateful they have taken it off our soil and out of our hills."

They all turned their heads as they heard the sound of big engines coming up the road. Chad went to the kitchen door and looked out.

"Mac, boots and coat. Let's go."

"Grandpa, go where?"

"The logs are here."

It was almost nine, and they all put on their coats and boots. Nora, Fred, and the kids trooped outside, and Bella gave Chad the key to the shed to get the lawn chairs so they could sit far enough out of the way. She slipped her mobile phone into her pocket, hoping she would remember to take pictures.

"That seems to be everything. Just you and me to go, boy," she said, grabbing Wizard's leash and opening the door.

As she stepped outside, she noticed Nora, Fred, and the children were standing with their backs against Wizard's favorite tree. He stopped and looked at Bella. She walked towards the front porch and pointed to the expanse of the forest. "You'll just have to find a new tree, Wizard." He did.

After hooking the leash to Wizard's collar, Bella walked over to where everyone was sitting. A deep rumble filled the air as the vehicles got closer to Drellag Caban, and at the back of the parade of two flatbed trucks and Arthur's crew, Bella saw a Chevy Tahoe; she wondered if it was Joshua. It was. Joshua honked and parked out of the way. He and Carla headed towards the group.

Carla hugged Bella. "We invited ourselves to the cabin raising. Hope it's okay?"

"Oh, Carla, Joshua! I'm so glad you came. I assumed you'd be at the store."

Joshua stepped back from hugging her. "We put a sign up: 'Closed: Family matter. Reopen by one p.m.'"

Bella pulled him back into a hug. "Oh, that's sweet, Joshua. Thanks. And good for you! I'm thrilled to have my new brother here." Chad had already gone to get two more chairs.

Carla stepped over to the group. "And soon to be sister-in-law. We talked to Pastor Fisk this morning, and he's going to marry us tomorrow morning. We want you all there."

Nora jumped up and hugged Carla and Joshua.

Carla returned the hug. "And we want you to sing, Nora."

"I'd be honored."

There was a loud, piercing yell of excitement from Mac as the boom arm on the truck started to lift the first log from the back of the truck. Everyone turned from Mac to the site of the new cabin.

"Pull up a chair, folks. The show is starting early." Bella was as excited as Mac.

Arthur came over and spoke to the group. "We'll take the logs off the flatbeds and then start lifting them onto the foundation. We'll do the logs of the cabin first. We'll brace across the top of them. The roof joists should be here on Monday. Should have it under roof by late next week. Questions, Miss Bella?"

"None from me. Anyone else?" Everyone shook their heads.

"Then enjoy the show." Arthur returned to his crew.

After an hour, Bella and Carla went into the cabin to make coffee and hot chocolate to go with the muffins Carla and Joshua had brought from Diane's Home Cooking. Bella brought out some lap shawls for Nora and Lilly. There was laughter, pointing, and exclamations of awe as each of the large logs was lifted as easily as someone picking up a stick for a dog.

Bella looked at Chad's family enjoying the time together and at the happiness on the faces of Joshua and Carla. She was grateful to feel her roots deepening through her own connections in these hills.

She had forgotten to turn off the outside bell on the phone, and its ringing shook her out of her musings. She jumped up quickly to answer it, but Chad was ahead of her. "I've got it."

Bella knew it probably was for him, but she trailed behind him to the door.

His dispatcher was on the phone. "Sheriff, good. Glad I reached you. Sir, Sergeant Whitehorse needs you."

"Fine. Put her on."

"Sir, we have received a message that Detective Williams was due at the residence where Agent Quinn is staying at nine last night. He has not arrived, and he is not answering his phone. We have put out an all-points bulletin across the region. He told her he was outside Maryville when he called around eight last night."

"We'll find Billy, Sylvia. I'll be there by one. If you need me before, call."

Chad took a deep breath and sighed then turned and saw Bella standing in the doorway. He wondered if she heard his part of the conversation.

She walked to him and put her arms around him. They stood together, swaying for several seconds. Bella couldn't help but wonder what might have happened to Billy Williams—she liked him.

"This job is demanding, Bella. Are you—"

She reached up and put her fingers on his lips. "We'll figure out how to navigate it together. Let's go enjoy the people who've come to be with us. And tomorrow we'll go help Joshua and Carla start their new lives together."

"And tomorrow night, I hope, we'll celebrate Mr. and Mrs. Johnson at the jamboree."

"And our tomorrow will be a new beginning for all of us. I love you." Bella smiled at him, took his hand, and they walked out the door.

"I love you, Bella Anderson. Here's to new beginnings."

May it ever be so. She smiled as four-year-old Mac ran towards her and his grandpa. *May it be ever so.*

About the Author

Jacque Jacobs resides in Vero Beach, Florida. She retired as Professor of Educational Leadership and Foundations from Western Carolina University in 2011. She is on the Board of several non-profits in Indian River County and deeply cares about community—a value she credits to her parents who were raised in the east Tennessee Mountains. She has completed the series "Love is a Cabin" and all six books will be available by the end of 2022. Her current writing is a detective novel.

Author's Note

New Beginnings on a Mountain has multiple hypothetical law enforcement agencies, law enforcement positions, and other acronyms. Several readers have suggested having a list of these to reference would be helpful. Here is a brief guide to help you keep the acronyms from becoming too much alphabet soup. Thanks for reading my work.

- AIC – Agent in Charge
- ATV – All-Terrain Vehicle
- CSO – County Sheriff's Office
- DA – District Attorney
- DEA – Drug Enforcement Agency
- IEA – Immigration Enforcement Agency
- LEO – Law Enforcement Officer(s)
- SBI – State Bureau of Investigation
- SAC – Special Agent in Charge
- IA – Immigration Agent